WHERE ARE YOU REALLY FROM

ALSO BY ELAINE HSIEH CHOU

Disorientation

你到底來自哪裡

周怡然

WHERE ARE YOU REALLY FROM

ELAINE HSIEH CHOU

PENGUIN PRESS   NEW YORK   2025

PENGUIN PRESS
An imprint of Penguin Random House LLC
1745 Broadway, New York, NY 10019
penguinrandomhouse.com

Copyright © 2025 by Elaine Hsieh Chou
Penguin Random House values and supports copyright.
Copyright fuels creativity, encourages diverse voices, promotes free speech, and creates a vibrant culture. Thank you for buying an authorized edition of this book and for complying with copyright laws by not reproducing, scanning, or distributing any part of it in any form without permission. You are supporting writers and allowing Penguin Random House to continue to publish books for every reader. Please note that no part of this book may be used or reproduced in any manner for the purpose of training artificial intelligence technologies or systems.

The following stories have been previously published, in slightly different form: "Carrot Legs" in *Guernica*; "Featured Background" as "Background" in *The Atlantic*.

Set in Adobe Caslon Pro
Designed by Christina Nguyen

LIBRARY OF CONGRESS CATALOGING-IN-PUBLICATION DATA
Names: Chou, Elaine Hsieh author
Title: Where are you really from : stories / Elaine Hsieh Chou.
Description: New York : Penguin Press, 2025.
Identifiers: LCCN 2024044529 (print) | LCCN 2024044530 (ebook) | ISBN 9780593298381 hardcover | ISBN 9780593298398 ebook
Subjects: LCGFT: Short stories
Classification: LCC PS3603.H686 W44 2025 (print) | LCC PS3603.H686 (ebook) | DDC 813/.6—dc23/eng/20250325
LC record available at https://lccn.loc.gov/2024044529
LC ebook record available at https://lccn.loc.gov/2024044530

Printed in the United States of America
1st Printing

The authorized representative in the EU for product safety and compliance is Penguin Random House Ireland, Morrison Chambers, 32 Nassau Street, Dublin D02 YH68, Ireland, https://eu-contact.penguin.ie.

Don't you think at the very center of the whole enterprise of storytelling is the fact that storytelling is an activity that faces in two directions? On the one hand, it's connected with an idea of truth. On the other hand, it's connected with an idea of invention, imagination, lies.

–SUSAN SONTAG

CONTENTS

CARROT LEGS • *1*

MAIL ORDER LOVE® • *29*

YOU PUT A RABBIT ON ME • *75*

FEATURED BACKGROUND • *143*

HAPPY ENDINGS • *177*

THE DOLLHOUSE • *209*

CASUALTIES OF ART: *A NOVELLA* • *245*

ACKNOWLEDGMENTS • *339*

WHERE ARE YOU REALLY FROM

CARROT LEGS

In America, I was not beautiful, but in Taiwan, I was ugly. I understood this before I even set foot in Taipei. On the way from the airport, I passed advertisements for skin-whitening creams, double-eyelid surgery, circle contact lenses. I hadn't been aware of all the variations of myself that lay dormant inside me, waiting to be enhanced. Growing up, wishing for naturally blue eyes or blond hair was pointless, so I never did. But in Taipei, the standard for attainable beauty had shifted and I alone was responsible for my ugliness.

The summer I turned thirteen, my parents decided I was old enough to visit my grandparents by myself. They had arranged a welcome dinner at a noisy seafood restaurant with all my aunts, uncles and cousins. They'd even rented a private dining room, with dark-paneled walls and ornate red carpet. I was seated next to my cousin LaLa. She was sixteen.

I had first seen her standing alone outside the restaurant,

checking her appearance in a compact mirror. She was pale and thin, with strawberry-tinted lips like the women in the ads. When she wandered into our private room, I thought she'd come in by accident, a beautiful stranger who'd gotten lost. But then she was calling me "mei" and clasping my shoulders while my grandparents scolded her for being late. I had wanted to hate her, but I loved her automatically, as if she were an expensive gift.

"LaLa will take care of you while you're here," Grandpa said.

"Biao-jie and biao-mei," Grandma smiled. "Together at last."

"But have you ever seen cousins who look so unlike one another!" Third Aunt exclaimed.

My family proceeded to catalogue the breadth of our difference. How much whiter LaLa was than me. How her nose bridge was high and mine was flat. How she was so thin, they could count the bones in her neck. How I was so fat, I was stirring their appetite.

Second Uncle squeezed my arm. "What are they feeding her in America?" he crowed. Everyone laughed merrily, as though LaLa and I weren't in the room.

LaLa leaned over to whisper in my ear, "Maybe we should kill them all."

I felt so grateful, I wanted to kiss her.

I was to share LaLa's bedroom at my grandparents' apartment. LaLa had lived with them since she was just a few months old. Her father, my mother's younger brother Kun, suffered from a drinking and gambling addiction and my grandparents had decided he couldn't be trusted to raise a child. When I met him at the restaurant, I could only stare at his pockmarked skin and blackened teeth, stained from chewing betel nuts. Throughout dinner, LaLa spoke little to her father and the times she did, her embarrassment betrayed itself in her lowered gaze. As for LaLa's mother, I had no idea what she was like because everyone, including LaLa, pretended as though she didn't exist.

We took a taxi back to my grandparents' apartment. By the front door stood a glowing fish tank, swirling with orange-white patterns. I noticed every sofa was covered in lace embroidery, every table in a thick pane of glass. Even with all the lamps switched on, darkness clung to the apartment's surfaces. LaLa showed me her bedroom, which looked like it belonged to a middle-aged man, not a teenage girl. The walls were lined in green felt and the wicker furniture felt both dusty and oily. A high window overlooked the metal box patio of the neighboring apartment, strung with laundry and faded plastic buckets. As in every room of the apartment, a wooden crucifix was nailed above the door.

I began to unpack when our grandma came in holding two glasses of papaya milk. I took a sip: the thick sweetness was nauseating.

"Why do we have to drink this?" I whined.

Grandma flapped her hand in exasperation and shuffled to her bedroom.

LaLa turned to me and squeezed her breasts underneath her nightdress. "To make them grow," she whispered.

That night, my cousin taught me her "beauty strength" exercises. First, we massaged the space beneath our armpits—that fragile tuck of skin—until it ached, which LaLa said would boost the papaya milk's benefits. Then we lay on our backs on the bed and shot our legs straight at the ceiling until they turned numb. "So fat doesn't drain down your legs and get stuck there," LaLa explained matter-of-factly. Finally, we ran our index fingers and thumbs down the length of our noses over and over, ending with a hard pinch at the tip for a "high nose." Afterwards, we looked as though we'd been sneezing all night.

"How long have you been doing this?" I wanted to know.

LaLa cocked her head. "Since I was ten, maybe younger." When she was a baby, she said, our grandma used to tug her hands down both of her legs each night before bed so she'd grow up tall and thin. I felt resentful I had not started the exercises sooner. Perhaps I would've looked like LaLa, too, if I had known the body was a moldable thing.

In the daytime, LaLa took me to fashionable Ximending or the congested Fuxing boulevards. We wandered past glassy buildings stamped with mismatched signs, down narrow alleys beneath a canopy of awnings where we poked at rows of clothes, phone accessories, cheap jewelry. I couldn't buy any of the clothes because they were only available in two sizes: S and M.

On my third day in Taipei, we passed a pastel photo booth. When LaLa saw me looking at it, she pulled me inside. I copied her poses: framing her face with her hand, lowering her chin and pretending to pout, bending at the waist and blowing a kiss. Afterwards, a screen displayed the photos, which had transformed our faces like magic: my skin was fairer and clearer, my eyes, larger and brighter. How awful and wonderful, I thought, to witness my idealized form when I had lived in ignorance of it. By contrast, LaLa—who already fit the photo booth's algorithm of beauty—looked more or less the same.

In the evenings, we went to Shilin night market and ate chewy green onion pancakes and oyster noodles swimming in gluey sauce. For dessert, hot custard pancakes and brown sugar boba tea swinging in plastic bags. The air was fat with smoke and the stink of fermented tofu. Underneath the pillars of neon light, we spit on napkins to wipe the stickiness from our fingers and linked our arms.

I liked looking at LaLa. The way she walked, as if she couldn't tolerate touching the ground. The way she closed her eyes in happiness whenever she bit into one of her favorite foods. When she ate a greasy meal during the day, she only consumed boiled water at night. When the sun was out, even partially, she carried an umbrella lined with UV protectant. She never drank anything with ice because it caused period cramps. She told me I had to stop this bad habit of mine, but I hadn't gotten my period yet.

In a clinically bright store near our grandparents' apartment, we browsed fat-burning lotions, vitamin C whitening masks and funny-looking massagers designed to shrink your face. They were a reminder that in Taiwan, beauty was a choice.

After the first time LaLa brought me to the store, I returned alone one afternoon. I brought a pack of eyelid tape to the register, then at the last minute, left without purchasing anything. The decision to try for beauty meant I could also fall short of it, which would be more painful than not trying at all.

Each night before we fell asleep, we lay in bed and stared at the ceiling as we talked. LaLa asked me about my life back home. I told her that my American friends were cruel, that they made me steal the teacher's test answers and lift my skirt up in front of a group of boys in the bathroom. That once, they had locked me in a classroom overnight.

None of this was true. At school, the boys were afraid of me and the girls ignored me. I had only one friend, Minnie, who was a grade below me and did almost anything I said. I often made her cry just to see if I could. I hated her easy devotions, including to me. Just before summer break started, I hit a boy in the face after he said something disgusting and untrue about Minnie and me. He'd even made up a song about us. On the flight over, the lyrics kept looping in my head, so loudly I worried the song would follow me all the way to Taiwan.

Instead of telling LaLa any of this, I preferred to let her believe I was a helpless victim. I liked when she turned to me with wide eyes and asked, "Zhen jia?" as though the cruelty of my classmates was so vast, she could not comprehend the size of it. I nearly clapped my hands in joy when she said she hoped they would die—that if she were there, they would never harm me again. She even made me write down their names in red ink on a sheet of paper. "John-A-Than," she sounded out. "Jen-Ni-Fer." All these American names possessed an evil energy, she declared, and I laughed until my stomach cramped.

LaLa adopted my heartache as her own, without question or hesitation. I lacked the words to tell her how much this meant to me, so I just squeezed her hand across the bed in a silent alphabet of thanks. But when I asked LaLa about her friends, she said very little. She let me spread out the altered pieces of my life all over the dark-green-felt room and kept her own packed away inside her.

CARROT LEGS

My grandparents owned three dumpling shops across Taipei, the original one located in the alleyway just below their apartment. The shop became our second home whenever we grew restless indoors and were unwilling to wade through the humid heat outside. LaLa said she didn't mind hanging out at the shop because of the constant air-conditioning and because, away from our grandparents' nagging, she could watch the TV shows they wouldn't allow.

The shop was narrow and dingy, with scratched laminate tables and maroon vinyl-backed chairs. The walls were bare except for an outdated calendar: Year of the Horse. At the front of the shop was a wide, flat metal surface where the dumplings were fried. Behind it was a glass-door fridge stocked with premade dishes: thousand-year egg on a bed of silken tofu, sliced bean curd, pickled cucumbers bathed in chili oil. Above the fridge sat a small TV, tuned to a soap opera set in the Ming dynasty. The women on the show wore blue eyeshadow. I asked LaLa how they got ahold of it back then and she told me I think too much.

At the rear of the shop, down a dim hallway, was a studio where the manager lived with his wife, separated from the kitchen only by a curtain of wooden beads. They had worked for my grandparents for as long as LaLa could remember. I was introduced to them the way we were to all adults: "ShuShu" for men and "Ayi" for women. I never knew their real names. ShuShu was a silent man with evil-looking eyebrows and wiry muscles. Ayi looked at least fifteen years younger than him. She was chubby and seemed slow, which aggravated me on such a visceral level, I didn't even pause to wonder why.

In the hours between lunch and dinner, Ayi offered to teach me how to make dumplings, but LaLa said she could show me herself. While Ayi watched, LaLa dipped a middle finger into a bowl of clear water and traced it around the circumference of the dough. Then she dropped a bundle of pork, garlic and cabbage into its center. Her long fingers stitched the dough into gentle folds, pinching lightly each time until eight pleats were embroidered into a fan. I liked that LaLa was good at making dumplings and that I failed at it, all my attempts lopsided or stretched too thin. As with other little incidents, it confirmed the hopelessness in comparing myself to her. This let me love her, I believed, selflessly.

When Ayi went to the kitchen for more dough, LaLa asked if I noticed her luobo tui.

"Her what?"

"Carrot legs! When legs look like carrots," she said, her voice tight with impatience. Whenever certain phrases went missing from my Mandarin, LaLa would stare at me as if she had only just remembered we were different in some ways and always would be.

Upstairs in our grandparents' kitchen, she yanked two daikon radishes from the bottom drawer of the refrigerator and placed them in front of her calves. "White carrots. See?"

Our grandma cooked the stocky vegetable in a cloudy soup with pork bones until the daikon turned translucent and white streaks pinwheeled out from its center. I thought the soup tasted delicious, both light and savory, while LaLa found it underwhelming.

From her tone, I understood carrot legs were undesirable.

"What about me?" I asked. "Do I have carrot legs?"

LaLa studied my legs carefully.

CARROT LEGS

"No," she said at last, "they're healthy legs. All girls in America play sports, don't they?"

"Yes," I lied. I didn't tell her that P.E. was my most dreaded class, a fact I didn't hide from the teacher, who seemed to punish me by always clapping his hands after me, yelling at me to pick up the pace.

LaLa's legs were straight and thin, just as our grandma had hoped they'd be. When I tried to imagine the equivalent for legs like hers, I could only think of bean sprouts or some other vegetable I could easily snap in half.

The next time we went to the dumpling shop, I paid special attention to Ayi's legs. I couldn't see them at first because she was either sitting down or abruptly appearing beside me to ask if I needed anything. Up close, her eyes were deep-set, her mouth a pink peony pucker, her cheeks high and round as apples dewy with sweat. Her attractive features came as a sudden shock to me. I didn't think Ayi had the right to a pretty face.

When she went outside to empty buckets of water, I finally saw she was bowlegged, her legs like two parentheses hugging each other. Her thighs met her calves without transition and a pale set of indentations was the only indication she had knees. I had never seen legs like that before, but I would begin to notice them everywhere in Taipei: waiting in line at the lunchbox restaurant across the street, gliding up the escalators as I exited the MRT station.

"I see her carrot legs now," I whispered to LaLa.

"Don't they make you angry?"

When I stared at Ayi's backside, it's true I felt an intense desire to bite her thick white legs or to dice them up into perfectly smooth pieces.

"They make me feel, zenme shuo, violent." I didn't know how else to say in Mandarin what I meant.

When Ayi wasn't looking, we would take turns pretending to chew on her legs by tilting our heads sideways and splitting our jaws apart. Or we would mime sawing them off with a large knife, our hands horizontal and clawed. We joked about Ayi in front of her, even in the presence of customers.

"What do you think legs taste like?" one of us would ask.

"Carrots!" the other would shout.

"What kind of carrots?"

"White ones, of course!"

Ayi said we were funny girls and smiled her peony pucker smile.

Later we started a new game: how to kill Ayi so we could chop off her carrot legs and cook them. When our grandma gave us some money, we ran to the 7-Eleven, half-delirious at the thought of cold bottles of Yang-Le-Duo and cream-filled buns. With our snacks in tow, we weighed our options at the playground, overgrown with banyan trees and a fine green moss that blanketed every stone surface. The playground was located at the end of my grandparents' alleyway, before the main intersection.

LaLa said that when Ayi went to the morning market, we could kick her in the carrot leg shins. I suggested that when she went to the kitchen, we could lasso her from the back door and drag her into the alleyway. Or, LaLa said, excitement spilling over in her voice, we could pour oil all over the bathroom floor, causing Ayi to slip and fall. This was our favorite plan.

But how to cook the legs? we wondered aloud. What was the recipe?

CARROT LEGS

The next time our grandma prepared her cloudy soup, LaLa joined her at the stove. She looked like a model in her matching baby blue skirt and top, her long hair snatched up in a high ponytail. I wore a boys' set of matching T-shirt and shorts in obnoxious yellow, an outfit I wouldn't dare wear in America.

LaLa stood on her tiptoes and leaned over our grandma, though she was already much taller than her. "How much salt? What temperature? And for how long?" she asked in her most serious voice. She pretended to take careful notes in her Doraemon notebook while our grandma demonstrated each step. When boredom set in, LaLa made pig faces at me. "Ai-ya, pay attention!" our grandma yelled each time she caught her.

But how to cook Ayi's legs was not the trickiest task, we later realized—it was how to chop her up without splattering blood and guts everywhere. LaLa fixated on this part of the process because she had a phobia of anything unclean. Even when I had stayed indoors all day, she wouldn't allow me to get into bed until I'd washed my feet.

"I know what we have to do!" LaLa said one afternoon at the playground. We were sitting at the very top of the jungle gym and drinking apple soda. "We need to make her slip in the bathtub."

"Yes," I said, picturing her naked. "She probably has giant cantaloupe breasts."

"With dark hairy nipples," LaLa confirmed. "She must have sour-smelling feet from standing in that sweaty little shop all day," she added, pulling a face at the thought.

"And old-lady underwear! The kind that go up to your belly button." I had seen them strung up on the back patio of the shop, sun-bleached and frilly as old-fashioned curtains. We were both quiet for a moment as Ayi floated naked through our minds.

"Then what?" I asked.

"Then we pour in boiling water, add the pork bones and salt and cook her *in* the bathtub! Less messy and more efficient."

I realized my mouth was watering. I swallowed and asked, "What does Ayi soup taste like?"

"Bitter," LaLa said without hesitation. "Bitter and greasy."

That night, I had just fallen asleep when I felt the warm glaze of saliva against my leg. I opened my eyes to see LaLa's perfect teeth flash above my calf.

"What does it taste like?" I asked sleepily.

She pulled her mouth away, releasing a soft popping sound.

"White carrots!" She cupped my calf in her hand. "Try it yourself."

I bent my head, brought my lips to my calf and licked. I thought I could taste the faint bitterness of daikon radish.

LaLa laughed. "Have you ever noticed calves feel like little breasts?"

I lifted up my leg and LaLa kneaded the swaying flesh with surprising strength, as if kneading dough for dumpling skins.

"Do you think ShuShu bites Ayi's legs?" I asked.

"Maybe carrots excite him. Maybe that's why he married her!"

"When they have sex, he has to rub his penis on her legs first."

LaLa laughed so loudly at this, our grandfather smacked his palm twice against the wall separating our bedrooms. She covered her mouth and pinched my ankle until it hurt.

After LaLa fell asleep, one arm thrown carelessly across my stomach, I realized that back home, someone like her would never have acknowledged me, much less touched me. How lucky she was mine and I was hers, by the grace of something as simple and illogical as blood.

My mother used an international phone card to call me every Saturday morning: her eight p.m. was my eight a.m. Every time I thought of the time difference, I pictured my mother in our house and below her, an upside-down me.

I took the calls in my grandparents' bedroom, since LaLa slept in late. I liked sitting at my grandma's vanity table, with its large seashell mirror rimmed in pink ceramic and a matching hand mirror. I examined myself in it, tilting my head this way and that, pursing my lips to make my nose appear smaller. As we talked, I wrapped the phone's ivory cord round and round my legs.

My mother was always occupied during our weekly calls. I could hear her clanking around in the laundry room or stacking dishes in the kitchen. It bothered me that she couldn't stop what she was doing for just ten minutes to focus solely on me.

She always started off the call by asking me what I had done all week and I always responded, "Nothing much." Then she asked what I had eaten, reminding me I shouldn't eat bread every day—did I know bakeries in Taiwan still used lard? Was I staying out of the sun like I'd promised?

I considered coming back home tanned and thirty pounds heavier just to spite her.

"Well, are you doing your workbooks?" She had snuck two of them, math and reading, into the front pocket of my suitcase. "Ninth grade math isn't like anything you've studied before."

Whenever my mother brought up my American school, I felt unwell, almost sick, as if I could feel a string in my stomach tethering me there, a string I'd previously been able to ignore.

Our Saturday morning conversations were short, aimless circles. I grew sullen because my mother reminded me my life in Taiwan wasn't my real life and she'd grow sullen because I was sullen. But she always ended each call asking, in English, if I missed her—as if some phrases were too sentimental for her native tongue.

"I miss you," I mumbled, disappointed by how predictable I could be, how I still behaved exactly the way a daughter should towards her mother.

LaLa's year-round school started again in August. Her school was in Banqiao, over an hour away on the MRT. After classes began, she would leave early in the morning and return after eight, sometimes ten if she had English buxiban. Whenever I asked if she wanted to visit a night market or watch pirated DVDs, she always said she was too tired. She fell asleep earlier, too, and we no longer talked every night. I had trouble imagining the contours of LaLa's life away from me—teachers, classmates, friends, crushes—none of whom she had ever mentioned. I resented them anyway.

My grandparents didn't want me wandering around the city by myself, so I passed the time helping out at the dumpling shop. With my cousin gone, Ayi tried to pour herself into the space left by LaLa. She asked me what my father did for a living, if I had a good relationship with my mother, if I had a boyfriend.

"Boys are disgusting," I told Ayi and she laughed that I was too young to understand, an ignorant dismissal that made me want to punish her. When I stubbornly didn't offer up anything about myself, she would continue chatting as though she'd been talking to herself all along.

Ayi sat close to me as I traced the dough with water, then passed it to her to seal into a neat pouch. I grew acutely aware of her presence, her bodily odor a mixture of sweat and an acerbic medicine my grandparents kept in the living room cabinet. Ayi often spoke in Taiwanese with the customers, a language none of my family could understand, which seemed to me an act of insolence since she never spoke it in front of LaLa or my grandparents.

One afternoon, a woman looked curiously at me as she spoke in Taiwanese. I understood through Ayi's pleased tone that the woman had mistaken us for mother and daughter. Ayi laughed and glanced over at me for my reaction but I held my silence in my mouth like a cough drop. I refused to grant her even this small joy.

On the rare occasion LaLa visited the dumpling shop, Ayi would fall quiet, though still cheerful and smiling, and we would resume our habitual positions, with LaLa sitting on my right. She didn't speak to Ayi unless she was ordering her to bring us cold soy milk or Hot-Kid cake cookies or anything else we desired. Whenever Ayi obeyed LaLa, my entire body would flush with hot, sticky heat—as if I'd witnessed a private, shameful act.

LaLa had been back at school for a few weeks when Ayi invited me to tea after dinner. LaLa had not come home that evening. In fact, I had not seen her for several days. Her absence had grown into an echo, ringing hollow and empty through the apartment. My grandma said LaLa had started sleeping at her father's place more often since he lived closer to her school. I could tell by her tone, as if she were trying to convince herself of her own words, that she didn't approve of this new arrangement.

I was reluctant to accept Ayi's invitation, but my grandma insisted I go. She made me bring a box of sun cakes, my favorite, flaky and layered with a sugary paste in the center. I wondered if Ayi needed a whole box for herself and considered giving her only a single cake and keeping the rest for LaLa and myself.

Without the chatter of customers and the blaring of soap operas, the shop seemed almost lonely. ShuShu slept in a chair with his back to the wall, his eyes crimped tightly shut, disgruntled even in sleep.

I hesitated before the wooden beads that spilled down from the doorframe, nearly turning back around, before I closed my eyes and quickly passed through them. The room was larger than I had imagined, with a bed shoved against the right wall and a sagging, plastic-covered sofa at the foot of it. A coffee table sat in the middle of the room, also smothered in plastic. Everything was painted in a harsh fluorescent light. Seeing where Ayi and ShuShu slept made me itchy with embarrassment.

When Ayi saw the sun cakes, she exclaimed I was "hao guai," an expression I hated because it reminded me of how people spoke to their dogs. She set the cakes down on a tray and poured us cups of jasmine tea. While I listened, she spoke about ShuShu's back problems, about their noisy next-door neighbor.

I was playing with a cake's cellophane when Ayi's voice shifted to a more careful tone. "Do you know how happy I am that you came this summer?"

I smiled and drank my tea, trying not to look at Ayi's bare legs.

"I've been meaning to show you something." She reached for a brown leather album underneath the coffee table and turned to a photo of five girls standing solemnly in a row, wrapped in white dresses with big bows like presents waiting to be opened. Ayi tapped the youngest girl on the left. "That's me." She slid her finger to the girl beside her. "And that's your mother."

Ayi passed the album to me. I squinted at the faded photo, impatient yet reluctant to recognize my mother's face. In the photo, her short hair curled inward at the ends. I had never seen my mother look so carefree. I felt annoyed Ayi had a connection to my mother, to myself, that I hadn't known about.

"How can I be sure this is her?" I wanted to catch Ayi lying, proof that despite her sweet face, something rotten lived inside her.

"We went to the same church in Taipei, the one your nai-nai still goes to," she explained. "I always thought your mother was beautiful. You know, you look just like her."

"No, I don't."

Ayi smiled at this, then pointed at the girl with long hair woven into two braids. "Do you know who that is?"

"No."

"LaLa's mother."

I couldn't tell if LaLa and her mother looked alike, though they were both tall and thin. I had always assumed LaLa inherited all her looks from her mother. My uncle's pockmarked face and stained teeth popped up in my mind like a mask in an old horror movie.

"LaLa doesn't look anything like her father," I commented, not knowing what else to say.

Ayi laughed and poured us more tea. Her laughter came out in small gasps. "Of course she doesn't!"

I passed the album back and positioned myself a little farther from Ayi on the sofa. "What do you mean?"

"Oh, you don't know?" Ayi looked very happy, almost ecstatic.

"Your uncle Kun and LaLa's mother were childhood sweethearts. But when she was sixteen, she became pregnant with her high school teacher's baby. The whole neighborhood knew. Everyone called her bad names. But Kun still loved her."

She took a sip of her tea.

"After the baby was born, LaLa's mother disappeared and Kun suddenly had a baby in his care. A beautiful little girl. No one spoke about the arrangements, of course, but everyone understood. Your grandparents were unhappy about the situation—very unhappy—but they learned to love LaLa like their own granddaughter. Thank goodness they're Catholic or she might have been left out on the street!" Ayi sounded out of breath.

"How do you know all this?"

"Oh, I've worked for your grandparents for many years. I know all kinds of things." She took another sip of tea and smiled with such neat satisfaction, I longed to slap her across the mouth. When I was silent, Ayi asked in an eager, nudging voice, "Didn't your mother tell you?"

"No." I ate another sun cake, now dry and tasteless on my tongue. "So I'm not really related to LaLa?"

"Not by blood, but by family, of course. You'll always be biao-mei and biao-jie."

I drank the rest of my tea in a single gulp to wash away the denseness caught in my throat. I stood up abruptly, not caring if it was rude.

"I have to go," I announced. "Wan an."

Ayi kept her head down as she started slicing an orange into quarters. "Wan an."

That night, I dreamt I was being cooked into a soup. An enormous pair of hands washed me underneath a faucet, patted me dry on a kitchen cloth, then spread me out on a wooden cutting board. Each whack of the knife sent a pulse of pleasure through me, as though someone were touching me between my legs.

When I saw LaLa a week later, she brought home a foreign smell with her: a blend of cigarette smoke, fried chicken and a new, tooth-achingly sweet perfume. During dinner, she was more talkative than usual, even telling our grandparents about her most recent literature assignment. I was waiting for her to finish eating so we could escape to our bedroom and I could finally tell her about my night with Ayi. I had even rehearsed how I would describe the sad little room, the plastic-covered sofa. How together we would laugh at Ayi's pathetic ploy for attention. I felt certain she had only fed me that made-up story so I would grow distanced from LaLa and closer to her. I could feel Ayi prying her way into me each time she called me "hao guai."

After her shower, LaLa closed the door to our bedroom. She wasn't shy about being naked in front of me and shed the towel around her body to dry her hair with it. Her breasts were perfect teardrops with pale pink nipples, unlike mine, which were more fat than breast, shapeless masses capped with fleshy dark brown. I didn't want her to know this, so I always changed facing the wall.

Instead of her nightgown, LaLa put on the same clothes she wore earlier, which I found strange. I thought she was coming towards the bed to hug me and my arms instinctively lifted, but then she launched herself on the mattress and twisted around.

"Mei! I have so much to tell you. I have a boyfriend now." LaLa clasped a pillow to her chest. "He drives a motorcycle! His name is Nianzhu."

"Oh." Disappointment suctioned the bottom floor of my stomach. I could picture it: an engorged, blotchy octopus.

When LaLa didn't say more, I made myself say, "That's great!" then hugged her and breathed in her soapy smell, familiar again after her shower. "How old is he?"

"Eighteen."

LaLa pulled away, flipped her long hair over and began untangling it with a comb. "I know you're going to like him, mei. He said he'll drive us to Danshui sometime, isn't that nice?"

"That's great," I said again, though the falseness of my enthusiasm was unmistakable even to me. I wondered how to introduce the topic of Ayi. Before, LaLa used to poke me in the stomach and ask when we were going to murder Ayi for her ripe fatty legs, but she hadn't for many days. "I have news, too," I tried.

"Tell me!" LaLa said through the dark screen of her hair.

"Carrot legs Ayi has been making up lies."

"Zhen jia?"

"It's true. She told me something about your mother—"

"Shut up," LaLa snapped. "What does that stupid woman know about my mother? Why do you repeat her stupid lies?"

For a few seconds, my cousin was unrecognizable to me, her lovely mouth distorted by a snarl. I had seen LaLa slip into cruelty as easily as slipping on and off a dress. But she'd never spoken cruelly to me. Maybe Ayi wasn't lying after all.

"I'm sorry," I whispered, "please don't be mad."

Two short honks disrupted the uneasy quiet of the room. LaLa leapt up and looked through the window from her tiptoes. She waved to someone.

"Don't wait up for me, mei," she said, her tone light again. This alone filled me with dizzying relief. I wanted to ask if she'd forgiven me, but I was afraid of misspeaking again.

LaLa went to the mirror, smudged on lip gloss and left the bedroom. I waited a few seconds, then followed after her into the living room. In the darkened space, lit only by the glowing blue fish tank, I stood still and listened to Nianzhu's motorcycle rip out of the alleyway.

LaLa returned just past four in the morning. I could tell she had taken another shower. As she slid into bed beside me, I pretended to wake up and yawn. "Jie? Is that you?"

"Yes. Go back to sleep."

"I'm not tired." I turned on my side to face her. "Where did you go?"

"A love hotel."

I pictured the one by the MRT station: it looked like a regular hotel, but LaLa had told me you could rent a room by the hour for just a thousand NT. She said all the rooms came with a bowl of condoms, like an adult candy jar. I felt, irrationally, like she had gone somewhere she had always promised to take me.

I unwrinkled the nerves in my voice into smooth nonchalance. "So, what did you guys do?"

"I licked him. And he licked me," she giggled.

"What does it feel like?"

She reflected for a moment. "Like melting. He eats me like I'm ice cream."

After a while, LaLa's breathing evened out. She lay sleeping with her eyes closed and a slight smile resting on her lips. I pictured her and Nianzhu lying on an unmade bed. I saw him lapping at her pink nipples, his mouth drinking greedily from between her legs. The image was so vivid, I felt like a bystander in the hotel room. I faced away from her, spit on my fingers and quickly masturbated.

As the end of summer approached, the afternoon rain showers grew unrelenting. When I went outside in the brief pockets of time it wasn't raining, mosquitoes pestered me until I sometimes cried. I hadn't seen LaLa since the night she'd snuck out to see her boyfriend. Every time I looked at the photo booth picture we'd taken, the two of us smiling side by side, I felt as if I'd been betrayed by the LaLa in the photo.

I spent my days hanging out at the dumpling shop, following my grandma on her errands and watching cartoons in Mandarin, which featured an unnerving, dreamlike intro of disembodied eyeballs on a woman's breasts. At night, when the garbage truck would sing its tinkly song, I'd look outside at the puddles of warm light as an overwhelming sense of loneliness gathered inside me.

Since I spent so much time alone now, my grandma gave me pocket money to go to 7-Eleven whenever I wanted. A week before my flight home, I bought two custard buns and decided to eat only one at the playground and save the other one for that evening, when I watched my cartoons. By then, I could understand almost all of the dialogue.

I climbed to the top of the jungle gym, unwrapped the first custard bun and ate it slowly and meticulously. One of the neighborhood boys stopped his game of jump rope to call me "zhu." Instead of coming up with a clever comeback, I ate the second custard bun while he watched. Insults no longer stung. I had become a visitor in the house of my body.

When I was walking back to the apartment, I looked up and saw a slim, pretty girl exiting the building onto the street. She wore a short red dress and white high heels. For a brief moment, I disorientedly thought I was back at the seafood restaurant from my first night in Taiwan. Then I realized I knew her.

"Jie," I cried, "you're back!"

"Mei," she said, hugging me. "I'm just picking up some clothes."

Only then did I notice the heavy shopping bag slung around LaLa's shoulder. She looked tired, her eyes bloated from lack of sleep. Before I could ask why she wasn't wearing her school uniform, she promised me on the following Thursday—the day of my flight home—she would skip school and we would spend the whole day together like we did at the beginning of summer.

"Wait for me at the dumpling shop," she said. "I'll come in the morning."

"Okay. Bring your knife!"

She looked blankly at me.

"To make the soup." I mimed slicing off my legs.

LaLa laughed but her head was turned away so I couldn't tell if it was sincere or forced. In her hair was an expensive-looking rhinestone clip. A gift from Nianzhu, I thought, jealous of this boy whose affection she received because she wanted it, not because she was obligated to.

"I have to go," LaLa said.

I nodded without playfully tugging at her hand and whining that she should stay, the way I would have earlier in the summer. Two nights ago, I had looked down at my underwear and found blood. There was a time when I would have told LaLa right away that I'd gotten my period. I knew better than to tell her now.

On Thursday morning, I got up early, packed all my belongings and dragged my suitcase to the front door. My flight wasn't until late that night but I wanted to have everything ready in advance. My grandparents would be asleep by the time I had to leave. They'd given me enough money to take a taxi all the way to the airport.

I unwrapped and rewrapped LaLa's present: a shiny ceramic daikon radish with a watery wash of green paint and real straw sprouting out of its head. I had found it at a cluttered stationery shop a few streets away. Inside the gift box, I had added blank paper and addressed envelopes so we could write each other letters.

My mother called to verify I had all the instructions for flying home. When she offhandedly mentioned a school notice she'd received in the mail, I nearly hung up on her. I couldn't bear to think about Minnie, who'd be staying behind at our old middle school, or the taunting boys in my grade who'd follow me like flypaper to our new high school. I told her I had to go, LaLa was waiting for me, and cut the call short.

When I went downstairs, LaLa wasn't at the dumpling shop. I slid into a seat at my usual table and a moment later, Ayi passed me a plastic tray with a dish of water, a stack of round dumpling skins and a bowl of ground pork filling. I put on the headphones of my portable CD player and began to fold, trying not to glance up at each customer who walked in. By noon, I had folded over a hundred lopsided dumplings and still LaLa had not come.

"Where's LaLa?" Ayi asked in a cloying voice. She kept lingering near me, which made me feel both irritated and needy for more attention.

When I didn't answer, she brought me a red bean ice cream pop in a clear plastic wrapper. I pressed it against a throbbing mosquito bite on my thigh before unwrapping it, then bit off its head with my front teeth. I welcomed the cold burn and wished it burned more.

"Don't worry," Ayi said. "She wouldn't forget about you!"

"I'm not worried she forgot. Something bad probably happened to her. Don't you know her boyfriend drives a motorcycle?"

Ayi didn't say anything, just picked up my tray of misshapen dumplings and brought them to ShuShu to fry. As she walked away, an unreasoned anger grabbed hold of me. I hated her milky skin, her peony mouth, her stocky carrot legs. The image of a large kitchen knife slicing cleanly through her hurled across my mind.

I continued making dumplings, hundreds more, as if in a stupor. Several of them were ripped in the side, the uncooked pork like a gash in a face. When my grandparents descended to say goodbye, they gripped my hands and wished me safe travels, but I could hardly pay attention and returned to my task as soon as they left.

When I looked up again, night had fallen and the dinner crowd had dispersed. Ayi brought me a plate of freshly fried dumplings and a small dish of thinly sliced ginger lying in a pool of black vinegar. The immaculate pleats pointed to Ayi's handiwork. She sat down across from me and urged me to eat.

Suddenly starving, I shoved a dumpling into my mouth, savoring the conflicting texture of crispy and silky skin. Then I felt upset I was enjoying food that bore the mark of Ayi's touch; it felt too intimate, like eating a part of Ayi herself. I finished chewing and pushed the plate towards her.

"Actually, I hate dumplings. They're oily and they make you fat. My mom won't even buy them," I added, wanting Ayi to know she made food unfit for people in America, even if this was blatantly untrue. I looked down at my hands and noticed half-moons of dark red. I'd scratched the mosquito bites on my thighs so hard, blood had caked under my nails.

Ayi smiled a little, then walked away. The beads on the bedroom door clicked softly against one another.

At some point, I fell asleep at the table. When I woke, all the lights in the opposite apartments had been turned off. The alleyway was empty. Even the next-door neighbor's anxious dog was silent. The clock next to the register read just after midnight.

"Ayi?" I called. When I realized she was gone, panic bloomed inside my chest. I didn't even care I had missed my flight home.

I turned around to see ShuShu sleeping in a chair at the back corner of the shop, frown firmly in place, arms crossed. Three empty green bottles of Taiwan Beer idled by his feet.

I stood up and walked towards their bedroom. I ran my fingers across the cool wooden beads and then, without thinking, I stepped inside and flicked on the fluorescent light. I opened and closed the dresser drawers with unhurried, disinterested movements, then did the same with the nightstand, finding only tissue packets, a nail clipper and hair ties with plastic fruit dangling at the ends. I looked in the bathroom medicine cabinet, in more drawers. I didn't know what I was searching for. I didn't care if anyone caught me. I lay down on the bed and pinched my eyes, commanding myself not to cry.

Eventually I heard someone come in. I looked up to see Ayi

setting down a striped pink-and-white plastic bag of apples on the coffee table before studying herself in the discolored mirror on the wall. Unburdened by her usual ingratiating smile, her beauty was even more striking. Then she saw my reflection in the mirror and turned around.

"Mei-mei? What's wrong?"

I thought Ayi would scold me for entering her bedroom without permission, but she only sat down heavily beside me. Her voice weighed with exhaustion and I wondered for the first time if, behind her smile, lived unhappiness.

"I'm sorry LaLa didn't come—" she started and I stopped her before she could say more. Even in my anguished state, I couldn't stand to hear a bad word against LaLa. I had nothing left but my devotion to her, a devotion I idolized as perfect and pure. I had to, since I had forfeited all my desires, all my dignity, to secure it.

Ayi handed me a tissue. "She's still your jie-jie."

"We're not sisters." We called each other mei and jie, but those words had been stripped of all meaning now. "Why did you tell me we're not related?" I asked Ayi. Saying the truth aloud released the tears I'd been holding hostage. Without the fact of our shared blood, I had nothing to anchor myself to LaLa.

"I don't know. Duibuqi." Ayi twisted a section of the bedsheet in her hands. "Do you want a sun cake?" she tried. "How about some milk tea? I can go to 7-Eleven right now and get your favorite kind."

I shook my head. Her kindness hurt more than any cruelty I'd ever bore. I was crying even harder now, the sounds coming out of me embarrassing. Ayi looked a little frightened. "Is there anything I can do?" she asked me.

I couldn't look her in the face. Her white T-shirt had puffy sleeves and a picture of a cartoon rabbit. I thought back to when LaLa and I sat cross-legged on our bed, talking late into the night about all the violent acts we wanted to subject Ayi's body to, as if, by slaughtering what we hated about her, we had proved that the good should only favor the beautiful.

"Let me see your nipples," I whispered. "Please."

At first Ayi didn't move. A flare of panic went through me as I pictured her dragging me upstairs by the arm, informing my grandparents that there was something deeply wrong with me. Then she lifted up her shirt and unhooked her bra. She kept her face hidden behind her shirt, stretched taut like a screen.

LaLa and I had been wrong; her nipples weren't fleshy and brown like mine, but delicate and pink like LaLa's. They were beautiful. I pushed my face into her breasts, inhaling the warm scent of Ayi's skin, my tears and snot sliding against her. Ayi patted the back of my hair and repeated, "mei guan xi." It doesn't matter.

After a while, she extracted me from her chest and told me to wait. I heard her turn on the faucet in the bathroom, then she came back out and told me to stand up.

Ayi knelt in front of me and undressed me like a child. First my shirt and my shorts, then my socks and underwear. She took my hand and guided me to the small bathroom. Gripping her arm, I slid into the bathtub and spread my legs until my feet lay flat against the green-tiled wall. Steam rose in spirals from the water's surface. I could smell my grandma's soup, cooked for hours until the daikon melted against my teeth. I cupped my hands, lifted them to my lips and drank.

MAIL ORDER LOVE®

The man paid for the order on Monday morning. With express shipping, it arrived from Taipei on Wednesday afternoon. The box was large and rectangular, measuring six feet in height, four feet in length and three feet in width. Air slits had been scored into the top and bottom of the box. A single FRAGILE sticker had started to unstick from one side.

The delivery person handed him a form on a clipboard to sign, then winked as he turned to leave. The man bristled not so much at the wink, but at its implication. He waited until the delivery truck had peeled out of his cul-de-sac before coaxing the box into his living room.

First, he peeked out the windows and closed all the blinds before dropping to his knees. Next, he pattered back into the kitchen for a pair of scissors. He prepared to slice the box down its middle, then froze, astonished at his own carelessness. He picked at the edges of the tape before severing the whole strip. Finally, he parted the cardboard flaps and held his breath.

Inside the box were hundreds of packing peanuts, seafoam colored, and a pink return slip. Frank (the man's name was Frank, after his father) frowned. He had imagined something a little more romantic.

Hello? he asked cautiously.

A pale hand shot up through the packing peanuts. The fingernails were polished bright cherry red. Frank grasped the hand and pulled a woman out of the box. She stretched, yawned and cracked her neck in two swift movements. Frank was startled—were women supposed to make such noises?

She wore a white wedding dress and square-toed high heels. He lifted her veil: her face looked just like the picture he'd seen in the online catalogue. In her hands was a limp bouquet; on her arms, a few silica packets. He gingerly brushed them off her.

Long flight? Frank asked.

The woman frowned. She didn't understand the logic of his question. She suspected they were speaking two different languages, beyond the literal sense. She'd been traveling for sixteen hours and badly needed the bathroom.

Toilet? she responded.

Frank stared at her for a moment before moving aside and pointing down the hallway.

When she finished freshening up, they went straight to city hall. The ceremony was quick and no-nonsense. Frank indicated where she had to sign and date. Inside a conference room, he slipped a diamond ring onto her finger, purchased from a different catalogue. The witness was a stout, unsmiling woman provided as part of the service. She took pictures of them on Frank's phone, gesturing impatiently for them to get closer, closer still.

When they were pronounced husband and wife, Frank felt too shy to kiss someone he'd known for less than an hour. His bride didn't seem to mind; she was busy counting the number of ceiling cracks. They shook hands instead.

Afterwards, the newlyweds stood on the steps of city hall, dazzled by the bright afternoon light, blinking like children awoken from a long nap.

During dinner, Bunny (selected because she liked the sound of it) told her husband half in Mandarin, half in English that she would like to open a checking and savings account.

Frank nodded agreeably.

Why, thank you, I *would* like some coffee.

Bunny made no move to make coffee. Instead she poked at the untouched hamburger steak, string beans and instant mashed potatoes on her plate, her chin cupped sadly in her hand. They were in Frank's dining room. A home-cooked meal had been his idea. Simple. Romantic.

Beneath the table, Frank worried his new wedding ring. He had paid for the premium package—in addition to all her vaccines, Bunny was supposed to come with an intermediate level of English. Her English, he felt certain now, was not intermediate. He wondered if he should make a formal complaint on the company's website.

Instead of talking to each other, they watched TV through the awning that fed into the living room. The channel was set to a news station: during a press conference, the U.S. president had accidentally said Taiwan instead of the Republic of China. The insinuation that Taiwan was a country was unmistakable. Now China was threatening to invade Taiwan, to bomb it if necessary, to reclaim what was rightfully theirs.

A wave of indignant rage washed over Frank, as if it were his country and not hers that was under constant threat of attack. He reached across the table to pat Bunny's hand.

You're safe here, he said.

She retracted her hand.

After he loaded the dishwasher, Frank led Bunny up the stairs to the primary bedroom, his cheeks flushed to a boyish pink. This was their wedding night, after all. Surely she had expectations, expectations he did not want to disappoint. He was a man who treated his husbandly duties with solemn reverence, though the mere thought of fulfilling said duties made him feel very tired and very old. He hadn't always felt this way, of course. With Susan—well, with Susan it had been different.

Bunny stood in the primary bedroom—taking in the four-poster oak bed, the faded floral armchair in the corner, the painting of a sea tossing about a ship—as if she were a real estate agent appraising a piece of property.

She abruptly turned around and poked her head into the hallway bathroom, the linen closet, Frank's daughter's bedroom. She had moved out after high school but Frank had left her room untouched. Twice a year, he dusted and vacuumed. His daughter lived across the country now, with her own family.

Here, Bunny said, and sat down on the polka-dot bedspread. A purple inflatable armchair was slowly losing its optimism in the corner. She studied the posters of boys on the wall: Boyz II Men, Boyzone, the Backstreet Boys.

I like it here.

Of course, Frank said. Whatever makes you happy.

He lingered at the door's threshold for a moment, unsure if Bunny wanted him to stay. Then she said she had to call her mother, the words carefully enunciated like a child reciting her memorized home address. Frank gestured at the clear plastic telephone on the nightstand, frantic with multicolored wires. Bunny produced an international phone card from her purse, punched in a long stream of numbers, then stared pointedly at him.

I'll give you some privacy, he said, and left his new wife alone.

The next day, Frank took Bunny to the mall. She possessed only the clothes she'd arrived in, but since she could not go shopping in a wedding gown with a three-foot satin train, she had borrowed a pair of jeans and an old summer camp shirt belonging to his daughter. They were a size too large for her.

When she came downstairs, Frank's hand froze, his spoonful of Frosted Flakes hovering uncertainly before his open mouth. He looked unmoored, a captain without his compass.

Bunny frowned at the soggy affair in his bowl.

Cereal's in the cupboard, Frank said.

She went to the kitchen and boiled a hot dog for her breakfast.

Did you sleep well? he asked.

Bunny replied in Mandarin, I had a dream I was flying over the Pacific Ocean. I wanted to swim, but when I dove into the water, I forgot how and drowned.

Ah. I'm glad to hear it.

Frank beamed at his wife across the table. He had a habit of smiling too frequently when nervous.

Bunny wondered aloud in Mandarin if he suffered from involuntary muscle spasms.

When she finished eating her hot dog, they got in Frank's car. The drive to the mall was only ten minutes long. Bunny sat up very straight and stared out the window the entire time. They drove past a billboard for a casino steakhouse, a miniature golf course, car lots with jewel-colored SUVs and blow-up men waving their blow-up arms in the air.

So, what do you think of Orange County? Frank chuckled good-naturedly. Is it everything you dreamt of?

Bunny made a strange noise, something between a *hum* and a *ha*, and they drove the rest of the way in stuffy silence.

Frank considered enrolling in Mandarin courses. Private tutoring. MOOCs. He wanted to talk to Bunny. He wanted to know what she was thinking. No distance should separate them, as it should be between husbands and wives, like salt and pepper shakers molded to fit together just so.

At the mall, Frank bought Bunny clothes, shoes, makeup, bras and underwear (he sweated enormously under the saleswoman's disapproving gaze), plus a few accessories. He put it all on his credit card, nodding pleasantly even as sweat trickled down his back and settled into his waistband.

Anything you want, he repeated when his Mastercard was swiped. Each time, Bunny would smile with all her teeth at him. A smile from Bunny was like winning a prize, the largest stuffed animal at the county fair.

On the drive home, Bunny sat in the back seat, snapping the

labels off all her purchases into a neat pile. Frank felt uneasy. He had already withdrawn funds out of his retirement portfolio. The website had not been transparent about the true cost of a mail order bride. He would not forget to include this detail in his online review.

But later that night, when Bunny was asleep in her room, Frank logged on to the website's review page and felt both nauseated and guilty, like the time he'd eaten an entire frozen pound cake. He had assumed the other reviews would focus on the timeliness and safety of the delivery, shipping conditions, hidden costs and other practical details. All the reviews, however, focused on the women themselves. What they looked like and what they didn't look like. What they were willing to do and what they needed convincing to do.

Truth be told, Frank was bewildered by the circumstances that had sanctioned Bunny's delivery in the first place.

Nine months ago, Congress had passed a bill banning all immigration. The Senate had ratified the bill and the president, a watery backboneless man, had not opposed it. At first, some immigration continued to trickle in through the borders of Canada and Mexico, but these soon petered out after the construction of two costly military zones. That seemed to be the end of that—what could anyone do? The bill should not have come as a surprise. It was not the first time America had closed her borders to parts of the world, though it was the first time she had done so to the world absolute.

But then a loophole was discovered: mail order brides, considered imported foreign goods, were an exception to the law.

Companies did not hesitate to exploit the loophole for profit. The mail order bride system, already in existence before the immigration ban, simply made a few adjustments: custom-made cardboard boxes, regulation air slits, packing peanuts for comfort and cushioning, silica packets to prevent humidity, adult diapers. The inability to eat and drink for hours wasn't ideal, one website conceded, but people fasted all the time for health reasons, didn't they?

The brides were packed into the cargo of planes, along with dogs and cats. The brides took the same medication as these pets, meant to subside anxiety and lull them into a gentle sleep. If a bride correctly followed instructions, she drifted off in one country and woke up in a new one, ready to wed an American citizen. The process was quite painless, another website reassured the public.

No one knew how long the loophole would continue before the government stepped in and tied it off in a firm knot. On some corners of the Internet, people speculated the president had personal reasons for leaving the loophole untouched: he'd been caught leaving a hotel with his mistress, a foreign-born woman.

America was a fool for love.

Frank sold vacuums for a living—the self-automated models that zipped around by themselves. At the next company party, Frank brought Bunny as his date.

Everyone, this is my *wife*, he announced, his voice damp with meaning.

His colleagues congratulated him, though they all had trouble holding eye contact with Frank and his new bride. She wasn't anything like Susan, a woman they still thought of with fondness. In the basement conference room, they raised their plastic glasses of sparkling juice in the air and passed around squares of vanilla sheet cake drowning in blue frosting. By the water cooler, a group of colleagues in his department speculated on how the two had met. A sizable age discrepancy stretched between them. Bunny looked not a day over eighteen (she was twenty-five). Frank looked like he was pushing seventy (he was pushing seventy). On everyone's mind was the loophole, though no one said so aloud—it would have killed the mood.

The women cornered Bunny and asked where everything had come from: her shoes, her dress, her purse, her eyes, her hair. A few of them tried to pet her. When they ran out of things to say, they brought up the Taiwan-China conflict, grateful a reliable script existed for them to fall back on.

Just *awful*, they said, clucking their tongues. Your friends and family must be *terrified*.

Bunny's friends and family were not, in fact, terrified. At least not in the specific, daily way that these women imagined. Because after a while, an unused threat ceases to feel like a threat and Taiwan had been threatened for the better half of a century. To live under fight-or-flight mode for years on end is unsustainable, so after a while, people simply choose not to. They work, they eat, they sleep, they go to school, they take vacations, they raise children. They plan for the future.

Bunny didn't know how to express this so she just shrugged. The women lined their smiles with pity—her English explains her rudeness; the poor thing has no clue what we're saying.

Across the office, the men clustered around Frank and asked him what Bunny was like in the places it mattered the most: the kitchen and the bedroom. He excused himself and told Bunny they were leaving early.

The truth was Frank did not know how to have sex with his new wife. His single attempt had involved various gestures and painfully enunciated words. The whole ordeal had played out like a guessing game at a party where everyone has drunk too much and no one can drive home. By the end of that night, Bunny—puzzled but mostly amused—had made him six different cups of coffee, each with varying levels of cream and sugar.

This one attempt out of the way, relief drizzled over Frank. Sex was a perfunctory side effect of marriage, an embarrassing bodily function much like coughing up phlegm. He was not very interested in it to begin with. Despite what his colleagues believed, sex was not the reason Frank had bought a wife.

Christmas in America wasn't at all what Bunny imagined. The weather stayed at a breezy seventy degrees and multicolored lights twinkled around the trunks of palm trees and the saw-toothed arms of aloe vera plants. Some of their neighbors displayed plastic snowmen on their lawns, but they looked in constant fear of melting, baking in full sunlight on the parched grass, their arms jutting out helplessly from their rotund sides.

Frank's daughter, Margot, came to visit the day before Christmas. She arrived alone, without her husband and her two children, who were staying with her in-laws in Rhode Island.

Frank and Bunny waited for Margot at John Wayne Airport. Bunny spotted her right away, from the photos on the refrigerator. She was dressed in three different shades of brown. Margot hugged her father, then took off her sunglasses to look Bunny over, as if she couldn't quite trust her eyes.

Well! she said. Here you are.

Yes, Bunny frowned, isn't it obvious?

Margot raised an eyebrow. She's a funny one, she said, not to Bunny but to Frank.

After leaving the airport, they stopped at KFC and waited in the drive-through line. Margot gripped her purse on her lap as if she thought someone might reach through the sealed window at any moment and steal it. She and Frank spoke in low voices. In the back seat, Bunny put on her headphones, hit play and slid down until she was about to hit the floor. She lowered the volume just enough to catch crumbs of their conversation.

It's a cultural thing, Margie. I think she misses home, Frank said.

Cultural? Margot sniffed. She snapped open and shut the clasp of her purse. Well, if that's the case.

They spread out their Christmas Eve meal on the dining room table: a bucket of dark and white meat (regular and extra crispy), mashed potatoes and gravy, biscuits, mac and cheese, coleslaw. Paper plates and cutlery were included, but Margot insisted on taking out the special china from Limoges, France.

These were my mother's, Margot told Bunny, looking hard into her eyes.

During dinner, Frank and Margot talked about people Bunny had never met. Who was pregnant, who had been fired or promoted, who had relapsed after spending a fortune at rehab, whose gallbladder stones were acting up again. Bunny watched them and pinched her thigh under the table each time she got the staticky, unreal feeling she was watching an American sitcom.

Every once in a while, Margot looked at Bunny from across the table and crinkled her eyes. Bunny assumed she had clinical dry eye.

Eat more, Margot kept saying. We need to get some meat on those bones!

The phrase made Bunny's stomach turn, especially when she was chewing on a drumstick. She looked at Frank, who didn't look at either of them but instead studied the pine cone centerpiece on the table with enormous concentration. Bunny noticed Frank was different around his daughter. Smaller and more apologetic, from the way he looked sideways at Margot to the way he cut her a square of brownie and passed it to her, as if it were an offering at an altar.

After Frank had gone upstairs, the two women stood at the sink. Margot washed and Bunny dried.

If you don't mind me asking, Margot began, passing her a wooden spoon, how old are you?

Bunny considered this. Age is just a number, she finally replied, a line stolen from a sitcom.

Margot snorted. She continued to scrub the plate in her hand, though nothing was left to scrub. Then she set the sponge down and turned to face Bunny.

He doesn't have any money.

What?

I just thought I should make that clear.

Margot turned back to the dishes. What I'm trying to say is—neither of you should stay in an arrangement made under false pretenses. Margot stared out the kitchen window into the yard. She seemed to say this more to herself than anyone else.

Okay? Bunny said.

After she finished drying the dishes, they went upstairs together.

Do you want to sleep in your old room? Bunny asked when they passed it. I don't mind.

Margot stepped inside and looked around. Her face instantly changed. This is where you sleep?

Duh. Another expression nicked from TV.

Margot laughed. A beautiful, full laugh, round at the edges. Bunny smiled up at her.

No, I'm just getting the air mattress from the closet, Margot said after she caught her breath. On her way out, she lingered at the threshold, running her hand along a daisy-shaped light switch.

Merry Christmas, Bunny said.

Margot turned around and blinked, as if she'd forgotten Bunny's presence.

Oh. Right, well—Merry Christmas, Bunny.

A month after her arrival in the cardboard box, Bunny announced she wanted to take the GED.

The GED? Frank frowned.

At a community college, Bunny said. On her way up the stairs, she paused to add, I want to get my driver's license, too.

Naturally, Frank was supportive. He was not one to stop a modern woman from pursuing her professional objectives or learning how to navigate the road without supervision. He brought home study books and quizzed Bunny on North American geography and basic algebra. In a Lowe's parking lot at night, they practiced parallel parking.

Most days, Bunny ate breakfast, then went straight to the community college. She was rarely home for dinner, not to make it or eat it.

Can I have twenty bucks? she asked one morning.

What for? Frank stood up from the sofa, concerned.

I'm going out.

With who?

Friends.

You have *friends?* Frank frowned even more deeply. Somehow, in all his preparation for Bunny's arrival, he had not foreseen this possibility.

The rare moments she was home, Bunny spent all her time in the living room watching Korean soap operas dubbed in Mandarin and smoking menthol cigarettes. She sat on the floor, a bag of garlic-flavored potato chips slit open beside her. The kitchen soon became cramped with cartons of Tsingtao beer and spicy instant noodles with a picture of a chicken on fire. Frank had tried them once and experienced forty-eight-hour indigestion. Instead of offering to drive to the drugstore to buy him Pepto-Bismol (did they have Pepto-Bismol in Taiwan?) she had offered him one of her imported beers.

With a gun to his head, Frank could never have predicted a wife quite like Bunny. He had imagined them making pasta together while listening to light jazz. Adopting a rescue dog and taking him on long walks, stopping often to let children fawn over him. Playing bingo at the community center and eating tacos on Taco Tuesday (she would order carnitas and he would order pollo, they would share). Tackling crossword puzzles on Sunday mornings and watching a rented movie on Saturday nights while enjoying low-sodium popcorn.

Susan used to leave him thoughtful (and occasionally naughty) notes on the refrigerator. She wore Jergens extra dry skin lotion and shapely orthopedic shoes. He liked seeing the little frosted pots and bottles crowding her side of the bathroom sink. He watched her pat on her cold cream with something akin to fascination. She was allergic to shellfish. Her birthstone was opal and her favorite color was lilac. She feared heights and stairs without handrails. She could only fall asleep with a night-light on in the hallway; not the bedroom, but just outside it. He knew her—completely and fully.

Frank made a decision: he would remove his heart from its safe little kennel. He would let it sniff around, take in the fresh air.

When he asked Bunny if she was available to watch his favorite film, *Tremors* (1990), she said she would check her schedule and get back to him. She never did. He bought Bunny tulips, which she carried to her bedroom and left to wilt on the dresser (she thought trying to keep something dead alive was foolish). He took her to his favorite Tex-Mex restaurant with the complementary tortilla chips, where she spent twenty minutes in the bathroom talking to a friend on the phone. Not wanting to be impolite, he waited for Bunny as his chicken enchilada platter congealed. He booked them a couples' tango class, where he watched her and the instructor, Sebastián, dance for an hour while he sat in a metal folding chair and recorded them on his phone. She wanted to review the steps later, she told him.

Still, Frank remained undeterred. He would work hard to wriggle into Bunny's daily routine, to position himself inside her life like a necessary but unobtrusive organ. A kidney, for instance.

At work, his boss called him into his office for a stern talking-to. His monthly sales were down. His monthly sales had never been down before. Frank admitted he had been distracted as of late. He spent most of his workday researching Bunny's motherland.

"What is QQ?" he asked the Internet. He typed on the keyboard as slowly and earnestly as a first grader. "What is strawberry generation?" He studied photos of the famous carved fatty pork and jade cabbage, housed at the National Palace Museum, trying to decipher the reason behind their importance. He lost an entire afternoon researching the February 28 incident and another to the White Terror. He only wanted to get to know his wife.

What are you thinking? he asked once, when she was chain-smoking on the sofa after returning home late again.

She shrugged and said, How I can afford a bachelor's degree without accruing student debt.

Since she had made friends, Bunny's English had greatly improved. Frank's Mandarin had not. The secondhand Rosetta Stone he'd bought still sat bulging in its plastic wrap. The boxed set looked intimidatingly at him from its perch on the bookshelf—like it wanted to take him out behind the schoolyard and knock him around a bit. Frank had failed French in middle school; he had not recovered.

I see, Frank said. He hoped she would ask him the same question: What are you thinking?

Instead, she got up and made him a cup of coffee. Five teaspoons of sugar, no cream.

That night, Frank logged on to the website's twenty-four/seven online customer service chat.

MAIL ORDER LOVE®
24/7 CUSTOMER SERVICE CHAT BOX

Sheryl: Hello! How can I help you?

Frank: I'm not connecting with my wife.

Sheryl: I'm sorry to hear that. Our studies show emotional connection takes six to twelve months to build. Did I answer your question?

MAIL ORDER LOVE®

Frank: No.

Sheryl: Would you like to buy our online marriage counselor services for only $99.99 per session?

Frank: [Typing . . .]

Sheryl: Are you still there?

Frank: No. I mean no, I do not want to buy the sessions.

Sheryl: Would you like to return your bride for a refund? (Disclaimer: after ninety days, full refunds are no longer available.)

Frank: No.

Sheryl: Is there anything else I can help you with?

Frank: Yes.

Sheryl: Please describe your issue.

Frank: On my wife's first night here, she made me six cups of coffee. I don't know if this is her way of saying she's upset with me? We have a bit of a language issue, you see.

Sheryl: I'm sorry, I did not understand that. Is your issue with 1. Refund 2. Reviews 3. Shipping 4. Marriage Counseling?

Frank: None of the above.

Sheryl: Have I solved your problem? Select: [Yes] [No] [Other]

Frank: [No]

Sheryl: [Typing . . .]

Frank: Hello? Are you still there?

Sheryl: I'm sorry to hear I have not solved your problem. I would like to offer you a FREE OF CHARGE excerpt from our marriage counseling service.

Frank: OK . . .

Sheryl: "Communication is key in any marriage. Don't be afraid to express your needs and how your spouse can meet those needs."

Frank: [Typing . . .]

Sheryl: Thank you for contacting MAIL ORDER LOVE®. Please rate my service on a scale of one to five stars.

The next time they practiced driving at the Lowe's parking lot, Frank broached the subject. He waited until he gave Bunny a dose of positive reinforcement ("very good three-point turn"), then folded his hands across his knees.

Bunny . . . Frank began, then tacked on "darling," because that was how one spoke to one's wife, wasn't it?

Bunny darling, we've been married for over a month and in that time, well—he cleared his throat and wished he'd brought a thermos of water—I haven't been getting what I need.

In the driver's seat, Bunny tensed up.

Frank continued, a little less sure of himself. What I mean is, a wife has certain . . . duties. Yes?

Bunny pictured a woman vacuuming, mopping, dusting. Mixing, stirring, baking, roasting, blending.

You want me to clean more? To cook? she said, not at Frank but at the windshield. A teenage boy and girl exited the store in a shopping cart. The boy squatted inside the cart as the girl pushed off with one foot, then hung on to the back of the cart as it sped down a stretch of empty lanes.

No, Frank said, more forcefully than he'd intended. He didn't know how to communicate taco night, movies and popcorn, a curly-haired dog named Jasper.

I understand. It's fine. Bunny's voice was flat.

Bunny—

But she was already starting up the car and reversing out of the lot.

Once more, Frank got the unsettling feeling that Bunny was unreadable. Perhaps unknowable.

MAIL ORDER LOVE®

Bunny did not think of herself as a complicated woman. She had wanted to move to America in the same way she wanted to try free-fall skydiving one day. She had seen movies that depicted its cold steel towers, its purple mountains and amber plains. She had heard rumors of tax rebates and lifetime guarantees. Gender reveal parties, farm-to-table restaurants, antique flea markets, monster trucks, DIY furniture, Crest Whitestrips—all of it was foreign to her. Exciting. New.

Bunny didn't like to plan too far into the future. Her GED friends said this was typical for an Aries with a moon in Sagittarius and a rising Gemini. She knew she was Year of the Dragon and AB blood type, but this distillation of herself, of her personhood, was foreign. Exciting. New. As though, having crossed the border into America, she had access to parts of herself she couldn't access before.

She thought Frank was a nice enough man. He let her do what she wanted. He was always asking if she was hungry or cold. He said a lot of funny phrases like "birds of a feather flock together" and "time flies when you're having fun." He encouraged her to take a daily multivitamin gummy. He worried whenever she left the house without a thermos of water—what will you do if you get thirsty and you can't locate a water fountain? he nagged her.

In some ways, he reminded her of her father, who had died when she was sixteen. She missed her mother. On WeChat, she asked if Bunny was being a good wife.

當然, Bunny typed with irritation. Her mother was so nosy.

Then, remembering the conversation in the car, she backspaced and texted, Mama, what do husbands like to do for fun?

Her mother replied with a sticker of a cartoon dancing pig.

The next day, Bunny invited Frank to Six Flags. Frank's heart couldn't withstand roller coasters the way it used to, but he was happy—elated, even—to be asked. His elation deflated, however, when they arrived at the entrance and were greeted by four of Bunny's GED friends.

Frank spent the day buying everyone soda from the vending machines, standing at the bottom of rides cradling their bags, hats and wallets, making sure they were reapplying SPF 45 sunscreen every forty-five minutes.

When Frank pulled into their driveway, Bunny thanked him. I had fun, she said. Remembering her decision to be a better wife, she asked, Did *you* have fun?

Frank could not look at her. Why did you tell your friends I was your uncle?

Oh. Well.

I am your husband, Bunny.

I know.

Frank gathered his courage. Can you love me one day? As your husband?

Bunny remained silent. She cleared her throat and lowered and raised then lowered the car window.

Frank fumbled with the car door before it sprang open. His shorts billowed around his pale legs as he sprinted towards the house.

After several minutes, Bunny resigned herself to going upstairs. She pressed her ear against Frank's bedroom door, then shrank back as if it had singed her. She thought she heard crying. It was not the first time she'd heard it. Bunny's stomach hurt. She felt tricked. Nothing had seemed permanent in this country. Here, sadness was supposed to be fixed with an over-the-counter product or by calling customer service.

She walked back to her room, sat on the squeaky inflatable chair and thought. Maybe, it was true, she hadn't been focused on her responsibilities as a wife. Maybe, it was true, she hadn't considered Frank as her husband. As a romantic partner.

An American expression came to her: "grin and bear it." The equivalent in Mandarin: "eat your bitterness." But a gray space had to exist, a space for compromise. That was another American virtue: negotiation.

Bunny sat up—she remembered that next week was Frank's birthday. She'd plan a party for him. With all of his favorite foods, which she could make, probably, if she watched some online tutorials. She'd invite his friends—though, now that she thought about it, most of them lived in retirement housing. Or his daughter and her family, his grandchildren—yes, that would make him happy.

Bunny slipped downstairs, passing Frank's bedroom on the landing. A pout seemed to radiate through the closed door.

She went inside his office for the first time. On his shelf were books about penguin migration, the habits of highly successful salesmen and how to make meals with five ingredients or less. On his desk were bills, receipts and coupons for a place called Sizzler. Underneath, she found a printout from the Internet, "A Beginner's Guide to Cross-Strait Tensions Between Taiwan and China" with highlighted sections. In spite of herself, a smile leaked from the corners of her mouth.

She opened his desk drawer and poked around. Nothing. She checked the second drawer: still no address book. Bunny was about to abandon her search when she spotted a carefully preserved piece of paper, pink and smooth to the touch.

WHERE ARE YOU REALLY FROM

MAIL ORDER LOVE® RECEIPT

CUSTOMER SERVICE NUMBER: 1-800-MAIL-LUV

Please keep this receipt as proof of purchase for returns and exchanges

ITEM: Mail Order Bride
Package Type: Premium
Country of Origin: Taiwan

ORDER DATE: October 12
ORDER NO: MOB400298548

SUBTOTAL: $3999
1-YEAR WARRANTY: $999
2-DAY EXPRESS SHIPPING: $550
DISCOUNT (FIRSTORDER10): 10% off
CA SALES TAX: 9.75%
IMPORT TAX: 6.25%
TOTAL: $5792.11

PAYMENT METHOD: MASTERCARD
xxxx xxxx xxxx 8142

RETURN POLICY
Refunds and/or exchanges are offered within the first 90 days of purchase (no exceptions).

Eligibility for Refunds and Exchanges

* The item must be unused and in the same condition that it was received.
* The item must be in the original packaging.
* A receipt or proof of purchase is required (no exceptions).
* Mail Order Love® does not cover return shipping costs.

Exchanges (if applicable)

* Items can be replaced only if they are defective or damaged.

Bunny stomped to her bedroom, the receipt crumpled in her fist. She shut the door with a bang, not caring if Frank heard. She had changed her mind about the birthday party.

MAIL ORDER LOVE®

Bunny learned to jimmy the lock on the garage side door. In her bed, she built a mound of clothes in the form of a body and crowned it with a Halloween-store wig. She crept downstairs after midnight and carried her shoes in her hands. With her GED friends, she climbed over gates into community pools and went swimming in her underwear. She learned how to make Jell-O shots and smoked weed out of a plastic water bottle, aluminum foil pressed over its mouth. She played Truth or Dare and chose Dare more often than Truth. Having friends turned out to be expensive, but one of them worked at Best Buy and got her a job as a cashier.

Bunny had been neglecting her studies in exchange for having fun. She had never experienced fun fit for a music video montage. Fun you could package and resell.

Sometimes her friends invoked the fuzzy outline of Frank in their conversations, like a hologram. They called him her "old man." How's your old man? they asked. Sometimes they made jokes like, Did Bunny have to change his Depends? Did she have to pick up his dentures when they popped out during dinner? Did everyone assume she was his adopted daughter? She would laugh, though it felt like she'd swallowed something laced with mold.

After Frank found Bunny passed out on the couch one morning, fully clothed and reeking of sour, day-old Smirnoff, Frank began to ask to see her cell phone when she came home at night. He limited her computer time to one hour a day, with the child protection mode turned on. He stopped asking her to play Scrabble. He took to drinking Bunny's imported Tsingtao beer and flushing her cigarettes down the toilet.

Come home straight after work, he said. And I don't want to see you hanging around with those low-life friends of yours anymore. They're a bad influence on you, to which Bunny had learned to roll her eyes.

Sometimes Frank trailed after her into her bedroom, asking, Have you even thought of applying to college yet? The SATs won't pass themselves, you know. You have to take your future seriously, young lady.

In Mandarin, Bunny told Frank she'd started having a different dream. She was floating on her back in the Pacific Ocean watching a plane tunnel and swoop through the sky. Suddenly she was inside the plane just as it spiraled into the water. The waves swelled around her magnificently, as tall as skyscrapers.

I can't understand you, Frank cried. What are you saying?

On the news, relations between Taiwan and China had worsened. A universal beauty pageant had printed TAIWAN on the Taiwanese contestant's sash instead of NEW TAIPEI. China was outraged. The U.S. president was flummoxed. Between defending democracy and annoying a superpower that manufactured a third of all American goods, his hands were tied. But rest assured, the White House formally announced, America considered Taiwan a great friend. As a show of said friendship, ten tons of Florida oranges were gifted to the president of Taiwan.

When Frank was vacuuming one day, he found a leopard-print bra underneath Bunny's bed. One he certainly had not purchased at the mall on Bunny's second day in America. He did not ask if it belonged to her or someone else. Instead, he threw it into the recycling bin. He bought a bestselling book, *How to Make Her Love You in Thirty Days*, and kept it locked in his nightstand.

Frank had bought Bunny in a similar fashion, on impulse. He'd

MAIL ORDER LOVE®

been midnight channel surfing on his corduroy La-Z-Boy when a Mail Order Love® advertisement shone on the screen, sandwiched between an infomercial for Precious Moments figurines and erectile dysfunction pills. As he watched the Technicolor advertisement—love at your fingertips, never be lonely again—he felt more awake than he'd felt in years. What a feat of the twenty-first century! This was the beauty of consumerism: a promise to ward off feelings you never wanted to experience again. Pesky out-of-control feelings that didn't come with a how-to manual.

Spring arrived. Frank had finished his rotation of office work and was back to in-person rounds for the next three months. Today he was in a suburb of Anaheim Hills, tidy-looking houses with stone siding, constructed in the seventies. A warm breeze brightened his step.

He knocked on the door of a yellow house with two lovely ceramic birds roosting in the corner. A woman answered it: she looked to be in her sixties, her hair in a bob so soft, he almost reached out to touch it. Her blue-gray eyes seemed kind. As he brandished the newest model of the ZipMaster3000 and asked if she could spare a minute of her time, he waited, as he always did, for her to disappoint him. Everyone was always busy or already owned a vacuum that worked perfectly fine. But the woman—Deborah, she said—nodded that yes, she had time.

Frank set the vacuum down and straightened his tie. He launched into his usual speech, noting the model's superior qualities, but—encouraged by Deborah's friendly smile—decided to improvise a little. Modern life—what a hoot, huh? Nobody had time these days, not like they used to, and he didn't blame them, it wasn't anyone's fault. Women didn't have time for vacuuming anymore because—for good reason!—they were busy doing things like getting the GED and exploring their sexuality. And that was where the ZipMaster3000 came in!

Deborah's smile wavered.

My wife, Frank said pointedly, is one such modern woman. And he respected her ambitions, he did. For example, she wanted to buy her own car and even though she still couldn't parallel park to his standards, he was fine—FINE!—with the idea.

Deborah closed her front door a few centimeters but Frank failed to notice, engrossed as he was in his monologue.

He supported Bunny through and through. When she'd insisted on buying the extra-large limited-edition Mountain Dew–flavored potato chips last week, he knew she would not be able to finish them before their expiration date, leaving him, Frank—whose doctor had restricted him to a limited amount of daily calories—to finish the chips, because, unlike her, he was not spoiled, he could not stand to waste food, he was from a generation used to *working* for things.

Speaking of which, what had happened to good old-fashioned *sucking it up*, pardon his French? True, no one *wanted* to spend their Saturday cleaning up their room, folding their laundry and loading the dishwasher, but who said everything in life was a picnic? If you agreed to something, you did it. Why *agree* to something you never intended to follow through on? Wasn't that awfully, awfully selfish? Did vows—spoken in front of a minister of the state, no less!—mean nothing? Was something like the sacred exchange of *rings* a meaningless act?

No one had any respect anymore—that was the problem! Teenagers lambasted their teachers on the Internet without consequence, people threw themselves in front of buses to file million-dollar lawsuits and won, politicians were constantly apologizing to their constituents for hurting their feelings. If a store was robbed, the owner couldn't call the police on the robber because of some hoo-ha about class and privilege. Everything was topsy-turvy. Nothing made sense anymore. What did Bunny expect from him? No, really, what exactly did she EXPECT FROM HIM?

Frank realized he had worked himself up into such a frenzy that his underarms were pungently drenched. He noticed, too, that Deborah was visible only by a sliver, she was closing her front door while murmuring about a casserole in the oven, thank you, though, she had the pamphlet, yes, all right, goodbye.

Then the door clicked shut and Frank had only the ceramic birds for company.

MAIL ORDER LOVE®

FREQUENTLY ASKED QUESTIONS

My M.O.B. and I are having trouble communicating.
If you did not order a Premium Package, consider enrolling your M.O.B. in adult English classes.

My M.O.B. talks about wanting to go home all the time.
Introduce your M.O.B. to your friends and family. Discover mutual interests and hobbies. Make her feel included in your day-to-day life.

I'm worried my M.O.B. only married me to get a green card.
We vet all our M.O.B.s carefully to ensure they signed up to be a part of MAIL ORDER LOVE® because they are invested in finding true love. If you feel that this is not the case, we encourage you to enroll in a counseling session with one of our licensed marriage counselors. If you feel that the sessions do not help, contact us for information on how to begin the refund process.

WHERE ARE YOU REALLY FROM

Bunny passed her driver's license test on the first try. To celebrate, her GED friends took her to Rainforest Cafe. A lanky orangutan creaked from the ceiling and a muscular gorilla leered at them over their booth. Artificial thunderstorms, animatronic creatures, a labyrinth of vines and other endless décor pulled at Bunny's attention until she was dizzy.

The restaurant offered a special promo every Saturday: if a customer spent over $50 on a meal, they were entitled to unlimited Safari Fries. Bunny, being an enormous fan of fries, decided to spend part of her first paycheck on a surf and turf platter, a milkshake and a lava cake. She told her friends to help themselves.

Their ponytailed server brought over a basket of Safari Fries. Five minutes later, they disappeared. Bunny asked for a refill and the server obliged, her lipsticked smile stretching wide.

Sure thing, honey.

Bunny could never get over how people here called complete strangers "honey" and "sweetie."

When the server came back, however, she was empty-handed. The kitchen was out of fries, she explained. Bunny's friends were already murmuring their understanding when she frowned and turned to the server.

Excuse me? she said. This is unacceptable.

The server looked around and kept smiling, as if Bunny were joking.

This is not a joke, Bunny added, to make herself clear.

Her friend Amanda, sitting beside her in the striped booth, patted Bunny's shoulder and said, Hey, it's okay. We ate a lot.

Her other friends echoed their fullness, their couldn't-eat-another-fry-even-if-I-tried-ness.

But Bunny was immovable. She crossed her arms. I want to speak to your manager, she said.

Her friends looked away as if they were Bunny's children and she was their disruptive mother who had drunk one glass of wine too many.

The server's smile departed entirely. No more "honey" or "sweetie." Fine, she said, and turned away.

Ten minutes later, a free meal voucher secured in her hand, Bunny and her friends loitered in the parking lot.

Why'd you make that into such a big deal? Kevin asked.

Her other friends waited to hear her response.

I want my money's worth, Bunny finally said.

She felt annoyed she had to explain such an obvious fact. Wasn't it an American virtue? Weren't people obsessed with getting their money's worth? Wasn't it why, when her friends went to a buffet, they stayed until their allotted two hours were up and not a moment sooner? Wasn't it why, when they had paid for three hours of parking, they hated leaving behind an hour of free parking to some freeloading stranger? Wasn't it why they threw their hands up in annoyance when they bought a new shirt or phone or video game and the very next day at the mall, saw that it was now on sale? Wasn't it why they treated Black Friday like a holiday more sacred than Christmas and Thanksgiving combined? Wasn't Black Friday, at bottom, not about getting one's money's worth, but getting that and more? Wasn't it really about fucking over someone— the idea that if they got less, and you walked away with more, you had won?

WHERE ARE YOU REALLY FROM

What did $5,792 mean?

What the fuck were you supposed to get out of $5,792?

Her friends were silent. No one knew what Bunny was talking about. Even if she explained, the only comfort they could provide would amount to *That sucks*. None of them had made the choices she had.

Frank was having trouble sleeping. Deborah—what a deceptively friendly smile she had!—had submitted a complaint about him. He woke up around three a.m. and puttered downstairs for a warm glass of milk. He stared at the backyard, drenched in blue moonlight, his thoughts an empty field of nothing. As he was heading back upstairs, headlights glazed the living room windows followed by the unmistakable sound of his car wheezing into the driveway.

Frank walked to the garage door just as Bunny came in, his car keys dangling from her fingers. It wasn't the first time she'd "borrowed" Frank's Buick without his permission, but it was the first time she'd been caught. It was four a.m. She stank of marijuana. He raised his voice at her. Bunny was so surprised, she cried—another first. When she cried, the commas around her mouth sank. She looked older, closer to her actual age.

Bunny's tears made Frank constipated with anger. He wasn't supposed to incite such helpless rage in her. The possibility was not even listed under the website's FAQ page.

Bunny cursed at him in Mandarin, calling him a dog's bark and a mixed egg, and—sick of hearing her speak in a language that rendered him a dumb uncomprehending child—Frank smashed his mug on the kitchen floor. It made an awful noise. The mug was styled in the likeness of a cartoon character, a deranged-looking Tasmanian Devil. Frank had bought it for Bunny at Six Flags. He stared at the broken mug, then his hands, his jaw agape.

Bunny ran upstairs to her bedroom and came back with a pink slip in her hand. Frank was still staring at the pile of broken shards.

Bunny waved the slip in Frank's face, livid. Why did you keep this?

She misinterpreted the look on his face for apathy, but it was a look of exhaustion. He was sorry he had yelled at her. What are you talking about? he asked quietly.

Bunny responded by ripping up the pink slip. The pieces floated downwards as if in slow motion, landing gently on top of the shards. Only then did Frank realize Bunny had found the receipt. Before he could say a single word, the slam of her bedroom door put a period on the fight.

Bunny discovered an online forum for women like her. It included information on what to pack, lists of breathable wedding dresses that didn't wrinkle in cardboard boxes, the best kind of sleeping pills with the least amount of side effects. Women traded notes on American etiquette: how they liked their hands to be gripped (firmly), how they liked to be looked at (in the eyes but with frequent breaks), how they liked to have you stand near them (a radius of some two feet). The women shared tips and advice.

Pros and cons of having a baby here. DISCUSS. **[520 comments]**

Group brainstorm: dinner conversation topics. **[67 comments]**

Are we "sugar babies"? **[1,093 comments]**

WHERE ARE YOU REALLY FROM

Domestic Violence hotline. **[18 comments]**

Do you ever feel lonely? **[44 comments]**

Bunny attended a meet-up in her area. She took a local bus to a bus station, then an hour-long Greyhound bus to a café in a shopping center adorned in fake plants. Everything was beige. The sofas were deep. The women sat in a circle drinking lattes and cappuccinos and Americanos. They met every month. Sometimes they would discuss a preselected novel. The novels were always about a woman trapped in bad circumstances, which ended with the woman either gracefully accepting her bad circumstances or murder.

And how are you feeling? a woman with a tight perm asked the circle. Don't just say fine, she chided. Tell us how you're *really* feeling.

Someone said, I miss speaking Vietnamese at home.

Someone else said, I miss the taste of my mother's dotorimuk. I found some at H Mart but it's not the same.

Another woman said, Yesterday, I tried to say "power strip" in Ukrainian and I forgot how. I still can't remember. Does anyone know how to say it?

The women shook their heads and looked down at the sugar-studded strudels and muffins on their laps.

When it was Bunny's turn to speak, she did not know what to say. After a minute, she pushed the word *Fine* out of her mouth like it was an insult.

The woman with the tight perm shook her head. Oh, honey, how are you *really* feeling?

The other women all looked at Bunny with big smiles and sad eyes.

She sighed.

I miss my mom and my friends in Taipei. I miss how it was never quiet in my alleyway and how the rain looked against the green glass in the kitchen window. Sometimes I even miss the café where I used to work. I miss ordering food without anyone asking me to repeat myself. I miss walking around at night and never worrying if a man in a white van was going to kidnap me. I miss knowing how to be funny—I'm funny in Mandarin, but not in English. I wanted to leave Taiwan but sometimes I—

Bunny stopped to drink from her iced Americano.

I have friends but sometimes they look at me funny because I came here in a box. Sometimes I hate the man who bought me. Because what kind of person buys another person? Sometimes I hate myself because I let it happen. Because what kind of person lets herself be bought?

A strangled choke came from the direction of the Ukrainian woman. She got up and ran to the bathroom. The meeting ended soon after. Bunny followed the woman, a packet of lotion-infused tissues in her hand, but all three stalls were empty.

Outside the bathroom, a willowy woman with a long gray braid was waiting. Bunny held the door open for her, but instead of entering, the woman thrust a yellow flyer into her hands. Her eyes looked wild. Before Bunny could say a word, the woman turned around and fled.

Bunny looked down at the flyer: *Are You the Victim of a Sex Trafficking Ring? Know Your Rights and Seek Emancipation Today! Call 1-800-Free-Her.*

Her cheeks burned. She balled up the flyer and threw it into the trash along with her Americano.

On the bus ride home, Bunny fell asleep and dreamt she was in a giant superstore. She needed to return a toaster, but the moment she stepped inside, she forgot why she'd come. The store was floating in the middle of the Pacific Ocean. None of the water flowed inside when the automatic doors slid open. The lights were white and very bright. Garlands of American flags crisscrossed the ceiling. Inside was everything Bunny could ever want. She could buy a lawn mower. A life-sized dollhouse. Two-in-one shampoo-conditioner and discount sneakers and bulk chocolate chip cookies in plastic tubs. Ugly things were for sale, too, like automatic guns and Halloween costumes that left a bad taste in her mouth. When she tried to check out, she couldn't leave. Every exit opened into another store. So they weren't exits after all. They were new doors, endless doors. She kept moving through them. She had come in search of something and she was going to find it.

Occasionally, the online forum was infiltrated by trolls. The first image Bunny saw when she looked up "troll" was of the children's toy: disturbing-looking creatures with neon poufs of hair. She could never picture them as anything else afterwards. She imagined these trolls, with their strangely mournful eyes and stubby hands, typing furiously at their pint-sized computer desks. Despite their funny appearance, the trolls did not leave funny comments.

> No one forced you to come here. **[29 upvotes]**
>
> If you don't like it here, just go back to where you came from. **[117 upvotes]**
>
> You made your bed, now lie in it (literally)! **[309 upvotes]**

The moderators did their best to ban the trolls but this was America, after all. Even trolls had a right to free speech. Bunny soon learned that no correct answers to a troll existed. Anything a woman might say would be met with another insult, another argument. Don't let the trolls get to you, everyone said. And yet they did—get to Bunny, that is.

At Best Buy, when she was restocking the shelves or stickering sale items, she found herself arguing with these imaginary trolls. She wanted to explain herself. She wanted to tell them that no, maybe she wasn't escaping a war-torn country on the brink of famine and the ravages of global warming. No, she wasn't diagnosed with a disease she could not afford to treat in her home country. No, she wasn't running away from an abusive ex-husband who had sewn trackers into the lining of her suitcase and would hunt her down at any moment.

When Bunny heard of America's immigration ban, she had felt stunned, then indignant. Why was she, specifically, shut out from this country? She never dreamt of moving to America. She just thought she'd visit, one day. Drive along Route 66 and sleep under a carpet of stars and check out Las Vegas and maybe try free-fall skydiving. But she didn't think America was *better* than her and yet the ban disagreed. A door had been slammed in her face, a door Bunny had been ambivalent about stepping through, but this only made her feel more entitled to what lay beyond it. That singular act led her to look up the Mail Order Love® website. To submit an application. She told herself that she wouldn't be chosen. She was chosen just three months later.

It wasn't so much that Bunny wanted to open the door, she simply could not stand it being closed. Her greatest fear was being cornered. Out of options. She wasn't always like this. She'd been too busy with the prosaic drama of daily life—school and exams, friends and crushes, arguments and makeups—to want more than she'd been given. But then her father died.

No, that was the sanitized synopsis that didn't scare her friends. What happened was a "business associate," a man she called "uncle" who she'd known half her life, had pulled a knife out on him while they were drinking baijiu and eating dried squid one night. Her father had laughed, thinking it a joke. It all happened so fast, in surprisingly intimate silence, that by the time Bunny and her mother realized what the uncle had done, he was gone.

The last time Bunny saw her father, he was lying on the living room floor, a look of utter disbelief on his face. As the paramedics pulled a white sheet over him, a fracture opened up inside Bunny's chest.

She never learned why that uncle had attacked her father, though she had her theories. Bunny's mother never told her and she never asked. The only thing she told Bunny was that she must never speak of what happened—not even to the police. She had to pretend her father's murderer was a stranger who'd broken into their apartment.

At the crematorium, Bunny's mother had remained silent until just before leaving, when she said offhandedly, You know, life will always be a little bit worse than it was before.

And she was right.

The next year, Bunny's classmates all headed off to different universities. She started working at a Family Mart convenience store, then Dante Café. She and her mother led inconspicuous lives, afraid of making even a single, inconsequential wave. When Bunny was twenty-three, her mother started dating a man nine years younger than her, raising eyebrows in their neighborhood, but Bunny could understand why. He wasn't assertive, he liked being told what to do. When her mother's boyfriend moved in with them, the boyfriend wore a frilly apron and matching slippers whenever he was home, gifts from her mother. The explicitness of their laughter, their private joy, penetrated through Bunny's closed bedroom door.

Instead of returning home after work, Bunny escaped to twenty-four/seven Internet cafés and read online manga where love and revenge were both easily won. She felt the fracture inside her chest split into finer and finer fractures and wondered what would become of her if it continued ad infinitum.

And then, the announcement of the ban.

Margot called her father every Sunday evening at five p.m. Frank liked to take these calls outside in the backyard, sitting on a lawn chair with a glass of iced tea cooling his hand. He tried not to let on how much he looked forward to the calls, how his productivity went out the window after lunch because his mind would be on the call. This Sunday, however, Frank sat on the lawn chair for the better part of the entire day, his mind stuck on that empty field of nothing.

Bunny was out, again. When he had nowhere else to be, he let her borrow the Buick because what was the point in convincing her to stay? She wasn't his prisoner. He hadn't suggested that they go out to the movies or a new restaurant in months. She never suggested it, either. When one needed something from the other, they communicated it with as few words as possible. More often than not, they left each other sticky notes on the fridge: "Be back late tonight." "Dinner is in the fridge, reheat at 350 degrees."

"We're out of dish detergent." Susan's loving and teasing notes seemed from so long ago, so beyond the bounds of his current reality, that Frank wondered if he'd imagined them.

A new cleaning chart announced whose turn it was to take out the trash or wash the car. When Bunny had tacked it to the fridge, Frank's heart had floated to the floor along with the note. Even if they lightly bickered about whose turn it was to empty the trash or wash the car, wasn't that a part of marriage? One of its small joys that, when taken away, you sorely missed?

Frank and Bunny had become nothing more than roommates. Barely speaking roommates. And yet Frank didn't hold it against Bunny, not in the slightest. But after the smashing of the mug and the ripping up of the receipt—all of it had been too disastrous of a mudslide, too treacherous of a glacier, to acknowledge out in the open, much less apologize for.

Frank's phone rang.

Hi, Dad, how are you? came Margot's soothing made-for-radio voice.

He listened as she caught him up on her work, her husband, the state of her garden. And of course, the kids, his beloved grandchildren.

What about you, Dad? How was your week?

Oh, it was fine. Frank sipped from his iced tea before realizing the glass was all ice, no tea.

Margot waited for him to elaborate. Just fine?

Yep.

On the other line, he heard a sigh. How are things with Bunny? Margot asked in an oddly prim voice. Frank sat up and wondered if he'd heard her right. Margot never asked about Bunny.

Oh, well—we don't have to—

It's okay, Margot said, more evenly. I mean, who else are you going to talk about it with?

Frank's gratitude for his daughter was so immense that his eyes smarted with tears.

He found himself telling her everything—the broken mug, the merry-go-round of notes on the fridge.

Margot listened patiently, then said, One gesture goes a long way. Show her that you care. That you're willing to talk and make things right.

One gesture, Frank repeated. He worried his wedding band. That's all?

You need to take the pressure off making this . . . marriage work. Just focus on making it bearable to live again in the same house. Make it fun.

The next day, Frank arrived at work feeling chipper. Bob had told him to come by the office before heading out for his rounds, but his thoughts were on tonight's surprise: he had reserved an enormous bouquet more expensive than most of his belongings, which he would pick up after work along with a box of chocolates (Bunny's favorite were liqueur filled). He was planning to cook dinner, too, the same meal he'd cooked on their wedding night: steak, potatoes and a healthy side of greens.

When he walked into the office, Bob looked at him the same way you looked at a horse you were about to euthanize and process into glue.

I'm sorry, Frank, was all he said, spreading his hands across his desk. They had known each other for too long to beat around the bush.

Frank sank into the chair across from him. Why?

Bob considered Frank for a lengthy minute, then turned his computer screen around, open to their company website. It's the reviews, Bob said. You know how much they're a stickler for reviews at the main office.

Reviews? Frank said in a barely audible voice.

★

Kept talking about his wife, who he doesn't want to drive. Highly unprofessional.

★

Spent an hour arguing that nothing is the same these days? He didn't even try to sell me a vacuum.

★★

When I called him to follow up on the ZipMaster6000 model, he asked me for marriage advice. Nice enough guy but I still don't know if the suction power of the ZipMaster6000 outperforms the ZipMaster3000.

I see, Frank said quietly. He sat back in his chair as Bob re-angled his computer screen.

You'll have full severance, of course.

Frank nodded, hardly listening.

Bob leaned over the table. Is everything okay at home?

Frank looked at Bob head-on. No, Bob, everything is not okay at home.

Then a light shifted in Frank's eyes. He stood up, shook Bob's hand, a startled look on his face like he'd just witnessed a miracle, and left to gather up his things in a cardboard box.

Bunny looked down at her phone: Frank was calling her again. She didn't answer. She was on her way to Long Beach with two of her friends to sign a lease on an apartment. Bunny wasn't sure how to tell Frank so she didn't. She'd leave the same way she'd arrived: alone. And how could he blame her? Frank was a grown man. He should know people came with no guarantees.

The bouquet was so large, it hogged Frank's entire passenger seat. At the store, he had added a few Mylar balloons because, why not? Three heart-shaped ones bobbed happily in the back seat. FM 104.7 was playing Eartha Kitt and the sky was turning that particular brand of Southern Californian pinky-orange, more a taste (Thrifty's rainbow sherbet) than a color. He would have rolled the windows down, if not for the balloons.

When he switched to the right turn lane, he checked his blind spot as he always did. The bouquet and the balloons made the task more difficult than usual, but he kept looking to make sure the next lane was clear, no oncoming cars or pedestrians or bicyclists. But, perhaps because he checked his blind spot a few seconds longer than usual, when he looked back out the windshield, the car in front of him—a white pickup truck—was no longer in front of him, but right up against him, exploding in an extraordinary shower of dented metal and broken glass.

Frank had always looked older to Bunny, naturally, but now, in his periwinkle hospital gown, he looked *old*. Both his legs were in casts. A bandage was wrapped around his swollen forehead.

His condition is stable, the nurse told her. He's just fallen asleep.

The nurse looked strangely at her, then at Frank, then back to her, but Bunny was too distraught to notice. She stared at the linoleum floor for so long, she had no sense of how much time had passed. She could not recall talking to Margot on the phone or her flight number. She had no sense, in fact, of being a body at all, if she was hungry or thirsty, hot or cold. When she finally looked up at Frank, his sleepy eyes met hers.

You came, he said, smiling a little. The gesture looked painful.

That alone was enough—Bunny started to bawl. She couldn't remember the last time she'd cried so hard.

When her cries subsided into soft hiccups, Frank spoke again. Could you do me a favor?

Right side of the desk, bottom drawer. The only drawer Bunny hadn't peeked in all those months ago when she found the receipt.

Inside were photographs, hundreds of them. A woman with hair the same color as Frank's favorite cereal. Was she his sister? A sister he had never mentioned before? They looked alike and were exactly the same height. Both their faces possessed the same hysterically happy expression many Americans possessed in photos, like each day was the best day of their lives. Their happiness had no caution—it was irresponsible. Bunny realized she had never seen Frank smile like that. Not since she had first grasped his hand when he pulled her out of the cardboard box. She squinted closer:

the woman's nose was thinner at the tip and her eyes were spaced closer together. Perhaps they weren't brother and sister after all.

The pictures contained a whole lifetime. Blowing out candles on a cake. Jet-skiing. Holding hands in a sun-dappled park while admiring geese. Posing in front of the Grand Canyon and doing a thumbs-up with their thumbs. And then, suddenly, a baby. Margot. Her head in a white eyelet bonnet. Shooting up like a weed in each successive photo. The three of them posing in front of a swimming pool, a fancy Italian dinner, Margot's high school graduation ceremony.

At the bottom of the stack was a gold-framed photo. The woman wore a cream dress and veil. Frank wore a powder blue tuxedo and bow tie. His pants were flared. Her hair was feathered. The lighting was soft and murky, as though the photo had been left out in the sun for too long. They weren't looking at the photographer, but at each other.

When Bunny returned to the hospital, Frank was sitting up and eating a cup of applesauce. The news was playing on the TV anchored in a corner of the ceiling: after months of threatening to bomb and invade Taiwan, China—in the end—had done nothing.

Bunny carefully set the framed photo on the bedside table. Next to it, she placed a stack of photos.

She's beautiful, Bunny said.

Her name was Susan.

They looked at the wedding photo for several moments.

Frank tried reaching for the photo suddenly, his spindly arms extra spindly under the punishing hospital light. Bunny leapt up and handed it to him. He held the picture frame in his hands as if afraid it would disappear.

What happened? Bunny asked, playing with a loose thread on her shirt.

She died.

Bunny's hands froze.

I miss her, Frank said. We loved each other very much. Have you ever been in love, Bunny?

She twisted the wedding ring on her finger. The look in Frank's eyes told her that he wanted very badly to be in love again.

If she said no, he might divorce her. He would repack her in the official box ordered from the website, fill it with squeaky packing peanuts and send her away by express shipping. He would receive a fifty percent refund on the original price he had paid, plus a complimentary ten percent off coupon for a future order. Her photo would be reuploaded onto the website at a discount rate, PREVIOUSLY OWNED stamped beneath her face.

For a moment, Bunny considered lying. Then, looking at Frank clutching the photo of him and Susan, she could not do anything but be honest with him.

I can't love you, Frank. I don't think you love me, either.

He didn't say anything.

We could be friends.

Still nothing.

Bunny pictured them eating frozen yogurt together at the park. Maybe, on a warm cloudless night, they could go to Lowe's—he'd sit inside the shopping cart and she'd hang on to the back as they flew through the parking lot, hair flying. She would agree to watch that movie he was so obsessed with, *Tremors* or *Terrors*, and she would make sure to laugh each time he laughed.

I want to be friends, Frank.

He smiled at her. I would like that very much.

Bunny smiled back as a tightly wound rubber band unsprang itself in her chest. All this time, she hadn't known how taut the band had stretched.

Frank handed the framed photo back to Bunny to set down on the table. She looked at the happy couple on their wedding day, at Susan's smile that lived on in Margot's.

How did she die? Bunny asked.

Frank didn't speak for a long time. She was sick, he finally said. Trouble with her brain, the doctor said, not enough happy chemicals.

Bunny's heart took a nosedive to the linoleum floor.

Frank continued, as if talking to himself. When I found her, you know, the thing is—well, she looked peaceful.

He blinked away a few tears. Isn't that awful? The only silver lining is that Margot wasn't home, she was working as a counselor at a summer camp. Anyway—

He lifted and dropped his hands, offered up a weak smile.

Bunny looked at Frank, her heart trembling like her namesake. Having witnessed death, they had both crossed a threshold they could never un-cross. Grief was the only commodity of the heart no one could bargain their way out of, though people tried every day and would continue to try for as long as the world spun. And why not? None of it would matter in the end. Boxes would be bought and returned. Borders would close and reopen. The ocean would rise and fall. People would come into your life and most would leave. But some would choose to stay.

YOU PUT A RABBIT ON ME

I moved to Paris to find myself. I didn't openly admit this, of course—to anyone who asked, I said I loved children, especially children with accents, which was why I had applied to be an au pair. And while I had nothing against children, accented or otherwise, I had primarily come to Paris to find the *real* me, to discover who she wanted to be, who she *could* be.

The American Elaine was old news, a soggy newspaper discarded in the rain. She had given America an honest chance and it hadn't worked out; it wasn't anybody's fault. They simply were not compatible. The relationship had been awfully one-sided, with America taking the lead and she unable to say, "No, thank you." And then one day, she woke up bewildered at how she'd ended up where she'd ended up. Without ever seeming to have made active decisions leading towards the definitive facts of her life, she had a job she hated in a city she hated, surrounded by people she hated. She certainly had no "joie de vivre."

During the ten-hour flight, I thought of all the ways I would open myself up to radical change. I made a list: Dare to make yourself uncomfortable. Say "yes" to everything. Ask yourself, what would the *French* Elaine do in this situation?

With this list in hand, I landed at Charles de Gaulle Airport feeling confident. True, my pronunciation was nowhere near where I'd hoped it would be after two years of community college French and my constitution could not tolerate unpasteurized dairy, but I had a plan and I refused to anticipate how that plan could fail. If I did, I would worry to the point of never leaving. I felt so inflated with confidence that I threw my list of Emergency Phrases, phonetically written out, into the trash can next to the gate.

But my confidence, it turned out, was unearned. At baggage claim, a full hour passed and my navy blue suitcase had yet to tumble across the carousel. After walking around in circles for some ten minutes, I located the Air France help desk, where the agent asked for my flight information and identification.

"Your luggage was reported as missing," he said.

"Oh. Well, I would like to pick it up now."

The agent tapped on his computer for an unusually long time and frowned. "Are you sure this is you? Elaine A———?"

I nodded.

"Someone already claimed your missing luggage."

"How is that possible?"

The attendant lifted and dropped his hands.

I pressed my backpack closer to my chest, now that it was all I possessed in this new country. "What should I do?"

The attendant looked baffled as to why I had entrusted him, a stranger, with so much unearned responsibility. "I do not know, mademoiselle." He smiled and looked behind me at the next customer. I was no longer his problem.

I was determined not to let this hiccup cloud my arrival in Paris. I would go to the host family's apartment in the 17th as planned. Magali had sent me detailed directions: take the RER B direction Orsay Ville to Gare du Nord, then ligne 2 direction Porte Dauphine to Villiers. By some miracle, I followed her instructions without getting lost or pickpocketed. My confidence resurfaced. So what if I was missing clothes and shoes and allergy medication? France had clothes and shoes and allergy medication, too, and no doubt classier versions of all three.

When I stepped out of the metro station, I momentarily forgot my purpose. I stood on the sidewalk and looked around, awestruck. Haussmann buildings flaunting curlicue iron culottes. Pharmacies flashing animated green plus signs. Little dogs trotting next to their owners and politely waiting at the traffic signals. The air smelled fresher and, somehow, elegantly damp.

I was here. I was actually here.

Magali's apartment was located in an eggshell white building with an enormous red door. Instead of a door handle that turned, a round brass knob stuck out breastily from the door's waist. Magali lived on the third floor, which apparently meant the fourth floor. I punched in the digicode, entered through a small courtyard furnished with dehydrated plants, then climbed the stairs and knocked on apartment number 10. A middle-aged woman opened the door and looked distractedly at me, as if I were interrupting an important activity, like bomb defusing.

"Oui? Je peux vous aider?" The quizzical look on her face destabilized me. She was a thin, harried-looking woman with remarkably intense blue eyes.

"Je suis l'au pair?" I tried.

Magali's face shifted into recognition, though it did not break into elation as I hoped it would. She scrutinized me as if she were trying to read a menu at a foreign restaurant. I got the feeling I was not what she expected.

"Ah, bah, oui, oui—entrez."

Magali ushered me into the living room, where I stood uncertainly while she gathered plastic dishes, toys and errant socks. Despite its old exterior, the apartment's interior looked recently renovated. The space was decorated in a modern, yet strangely unsophisticated and color-clashing manner: excessive dark magentas, grays and purples, with sudden jolts of lime green in the form of place mats and mugs. A lot of circular patterns and chenille textures. Nothing looked like it had been made before the last decade.

"Do you need help?" I asked in French, but apparently I was incomprehensible because Magali continued tidying up alone as she spoke in a single breathless rush.

I pieced together that she was a single mother, her son's *inutile* father had left them three years earlier to bicycle up and down the Saint-Jacques-de-Compostelle pilgrimage, can I imagine that?, and yes, yes, the government is nothing but a circus of overpaid bureaucrats but at least she qualified for this subsidized program, *une au pair américaine*! Can I imagine that? Never in her life did she think she could afford one—they were for *les familles riches*, but oh thank god she qualified because she is at a loss over her son, he is completely beyond her, the older he gets, the more he is convinced he can parent himself better than she can parent him—

At the mention of her son's existence, she seemed to remember he was the reason I was standing in her living room.

Magali paused her tidying to hug her long cardigan tightly around herself. "Hippolyte!" she shouted into the hallway's ear canal. "HIPPOLYTE."

After a moment, a small boy of seven appeared in the doorway. "Oui?" he answered. His chestnut hair was neatly combed to one side.

"Come meet your au pair, Elaine." She pronounced my name like Hélène.

Hippolyte came forward and delicately shook my hand. "Enchanté."

"She is here to take care of you and teach you English, remember?" Magali continued.

He nodded and regarded me openly, without any of the usual shyness children exhibited towards strangers. "I hope we get along," he said.

"Oh, well—yes—moi aussi."

"You have very bad posture," he remarked.

I blinked. "Thank you for telling me."

"You're welcome."

A moment passed as we all stood there, wordless, before Magali told her son to finish his homework. Then she informed me of my duties: I would arrive at the apartment at 7h30, I would prepare Hippolyte's breakfast, then I would accompany him to school. At 16h30, I would pick him up, bring him home and prepare his afternoon goûter (except on Wednesdays, when I would pick him up at 12h30, lunch at home and bring him to his Les Jeunes Historiens extracurricular club). I would supervise his homework and if he finished early, play or read with him. Then at

19h00, I would cook Hippolyte's dinner and clean up before I was free to leave at 20h00.

"Free to leave?" I repeated.

From my research, I had assumed I'd be staying with the family, in one of the quaint *chambres de bonnes* located on the top floor. In fact, I had hoped I would—everyone said living with the host family made immersion into French life that much richer.

"Chambre de bonne?" Magali screeched. A sharp laugh folded her body in half. "Ah bah, non, mademoiselle, c'est pas Versailles ici, hein!"

I wondered if this meant I would have to pay for my own apartment out of my modest stipend of five hundred euros a month. Magali seemed to enjoy watching panic ripple across my face, waiting for several seconds before adding that she'd already found me a furnished apartment on Leboncoin. How lucky for me that au pair contracts stipulated it was the host family's responsibility to provide housing, she said. When I realized Magali was waiting for a response, I agreed I was very lucky indeed.

My apartment turned out to be a studio, though a fairly spacious one that overlooked Parc Monceau. Curiously, a long black curtain divided the space in half. On one side was a clic-clac futon that opened out into a bed and on the other side, a second identical clic-clac. In the center of the room, tucked against the mansard window, was a TV on a low console with wheels. The kitchen consisted of a two-burner hot plate and a yellowing fridge half the size of a normal one in the U.S. In the bathroom, a miniature pale blue sink squatted directly above the toilet. The shower was a kind of plastic tube that looked like it had come preassembled at the store, ready to be brought straight home. Even the shower knobs were plastic. The only possessions the previous tenant had left behind were an I LOVE LONDON magnet and a small desk fan. I tried to turn it on, but it was out of batteries.

"Alors? What do you think?" Magali asked.

"It's . . . clean," I said, not wanting to disappoint her, as I was starting to understand that Magali was easily disappointed.

She nodded in agreement. "Enjoy the space while you can, your roommate is arriving next month. She's finishing out her old lease."

I stopped mid-walk. "Roommate?"

"You don't think I could afford this place without a roommate, do you?" she cried and folded in half again, evidently overjoyed each time I misunderstood the slightest thing.

The black curtain made perfect sense now.

"Well, who is she?" I asked, hoping to ground myself with some information about this stranger who I'd be sharing twenty square meters with.

Magali pushed a pocket of air from between her pressed lips. The sound was, I think, an approximation for: *The hell would I know.* She said she had to go—Hippolyte was doing god knows what unsupervised, probably rearranging the medicine cabinet—and closed the door behind her, leaving me alone in my new shared studio. I unpacked, which took all of five minutes, and realized I had forgotten to ask Magali where I could purchase clothes, shoes and allergy medication.

So my life in Paris commenced in earnest. Hippolyte's schedule scaffolded my days, like two sturdy bookends. To my disappointment, he was an exceptionally well-behaved child. Before meeting him, I had already planned how I'd win him over: When he'd beg for a sugary snack, I would relent after a single protest. When he asked to watch television instead of studying, I'd do the same. All in moderation, naturally. With this foolproof technique, he'd think I was both generous *and* fair.

But Hippolyte was appalled by rule breaking. When I asked him if he wanted two pieces of chocolate inside his baguette for his goûter, he looked at me angrily and asked, "Do you think this is a party?" then firmly restocked the second chocolate bar in the cupboard. I felt so chastised, I actually hung my head down.

Another time, when Magali was kept away by a work dinner, I served him orange juice to accompany his chicken nuggets and he lectured me for nearly half an hour. "Jus d'orange à cette heure-ci? Mais c'est atroce!" I wasn't sure what "atroce" meant but issuing from Hippolyte's small pursed mouth, it sent a veritable chill down my spine. He claimed I was not thinking of his sleep schedule by serving him extravagant portions of vitamin C before bedtime, then watched in silent horror as I drank it instead.

I had never met a child with such a severe sense of justice. When I sliced strawberries for the two of us, he stood behind me, watching intensely to ensure we received the exact same amount. If one of my strawberry slivers was slightly larger than his, he made me "even it out" by cutting another strawberry. If that failed to correct my former miscalculation, he made me do it again. As a result, I often went through entire barquettes of strawberries.

Despite this, I found my young ward *adorable* (pronounced en français), a description I was certain would infuriate him. Hippolyte was obsessed with fossils and when I asked why, he looked at me as if I were his pupil who had asked him an unspeakably obvious question and said, "Because they are *interesting*, Elaine," to which I duly reprimanded myself. I was surprised by how much I craved soupçons of Hippolyte's approval, like a dying patient being fed broth. I was ambivalent about having children of my own, but with Hippolyte, I started to understand the appeal. Children could be cruel but at least they were honest.

When I wasn't spending time with Hippolyte, I took mandatory French classes in a sterile white room at a Centre de Formation Continue in the 15th arrondissement. The instructor, Paul, a balding transplant from Marseille whose singular passion was trash-talking Paris, forgot my name every class. Some weeks I was "Ellen," other weeks, "Lane." I don't know if the other au pairs noticed. They were all younger than me, girls who had recently graduated from high school to embark on a gap year before college. They spent their off-hours frequenting bars in Saint-Germain-des-Prés and drank through three-euro bottles of wine on the banks of the Seine. I had hoped to make friends with the other au pairs, but being the oldest in the class, they never extended their invitations to me. I told myself that this was for the better. I hadn't come to France, after all, to regress to a younger version of myself. That Elaine—desperate to fill herself up with the personalities of others—had long been erased.

I spent most nights pigging out on videos of Americans sightseeing around Paris. I took mental notes of places to visit, though I never bothered to write any of them down. I stared at the other clic-clac across the room and tried to imagine what kind of person would occupy it. My roommate would arrive in just another week. In the daytime, after French classes ended at 12h00, I could have gone to museums, landmarks and other must-see spots around the city. Indeed, people all over the world devoted a considerable amount of resources to travel to Paris with the express goal of visiting museums, landmarks and other must-see spots. And yet it seemed like an awful lot of work, so I found myself more often than not wandering around a three-story Monoprix.

Monoprix was the supermarket I had found my first night in Paris. Except it transcended a supermarket—it sold clothes (and shoes!), roasted chicken, premade sushi and even boasted its own fromagerie. I could spend up to two hours reading the labels of different products, then hunting down the definitions in my pocket dictionary. In this way, I told myself I *was* learning about French culture and I *was* trying new things. Looked at in a certain light, I had opened myself up to change—hadn't I?

Change was difficult to measure when I didn't possess a solid understanding of myself pre-change. My phenotype and gender had never felt like adequate approximations of myself and yet I deferred back to them because finding a legible receptacle for my slippery insides and formless thoughts was easier, more socially acceptable and fun at parties, than having them flop around on the floor.

All I wanted, really, was to find the bottom of myself. Like a perfect reduction, in the gastronomical sense: heating myself down in a saucepan until I reduced and reduced and reduced, until I couldn't be reduced any further. Lately, though, I had begun to worry I would never find myself in Paris. Maybe I would return to the U.S. after one year exactly the same as I had been: a passive witness to my own life. Maybe finding yourself in a foreign country was a fool's errand—you simply were you all along.

YOU PUT A RABBIT ON ME

Imagine my utter astonishment, then, when I found myself one afternoon in Monoprix. Exactly three weeks had passed since my arrival. I was pondering the yogurt aisle—an enormous, seductive selection of fermented dairy including dessert pot de crème and fromage frais—when I looked in the glass of the refrigerated door to see myself bending down to examine the price of a probiotic yogurt value pack. Except I was not, at that moment, bending down to examine the price of a probiotic yogurt value pack. I turned around to see a woman my height. Her black hair, clipped just below the shoulders and parted on the left side, was the perfect facsimile of mine.

When she stood up, I gasped. It was me.

"Elaine?" I whispered. I couldn't breathe properly.

For a moment, the woman did not move. Then she nodded yes. As she sized me up, the expression on her face suggested amusement rather than shock.

"I'm sorry, your name is *Elaine*?" I had said my own name aloud as a reflex. I had not expected her to answer to it.

"Yes, I'm Elaine," she replied in English. "Let me guess, you are Elaine, too?"

I circled her, waving my hand in her face—perhaps she was a projection.

She jerked away from me. "Tu fais quoi, là?"

So she was French—her English was charmingly lilted and her French was faultless.

"Aren't you—aren't you in a state of disbelief?" I patted my cheeks, half expecting her to do the same. Without realizing it, I had raised my voice. A few shoppers had stopped at the end of our aisle to gawk at us.

"Don't make a scene," she said, then sighed the most fashionable sigh I'd ever heard. "You Americans are so dramatic."

I didn't know whether or not to feel offended.

"Viens," she said and grabbed my arm.

At a brasserie across the street, the waiter looked us over and winked. "Ah, les jumelles?"

"No," I started to say, we were not twins, before Elaine spoke loudly over me. "Oui, c'est ça."

She ordered a decaf espresso without looking once at the menu. I was already annoyed she seemed more collected than I was. I was also disturbed by the realization that our synonymy was obvious to others. During the short walk from Monoprix to the brasserie, I had hung on to a morsel of hope that I was hallucinating. Time had gone wonky; I wasn't sure if minutes had passed or an hour.

As Elaine stirred sugar into her espresso, I took the opportunity to examine her in finer detail. Yes, we seemed identical down to the number and location of beauty marks on our face and neck, but our aesthetic differences were undeniable. Elaine wore red lipstick, white sneakers, not too pristine and not too soiled, simple gold hoop earrings. She looked both smartly put-together and devastatingly casual. In other words, she looked perfectly . . . *French*. In comparison, stuffed into my old college sweatpants and sweatshirt, I looked like a sofa with extendable arms and legs.

"So, tell me about yourself," Elaine said. In response to my dumbstruck silence, she went on, "I doubt we'll figure out a logical explanation for this so we might as well get to know each other." More silence. "Bon, I guess I'll go first," she said, as if she were placating a child.

Elaine was a student at La Sorbonne Nouvelle. She was studying for her M2 in Monde Anglophone, not to become an English teacher like ninety percent of her other classmates "sans talent," she added, but to eventually move to the U.S. and work as an interpreter.

"Move to the U.S.?" I laughed, punctuated by a knee slap. "Good one!"

Why would someone willingly leave behind France—the land of art, sophistication and five weeks' paid vacation plus bank holidays—for the land of store-bought AK-47s, bleached milk and two weeks' unpaid vacation? When I noticed Elaine was not laughing along with me, I asked her exactly that.

"France is stuck in the past," she said with a note of finality.

"In what way?"

Too difficult to explain, Elaine suggested, by way of an artful hand gesture. Then she added, as if to herself, "Liberté, égalité, fraternité c'est un mythe, c'est tout."

I nodded, unsure how to respond to something I had no context to interpret.

"And you?" she asked. "Why did you come to Paris?"

I was too mortified to tell Elaine the truth—that I had come to Paris to find myself, which I had apparently accomplished today in the yogurt aisle—so I told her instead that I loved children, particularly children with accents.

She leaned back in her chair and narrowed her eyes. "You don't seem maternal."

I wanted to unpart the velvet curtains to Elaine's life—her

parents in particular, I was dying of curiosity about—but she drained her cup of espresso and pulled a few euros from her purse. She hadn't even eaten her complimentary cookie. "I have to go—j'ai un rendez-vous."

"Wait! What about—well, your parents, for example. Do they live here? Can I meet them?" Other questions stacked up inside me, one after the after: Are they the same as mine? Are we the same ethnicity? If her parents had immigrated to France, presumably like mine had immigrated to America, what country had they left behind? Was she, like me, an only child? Did we share the same birthday? An incessant panic, like I should call the police or alert the newspapers, ensnared the back of my neck and would not let go.

Elaine looked at me as if I had told her an obscene joke. "Soit pas ridicule."

"But—"

Exasperated, she handed me her phone. "Here, put your number in," she said before excusing herself to use the restroom.

Relief expanded into my lungs with each breath I took. We would see each other again; my questions would not go unanswered. And yet as I typed my number into her phone, saving myself as Elaine A——, I also felt a keen sense of disturbance, an unsettling sensation like my lunch was having a tickle fight inside my stomach. I wondered if by staying in touch instead of letting this incident become a singular one in history, to remember but never relive, we were ruffling the universe's feathers.

Elaine returned from the bathroom. I handed her phone back, my number safely saved inside it, but not before sneaking a peek at the name of her social media account: *la_bordelique*.

"By the way, what should I call you?" I asked her. "We can't both be Elaine, can we?"

She tilted her head. "Since my name is Elaine B——, why don't you just call me Elaine B?"

I nodded, a little stupefied at how quickly she'd adjusted to the situation.

"I'll text you," she smiled—was it my imagination or did smiles look better on her?—then slipped out the heavy glass door. I stared after her shrinking figure in awe. Elaine B was confident and self-assured. She knew exactly what she wanted and what she didn't. She was who I had always wanted to be.

The next few days passed by with chest-aching slowness. I waited for Elaine B to call me with as much anticipation as waiting to hear from someone I was newly dating, giddy with hope at each chime from my phone. But it was always Magali telling me what to prepare for Hippolyte's dîner, interspersed with complaints about her day at work, which was as an administrative assistant for the national train service, SNCF. Ironically, Magali was one of the "overpaid bureaucrats" she was fond of complaining about.

On the fifth day, when I still hadn't heard from Elaine B, disbelieving outrage phlegmed in my chest. How could she walk away from what was no less than a metaphysically impossible encounter? Though I had avoided looking up her social media for fear of turning into a desperate stalker, I now felt I had earned the right to sift through it.

Elaine B's account was public. She had perfected an effortless je ne sais quoi in every photo. Whether it was of her, braless and rain-soaked in a silver slip dress, or of half-eaten meals sprawled promiscuously out on the floor, or out-of-focus snapshots of her equally untouchable friends foregrounding a neon-lit bar at night, the vice of self-consciousness had apparently spared her. She rarely looked into the camera, as if she spurned its adoring eye. Every photo was over- or underexposed. Her captions were either nonexistent or alluringly cryptic.

By contrast, I had never dared to make a social media page. Why would anyone care enough about my life to follow its digital trace?

Another week passed and still I had not heard from Elaine B. The initial anger I felt distorted itself into incredulity, then a kind of sulking hurt, then forced nonchalance. By the end of the week, I had wrung myself through such a broad range of emotions that I felt emptied of them.

When Elaine B posted pictures of herself and her friends, blissfully wasted at some satirical American-themed party (cheeseburger sliders, cupcakes decorated with little flags and handguns, terrifying plastic masks of the latest frauds in office), a forgotten childhood pang surfaced in my chest, as if I were ten years old and the only one in my class not invited to a birthday party. She had made the conscious decision to close the case on what we might have uncovered between us. I overindulged in a bottle of second-shelf wine and deleted my burner account.

Whenever I thought back to the encounter with Elaine B, it started to take on a dreamlike quality, indistinct around its bleeding watercolored edges. I couldn't pin down for certain all the details of that day: Had she been wearing blue jeans or a blue dress? Had she been looking at yogurt or cream cheese? And because the grip of rejection had tightened into a chokehold, I decided it really *had* been a dream. When I tried on the occasional swimsuit at Monoprix, I didn't let myself wonder if it would flatter Elaine B's body more than mine. I forced myself to stop walking past La Sorbonne Nouvelle. I turned my attention to Hippolyte, to my French classes. I would focus on what was within reaching distance. I could find myself—whoever that was—on my own.

And yet, just as I vowed to be more present in these other aspects of my life, they brought frustration. My English lessons with Hippolyte were progressing so poorly, they were nonexistent; they'd somehow morphed into French lessons (for me) after discovering Hippolyte hated to be corrected on his mistakes but absolutely loved to correct mine. He seemed to grow a centimeter taller each time I used the wrong verb tense. When it came to food, his new favorite activity consisted of criticizing anything I fed him. He grew suspicious of my cooking and insisted on overseeing the entire process, which piqued more than I let on. I felt myself doing hopeless pirouettes around Hippolyte, desperate to win his approval as if he were my stern ballet instructor.

When I sought Magali's advice, she simply pushed a pocket of air from her lips, a signature gesture of hers. Troublingly, she seemed more concerned with workplace gossip than her son's nutrition. Every day after coming home from work, she boiled over with complaints about her colleagues, which she unloaded onto me to such an extent that they began to metamorphose into my own problems. I knew who Ghislaine and Didier were and what they had said to Magali at the pot de rentrée and I sincerely wished I did *not* know. But I never dared say anything that might have insinuated Magali wasn't an exemplary mother. After all, the entirety of my legal status in France depended on working *en harmonie* with the host family, as defined by the host family—Magali.

The situation wasn't much better in my French classes. I had failed my most recent quiz, having flip-flopped le subjonctif for le conditionnel. Paul, who never displayed any favoritism among the au pairs, let loose a disparaging whistle as he handed me my quiz. In the lobby next to the instant coffee machines, I thought of asking the other au pairs how they had fared on the quiz, but changed my mind when I overheard them chattering about their La Toussaint plans.

After class, I decided to walk the forty-five minutes home. Sometimes, when I was adrift in a fog of French, I experienced a new kind of solitude: soft and welcoming. I realized the de facto solitude of living abroad was exactly what some foreigners sought out because it was acceptable, even expected, whereas back home—in the place you grew up surrounded by friends and family—it was a personality flaw. I was just settling into solitude's embrace when a man in a black Renault pulled over and asked me, "Combien?"

That night, desperate for even a single drop of kindness, I did something I swore I wouldn't do after gorging on unhealthy servings of true crime documentaries. I downloaded a dating app and swiped right on everyone who flashed across my screen, as long as he was between the ages of twenty-eight and thirty-eight. I did not so much want a man in my life as I felt I needed something to replace the awful deficit in me and a man seemed like the easiest and most socially acceptable solution.

I was in this state of frantic swiping, hunched on my clic-clac in my underwear and an oversized T-shirt while diligently making my way through a packet of chocolate Prince cookies, when I heard someone fumbling with the lock on my studio door.

With weak-kneed steps, I tiptoed towards the corner of the studio where the curtain hugged the wall, then hid behind it. I looked around for a heavy object, finding only my laptop charger, then waited as my heartbeat thrummed in anticipation. When the door groaned open, I lifted the charger high in the air, ready to smash it into the intruder's head.

"Âllo? Il y'a quelqu'un?" a voice called.

I touched my fingertips to my lips. Had I just spoken?

I stepped out from behind the curtains to see an eerily familiar figure standing in the doorway. Next to her was an eerily familiar navy blue suitcase, last seen before I'd boarded my flight to Paris.

"Elaine!" she called out, dropping an oversized canvas bag. To my shock, she walked over and gave me the bises. Strange—her face against mine felt like slipping on a well-loved sweater. "Ça va?" she asked, as if we'd only seen each other yesterday.

"Where did you get that?" I asked carefully.

Elaine B followed my gaze. "Ça? I picked it up at Charles de Gaulle a few weeks ago—"

"Why were you there?" I hastily interrupted her.

"—when I was coming back from Berlin," she finished. "I have the exact same suitcase, mais c'est trop bizarre, when I opened it, it was not mine?" She shrugged. "Whoever owned it did not have very good taste."

I changed my mind about sharing this remarkable coincidence with her. "Why didn't you call me?"

"My phone broke," Elaine B said breezily. I knew that was a lie, since before I had stopped stalking her on social media, I had seen all her updated photos.

"Okay, that was a lie," she confessed. She made herself comfortable on the clic-clac beside me and plundered the packet of Prince cookies without asking if she could. We were so different, Elaine B and I.

"Franchement? J'avais peur."

I blinked at her in surprise—was this a genuine admission of vulnerability or a manufactured one?

During our first encounter, Elaine B explained, she had been more disturbed than she let on. But seeing as I was so disturbed, she thought that if she revealed how disturbed *she* was, we would have risked acting out of our minds, giving ourselves over to hazardous and irreversible urges like testing the laws of physics—if I slice your arm with a knife, would I feel it, etc.?

The mechanics of her thinking were so wild, I was reassured that for all our identical appearances, we were not the same person. And even *if* Elaine B were me, she was the me if I had been born and raised in Paris, under the circumstances she had been raised.

Still, I was relieved her nonchalance had been a calculated decision for both our sakes. I was not alone in believing how law-defying our situation was. I must have been waiting for Elaine B to confirm my reality because I now felt instantly realigned, as if a piece of food in my throat had become dislodged and I could resume normal breathing. I decided at that moment, watching Elaine B finish off my Prince cookies, that succumbing to the madness was easier than resisting it. Well, I would not so much succumb to it as I would let it envelop me as I stayed motionless. I imagined the madness as an ever-expanding pink foam.

Elaine B stood up and looked around the studio. "So, you're the mysterious roommate? How funny we keep meeting." She turned to look at me; the intensity of her gaze made me blush a little. "C'est bien. We shouldn't run away from each other, non?"

And indeed, as I helped Elaine B unpack, her arrival seemed not only inevitable, but necessary. In addition to reuniting with my lost suitcase, I had bought too many forks and not enough spoons; Elaine B had too many spoons and not enough forks. I had coffee filters but had run out of coffee; she had no filters despite owning an unopened canister of 100% Arabica. The remote-controlled fan still lacked two AAA batteries; she produced exactly two AAA batteries from the pocket of her bag. This uncanny configuration felt predestined, as if all this time, I had unknowingly chiseled out the precise shape of Elaine B and when she reappeared in my life, she fit perfectly inside it.

As we lay on our matching clic-clacs that night, Elaine B said, "Let's be friends."

I couldn't help but ask why.

Elaine B turned on her side to face me. "Because I'm interested in myself. So by definition, I am interested in you."

Soon, the scope of my world narrowed down to Elaine B.

Instead of hanging around Monoprix, we walked for hours through different arrondissements. Her natural pace of walking was a second faster than mine, but we compromised, me walking a half second faster, her walking a half second slower. She taught me how to skip paying the metro fare, how to distinguish an industrial boulangerie from an artisanal boulangerie and a personal interest of hers: how to use odd French idioms like "avoir des casseroles au cul." She brought me to her favorite restaurants, cafés and shops. Everywhere we went, we spun heads. People exclaimed they had never seen two such identical twins. Even when I was at French class or taking care of Hippolyte, I was only physically present—my real self was with Elaine B.

We did everything together: we brushed our teeth side by side in the morning and at night. Predictably, our periods arrived within the same twenty-four-hour time frame. We watched funny video clips and our favorite music videos together, sharing a pair of wired headphones. When we walked down the sidewalk and someone shouted, "Ni hao!" or "Chintok!" it was shouted at the both of us and so at least we bore the indignity together. We even started to fall asleep on the same clic-clac. Sometimes I'd wake up and find Elaine B's hair homogenously tangled in my own. When Elaine B came down with a stye in her left eye, I did, too. Twice a day, I laid my head in her lap as she squeezed antibiotic drops into my eye, then I into hers. The only thing we avoided was coordinating matching outfits; it was a cutesy gimmick and neither of us felt that whatever we had was cutesy or a gimmick.

The people in my life were so few and far between that all the inordinate amount of time I spent with Elaine B went unnoticed. Only Magali commented that my skin looked clearer; had I at last developed a taste for water (she believed most Americans abstained from it) or was I using the new La Roche-Posay skincare line she'd recommended? As for the people in my life back home, I had been so sloppy at keeping in touch to begin with—a brief email here and there to my modest number of friends, a video call to my parents once in a blue moon—none of them noticed, either.

By contrast, everyone in Elaine B's life noticed. Her parents lived in the suburb of Vitry-sur-Seine. She visited home two or three times a month but hadn't at all this month; I overheard them complaining about it to her over the phone. When we were together, I often saw her phone glow with text messages and social media notifications from her friends, but she stopped answering them. We debated telling people the truth, but we agreed it was better not to; doing so would only invite unanswerable questions.

I was worried Elaine B might start to skip school or study less, but her M2 final exams at the end of the year were far too important. Her current moyenne was at a precarious 11/20, with 10 being the minimum to pass the entire year, not because she didn't understand the material but because her teachers were biased against her. When I asked why, she shrugged and said, "My English is superior to theirs." Since l'école primaire, she explained, her classmates and even a teacher in sixième had mocked her for speaking English with an American accent. Everyone else leaned into their French accents, embarrassed to try for accuracy.

"Don't you miss your friends and family?" I asked Elaine B one evening, emboldened by two aromatic glasses of diluted Ricard.

"I have my whole life to see them," she said, "but you are here for less than a year." Her words telegraphed a frisson of happiness down my spine, but the truth of my situation—my au pair visa with its expiration date printed in bold—circumvented the feeling. I changed the topic.

"What about dating?" I asked. Elaine B had mentioned she had an ex-boyfriend, Thibaud, who she occasionally slept with, but I didn't know if she'd cut contact with him.

The sly smile Elaine B always wore, as if she'd swallowed a delicious secret, stiffened. "Can I tell you something I've never told anyone?"

I nodded.

"I've never had a boyfriend for more than a few months." She paused. "Maybe something is wrong with me."

I had to stop my jaw from dislocating. "I'm the same. I've always worried something is wrong with *me*."

Elaine B looked at me for a long moment. "Bon, c'est pas grave," she finally said. She slipped back on her deliciously secretive smile. "Who needs men when we have each other now?" She laughed at her own joke. I did, too.

When I had a particularly difficult time with Hippolyte one evening, I came home in a sour mood. It was the end of November. Hippolyte had told me exactly what he wanted for dinner (a single boiled potato garnished with butter), but when I served it to him, he took one bite and spat it out into his napkin. I watched in disbelief as Hippolyte dumped the perfectly good meal into the composting bin before scolding me. Did I know a potato had to be heated to one degree below the local boiling point? Why hadn't I used a thermometer? Had I really gone to university or did they not teach basic science in America?

Until this moment, I had never felt the urge to lightly smack him on the hands and though I never would, I was ashamed something like violence lived inside me.

Without having to say a word, Elaine B declared we weren't going to stay inside and mope all night. She was taking me to a movie and we were going to consume full-butter popcorn and non-diet Coke and Kinder Surprise, which were banned in America because our children were unable to differentiate toys from chocolate and we were going to remember it was okay, more than okay, to buy a ticket out of your own life from time to time because otherwise you'd shoot yourself in the head, no sane person could be checked in to every waking moment of their life. Even though the movie was a saccharine and clichéd affair about a family vacation gone wrong, I ended up sobbing.

As we exited the theater, I asked Elaine B if we could do this every month. For an answer, she slung her arm around me and kissed me on the cheek.

My old friend (all-consuming self-consciousness) never visited when I was with Elaine B; somehow I just knew that when I was feeling a particular way, Elaine B was, too. I didn't necessarily need to communicate it aloud and neither did she. I had once read that if two people felt alone when they were together, it meant they had found real love. I tweaked my earlier hypothesis: maybe Elaine B and I were the same person in spite of having been raised in different countries. The questions that had originally eaten away at me—what was her birthday? where exactly had her parents immigrated from? what did they look like?—shrank from my mind until they were zapped out of existence.

But interestingly, I lost sense of the things I originally liked or disliked, as if they'd had fallen out of my purse one day. I couldn't remember if I was someone who removed pickles from my sandwich or added extra. I started to question even the simplest facts about myself. Was I really a size 7 shoe, 37 in France? What was the name of my first pet growing up? Elaine B's was a rabbit named DouDou and now I could only remember that my first pet had also been DouDou.

Rather than feel discomforting, though, this blurriness had the exact opposite effect. I no longer had to carry the weight of myself all by myself. Someone else could do it for me, too. And in a way, being myself—the never-ending accountability of it—was exhausting. I had doubts I'd ever excelled at being Elaine A to begin with and I suspected Elaine B could do a better job of it than me. So when she informed the server without hesitation that we did *not* want les cornichons with our duck pâté sandwiches, I felt overwhelmed with gratitude. In fact, I couldn't fathom how I had ever lived without her.

The next time we went out for lunch, Elaine B prompted me to tell the server, "On veut pas de cornichons, merci." During our interaction, the server spoke to me entirely in French, a first. Most of the time, servers insisted on speaking to me in barely comprehensible English.

"Maybe he thinks I'm French," I told Elaine B, overjoyed.

She looked blankly at me. I couldn't tell where the arrow of her expression landed and I wondered if I had said something to offend her. Then she smiled and told me, yes, surely he did.

One night in December, we were co-eating an obscenely giant bowl of cassoulet and guilty pleasure–watching *Tellement vrai* on my clic-clac. During the commercial break, my phone buzzed. I instinctively waited for Elaine B's phone to buzz, as well; it did not.

"Aren't you going to see who it is?" Elaine B prompted me.

I reluctantly checked—Magali, no doubt, with another update about her gastro—but it was a man named Thibaud from the dating app.

"Tu veux qu'on se voit?" read his message.

I blinked several times before remembering I had swiped right on him. For all my furious swiping that night, I had incredibly received only a single match: Thibaud. Probably because I had not uploaded any photos or information besides my age and gender.

"His name is Thibaud—isn't that funny?" I said.

If Elaine B was shocked he shared the same name as her ex-boyfriend, her lack of reaction was award-worthy. She gestured to see my phone. As she scrolled through Thibaud's profile, I studied her expression. Her bottom lip twitched slightly. "He's not bad," she said slowly.

For the first time since she'd moved in, I got the feeling Elaine B wasn't being entirely honest with me. "Really? I don't know anything about French men."

"There is nothing special about French men, that is a lie made up by the American media," she snapped. "They are just as unremarkable as any other kind of man."

I held back a smile. "Well, what should I say?"

She shrugged and turned back to the TV. "Whatever you want."

Part of me wondered if letting someone else into my life would throw off its balance with Elaine B, our perfect little temperature-controlled terrarium. But then I remembered the list I had compiled on the plane ride over: Dare to make yourself uncomfortable. Say "yes" to everything. Ask yourself, what would the *French* Elaine do in this situation?

I messaged Thibaud: "Quand?"

He answered back quickly: "Demain à 19h00."

I put my phone down to see Elaine B looking straight at me. "What kind of men do you like?"

I laughed, awkwardly. When I realized Elaine B was waiting for a response, I said, "Probably the kind of men you like?"

She smiled. "So how do you like to be fucked?"

I realized then that I knew Elaine B's body as well as I knew mine. I knew where she liked to be touched and where she didn't. What repulsed her and what made her lightheaded with lust. As I watched the same thought leisurely stroll around her mind, the distance between us on the clic-clac grew infinitesimally small.

Before I followed that thought further and answered the question in Elaine B's eyes with a regrettable action, I said I was tired and closed my eyes. A little while later, I heard the steady rhythm of Elaine B's breathing. I turned to look at her face, still illuminated by the TV. Asleep was the only time she looked ill at ease in her skin. I picked up the remote to turn off the TV, then—remembering Elaine B's unnerving behavior—set it back down.

Very carefully, I slipped out of my clic-clac and winced towards Elaine B's side of the studio. I looked under her pillow, then her mattress. Nothing. I wasn't sure what exactly I was searching for until I found, inside the inner pocket of her school backpack, a black leather-bound journal. I glanced over at Elaine B's sleeping form, then brought it to the bathroom, locked the door and pulled the chain to the light.

As I sat on the toilet, I pictured myself returning the journal. I pictured thinking to myself, "This is a violation of Elaine B's privacy and I would never forgive her if she did the same thing to me." And yet no amount of visualization stopped me from opening her journal, my heart stammering wildly.

The entire journal was, of course, written in French. I felt motion sick just browsing the pages. The journal was three-fourths filled up and Elaine B's handwriting was messily sloped to the right, rendering any translation even more laborious. A sudden whine from the squeaky clic-clac made me freeze. When I heard no further noise, I quickly flipped to the latest entry. It was dated only a few days ago.

"Moi, je pourrais jamais être aussi naïve qu'elle. Quand elle decouvre quelque chose de nouveau, elle est tellement mignonne, elle me rend folle. Je sais pas ce que ça veut dire. Si je veux l'embrasser, ça va dire que je veux m'embrasser ? Est-ce que je suis une grosse narcicisste ? Ou, est-ce que ce désir vient du fait que l'embrasser serait tabou ? J'ai peur de lui dire. Elle me fait trop confiance."

Me, I could never to be also naive as her. When she discovers something of new, she is so cute, she renders me insane. I do not know what it wants to say. If I want to embrace her, that goes to say I want me embrace? I am a fat narcissist? Or does this desire coming of fact that to embrace will be taboo? I have fear of her to tell. She me makes too much trust.

I closed the journal, my hands limp. I thought back to last week when I had been taking a shower and Elaine B walked in. She had lingered at the threshold without embarrassment or apology. Lingering instead with what I now recognized as desire.

The journal entry was undeniable proof that Elaine B and I were spending too much time together. I figured it was good, for both our sakes, that I was going on a date tomorrow.

I met Thibaud at the McDonald's on the Champs-Élysées. I was skeptical—very skeptical—about rendezvousing at an American fast-food chain for our first date, but to be fair, when I stepped into the McDonald's, I thought I had gotten the address wrong and had landed in a midrange, two-dollar-sign establishment.

Thibaud secured a table for us on the terrace. He had a disarmingly open smile that made me reflexively smile back at him, with all my teeth. His dark hair was shaved close to his scalp, framed in exact and precise lines around the edges. He wore a matching brown tracksuit and a small Velcro satchel across his shoulder.

"I ordered for us," Thibaud grinned.

"Mer-ci?" I said, suddenly feeling like I had forgotten all my French. When our cheeseburgers and fries arrived, I was glad for an excuse to avoid talking but I needn't have worried: Thibaud was an open book. He had grown up in the "92" (this was said with a meaningful look that was lost on me) and in an HLM (this, I did know, meant government housing). His grandparents had immigrated from Algeria. He hated his first name ("the pressure to assimilate broke my parents") and was planning to legally change it to Farid. He had a lycée bac pro and had trained to work in hotel hospitality, which he did until two years ago. Now he was first and foremost a political organizer living on unemployment SMIC.

"Tu vas en manifs?" he asked.

I shook my head halfway no, then yes.

"Malheureusement, there is no shortage of atrocities to protest in France." At first, I thought Thibaud was attempting an ill-conceived joke, but his face was perfectly stoic. He started listing some of the atrocities—la brutalité policière, l'islamophobie, les ventes d'armes, le traitement des anciennes colonies, la peur du communautarisme—as I struggled for the English translations. I regretted having judged his restaurant choice; he appeared to me now as someone awfully upright.

After dinner, we walked down the lovely light-filled boulevard, refashioned for the annual marché de Nöel. The boulevard was stocked with hundreds of vendors selling vin chaud, thick stacks of nougat, tarte flambée and roasted chestnuts. The scent of fried dough, candied oranges and, inexplicably, fresh snow, sweetened the cold air. Behind the vendors were carnival rides, spinning spheres of neon sending up happy screams that waxed, then waned. I was surprised by how identical they were to the ones found at American boardwalks.

We stopped at a crosswalk. "Why did you swipe right on me?" I finally asked Thibaud. "I didn't list anything about myself on my profile."

"It was a little experiment—people these days, they are too obsessed with l'apparence, tu sais? Lucky for me, t'es mignonne," he grinned. When Thibaud smiled, his face was so symmetrical it nearly had the effect of being unsexy rather than sexy.

"Why *are* filets mignons called 'mignon'?" I inquired.

"You are funny woman," he suddenly said in English I strained to understand. "I like American girl."

"Why?" Panic swept through me—were American girls known for being particularly one thing or the other in France?

Thibaud switched back to French. "In the U.S., you talk truthfully—about les sujets difficiles. Here, you cannot."

I didn't press him for more information but I noticed his answer echoed Elaine B's when I'd asked why she was bent on leaving France.

At the entrance to the metro, we kissed, the logical conclusion to a pleasant evening. I found I didn't dislike it; I think I might have even liked it. And just like that, without any discussion, I was Thibaud's petite amie.

"Alors, c'était comment?" Elaine B asked me the next day.

I was going to tell her the truth—that the date with Thibaud was perfectly pleasant but nothing more—and yet I found myself telling her that I had met the man of my dreams.

"C'est clair," she smirked. "You just say that because he's French.

WHERE ARE YOU REALLY FROM

You have all these ideas about French people—you romanticize us. It's insulting."

"What are you talking about?"

Elaine B opened up her laptop. She wanted to show me a clip from the French dubbed version of *The Mask*. She said all American movies were dubbed since nobody in France read subtitles; an entire economy of voice actors relied on this collective laziness. I told her I wasn't in the mood to watch it, but after she insisted, I reluctantly put in one half of her headphones. In the scene where Stanley turns French, clad in a striped shirt and red beret, he cannot put on a French accent because he's already French. Instead, he speaks with *un accent italien*.

"See?" Elaine B said loftily. "Every time Americans invent a stereotype about French people, we think it's a stereotype about Italians."

"I guess." I went to the kitchen for a glass of water.

I could tell Elaine B was disappointed, that she had hoped we would mock my McDonald's date in the most touristy spot in all of France, the equivalent of Times Square. As she picked up her backpack to go to class, I told Elaine B I'd tell her more about the date later that night and she smiled at me, it seemed, in relief.

But our conversation never picked back up. I was still unnerved by Elaine B's journal entry and, for once, did not want to indulge her desires. I felt an urgent need to expand my life beyond the confines of Elaine B. I needed something that was mine and mine alone. In other words, I needed a hobby. And while an abundance of hobbies existed for me to choose from—from adult coloring books to accordian lessons to an expensive drug dependency—I decided to make Thibaud my hobby.

Fortunately, being someone's *petite amie* in France was very time-consuming—healthy friendship-relationship-work-personal-time balance wasn't a popular concept here. I wasn't used to men texting me immediately after I texted them; I was used to American men hijacking dating into a game of disinterested interest for months on end. But Thibaud wanted to see me every day. We met up after I dropped Hippolyte off at school or after my French classes ended or after I left Magali's at night. He lived in a modest one-bedroom apartment in the 18th arrondissement near Marx Dormoy station. We spent most of the time listening to music or watching videos on the Internet or eating takeout from the doner kebab place downstairs. I learned Thibaud was exceptionally meticulous about his hair, both the kind on his head and his face. I learned he couldn't stand the texture of mushrooms as much as he couldn't stand to inconvenience others, so he always picked them off of his food. I learned he loved his family, deeply, and visited his relatives in Constantine every August.

Most nights, we ended up kissing on his couch, sampling each other under our clothes like teenagers, but I was surprised Thibaud never initiated sex. When I asked him why, he said he did not take sex lightly, that in fact, he hoped to wait until marriage. He was worried I would find this off-putting, but once more, it simply made me view him as an awfully upright citizen.

Dating a French man turned out to be a crash course in French culture. I had known about their famous dead poets, artists, writers and so on, but soon realized this was a tourist's uninformed impression of French culture. For one thing, America had invaded the majority of it. I heard American music everywhere I went, American TV from *Malcolm in the Middle* to *Monk* still replayed on French TV channels (dubbed, naturally), more American storefronts popped up each year and more American phrases infiltrated the language faster than L'Académie Française could deport them.

After I kept missing references in the French media, Thibaud took it upon himself to lead me through a history of French rap from IAM and NTM to Oxmo Puccino and Kery James. By understanding French rap, he explained very earnestly, I could understand France's ugly history of social inequalities, and the only way to understand French rap was to learn verlan, which felt very unfair—how was I supposed to learn an inverted version of French when I had yet to master the latter? Thibaud spent another full day introducing me to key pop culture moments: Jordy, Mylène Farmer, Les Bronzés, Alizée's dance on *Top of the Pops*, "La Tribu de Dana," the TV series *H, Un gars, une fille, Kaamelott, Star Academy*, Nabilla's "T'es une fille et t'as pas de shampooing, mais âllo, quoi?"

When it came to la gastronomie, he took me to his favorite bakery in Asnières-sur-Seine, where we ate honey-soaked and almond-packed confections, and a Moroccan restaurant where I tried chicken tajine, spiked with plump dates and tangy olives, for the first time in my life. Thibaud was rabidly curious about everything and wanted to taste every type of cuisine in the world, and yet—like the opposite of Hippolyte—generally subsisted on junk food, industrial-sized bags of madeleines and halal steak haché bought in packs of ten from Lidl. Remarkably, since coming to France, I had eaten very little French food.

The only part of Thibaud's personality that felt stereotypically French was his obsession with le foot. Whenever PSG lost a game, I knew he'd be irritable all day. The only other time he grew irritable was when he watched the news. Once, after news broke that three police officers had beaten a man so badly that he'd died in custody, his eyes dewed as he said, "Liberté, égalité, fraternité mon cul." It sounded familiar, though I couldn't remember where I'd heard it before.

When Thibaud spoke about the latest societal breakdown in France, his eyes and gestures freighted with emotion, I kept hoping it would unlock a sealed door inside me. I, too, wanted to boil over with sorrow and anger—not the kind I was accustomed to, but the dignified, impersonal kind. I, too, wanted a purpose greater than "finding myself," which, the more I thought about it, the more I had to admit was nothing more than a comically American delusion.

Given Elaine B's general nonchalance, I thought she wouldn't begrudge all the time I was spending with Thibaud, especially since she practically cohabited with the books at the library, cramming for her upcoming exams. I even wondered if she was tired of spending so much time with me—she was the more interesting Elaine, she had a whole life here, replete with friends and family, compared to my part-time life here. Perhaps she found me clingy and burdensome, and would welcome my absence. Perhaps, like a child cleaning out her closet of scuffed dolls, she'd discard me as easily as she'd adopted me.

In late February, I was packing another set of clothes to stay over at Thibaud's. It was his birthday and as a surprise, I planned to cook him his favorite meal (cheeseburgers, fries and les frozen nuggets). I asked Elaine B if we could postpone our monthly movie outing, a rescreening of her favorite film, *Dikkenek*, for next week. We were supposed to watch it last Thursday but I'd been forced to cancel because another one of Magali's work dinners (dinners I suspected were in fact dates) had run late.

"Tu m'as encore posé un lapin?" Elaine B demanded. Before I could ask what putting a rabbit on her meant, she went on: I was treating our home like a hostel, I was never there for her anymore, I had kicked her down to the bottom of my priorities.

"You still haven't introduced me to Thibaud even though I keep asking you to," she added, pouting.

This felt a little unfair, given our mutual agreement to put an embargo on introductions. Yes, I could tell Thibaud the identical twin lie, which I had somehow neglected to mention in all the time we'd been dating, rather than confess we were strangers who had met in September, but I wanted to avoid lying to him. He was always going on about the government's lies and, knowing this, I felt certain he would not look kindly upon personal lies.

But the other reason—the real reason—was because the way Thibaud spoke about France mirrored the way Elaine B spoke about France. In fact, the more my French improved, the more their political and social synchronicity became unmistakable. If they met, I feared they would have too much in common, to such a degree that their similarities would keep infinitely snowballing until they pushed me out of the room entirely. At the end of the day, they were French and I was not. What if all the incongruities Thibaud found in me, he would never find in Elaine B, and vice versa? With each other, they would never have to pause the sketches on StudioCanal every thirty seconds to explain their subtext and the subtext's subtext.

"Vas-y, vas-y," Elaine B said to my silence. She said this whenever she was hurt and resigned to being hurt. She noisily yanked the curtain across the studio, then retreated to her clic-clac. I could hear her chewing loudly behind it.

"Elaine," I tried, "I'm sorry, but don't you think we should avoid being, well, too codependent on each other? Thibaud says—"

I realized my mistake a second too late. The curtain whisked back to reveal an incensed-looking Elaine B, one of her hands gagging the neck of a Curly puffs bag, the other stained with peanut powder.

"T'as parlé de moi à Thibaud?"

I instinctively took a step back. "Well, not exactly—I haven't explained all the circumstances . . . Just that you're my roommate."

Elaine B looked at me as if I had tried to shove her out of our seventh-story window. "Alors, je comprends. Je suis juste ta 'roommate,' c'est ça?"

When she was angry, she only spoke in French. She abruptly went into our minuscule bathroom and latched the flimsy lock.

I couldn't believe it—she was acting like Hippolyte. No, she was acting in a way my seven-year-old ward would not deign to act. I packed up a few more of my belongings in irritated silence. Before leaving, I passed by the bathroom and heard a sound I instantly recognized: the sharp snip of scissors. So this was Elaine B's juvenile protest, her attempt at proclaiming, "We are not the same person." I supplicated my head against the door, wondering if I should try to make amends with her. Or would I only be giving in to her increasingly impossible demands?

I decided a line had to be drawn, and because Elaine B would not pick up the pen, it was up to me. As I closed the front door behind me, I told myself I was doing this for her, or really, for us.

The next day, I walked into the apartment to see Elaine B wearing my checkered dress, the one I had bought for my three-month anniversary date with Thibaud. The style wasn't Elaine B's in the slightest; I knew she was only wearing it to spite me.

"I didn't say you could borrow that."

"It suits me better," Elaine B retorted.

As she did her makeup in the bathroom mirror, I felt a sudden seasickness, the floor beneath me buckling above water. The way she tucked her hair in the mirror, the way she smiled—cautiously rather than secretively—the way she dangled her arms in front of her chest, as if apologizing for having breasts . . . I realized she was copying my mannerisms.

"Quoi?" she demanded. She had caught me staring at her.

"Nothing." Elaine B had given herself bangs the night before and this new difference between us helped me reorient myself. I had always assumed I couldn't pull off micro bangs, but seeing them on Elaine B, I realized I could have all these years.

I watched in silence as she made breakfast, humming to herself. I suspected the dress *did* look better on her. Comparing myself to Elaine B defied every manner of logic and yet I craved the wounds it opened up, as if I had a kink for hurting my own feelings. I tried to pick out her imperfections—surely they were more imperfect than mine? But every time I found one, a blemish or an ingrown hair, the imperfection seemed tenfold worse on me. And yet, if Elaine B was beautiful, didn't her beauty reinforce my own? When things were good between us and she looked particularly lovely on certain days, I used to glow inside with a kind of warm, preening pleasure. Now it made me feel spiky twists of jealousy.

Sometimes, when she looked at me with an illegible expression, I wondered if jealousy pricked her, too. All this time, I had avoided even thinking that word. I was afraid that the moment it entered my field of consciousness, jealousy would sprout vicious barbs inside me and resist all attempts to expel it. Perhaps now it would.

Elaine B left her dishes in the sink without washing them, then turned off the kitchen light, leaving me in the dark, and left.

"REALLY?" I shouted through the door.

Elaine B was without a doubt punishing me. She was rarely at the apartment now, and when she was, her headphones were permanently attached to her head. She started labeling all of her food with her initials: E.B. She made a point to take long, environmentally irresponsible showers, emptying the chaudière so that I was left with frigid water.

I could tell Elaine B was stressed over her upcoming exams. She was always huddled over her laptop, murmuring phrases in English aloud, her assigned literature and history books marked up with numerous multicolored sticky notes. I wanted to offer my help, but how could I when she refused to acknowledge me?

To my distress, we really had become nothing more than roommates. Each night before I fell asleep, I tortured myself by replaying select moments between us and imagining how, if I had only adjusted my words or facial expressions a degree or two in another direction, I could have bypassed her ire. That the present could be so vastly altered through a few slight changes in the past deeply troubled me. For so long, my life had felt out of my control and now that it felt entirely *too much* in my control, I wanted to fold it up and return it in its original box, as if it had never been opened in the first place.

WHERE ARE YOU REALLY FROM

My latest endeavor with Hippolyte's ongoing culinary troubles was pretending we were running a restaurant called "Chez Hippolyte." I took orders from him as his dedicated sous-chef and asked him each night, "Alors, chef, c'est quoi le menu ce soir?"

Hippolyte would fold his hands together very solemnly as he reflected. He'd toss out nutritionally wanting ideas while I suggested vegetables that might accompany "des pâtes avec des Knackis." I didn't dare let Hippolyte handle knives or go near the stove, and explained that in all Michelin-starred restaurants, the chef didn't cook, they just ordered around the sous-chef, to which Hippolyte struck a haughty hand on his hip and said he already knew that. In a too-large denim apron, he'd stand on a stool next to me at an appropriate distance and tell me when to add the salt and the pepper. Any other seasoning, he hated.

After I served Hippolyte his Knacki pasta with a side of spinach, he ate it all. I couldn't help but hug him. I even felt a little weepy-eyed. I thought the only culprit was my relief, but then he asked me, "Ça va, Elaine?"

He placed his little hand on mine and I began to cry. "Ça va pas, Hippolyte, ça va pas."

His expression dipped into great seriousness and he demanded I tell him what was wrong. I used his napkin to blow my nose. I carefully admitted I was having roommate troubles and hoped he would not ask further questions. But this was Hippolyte.

"What is she doing to you, Elaine?" He wadded his hands into small fists and placed them on either side of his plastic dinner plate.

Because I had no one to talk to, the truth spewed out of me: the numb, sneezy showers, the labeled food in the fridge, turning off the lights when I was still reading, laughing very loudly to something she was watching but not inviting me to watch with her.

Hippolyte shook his head. "Elaine, you must go to war."

He proceeded to tell me that at his Les Jeunes Historiens club, they had watched a children's educational video about *The Art of War* and he had learned that one must appear weak when one is strong, and strong when one is weak.

I was momentarily rendered speechless. French education was truly something else.

"Alors?" he asked. "Are you listening, Elaine?"

"Yes . . . Yes! Thank you?"

He stood up to place his dish in the sink. "Avec plaisir."

Ever since I was a child, I never argued when someone no longer wanted to be friends with me or when someone no longer wanted to date me. I hated that about myself—how easily I forfeited being loved. And I hated to act so petty, but because I could not see a way out of the predicament we'd become entangled in, I resorted to punishing Elaine B back. Like Hippolyte said, I had to appear strong now more than ever, when I felt so dreadfully weak. I started to label my food in the fridge, too, and took it one step further by labeling my shampoo, conditioner and body wash in the shower. I purchased a small trash can and housed it next to the other trash can, but only emptied mine. I wore one of Elaine B's most expensive-looking silk dresses without asking. And finally, I went into the bathroom with a pair of scissors to give myself bangs identical to hers.

I was certain that the accumulation of these small attempts at warfare would propel Elaine B back into my orbit. Was she really the kind of person to let something so trivial as missing a movie night decimate everything we had? And yet I knew in my heart that she was—and that this was what made Elaine B so Elaine B. Everything was operatic, a matter of life or death. *She* was the dramatic one.

Two weeks passed. None of my attempts vexed Elaine B enough to thaw the cold spell between us. She had reduced me to a ghost haunting my own apartment, but unlike a ghost—whose shenanigans would surely provoke a reaction—I had no effect over Elaine B.

On the last morning of the two-week period, I cracked. "Please, Elaine—this has to stop," I petitioned over breakfast. "We have to talk to each other!"

But she simply looked past me as if I were another object on the kitchen table and poured more milk into her bowl of Banania, a brand she'd previously told me she could not support because of its inexcusable racist marketing. Who was this person sitting across from me? I studied Elaine B: she looked better than she ever had. Unlike my anger, which manifested in geriatric bags under my eyes and teenage acne breakouts, Elaine B wore her anger like a fur coat, timeless and luxurious. It was so unfair.

The next day, I texted Magali to say that I had come down with a deathly flu. She scolded me, writing back in all caps that this was clearly a result of not drinking enough water, but nonetheless sent me a detailed list of OTC medications to buy at the pharmacy. I pretended to be asleep as Elaine B prepared for the day, brushing her hair, conspicuously eating a probiotic yogurt. The second the door shut, I leapt out of bed, haphazardly dressed in yesterday's clothes and accessorized my ensemble with a baseball cap and a pair of prescription-free eyeglasses.

I followed Elaine B to La Sorbonne Nouvelle on rue Santeuil. She walked through the main gates, then up to the third floor. I followed just a few paces behind her. Tailing Elaine B was easier than I thought, until she entered her classroom. I couldn't follow her in and I couldn't stay in the hallway for fear of her classmates noticing me. I decided to head back towards the gates. Since the university had only one entrance, she would have to exit the same way she came in. I tried to stay incognito by holding meaningful eye contact with a notebook, my hat snug over my head, but a couple students still looked at me as if wondering where we'd met before. Perhaps my body language had started to speak Elaine B's without even realizing it.

After two hours, I saw her walk down the main steps and exit the campus. I was impatient to know what Elaine B was doing with all her time now that she wasn't spending it with me. Did she go to the movies alone? Sob into napkins at bars? Had she reconnected with her friends? With her ex-boyfriend?

She walked quickly towards ligne 7 at Censier-Daubenton. On the platform, I waited as far away from her as I could while staying close enough to steal into the same car. When she selected a seat at the far end, I sat at the other end, facing the back of her head. She put on her headphones and I wondered what she was listening to. A pang of nostalgia bit into me so deeply that I cupped a hand to my side.

At Porte de Choisy, she exited and switched to the T9 tram. I sat behind her and studied the tram map: we were leaving Paris proper. Where on earth was Elaine B going? When we passed la périphérique, I finally realized: we were going to Vitry-sur-Seine.

WHERE ARE YOU REALLY FROM

Elaine B's parents lived in a modest brick house that shared a wall with an adjacent house. I watched her open the gate, dig her keys from her backpack and enter the front door. I stood on the sidewalk for several moments, at a sudden loss. A child playing lonesomely in the yard of the house across the street stared at me. What was I doing? I couldn't ring the doorbell. I could try calling Elaine B, but I knew she wouldn't pick up. I felt foolish for having planned so little in advance and yet I also felt acute twitches of excitement.

There was nothing left to do but lift up the latch of the gate as if I had done so countless times before. I hastened past the left side of the house, paved with loose rocks, and found myself in a threadbare yard. The back of the house had a sliding glass door and two windows: one large on the left, one smaller and higher on the right. I decided I could be less easily spotted through this petite window. I carefully positioned a lawn chair beneath the window, climbed onto it, then held my breath.

I was looking at a cluttered kitchen. An overburdened wooden cupboard faced a vinyl-covered table sitting atop rusted metal legs. To the left was a slice of the living room: a TV, a greenish sofa and two pairs of legs in slippers. Elaine B's parents. My heart nearly stuck in my throat when I saw Elaine B enter the kitchen from the hallway, crossing it on her way to the living room. I ducked and counted ten seconds.

When I dared to look up again, Elaine B was sitting on the floor, next to the coffee table. On the table was a circular glass serving dish with three different compartments: almond cookies studded with cherries, chewy brown nougat, sugar-coated pecans. A spasm of déjà vu nearly knocked me out of the chair. Didn't my parents serve the exact same refreshments when guests came over, in the exact same dish? Or was I once more mistaking Elaine B's memories for mine?

I don't know how long I stood outside Elaine B's window. Only suddenly, I knew I was cold and hungry and desperately in need of the bathroom. I contemplated peeing into some weeds near the side of the house, then talked myself out of it.

I was disappointed. I had only glimpsed the entirety of Elaine B; her parents had stayed seated on the sofa the entire time. I couldn't pinpoint the exact reason behind my curiosity—maybe it would give me an illusion of power over Elaine B because I would have glimpsed a desperately private part of her life that she was intent on keeping private.

I climbed down from the lawn chair and quietly slipped out the front gate. The sun had started to lay her head down for the night, taking the temperature with her. All the houses in the neighborhood were constructed with the same dull red brick as Elaine B's house. Occasionally, graffiti crawled across the low chalky walls separating the sidewalk from the front yards. I had only walked a few meters before I met an intersection and had to look up directions on my phone, having failed to memorize them on the way over. I groaned; with the tram experiencing delays, I'd have to walk some twenty-five minutes to the closest ligne 7 station. My phone redirected itself and I turned around, running straight into Elaine B.

I yelped and dropped my phone. I waited for her to slap me

across the face—I wouldn't have even blamed her—but Elaine B calmly retrieved my phone from the ground, dusted it off on her jeans and handed it to me.

"I'm sorry," I said, my voice more plaintive than I'd ever heard it. I told her I had acted stupidly and childishly (yes, I had taken advice from a child). I told her she was the most important person in my life. I told her I would take her to the movies and we could order all the popcorn, Coke and Kinder Surprise that we could stomach. I wanted us to return to our perfect ecosystem, that safe little terrarium sustained by just the two of us.

To my surprise, Elaine B's eyes softened. Then she drew me to her and kissed me. How to describe the sensation? Kissing myself made me dizzy and flipped inside out, as if all my internal organs had been exposed. I pulled away.

"Why did you do that?" I felt as if she'd committed a grave transgression.

I watched as anger spread open like a fan across Elaine B's face, slow yet deliberate. "Why can't you admit what you want from me?"

"I don't feel that way about you . . . I love Thibaud," I blurted out.

"No, you don't. You are using that poor man as an excuse to stay away from me."

This was so clear to both of us that I didn't even bother to refute it.

Elaine B took a step back and made a noise, an immaculate French scoff that I would never master no matter how many years I lived in this country.

"You are obsessed with me," she said. "You only eat the food I eat, you only go to the cafés I go to. You copy how I talk in French. You cut your hair like mine. You wear my clothes. You follow me to my university. You come to my parents' house. Why? To replace me?"

"What?—I—no—" I was out of words and grasped the first handful that came to me. "You're insane!"

"No, it is *you* who are insane. It's so clear to everyone that you want to be me." Elaine B took a step towards me. I couldn't move so much as a facial muscle. She held my face in both her hands like a lover's. Her touch was a warning, cool and dry. "But you will never be me. Unfortunately, Elaine, you will always be you. Nothing more and nothing less."

I punished Elaine B the only way I knew how, by spending more time with Thibaud. But this alone was no longer enough. I had to resort to something I had never done before: invite him to sleep over.

By sneaking a look in her planner, I knew exactly when Elaine B would be staying late at the library. I selected a Thursday night and asked Thibaud if he wanted to see my studio. He didn't need any convincing. When Elaine B's key announced itself in the lock just after midnight, Thibaud was in the shower, singing.

Elaine B took one look at me, sitting up naked under the bedsheets, then at Thibaud's pile of clothes on the floor, and slammed the door. From our window, I watched as she walked down our street and rounded the corner, her gait determined. I waved au revoir and smiled: I had upset her.

Thibaud and I hadn't had sex but we'd fooled around like we always did. Afterwards, I suggested he take a shower. I wasn't in love with Thibaud, true, but I did admire him, which I reasoned might be even better than love. I wondered if this was how people felt when they were smitten by public figures like Mother Teresa or Martin Luther King, Jr. Thibaud was passionate about social issues to a degree I'd never known. Unlike Elaine B, whose solution was to abandon her country and its problems, Thibaud wanted to stay and solve them.

The next evening, I asked Thibaud if I could come over but he was meeting with his fellow organizers to plan a massive protest at Le Trocadéro. The news had just broken that the three cops who had beaten the young man to death had not been arrested and were back patrolling the streets.

Part of me dreaded going to the apartment, where Elaine B would be sulking, but another part of me felt such an incessant desire to see her that it was physically agonizing. I was perpetually surprised when I came home to find her belongings still there; I half hoped that this, her not moving out, signaled a desire to see me that paralleled my own. But I was tired of my desire, the embarrassing nakedness of it. Like a child forced to wear shoes that broadcast their presence with each step. Everywhere I walked, my desire went *squeak*.

After leaving Hippolyte and Magali's apartment, I opted to pass the time at Monoprix instead of going home. Entering the store, I felt instantly calmer. When I reached the yogurt aisle, I found myself tearing up. It was nothing short of a miracle to find myself in France and now I was letting it slip through my fingers. For—I hated to think it—a man I wasn't even in love with?

I splurged a portion of my meager salary on a roasted chicken, premade patates dauphinoises and pistachio ice cream. I would surprise Elaine B, we would make up, finally watch *Dikkenek* and weld shut the schism that had opened between us so tightly you'd never know it existed in the first place.

On the way back home, I waited for the metro at Villiers, my shopping bags digging welts into my palms, but setting them down on the platform was out of the question; the smell of ancient urine permeated the entire station. The clock read one minute, but kept reverting to one minute just before it reached zero. Finally, after some ten minutes of waiting, the metro car barreled into the station with a hot blast of air. The green doors unlatched and the commuter crowd elbowed their way out. Obtaining a seat was tantamount to a competitive sport, and I eyed one in the left corner that looked like it was soon to be vacated. Before I could step onto the car, however, I witnessed a violation that made me lose my balance and my bags. I stumbled backwards as the people behind me surged forward.

Surely I was hallucinating? Or had I actually seen Elaine B clasping her arms around Thibaud's neck, mid-kiss?

I had to choose who to confront first: Thibaud or Elaine B.

Elaine B, I knew, was far more cunning and wily than Thibaud. She'd be able to wriggle out of this traitorous situation with zero qualms about lying to me. Thibaud, on the other hand, with his high code of ethics, probably didn't possess the ability to lie.

I went to his apartment in the 18th arrondissement. He had given me the digicode, so I made myself comfortable on the staircase landing outside his apartment. A few of his neighbors tossed disapproving looks in my direction; I had gotten so hungry while waiting that I had devoured half of the rotisserie chicken with my hands. The ice cream had melted into a milkshake, and, giving in to my thirst, I drank it straight from the carton.

Around 12h40, Thibaud arrived. "Mais qu'est ce que tu fais là? Ça va?" He pulled off his headphones and rushed over in concern. He sat down beside me and looked me over, checking for injuries. He was a good man. I wondered why I didn't love him more than I did. What did this reveal about me? Then I felt bad for making my mistreatment of him about myself. The chaos of my emotions frustrated me so much, my eyes started to water.

"Where were you?" I asked.

Thibaud looked at me with an excess of tenderness, which finally sent my tears running. "But what are you saying, mon petit lapin?" He enfolded me in his arms. "I was with you."

"What?" I could barely speak.

Thibaud chuckled but continued as if he were humoring me. "When we said goodbye outside the metro, I asked if I could accompany you home. You said not to worry." He looked at the Monoprix bags, perplexed. "When did you have time to go to Monoprix? Did you change your clothes?"

Thibaud was telling the truth; he hadn't deceived me. Of course he hadn't.

"Désolée," I mumbled, "I don't know what's gotten into me."

"Hey, hey, it's okay." He rubbed my back, then leaned in close. "J'arrête pas d'y penser." *I can't stop thinking about it?* I pulled away. What did he mean by that?

Scenarios whipped through my mind: Had Elaine B slept with Thibaud? Had she taken him to our studio? A wild possessiveness took hold of me, babyish and out of proportion. In spite of the loveless state of my feelings for Thibaud, he was still *mine*.

"I can't stop thinking about it, too," I said, hoping to glean more information.

He kissed my neck. "Did you really mean what you said?" Despite his large frame, Thibaud suddenly appeared shy and small. "Toi et moi . . . mariés?"

I thought I was going to vomit. The rest of our conversation kept fogging up with the cloudiness of my thoughts; I couldn't hear or think clearly. All I remember was Thibaud telling me he couldn't wait to tell his parents the happy news, and then he closed the door, smiling his kind, handsome smile.

Impatient to confront Elaine B, I took a taxi back to the 17th and swallowed the costly expense. I ran up the apartment stairs and flung open the door, my chest heaving. She had crossed an unspoken line, a line so clearly delineated that we'd never had to acknowledge it.

When I flicked on the studio lights, I stood perfectly still. The nightmarish episode on the subway platform—all my bearings stripped away from me—was happening all over again.

The apartment had been cleared of Elaine B's things. I looked under her clic-clac and around her side of the room. I checked the fridge and the bathroom cupboard: nothing, not even a forgotten piece of old fruit or a stray Q-tip. Her presence seemed to have never graced the apartment. I took several breaths to steady myself, then tried calling her. It went straight to voicemail—she had blocked me. I collapsed on the floor as my dinner strained to exit my throat.

How had Elaine B successfully passed herself off as me? Didn't

Thibaud know me well enough to know it wasn't me, or was Elaine B much more similar to me than I thought? Was their embrace on the metro their first kiss or one in a long line? And in spite of the deadlocked nature of our relationship, how could she—and in a sense, I—do this to me?

The thought finally sent me tripping over myself to the toilet.

I decided Elaine B was not the only one who could cross lines. The next morning, I dropped Hippolyte off at school and practically marched to La Nouvelle Sorbonne. After studying the campus map, I located the administrative office of the LLCE en anglais program on the third floor.

The hijab-clad woman with impeccable nails behind the desk recognized me right away. I mumbled that I'd lost my class schedule, praying my French had improved in part from my French classes but mostly because of Hippolyte's severe instruction.

The woman remarked curtly on my carelessness, but nevertheless printed out a new copy for me. I thanked her and tried not to overthink the vengeful thrill I felt in my chest, what it said about me and the kind of person I was.

Elaine B's final exam was on a Friday afternoon. I made sure to arrive early so as to be the first Elaine present in class. For visibility, I chose a seat directly in line with the vertical window in the door. Around 9h25, Elaine B finally appeared. We caught each other's gaze. She looked at me through the window and I looked straight back at her. In spite of myself, I smiled. I couldn't unriddle her expression (how did I feel when *I* made that face?) because she departed without a word.

When I received the exam, I was surprised to discover that the subject was a familiar book: *Frankenstein*. It had been years since I read it, but skimming over the exam, I knew I could answer the short essay question with a decent degree of knowledge.

> *The novel is told through three different narrators: Victor, Walton and the Creature. How does the reliability of each narrator influence, distort or contradict the reliability of the other narrators?*

But of course, that was not why I was here.

The teacher, a glasses-clad man who looked barely into his twenties, raised his eyebrows when I stood up an hour early.

"Déjà terminé?" he asked.

Remembering Elaine B's hours of studying, I hesitated before I handed him the exam. But then I thought of her and Thibaud's passionate embrace on the metro, of what they had done before or afterwards. I set the exam down on his desk with a smile.

"C'était trop facile."

Thibaud texted: the manifs were planned for tonight. Did I still want to join him and his comrades?

I did. Losing myself in a crowd, setting a cop car on fire and getting tear-gassed sounded fun; as a bonus, it would also get me out of my head. I knew these were all the wrong reasons to join a protest, but I also knew I wouldn't go in the end. The thought of seeing Thibaud sent me into a queasy spiral. I was horrified he'd accuse me of doing things I hadn't done, or perhaps he'd fall even more in love with me because of things he thought I *had* done.

"J'ai une cystite," I texted him, hoping his response would shed light on what had transpired the other night. But when he simply texted back to take care of myself, I learned nothing.

I didn't know what exact grade Elaine B received on her exam, but her latest social media post suggested it was bad: a photo of a dead rat, his poor two-dimensional body defaced with a tire imprint.

I felt guilty, and yet the feeling was outrivaled by another: happiness. Elaine B was back in my life and I was back in hers. Our lives felt yoked together in a way they had not been in a very long time. The feeling was almost as good, maybe even better, than when we were inseparable. I bore the consequences of her actions and she mine. What could unite two people further?

I shouldn't have been surprised, then, by what happened next.

The day Elaine B's exam results were released, I went to fetch Hippolyte from school. The week prior, I had been in such a state of hyperactive anticipation, I could practically feel my mind drooling. The anticipation was heightened because, now that she'd moved out, I couldn't guess what Elaine B was feeling.

My afternoon school routine was always the same: I stood by the front gate with all the other guardians and au pairs. Hippolyte, being the exacting child he was, abhorred tardiness. At precisely 16h31, I'd see him walking through the school's main doors and down to the gate. Like a little gentleman, he always politely waved goodbye to his teachers and friends.

This day, however, I was running late and arrived at 16h32. I waited until 16h35, then 16h40. By 16h45, I knew exactly what had happened. I nearly cried from some strange mixture of admiration for Elaine B's willingness to hurt me and fear for Hippolyte's safety, primordial fear I felt down to my bone marrow. At the same time, I tried to convince myself that because I would never hurt a child, Elaine B wouldn't, either. Or had I completely, and willfully, misunderstood the depth of our mutual understanding?

The mere fact that I had to debate this question pushed me off the small edge of reason I was clinging on to. In a barely controlled voice, I asked the recess monitor if she had seen someone picking Hippolyte up. She looked at me oddly. "Bah, oui—toi."

Of course; it was foolish to have even asked. I exited the school grounds and paced back and forth on the sidewalk. Worry prodded at me like two insistent fingers, now in my ear, now in my nose. I had to lace myself into Elaine B's uncomfortable shoes. If she were trying to torment me without endangering Hippolyte, what would she do?

I was staring at the patch of dirt around a lone tree when the thought came to me: Hippolyte's favorite place in all of Paris was the Muséum national d'Histoire naturelle. Elaine B, at a loss of where to take rule-loving Hippolyte, might have asked him where he wanted to go.

I took the metro to Jussieu. The museum was only open for another hour, but the attendant sold me a ticket after I claimed to be a tourist leaving Paris tomorrow morning. At this time of day, the crowd was thinning out. The first gallery was the grand gallery of evolution: an enormous glass-domed wonder, with intricate iron railings housing animals in both skeletal and stuffed forms. I breathed in the scent of polished wood and mothballs, momentarily struck by the brutal awesomeness of the displays and in comparison, my own crushing irrelevance.

I raced through the first floor before a docent barked at me to stop, then tried to discreetly speed-walk through every level in the first gallery before hitting the other galleries. An awful nagging sensation at the base of my spine kept me continually glancing over my shoulder. The problem was these damned glass surfaces all over the museum. I kept thinking I had seen Elaine B standing behind or just ahead of me, but of course, the reflection turned out to be my own.

An hour passed as I deliriously searched to no avail, coming across only my own reflected shame and the secret thrill that Elaine B was playing a game with me. In the jardin des plantes, a docent announced that the museum was closing in ten minutes. The scrubbed gray sky felt hostilely cold.

I was out of ideas. Only one recourse remained: retreat to Magali's apartment and wait for her to come home.

On the metro ride over, I considered for the first time in a long time what it meant to have met Elaine B. I was strung out and sick with fear, yet somehow my mind felt exceptionally clear. And indeed, meeting Elaine B had brought clarity into my life in the sense that my life now felt real and complete. I wasn't just a collection of vague and contradictory thoughts. If I ever felt unsure of myself, that old suspicion that I had been fastened into someone else's existence and not my own, I could look at Elaine B and feel grounded, utterly and completely, because if she was real, then I was real.

I walked up the stairs to Magali's apartment with heavyhearted steps. As my footsteps drew closer, I thought I heard a noise and walked more quickly, hope teetering before me.

I pressed my key into the door, opened it and nearly fell to the ground with relief. Hippolyte was in the living room completing a fossil puzzle. I ran to him, picked him up and, having never felt the inclination before, showered him with kisses on his head, his cheeks, his little hands, breathing in his clean scent mixed with the softest hint of No. 2 pencils.

When I set him down, Hippolyte looked at me as if I had lost my mind. "T'es malade, Elaine?" he asked, genuinely concerned. I knew in a minute I would get a lecture about abusing his country's universal healthcare. I shook my head no and looked up to see Elaine B standing in the darkened hallway, watching me.

"Go back to your puzzle," I said to him in the most poised voice I could muster. If he turned his head just twenty degrees, he would realize two of me stood in the room, inciting an existential crisis I doubted he could ever recover from. Unlike the majority of children his age, Hippolyte could not be tricked with empty platitudes in the vein of "You were just imagining things."

I motioned with my head to Elaine B: *Go that way.*

She smiled, clearly delighted to have driven me to such emotional volatility, then casually walked down the hallway to the bathroom. I followed after her and shut the door behind us, grateful the bathroom was at the far end of the hallway where Hippolyte would be hard-pressed to hear us.

We stared at each other in the eggplant-colored bathroom. Because it seemed we already knew what the other would say and then say in response, neither of us spoke at first.

I had not seen Elaine B up close for some time. She looked sleep-deprived and, like me, was dressed in a dark hoodie and dark jeans; this seemed a genuine coincidence. Our haircuts were more or less identical again. The same old innate pull towards her still lingered and I instinctively wanted to touch her. But an unfamiliar intruder had entered the room: horror, the kind derived from witnessing the deeply unnatural. A person crawling backwards. A head facing the wrong way on a neck.

"I'm going to take Hippolyte to his room," I said carefully. "Then count to ten and leave, *quietly*. Okay?"

Elaine B looked at me unperturbed, opening and closing a glass container of cotton rounds. "And if I don't?"

"How far do you want to take this?" I hissed.

"I can go as far as you." She smiled and swung the bathroom door open, then walked down the hallway.

I bit my lip so hard, it drew blood. *Please do not see her, Hippolyte, please.*

Then I heard his sweet, clear voice call out, "Elaine? Where are you going?"

The front door slammed.

Elaine B had trapped me in the bathroom. I'd either have to let Hippolyte believe I'd just walked out on him sans explanation or scale the fourth-floor apartment, drop down onto the sidewalk below and reenter (1) alive and (2) without being noticed. For several moments, I simply stood in the bathroom in a doomed state of immobilization. I hoped everything would resolve itself if I simply concentrated hard enough without moving a millimeter. Then I heard the discordant jangle of keys in the front door: Had Elaine B returned? Had she finally stopped this madness and come to her senses?

The breathless stream of indignant French that followed, however, belonged to Magali. "Alors, elle est où Elaine?" Silence. I imagined her son shrugging. Was he covering up for me? "Réponds-moi, Hippolyte," she insisted, her voice stern.

I knew Magali was one second away from having a full-on

crise. I opened the bathroom door and walked down the hallway into the living room. "Je suis là."

Magali glanced at me without a hello, then promptly complained that dinner wasn't ready, and why were all of Hippolyte's gladiator figurines on the floor, did I not realize that if he stepped barefoot on them, they could puncture through skin, which would lead to gangrene, and did I want to take him to les urgences at this time of night, when all the drug addicts and alcoholics were crammed together in the waiting room—

I looked over at Hippolyte. At first, his expression seemed unchanged. But then his eyes shifted from the front door to me and back again and I realized what the little crease on his forehead signified: fear. I came over and hooked a comforting arm around his shoulders.

"Ça va, Hippolyte?" Silence. "C'est moi, Elaine. Ta copine."

The words hardly had time to leave my mouth before Hippolyte ran from me as if I were cursed. I looked after him, devastated.

Magali was asking me something in a sharp falsetto but I could hardly hear her. An unbelievable rage towards Elaine B came over me that soon transformed into a clear-eyed epiphany. Of course the two of us could not exist at the same time. Look what had happened because of her recklessness—my recklessness. The situation had become untenable and I meant that in the most literal sense.

I saw only one solution.

Killing Elaine B was trickier than I thought. First, because I knew she had already gotten the same idea. Second, because I had no way of tracing her whereabouts. I knew she wasn't staying at her parents' place anymore because she didn't want us to meet and I had no idea where she'd gone afterwards. She had even deleted her social media account.

As I left Magali's apartment and started walking home, everything clicked into place. There was one clear out for Elaine B, an entire life waiting for her in California that she could slip into with no questions asked. All she had to do was hop on a plane and show up, then explain to all my friends and family that I had quit my au pair job early. My French had gotten so good, she could claim, that my English was forever accented. They might think I was experiencing some kind of glamorous post-life-abroad identity crisis, like actors who shoot a film in a foreign country and adopt the local accent. But they'd accept she was me—what other choice did they have?

The second I got home, I grabbed my passport from my nightstand, all my cash and a few other essentials, stuffing them haphazardly into my backpack. I felt a brief blip of gratitude that Elaine B hadn't taken my passport—but I knew every gift of hers came with a built-in catch. I flew down the stairs and would have missed Thibaud waiting outside the apartment building if it weren't for his signature scent of Scorpio cologne. As I turned around, I was struck by his handsomeness as if for the first time.

"Tu me réponds plus." He spoke in an uncharacteristically boyish voice. Even his hands were corralled into his pockets.

"Je sais," I conceded. He didn't deserve to be lied to. I thought of feeding him an American line: It's not you, it's me, I can't love you if I don't love myself. Instead I told him thank you, for being my first boyfriend in this country, for being in fact the most decent man I'd ever dated.

He was confused; what about the plans we made the other night? What about meeting his parents to tell them the happy news?

"What I said . . . It wasn't me. I can't explain it, but you just have to believe me." I blamed Elaine B for breaking Thibaud's heart; it was an easier pill to swallow than pointing the finger at myself.

Thibaud looked at me for a long time, as if trying to parse out the truth. Finally, he nodded.

"Good luck with the manifs and with . . . everything," I said, knowing full well how empty the sentiment rang.

Thibaud didn't press further. His eyes were somber as he turned away and repeated the first words he'd ever said to me.

"Salut, Elaine."

I took the metro to Gare du Nord, then the RER B. At Aulnay-sous-Bois, a mother and her son boarded the train and sat across from me. She unearthed a packet of berry compote from her enormous bag and held it out to him. As her son gulped it down, I couldn't help but smile. I thought of Hippolyte and hoped he would forgive me, or if not forgive me, remember me as the strange American au pair who had briefly entered his life and left it, leaving him no better or worse off than before. I thought of Magali and hoped she would not form a disparaging opinion of American au pairs, especially ones who looked like me, but I already knew this was a foregone conclusion.

The next flight out of CDG to LAX was American Airlines leaving out of Terminal 2B. I didn't see Elaine B at the airline counter, which meant she'd already gone through security. This was all based on the assumption that if I knew what I would do, I knew what she would do—a rationale that had yet to fail me. Because I had nothing else to go on, all I could do was fully commit to this lopsided logic. All I could do was abandon myself to the madness, that pink-foamed monstrosity.

I bought a ticket on my credit card and flinched; the cost of a last-minute flight was criminal. When I got in line for security, I looked around, my nerves frayed to a crisp—perhaps I had completely missed the mark and Elaine B, posing as Elaine A, was with Thibaud at this very moment, destroying public property and launching Molotov cocktails at cop cars as France 24 blasted my face across the news, effectively barring me from ever extending my visa.

But then I saw a familiar silhouette: Elaine B unloading her wallet, passport and phone onto a gray plastic tray. I thought of calling out to her and assessing the look on her face—she'd be surprised, no, *pleased*. She wanted me to pursue her and I wanted her to want me to pursue her.

By the time I arrived at the security conveyer belt, Elaine B had already headed off to her gate. I told myself to stay calm—neither of us could exit this terminal except by stepping foot on a plane.

When I passed through the body scan machine, the woman in charge looked at me and shook her head to herself as if to say: *I need to get more sleep.* I walked towards Gate 33B feeling oddly lighthearted. This is what I had wanted from the start—radical change. And after I had done what I needed to do, I could safely say I had achieved just that.

The terminal was uncannily empty at this late hour. I felt as if I had stepped into some liminal space. People dozed on black vinyl seats, others gaped red-eyed at their phones. The fluorescent light cast a defeated glow on the automated walkway and shuttered shops.

A mixture of duty-free perfume and the stale smell of the only restaurant still open, McDonald's, wafted along the currents of the AC.

When I neared Gate 33B, I passed by the bathrooms and, as if a lightbulb-studded arrow were blinking above it, understood exactly where I had to go. I looked around, opened the family restroom and stepped inside where Elaine B was waiting for me.

At that moment, I remembered I had not brought any weapons with me—naturally, I could not pass a knife through the security checkpoint. But, at least, neither could Elaine B.

We stared at each other.

I started to think—did she also?—that a way out of this predicament was within our reach. Maybe we could both exist at the same time if we made a blood pact or signed an NDA. Or was that wishful thinking? Maybe I'd simply have to follow Elaine B back home to California and bide my time before suffocating her in her sleep with my memory foam pillow. Or maybe I had to be creative right now, in this single-stall family bathroom with a changing area for newborns.

We lunged at each other at the same time. Elaine B's physical strength was no different from mine—neither of us exactly athletic, neither of us exactly weak. She kicked me in the stomach and acid reflux shot up my throat. I caught her head midair and whirled it into the hand dryer, setting it off—a sound I knew we both found unbearably grating. Her fist clocked me clean in the jaw and my head spun on its axis, before she body-slammed me into the tampon dispenser. Blood spiked my mouth. I cinched my legs into a vise around hers, tugged with all my strength, and she toppled down towards me. When she tried to jerk away, I gripped her tight by her hair and yanked backwards. I climbed on top of her and throttled her throat in my hands before she knocked me to my side, my head smacking hard against the floor, and did the same to me.

I was finding it difficult to breathe. My vision swayed to and fro. My ribs had been tenderized into rubber. I wondered, a little belatedly, if killing Elaine B would result in my own death. I guess there was only one way to find out. Staring at each other on the cold blue-tiled floor—inhaling a mixture of adrenaline, exhaustion and soiled diapers—I couldn't tell where I stopped and Elaine B began. Staring at her felt no different from staring at myself. I suddenly felt thankful I was dying by my own hand—there was something inherently generous about it. Something beautiful in its symmetry.

We smiled at each other as our hands flexed around our throats, tears leaking down our cheeks. I felt very faint from Elaine B, from myself. I felt something akin to resignation or, at least, rest.

When I opened my eyes, I was alone in the dark. The automated lights blinked on as I stood up. Every inch of my body screamed. I looked down at myself to tally up the damage: My arms and stomach were badly bruised. The back of my head was matted in liquid I didn't dare examine closer.

No sign of Elaine B.

I arched over the sink and flung handfuls of cold water in the approximate direction of my face. The bathroom lights were nosebleedingly bright and the AC sounded like a buzzing beehive. I tried to recall the classic symptoms of a concussion, but then I heard a voice calling my name on the intercom in English, then

French: "Elaine A——, your flight is boarding at Gate 33B. This is your last call. Elaine A——, dernier appel, votre vol est prêt pour l'embarquement à la porte 33B."

I flung open the door and raced towards the gate. Curiously, the entire airport was empty. Only a round automated cleaner nipped at the floor. At the gate, I dug my crumpled boarding pass from my pocket and shoved it at the two attendants. "Desolée!" I cried.

Rather than order me to stop, they waved me aboard and wished me "Bon voyage." I dashed down the jet bridge before they could change their minds. I pulled my hoodie over myself, a blast of icy night air assailing me in the face, and entered the plane with my head down. I only walked a few paces before sinking into the first empty seat. The crew must have been waiting for me because the second I sat down, the doors snapped shut, the plane shifted gears and a few minutes later, it was reversing and navigating down the runway.

I kept my hoodie on and my eyes closed as the safety and emergency instruction video played on the screen in the seat before me. The combination of light and noise was going to kill me. Was it wise to be up in the air, thousands of miles away from a licensed medical practitioner? How many hours was the flight to California? Ten? Eleven? Then the lights dimmed and my back was thrown against the seat as we ascended into the air with a thunderous drone. Lines of diffuse blue lighting flickered on beneath the overhead compartments. I knew I should rest until I felt more stable before verifying if Elaine B was on the flight, but I couldn't wait. I touched my hand to the back of my head and it came away soaked in fresh blood. I felt the edges of my consciousness going in and out, like faintly blinking stars. I worried if I closed my eyes, I would not be able to open them again.

I forced myself up. This alone made my vision lose focus. In the fuzzy darkness, I could hardly see; examining each row for Elaine B was out of the question. I stumbled towards the rear of the plane, where the flight attendants were gathered.

A brunette attendant turned towards me. "Je peux vous aider, mademoiselle?"

"Yes! I'm looking for a passenger, Elaine B——. She looks like me."

The attendant frowned ever-so-slightly before smiling again. "Elaine B——?"

I nodded vigorously. She smiled at me for a few more moments, then asked to see my boarding pass. Annoyed, I pried it from my pocket. "Why do you need to see it? Sorry, this is very urgent—you must tell me if an Elaine B—— is on this flight."

The attendant smoothed the piece of paper against her thigh, then held it up to her eyes, peering at it in the low light. Her spotlessly made-up face brightened in an instant.

"Mais c'est vous, mademoiselle!" She patted my arm and led me back to my seat. I was helpless against her authoritative grip.

"What do you mean, it's me?" I asked fearfully.

She held the ticket out to me. The passenger name read: *Elaine B——*

"You see? So there is nothing to worry about!" she insisted.

I twisted out of her grasp, pushing past a mother holding her baby. Behind me, I heard her cry out in anger. The bathroom—I had to get to the bathroom. The corridor of the plane, limned in pinpricks of white light, unfurled like an endless tongue before me. It looked alive, pulsing hideously. The air had sprouted minuscule fibers that clung to my every movement. I forced myself to keep going, my knees buckling with each step, as I grabbed the heads of the seats before me to wrest myself forward, inciting more annoyed shouts. Just before the brunette flight attendant caught up to me, I yanked open the bathroom door and locked myself inside.

I fixed my gaze on a spot on the linoleum floor for a long moment, hoping it would tame the vertigo and mute the attendant's furious knocking. But the jaundiced light and the cocktail of blue toilet disinfectant and bodily emissions in the airless space only aggravated it. I closed my eyes and repeated to myself, "I know who I am. I know who I am. I know who I am."

Finally, I opened my eyes. Looking back was Elaine B.

I reached up to touch my hair, my mouth. Elaine B reached out to touch her hair, her mouth.

"Bonjour," I said to my reflection.

"Hello," said the woman in the mirror.

FEATURED BACKGROUND

Gene called them his good-day-bad-day bagels. When he was having a good day, he'd allow himself a bagel, and when he was having a bad day, he'd also allow himself a bagel. How he landed on bagels was a matter of both convenience and health: New York had no shortage of them and donuts upset his blood sugar. But bagels, on the other hand—they possessed an inoffensive, neutral quality. The problem was he sometimes swerved between good and bad so frequently that he ended up consuming three bagels before dinner. Though Gene believed in waiting until the end of the day before declaring it one or the other—sticking a nice, firm label beneath it—waiting defeated the purpose of an immediate, edible consequence.

Gene measured out every moment of his life into a series of punishments and rewards. If he missed the subway at the precise moment the doors pinched shut, he let himself forgo eye contact with the homeless woman jiggling her paper cup. If he skipped the subway fare because a charitable stranger had propped open the emergency exit door, his punishment (awful to consider it punishment, he knew) amounted to coughing up a dollar along with the eye contact.

Mentally taxing to approach life like an escalator of fluctuating numbers, yet Gene found a neat satisfaction in balancing out the sum. When the positive and negative points canceled themselves out into a flawless zero, it proved he wanted for nothing. Besides, stopping was out of the question. A system of measurements designed to keep himself on the straight moral path because he couldn't always keep it straight on his own—this was his self-prescribed treatment.

Today, the day he rode the N train from Astoria and boarded the bus on East Thirty-Ninth and Second, he'd tallied zero ups and two downs, meaning he was allowed two ups: an everything bagel with green-onion cream cheese (he counted them separately; he didn't like to cheat the system). At the bodega, he'd considered ordering a second bagel, because today—surely, today of all days?—he would have reason to celebrate.

He opened his brown paper bag as Napoleon parked himself in the seat beside him. "My doctor said I have the heart of a sixty-year-old," he said by way of hello. Given that Napoleon had turned sixty last month, Gene offered no response, instead politely listened as his companion denounced the toxicity of Western medicine and Big Pharma. Napoleon interpreted Gene's silence as a reproach. "What's with you?"

"Nothing," Gene lied. "My stomach hurts."

Napoleon rummaged through his satchel, a counterfeit Louis Vuitton, and produced a bottle of Po Chai pills. "Take two of these. With lukewarm—*not* cold—water."

FEATURED BACKGROUND

Gene waved him away. "I'm fine."

"Suit yourself." Napoleon eyed Gene's paper bag. "What do you got there?" Gene reluctantly admitted to the everything bagel as Napoleon theatrically clutched his stomach. "I haven't eaten since last night. We wrapped at four in the morning. I took a nap on the 6, didn't even have time to go home and shower—"

Gene handed the bagel over.

"You sure you don't want any?" Napoleon said, already tearing through the wax paper.

"I'm sure." Gene meant to ask how bagels fit into Napoleon's anti-Western cleanse, but was distracted by a familiar face boarding the bus—a woman he'd once been coupled with at an overpriced Szechuan restaurant on the Lower East Side. He turned in his seat and recognized other faces before the vertigo of familiarity was heightened by a new realization: everyone present had been selected because, from a blurred distance, they could be related.

Napoleon noticed, too. "I bet you it's a Japanese World War II movie."

They had met on the set of *Law & Order*. Napoleon (his parents had named him with misguided hopes) played ILLEGAL IMMIGRANT while Gene played UPSCALE LAWYER. How their respective identities factored into this casting decision (Napoleon being a little more Southeast to Gene's East) was understood but left unspoken by both men. Standing in line to get propped—Gene with a slick leather briefcase, Napoleon with a soiled cardboard sign—Napoleon had offered to lift Gene up. He'd agreed under the impression he was joking and a moment later, found himself fully hoisted into the air, legs flailing. Apparently Napoleon's shortcut to making friends was lifting people up, including the six-foot-three man standing beside them who played SECURITY GUARD, somehow stunned and satisfied each time he managed it.

Gene continued to run into Napoleon on set, not unusual when few background actors shared their narrow demographic. Without having exchanged numbers once, Gene suspected he was on more intimate terms with Napoleon's catalogue of health problems than Napoleon's full-time friends—one of the perks, or pits, of the job: endless hours to kill when the only weapon around was small talk. But the transitory nature of these interactions was also their beauty, which freed you up to confess more than you'd otherwise dare because after twelve consecutive hours together, you'd simply say, "Nice talking to you," and walk off, you with their confessions and they with yours, safe in the degrees of separation that stretched between you.

Gene had been doing background for two years. When asked how he'd gotten into it (a stock question extras passed around between takes), he would say he'd always been interested in acting, and wasn't a late start better than none? That wasn't entirely true, though. Actually, it wasn't true at all. He'd signed up to do background because of his daughter, Athena. Like Napoleon's parents, Gene had named her with hopes she'd achieve magnificence, and then, to his bewilderment, she did: *Winner of the Nicholl Fellowship in Screenwriting. Voted Best Narrative Feature at SXSW. Premiered at Sundance Film Festival.*

He once asked the Internet for information about his daughter and it had responded with her professional bio: "Athena Wu is a writer and director. The daughter of immigrants, her work interrogates the intersection of race, sex and violence. She lives in Los Angeles."

"The daughter of immigrants." He read the line twice to make sure he hadn't hallucinated it. That she had taken on her mother's maiden name was bad enough, but what had compelled her to lie? Like Athena, Gene had been born in Michigan. He'd grown up in an industrial town on the outskirts of Detroit, pretty painlessly, all things considered. After Athena turned five, he'd moved his little family to New York. He had plenty to be grateful for, all things considered. But Athena—she refused to acknowledge that her accomplishments, all the awards and fellowships and titles, had been made possible through an unbroken line of others suffering more than she ever had. A line drenched in unspeakable terror and bloodshed, all so Athena could make derivative art about it from the comfort of her tastefully decorated apartment. In her "body of work," she never failed to adopt their suffering as her own. He sometimes wondered if Athena secretly hoped a horrific event would befall their community because, should tragedy's well run dry, what else would she write about? If such a thing as a surrogate of misery existed, that was his daughter.

How to explain he was terrified of her? Not just terrified but stunned he'd had any involvement in her upbringing, let alone her existence. In an interview, when asked why she'd gone into filmmaking, Athena had answered, "I've always been interested in controlling my environment. I guess you could say it was an affect developed in childhood." The last line had made him squint sideways at his phone.

Gene wasn't an ambitious man himself—he looked for meaning in the hours spent clocked out of his job more than in the job itself, which was, at the moment, driving part-time for Uber. He and his cousin split custody of a slate-blue Toyota Camry with jaundiced headlights; he had the weekends and his cousin, the weekdays. He rented the second floor of a duplex from a married couple half his age, a painful reminder he had yet to enjoy the financial security his daughter did.

He led a noiseless life, though it was a little lonely and monotonous, true, and he would have liked to live closer to his only immediate relative, that is to say, Athena. But doing background, he'd been a NASA scientist, a doctor and a UN ambassador without having to train for any of it. Lately he'd even started to entertain going out for speaking roles. Nothing major, of course, but he could play a security guard or valet with a line or two. The other day, he saw an ad for Beginning Acting classes at the 92NY, "open to all ages and levels of experience," and thought, why not? Really, why the hell not? For the first time in years, hope no longer beckoned like a trap but a challenge.

He knew what Athena would think if she got wind he wanted to act. *You? Stick with one job?* But that was the appeal of acting: it was a Russian doll that contained countless jobs. Staying loyal to a single profession had never been Gene's strong suit. When Athena was younger, he'd been a security-desk attendant, a truck driver for a restaurant-supplies company and a maintenance-crew member, just to name a few. In between jobs, he'd participated in paid surveys about products he could never afford and swallowed clinical-trial pills his nonexistent health insurance could never cover. He'd had no time to tend to a "career."

But Athena—she'd always known what she wanted. Barely in second grade and already marionetting her toys in elaborate three-act stories. Other little girls wanted clothes and stuffed animals; his daughter had coveted a Sony camcorder with infrared night vision. Other daughters were devoted to or at least tolerant of their fathers; his had abandoned him when he needed her the most.

The bus squeaked onto 495 and spat them out on Long Island, at an immense movie studio Gene hadn't known existed. All these years and New York kept pulling scarves out of her hat, discount-magician-style. He could never come to grips with the city, which thrived on chaos rather than order. But maybe that was why he couldn't quit his co-dependent relationship with the city. She was forgiving, built on second and third and fourth chances.

In the parking lot, everyone stretched, yawned and obediently shuffled in the direction of neon orange signs pointing to holding—a demoralizing room with ten fans in lieu of functioning AC. Nonunion's breakfast was already waiting for them. Warming trays on one table accommodated sausage patties, bacon, scrambled eggs, pancakes and home fries, while a second table housed juice boxes, granola bars, some battered-looking fruit and mini boxes of cereal. The granola bars were always pocketed in seconds. Gene had forgotten this and by the time he wandered over, only unsalted peanuts greeted him.

"Decent spread."

Gene looked up. Napoleon had sauntered in with his SAG-exclusive breakfast, served upstairs: eggs Benedict, shrimp cocktail, sliced avocado and a salacious chocolate muffin.

"Didn't want to eat with *them*," he sneered, though Gene failed to understand why since he never let anyone forget he was SAG. *"Where's the line for SAG?" "Sorry to cut, I'm SAG." "Is SAG getting bused home?"* Gene hated to be reminded he wasn't SAG—another point docked off.

He took a bite of flaccid pancake as the second AD swept into the room, his movements so frenetic that the NDAs fluttered in their piles on the conference tables. Gene waited for "Janek but you can call me Jack" to speak. He did not. To Gene's amusement, Jack waited until all the NDAs were signed and collected before opening his mouth. From that moment on, the extras were bound to silence.

"Okay, so _____ happens over the course of twenty-four hours. It's made up of three vignettes, each one based around a different _____ in New York. I said *vignette*, not *vinaigrette*."

Most of the time, nobody on set bothered to explain anything to them. Most of the time, they were corralled and herded around like livestock, with no sense of where they were going, why they were going there or when they'd be back. On the rare occasions explanations were offered, the film was either big-budget or art-house.

"And our eyes and ears, _____, he's the thread that connects them all. You still with me? Okay, so today we're shooting three scenes." Disappointment dribbled through the airless room. "I know, I know, it's going to be a long day, but trust me, we want to get you out of here as fast as we can." Translation: *We don't want to pay you a cent more than we have to.*

Someone raised her hand. Jack pretended not to see.

"So in this vignette, everything takes place on a _____. In the first scene, it's a normal day. You're all waiting for the _____ like it's going to come any second. Yeah? In the next scene, it's the same scenario but you're getting a little _____ and you all _____. In the last scene, imagine a _____ or _____ has just happened. This is when _____ starts to go haywire. He's been _____ throughout the day, ____ on, called a _____, and now he completely loses it. Got it?"

Gene set down his fork, his appetite hijacked. Why was Athena so seduced by tragedy?

A metal chair screeched back against the floor. The elegant hand gripping it belonged to Hiriko, an attractive, widowed woman of undisclosed age. Gene had met her a couple of months back, when they played ND PEDESTRIANS during an alien invasion. She had a habit of bringing an enormous paperback to set, opening it up, then ignoring it for the rest of the shoot, and kept an engraved flask in her purse from which she stole small, satisfied sips.

"Do you know who's playing the lead?" she asked him, eyes twinkling.

Gene could never tell if she was flirting. He wasn't sure if he wanted her to flirt. He had not dated anyone in a very long time. His last attempt had resulted in a minor catastrophe: a misunderstanding, a clumsy waltz, a fractured toe. He'd stowed dating on a high shelf and was undecided on ever taking it back down.

When no one responded, Hiriko indulged them: "That young man everyone's talking about, _____."

He was said to be the next (the first?) great Asian American actor of their time, the one who'd raise them from obscurity into, well, something beyond obscurity. His résumé ran the gamut from superhero action flicks to romantic comedies, and now he was, unsurprisingly, segueing into serious dramas. And Gene's daughter had nabbed him as the lead in her film. *His daughter*—the words tugged on his tongue's line. He reeled them back.

"He's dating what's-her-name, the actress who played the last Wonder Woman," Hiriko added.

Gene's mind sketched a rough impression of her: blond, full-figured, legs up to here.

"No way," Napoleon said in between vigorously attacking his eggs Benedict, as if he hadn't desecrated a bagel thirty minutes ago.

"Isn't that something," Gene offered.

"That's exactly what I thought," Hiriko said.

The three chewed in silence. No one said aloud the obvious thought hanging over the table, *That would have never happened in my day!*, because it would have conceded the world was zipping in a different direction while they feared they were affixed to the same spot.

The wardrobe assistant took one look at Gene and asked if he'd brought a change of clothes. He couldn't help but feel a little insulted; his clothes were brand-name, from T.J. Maxx. Gene did nearly all his shopping at T.J. Maxx, a store that was neither positive nor negative but a net neutral, which he appreciated. He shook his head no without bothering to trot out an excuse, then couldn't help but cut his eyes at Napoleon and his knockoff Louis Vuitton luggage. Napoleon pulled out five full sets of options in garment bags as wardrobe fawned over him. When Gene dislodged his gaze, the assistant was holding out a drab outfit. He sighed and exchanged his release form for it.

Inside a portable dressing room that refused to zip up all the way, Gene struggled to shuck his pants from his body without knocking over the flimsy nylon contraption. He cursed himself for ignoring the wardrobe notes from the previous night. *"No bright whites, no brand names, think grimy, interesting patterns ac-*

ceptable, nothing that causes strobing, though!" Bad Gene, failing to honor his duties as a background actor. Surely that warranted a subtraction of points.

At hair and makeup, his hair was combed through and spritzed. Makeup devoted more time to dusting him in a fine layer of soot-colored powder. "You have great eyebrows," the makeup artist complimented him. She kissed her brush into a cake of gray and gently stabbed his forehead.

Gene twisted around to look up at her. She had purple hair, a rose tattoo brambling across her neck. "Thank you," he said tremulously. He wished he knew her name.

She looked a little put off by his sincerity. "Sure thing."

Add three points to the day. *He had great eyebrows.*

She stepped aside to let him review her work in the mirror: He looked poor. Poor and old.

When the availability request had popped up on his phone, it had only said "BYSTANDER" for "UNNAMED PROJECT." His eyes had snagged on the text. Something about it crackled, its very nondescriptness setting it apart from other requests.

Gene had almost turned it down, had almost given up hope he'd ever land on one of his daughter's sets, but then he remembered she was scheduled to be in New York. He'd figured it out by skimming the comments section after Athena posted a snapshot of the Manhattan skyline on her social media.

He'd last seen her at the Atlantic City bus terminal, seven years ago. Their goodbye had been benign, even pleasant. When she handed him the envelope of cash, she hadn't cut any of her usual backhanded or reproachful remarks. And just before they parted, she'd even gripped his arm and said, "Good luck." *Good luck,* in any language, signified well wishes, didn't it?

Not until weeks, then months, later—time marked by earsplitting silence in response to his calls, texts and emails—did he obsessively rewind and freeze-frame the moment. Trying hopelessly to pinpoint when in the course of an hour their relationship had curdled and spoiled. When they stopped for Subway sandwiches? Waiting in line for tickets?

But that was absurd. He wasn't so naïve as to believe the first thread had unraveled at the Atlantic City bus terminal. No, Athena must have decided sometime before (when? the phone call that precipitated the envelope?) to "estrange" herself from him. What a funny word, estrange! Gene thought it sounded unnecessarily fancy, almost French, since it called to mind *escargots*. But smuggled into the belly of the word was *strange*, and yes, *strange* was the word for a part of yourself going off into the world, scaling magnificent heights, while the other part remained a distant spectator. If Gene had to describe the sensation, he'd say it was like catching a glimpse of your nose on someone else's face and wondering, *Now how did you end up there?*

Three PAs darted around set but theirs, the one charged with wrangling them like docile livestock, was named Beckett. He wore the standard PA uniform: sneakers, jeans, hoodie and a holster slung low around his hips where a walkie-talkie took the place of a gun.

Gene felt paternal towards the PAs, who were invariably twenty-somethings who'd moved to NYC to become screenwriters and considered sleep a fun activity they'd try someday. When an unusually thoughtful PA asked, "Need anything? Everything okay? Let me know if you want water," Gene had to stop himself from asking, "Do *you* need anything? Is everything okay with *you*? Let me know if *you* want water."

Beckett, unlucky fellow, was not a PA with a natural loudspeaker jerry-rigged into his lungs. Gene caught the first leg of his sentence as he crossed the room, his voicing wilting halfway through: "If you have *not* had your picture taken—"

"What?" Hiriko called. "What was that?"

The question landed on the floor, unanswered, as they shuffled in groups of five to the front of the room, where they were transferred into the care of another overworked PA.

Tian formed the start of the line, the portrait of serenity. Of all the people Gene had ever met on set, Tian had been doing background the longest. He never scrolled through his phone between takes or tried to negotiate sitting down in a scene. He'd never dream of sneaking off to holding, pretending he hadn't heard his number called. He even paid attention to scene continuity. The consummate extra, in other words.

Gene nodded hello to him, as did Hiriko. Napoleon ignored him; he was convinced they were locked in stiff competition. The PA took their picture, then asked for their numbers.

"Two," Tian chimed in his clear voice.

"You're featured background today?" the PA clarified.

Tian nodded.

As if sensing that this news might upset Napoleon, Hiriko asked him how auditions were going. Unlike her and Gene, Napoleon was an *acteur*, meaning he'd somehow convinced an agent to secure him auditions, self-taped most of the time, but occasionally held in demoralizing rooms not unlike holding.

"I just got a callback for a commercial," he said, loud enough for others to hear. "A national one." Gene and Hiriko exchanged

Aren't we special? glances. "For gastritis, which, sure, isn't what I planned on for my acting debut, but I wouldn't have to work for a year. $50,000 on average is what I'm hearing. And don't forget the residuals."

If Napoleon lucked out, he'd be guaranteed a lifelong job. Then again, he'd be forever known as the face of gastritis. Which put him out of the running for arthritis guy, ulcers guy, etc.

"I hope you get it, Napoleon, I really do." Gene mostly meant it. As they sat back down at their table, he wriggled free the bag of peanuts from his pocket, scrutinized it. Did he deserve a reward?

"You're just—what—one voucher away from joining SAG?" Napoleon nudged, though he'd asked Gene this question before.

Another point docked. "Mm-hmm." Peanuts, it was.

Hiriko's eyeglasses skated down her nose as she arced forward. Gene caught her perfume's bouquet: not spiced and musky as he'd imagined, but girlishly floral. "You have to learn a special skill. Sign language. Playing dead. Tap dancing. You know, I once tangoed with Sessue Hayakawa." She winked at Gene as he struggled to recalculate her age based on this new scrap of information. He wasn't imagining it—Hiriko was flirting. She cracked the spine of her paperback and scanned Gene's midsection. "Or just invest in an NYPD costume. You have the build." Maybe not.

"You know what you got to do?" Napoleon teased. "Insert yourself."

A few legendary extras had snatched up speaking roles by shouting a line so good, so felicitous, they'd rendered themselves indispensable. Infamous among extra lore was the *Being John Malkovich* scene when a guy whips a beer can at John and hollers, "Think fast!"

Hiriko pursed her lips. "What do you mean?"

Gene recounted the anecdote, pleased as anything, as if it belonged to him and only him.

"Oh, that? That's been debunked." Hiriko sipped gaily from her flask. "You didn't know?"

Gene sighed with inordinate disappointment. Now why did she have to tell him that? He preferred the false version. The better version.

By noon, Beckett's voice had been reduced to a rasp. "Everyone, numbers one to seventy-five, follow me. We are going to set *now*. Leave your stuff here. No one will steal your umbrella, I promise. Yes, go to the bathroom now. Bring your IDs to get propped. I said, BRING YOUR IDs."

Beckett escorted them through an artery of hallways that funneled into a massive warehouse. Rows of horizontal lights spanned the length of the walls, tricking the eye into the collective fiction that broad daylight saturated the warehouse. Extraordinary, the amount of muscle and sweat sacrificed in the name of movie magic, Gene thought. And it was extraordinary, to the point where he'd look around set and grow a little clammy-eyed. I'm a part of movie magic, he'd think, and if I so much as step in the wrong direction, I can break the spell.

They passed by a construction area—sawing, hammering, sanding—before entering the set, a replica of a New York City subway station. The uncanniness was surreal: everything, down to the grimy tiles and weeping metal beams and balled-up trash, had been cloned to perfection. Only the smell was disorienting. Instead of weed, spilled coffee and an unnameable l'eau de sewage, Gene breathed in fresh paint and sawdust.

He stood in a corner and canvassed his surroundings, angling for a three-hundred-sixty-degree view. The set was chaotic with crew members wrangling their respective gear: cameras, lighting, sound, hair and makeup, the person who stuck neon tape on the ground (how was he named in the credits? Gene had always wondered). He spotted Jack yapping into his headset, a different PA reprimanding Beckett, Napoleon hitting on a guy half his age, and then, and then—he saw her.

She was seated in a raised folding chair, eyes locked on a monitor. Her hair was short, chin-length, not long as she'd always worn it. She looked tired. She looked awfully young compared to everyone around her. She was dressed like a PA. Did she need water? He could have cried.

"You." Beckett snapped his fingers and pointed to a spot a few yards away from Athena. "Here."

Her outline flitted in the corner of Gene's vision.

Napoleon elbowed him. "What are you doing?"

Gene realized everyone was grudgingly lying down. "Which scene is this?"

"How the hell would I know? They never tell us shit."

"If wardrobe says I ruined this coat, it's not my fault," Hiriko murmured. She took off her glasses and tucked them away, then looked at Gene for approval. He offered up a noncommittal noise.

As soon as Athena's attention was stolen by the DP, Gene carefully lowered himself down; he couldn't bear for her to catch him panting and fumbling, the spitting image of the old man he suspected occupied her imagination. He stared up at the enormous ceiling. The floor beneath him was cold and yet it might as well have been a heated blanket. He felt lightheaded, giddy as a schoolboy. *They were in the same room.*

FEATURED BACKGROUND

The stand-in for the principal actor was shuttled off as Jack's voice descended from above. "Okay, so this is before _____ has entered the station. Think of it as the ____ before the _____. Right now we want to create a _____ mood. Got it?" He was met with blank faces. "Lie still, but move around. Scratch something, cough—no, *mime* coughing—just don't look dead. Okay? Now let's make a movie!" Jack clapped his hands once, an exclamation point on his pep talk.

Gene struggled to make sense of the film. Was it abstract? Athena's first film had been abstract. When the words "Written and Directed by Athena Wu" unscrolled across the screen, the hairs on his arms had bristled with pride, but it wasn't long before confusion seeped in and supplanted it. The film, which had one of those pretentiously long titles, featured an excess of neon signs at night, decadent food left uneaten on tables, opaque conversations. Even the deconstructed timeline seemed intentionally convoluted and self-important, as if looking down its nose at the audience.

At the same time, the film was the very opposite of abstract, given that ten out of its ninety-two minutes were devoted to the gang rape of a girl. A girl who looked not unlike his daughter. Gene's first instinct was to flee the theater mid-film, and he might have if his body hadn't congealed into an inanimate block of flesh. Later, in the theater's lobby, he used the free Wi-Fi to scrape the Internet for information on how he was supposed to feel. However illogical, he couldn't help but suspect Athena planted signs for him in her art. If she'd tried to telegraph him a message in her first film, what on earth was it?

When interviewed about the film's explicit violence, Athena had answered, "I had to show the truth. This *happened*. We can't look away from it," referencing a 1985 news story out of San Francisco's Chinatown. Gene understood this; he did. At least on an intellectual level. But who was it for? Who wanted to watch it? He certainly didn't want to see five white men gang-rape a girl who looked not unlike his daughter. He could've lived his whole life without seeing it. Happily. But maybe he was a philistine. He favored comedies. Animated movies. Black-and-white classics. He was a sucker for unambiguous endings.

In the lobby, he'd stowed away his phone with an uneasy heart. The public persona Athena had constructed was unrecognizable to him. Whenever Gene watched her interviews, she came across as angry. Angry and self-righteous. The combination made him profoundly sad. Wasn't she tired? He wanted to tell her to take a break. To allow herself carefree stupidity, the birthright of anyone her age. But his daughter was on a crusade (against what?). She was terrifying. She'd always terrified him.

"Napoleon?" Gene whispered.

"Yeah?"

Napoleon's head was positioned just above his. Tiger Balm wafted from his forehead; the man was morphing into an apothecary. "I ever tell you I have a daughter?"

"QUIET ON SET."

The urge to toss it all out the window seized Gene. To chuck a beer can and yell, "Think fast!" Gene licked his chapped lips. "She's the director."

Napoleon twisted around in disbelief as someone barked, "Stay in your first positions."

"No kidding?" Napoleon was uncharacteristically silent as this revelation sank in. Then he fished for the miniature headshots kept in his wallet. "Hey, introduce me."

Gene swatted his hand away. "She doesn't know I'm here."

"What the hell are you talking about, Gene?" Napoleon demanded, abruptly a full Staten Islander, a fact he suppressed until he couldn't.

"HOLD THE TALK. LAST LOOKS."

Napoleon finger-combed his hair and sucked in his cheeks.

"Pictures up . . . Rolling . . . Background . . . Action!"

Everyone shushed.

Action! was the sacred word that recontextualized the set into a nearly religious space. Every second carried weight and they all bore it, each and every one of them, for a common purpose, and surely such collective devotion gestured at a kind of religion, didn't it?

Gene noticed only then that the principal actor had materialized. They tended to wait until the last minute, apparently unable to bear proximity to him and his fellow background actors for longer than necessary. Gene startled a little in recognition—so Hiriko had been right.

The principal actor crumpled to the ground, moaning and writhing, before crawling over the extras. His foot nearly grazed Gene's chin. After a while, his wails echoed against the false subway tiles. In Gene's opinion, he was overdoing it, his notion of drama prefixed with melo.

"Cut!" At the sound of Athena's voice, Gene's heart did a jumping jack.

"RESETTING."

For the next two hours, while the camera was moved into every conceivable position, Gene remained suspended in a state of anxiety so intense it bordered on elation. When Jack called, "Checking the gate!" his posture caved with relief.

Beckett allowed the extras to stop by the crafty truck and the honey wagon before heading back to holding. Gene unstacked his spine, touching his hands to his toes and slapping his arms awake, loitering until the others had filed off set. He felt oddly light and heavy at once, as if he were a helium-filled balloon dipped in iron. He steadied himself and walked towards Athena, the calm locus in a cluster of moving parts, her headphones curving off one ear, still staring intently at a monitor.

He couldn't talk to her. He couldn't.

Gene kept his eyes lowered as he passed, chastised by his own cowardice, but at the last minute, all conscious control over his actions fled his body and what do you know, when he lifted his gaze, she was looking right at him.

"Dad?" she said, not unkindly, not even so much in surprise.

"Athena!"

Her stare washed over him like a flashlight, accusatory. "Follow me," she hissed.

From the back, she looked very thin—malnourished, practically. Her walk still listed towards the left, a bad habit inherited from her mother. She led him behind the set, lights blaring synthetic daylight above them, over electrical cords and past carts stocked with bottled water, through a set of double doors to the parking lot. Outside, it was drizzling.

Gene's hands quaked; he was on the verge of splitting apart from happiness. He'd planned out this moment hundreds of times. The apologies. The forgiveness. The reunification, like two weary factions after a civil war.

"You're sick," she said.

"I've missed you."

"What are you doing here?"

"I'm acting," he smiled.

She smiled back like she wanted to run him over with a truck. "I could have you arrested."

"No, you can't," he said lightly, and even she looked struck across the mouth by this truth.

"Please leave."

"You look great, Athena."

"You have no right—"

"I have every right."

At this, Athena laughed unconvincingly. The skin around her eyes had already started to sag. She's only twenty-seven, he thought.

"I have no obligation to you," she said.

"I disagree." Gene's voice had lost its friendly edge, as if he'd accidentally let it out of his sight.

"Your opinion doesn't matter here."

"'Opinion?'" he repeated skeptically. "Who's talking about opinions? You're my daughter—"

"Stop."

The hardness etched into the word was so startling, he took a step backwards.

"I will not engage with you on your terms. You will not cross the boundaries I've put up to safeguard my well-being." She had switched to the even, clipped register of a therapist. Wielding this foreign language against him—language she'd learned in the time they'd spent apart, language *he* certainly hadn't taught her at home—was an affront.

If she would at least cry, if she would at least scream! Anything would have been preferable to this phony wall of talk therapy. And yet he sensed the wall she'd patched together was fragile, the thinnest of paper barricading a deluge. If he just pressed a little further—

"I'll leave you alone if you give me a legitimate reason why," Gene countered. He was convinced he'd engineered an indisputable work-around, because reckoning with the contrary, leaving her alone for good, was inconceivable.

Instead, he stood dumbstruck as Athena fired terms at him like *emotional abuse* and *parental neglect*. As proof, she brought up the money, though she'd assured him in Atlantic City that she wanted to—what was it?—*put him on the road to recovery*. She told him she'd been going to Al-Anon for two years after realizing none of it was her fault.

Gene frowned. Al-Anon?

She'd always blamed herself, did he know that? As a child, she had to do everything, she had to track his purchases, his whereabouts, minimize his blunders for the sake of her mother, junk the empty bottles, open the windows in the morning to air out the stink. Keeping their family from collapsing in on itself had fallen to her, but if she so much as asked for a packed lunch, she feared she was acting selfishly. She existed on perpetual tiptoe, terrified the slightest misstep would set him off, too on edge to fall asleep because she was waiting, she was always waiting. At school, she had to pretend she had normal kid problems, invent excuses for why she'd dozed off during class again or why Gene had missed another parent-teacher conference. For years, she'd shouldered shame and guilt that were not hers, they were his and his alone. Thanks to Al-Anon, she had finally started to heal.

Heal. The word alone was a condemnation. His younger self might have raised his voice or collided one object against another to shake loose her sensationalized version of events and steer the narrative back towards reason. But this version of himself—tired, lonely, and tired of feeling lonely—could only grab a handful of empty words: "I see." He couldn't even bring himself to apologize. He loathed himself for it. But folding his cards would cede to her version of the truth.

When Gene didn't say more, Athena blinked in surprise. "Well—yes. And I need you to respect that." In the pregnant pause that followed, he thought she was planning to say something else, but then she abruptly walked past him towards the doors.

Gene turned around and called out, "I wanted to say I'm happy for you." The tremor in *happy* sickened him. He'd tried so hard to sound convincingly cheerful.

Athena slowed her steps without stopping. He started subtracting points, then lost count.

A year before they parted at the Atlantic City bus terminal, she'd been the same at her mother's funeral. Withholding. Cold. Distant. Gene knew parents could be withholding, cold, distant. He didn't know children could be, too.

Athena handled all the funeral arrangements, and for that, Gene was grateful. Well, more accurately, he felt blips of gratitude, bright buoys in the sea waving to him from afar through a haze of near-constant inebriation. From the hospital to the church, he was awash, afloat on a neat little mixture he'd concocted of suanmeitang and whiskey, while Athena rushed around in a dark pantsuit (where had she procured a pantsuit at a time like this?) making calls, answering the door, heating up leftovers. He was inconsolable. He would have liked to drown. He couldn't think of Bi-Ling's wasted body without thinking longingly of the pain-free place she now inhabited, a morbid breed of jealousy. The few times clarity visited before a numbing headache displaced it, he'd wonder, Why aren't you inconsolable? My busy daughter. My oh-so-efficient daughter. Why have you left me flailing alone in this watery grief?

The night before the funeral, he woke on the sofa when she noisily thunked a bottle of Pedialyte on the coffee table next to his head. Later, he thought he heard muzzled crying in the stairwell. But he couldn't be sure if he'd dreamt it, or if the pitiful whimpers had wrung themselves from his own mouth.

Gene sometimes wondered, in a fit of delusion that oscillated between self-indulgence and self-pity, if Athena would ever make an autobiographical film. The thought both tickled him with delight (she couldn't forget him!) and paralyzed him with fear (she couldn't forget him). Legally speaking, his permission was required if she were to base a nonfiction character on him; he felt pleased she still needed him in that regard. Or maybe she'd spin just enough details to slide the character into the safety net of fiction.

This aside, what preoccupied him the most was the question of how she'd portray him. He hoped she'd at least cast a decent actor. He didn't need to be played by some swanky A-list star, he just didn't want to be unfairly depicted. He didn't want to look up at himself on the silver screen only to see a monster.

Gene caught up with Napoleon and Hiriko at the crafty truck.

"Where the hell were you?" Napoleon said too honkingly, too Staten Island–y, then coughed and fine-tuned his voice. "Did you talk to her?"

Gene's former desire to confide in his part-time friend had

FEATURED BACKGROUND

packed up and left. "No. I mean, yes." Napoleon and Hiriko exchanged pointed looks. "Go on ahead," he insisted. "I'll see you inside." They walked off, briskly (it was drizzling, after all) but not so briskly as to be rude.

Gene faced the truck's window. "Hi, yes, one black coffee, cheese crackers, a Rice Krispies Treat, and . . . Sorry, what do you have back there?" He sensed the line behind him twitching with impatience. "And a granola bar. Wait, never mind—a fruit cup," he said sagely. He hated fruit cups. The points demanded a punishment. Or a reward. He no longer knew.

Gene had conceived of the good-day-bad-day-bagel system after attending his first, and only, AA meeting. First and only because he just couldn't look himself squarely in the eye in the unforgiving light of day. If he looked at a problem aslant, it didn't fully exist and therefore it couldn't fully annex his reality. Pathetic, he knew. But in his own way, he had managed, hadn't he? The points system, however faulty, kept him from sliding too far off in any given direction. If his life were a seesaw, he didn't want it to see or saw. He wanted it to lie perfectly flat.

"You don't want the other stuff?" The cook didn't sugarcoat his exasperation.

"No, I do," he sighed.

Arms full, coffee sloshing onto his borrowed shoes, Gene walked back to holding.

Napoleon was keeping Hiriko hostage as he swiped through his phone's photo album, flaunting screenshots of himself as an extra on various TV shows and films. Since Gene didn't have cable or memberships to any of the streaming services, he had no proof he'd ever played a NASA scientist, doctor or UN ambassador. Helping him figure out how to take screenshots was the sort of thing a daughter should have done for her father, good-humoredly annoyed at his tech ignorance. And yet.

"'Impact over intention,'" Gene said, interrupting Napoleon's photo parade. "What does that mean, anyway?"

Napoleon shrugged as Hiriko turned thoughtful, flipping through the pages of her book without glancing at them. "Do you have an example?" she asked.

"That's what I'm saying—it doesn't have any meaning. You can't disagree with it. Like an ace card." Gene stared suspiciously at his empty fruit cup—when had he eaten it?

"You okay, buddy?" Napoleon asked with unusual sympathy. As if Gene were unwell. Or worse, senile.

Before Gene could answer, Beckett called them back to set. As they filed down the hallway, Hiriko held out her flask. Just by its heft in his palm, Gene knew it was a third full—funny how an old instinct kicked right back in as if it had never left. He hesitated for a second, then cleared it in a single gulp. He had pinned Hiriko for a sherry drinker, but it was straight gin.

She raised an eyebrow. "One of those days?"

If there was one thing Gene could not abide, it was being smudged away. That's how Athena looked at him—like a smudge on the pristine glass of her life. Detritus from her pre-famous past she'd never have to set eyes on again simply because she could choose not to, so low was he beneath her line of sight. How foolish to think she breadcrumbed messages for him in her art. She didn't think about him, let alone have anything to say to him. And she had made up her mind to continue on this path of no contact until he or she died first. Unbelievable that she'd denied the fact of their biological relationship. Of course, she'd packaged it in different terms: *chosen family* and *personal autonomy*.

Nonsense was what it was.

But he shouldn't have been surprised. Athena had always rewritten reality to suit her preferred version of it. Though her mother had died from a sickness hoarded in her genes—the Huntington's so engulfing, it swallowed her personality—Athena claimed the disease had been triggered by Gene. The last week they spent at NewYork-Presbyterian, she launched accusation after accusation at him: That Bi-Ling had abandoned her family and friends in Taiwan to move eight thousand miles for him based on promises he never intended to keep. That she'd lived a miserable and isolated life in this inhospitable foreign country. That Gene, as self-centered and responsible as a teenager, couldn't see it. Yet Athena couldn't see past the narrow categories she'd sorted him and Bi-Ling into: Gene, an *American-born* and *privileged man*, versus her mother, an *immigrant* and *oppressed woman*.

Athena had been downright exhausting during this period. Gene could not have fathomed engaging in a real conversation with her about her mother's illness or what might happen if her mother succumbed to it. So they didn't. Instead, Athena talked at Gene while he sat there, mute and defenseless against her college-educated diatribes. The night Bi-Ling passed, his wife had gripped his hand with something synonymous to tenderness and, Gene hoped, absolution. Meanwhile, Athena glared at him from across the hospital bed, outraged her mother didn't share in her hatred of him.

The year following Bi-Ling's death was a sodden blur. But

after Atlantic City, Gene had decided to start fresh, to become someone . . . fresher.

He was a good man. Not a perfect man, no. He'd had a mercurial temper when he was younger, he could admit to that. And the drinking hadn't helped (harder to admit). But he found it laughable that some people believed a single instance of human error could cancel out love. His own father used to beat him, even when Gene was old enough to fight him off. And yet he'd forgiven him, in the sense that he had not known his father's fists warranted forgiveness.

He'd been five years sober—until now, anyway. He'd forgotten to tell Athena in the parking lot. He wanted nothing more than to pocket her pride in him, to be able to gaze upon it in the center of his palm anytime he wanted. He waited for something akin to momentous sorrow to wash over him, his hard-won sobriety erased in a blip, and yet the reality of what that sip portended seemed very far away.

Points lost, points gained.

He decided he would not give it any more thought and that was that; Gene had always excelled at compartmentalizing. He studied his aching legs instead. He should have worn his compression socks. Or maybe the feeling was heartburn. Where was Napoleon with his Po Chai pills when you needed him?

They were shooting the last scene of the day. Two hours ago, they'd wrapped the third (or was it the first?) scene and passed into the lucrative valley of overtime, but what would Gene have given to just go home already. It was a mistake to have come. A mistake to assume knowing could ever substitute the yielding softness, the generosity, of not knowing.

Jack was bouncing up and down, somehow even more animated

than at the start of the day. Gene would bet money he'd been subsisting on a steady dose of Adderall.

"So in this scene, you're all exhausted, okay?"

Napoleon snorted.

"But this is the moment we've been building up to, when _____ is finally going to _____. Remember he's been _____ on, _____, _____ around, and he's had it up to here. It's an emotional scene, a highly charged scene, and I want you all to *feel* it."

The extras were to stumble haphazardly around the subway station—easy when everyone was suspended in a fugue state at this twelfth hour.

Jack moved them into their first positions. "Don't be afraid to run into each other—I mean, don't hurt yourself," he quickly amended, no doubt thinking of lawsuits, "but act like you can't see where you're going. Okay?"

"If I ruin this coat, it won't be my fault," Hiriko murmured again. She looked at Gene for affirmation. He was in no mood to give it this time.

Commotion was developing farther up along the set, where the stand-ins and stunt coordinator were situated, but came to a pause when the principal actor emerged from who-knows-where. His hair and makeup team lagged behind him, spraying and smoothing and powdering, as he carefully avoided eye contact with the background actors, then checked his phone before stowing it in his pocket.

Unbelievable, Gene scoffed, the gin magnifying his disdain into outright anger. The shape of the phone would trace itself through his pants. He hoped it was on silent at the bare minimum. God, the disrespect was appalling. Acting was an art form. No, it was something more: it was the only time you could offer up a slice of reality that would outlast reality itself. And here their supposed savior was, treating it like a minimum wage job he was dying to punch out of.

Athena huddled up with the principal actor and the stunt coordinator, the three of them conferring in agitated tones. Then the stunt coordinator called "Number Two" and Tian walked over to join them. Gene trained his gaze on Athena, willing her to look his way. She refused. After a few minutes, Tian returned to his first position.

"Pictures up . . . Rolling . . . Background . . . Action!"

Gene zigzagged across the set, half-blind without needing to act. The gin coursed agreeably through him. He slammed his shoulder into several people, Napoleon included, who doled out a pitying look in his direction. He picked up his pace, everyone's features smearing together in a flesh-toned spin cycle, then slowed his steps when he heard the principal actor's voice.

The principal actor gripped Tian by the collar, then sneered a slur in his face and knocked him to the ground. He mimed kicking and punching Tian for an excruciatingly long time as Tian wailed. Gene looked at Hiriko—she had broken protocol and closed her eyes in protest. The sudden violence in the scene, in the warehouse, came as a terrible intrusion. Nothing, not even Jack's hyperactive explanations, could have prepared them for it.

"Still rolling!" the second AD called. A PA intercepted the principal actor with an unlabeled bottle and squirted milky liquid into his mouth. He leaned back, about to spit in Tian's face. Gene's stomach clutched.

"Stop," Tian said flatly. "I can't."

A few extras stalled in their movements, unsure if he was speaking as himself or if he'd been anointed out of the background masses at long last to a speaking role.

"Cut!" Athena called. She hopped down from her chair and walked over. "What do you mean you can't?" she said with a hint of annoyance. Her hands flowered open and closed, open and closed—a nervous habit.

"I don't understand why we're hurting each other," Tian frowned. "It doesn't make sense."

Behind Gene, two PAs were whispering. "She thought a _____ actor was too 'controversial' and a _____ actor was too 'predictable.'" The other PA whistled under his breath. "Apparently, she said the 'safest choice' was an all _____ cast."

Gene grimaced—his daughter's vision of society was awfully reductive. But for whatever reason, she must have derived comfort from reducing it down to manageable parts. Was it so different from his good-day-bad-day-bagel system? There was no manual for How to Be a Good Person. At the end of the day, everyone was winging it.

"I want to call my SAG rep," Tian said. Not the consummate extra, after all.

The principal actor vainly suppressed an eye roll.

Another extra addressed Athena. "What exactly are you trying to accomplish here?"

She looked caught off guard and reached for an academic tone. "Well—abuse against elderly _____ is on the rise and—"

"And your solution is more abuse?"

"But it's not real," Athena said softly, as though to herself.

Tian laughed. "Am I not real?"

The question skipped through the crowd of extras, from one person to the next like a live electric current, before dissent broke out in murmurs.

For a fleeting moment, Gene thought of calling out, "Impact over intention, Athena! Isn't that what you said?"

She was no doubt wearing the same contemptuous mask she'd worn in the parking lot, but when he looked in her direction, her expression spelled horror. Authority leaked out of her by the second. She looked so small. She looked so young.

In elementary school, Athena used to film him and Bi-Ling with a cardboard camera constructed from toilet paper rolls. He'd crushed it in his hands one night, hostile and drunk and then hostile because he was drunk, but the next day, he'd bought her a used Sony camcorder with that week's paycheck, which meant he'd have to skip meals twice a day, but she'd thrown her arms around his waist and it had been worth every spasm of hunger.

When she'd asked him in her little-adult voice (terrifying, she'd been, even then) if they had enough money to afford the camera, he'd lied. "Whatever you want, I'll get it for you" was his favorite refrain, even when Bi-Ling scolded him for turning her into a bottomless person, someone whose desires have no end.

He never told Athena about the illegal gambling that had paid off her mother's hospital bills. About the months he spent processing fake IDs in Jackson Heights as a second source of income. About the time when, during her freshman year of college, his bike was stolen and he lost his job as a deliveryman and spent six dehumanizing weeks homeless, fishing congealed food out of trash cans and sleeping in intermittent spurts in subway cars. She believed what she wanted to believe. No, she believed what he'd let her believe. Maybe both were true.

He realized, with sudden, searing clarity that cut through him like light, what Athena had meant in her interview. Directing brought her control over her environment because it offset the chaos he brought to it. When she zoomed in and out on her camera, perhaps she left their apartment in Astoria. Perhaps she traveled somewhere else entirely—to a safer, better place.

If he were the director of his own life story, he'd play things out differently. He wouldn't pulp the toilet paper roll camera in his hands. He'd help Athena construct a better one, twice as large and three times as intricate, with sturdier cardboard, and they'd spray-paint it gray on the sidewalk, and then he'd salvage more cardboard to make one of those black-and-white clapper boards because an aspiring young director needed a clapper board. He would have been his daughter's first audience and her biggest fan, from the very beginning.

"I'll do it." Gene walked into the heart of the commotion.

"What are you doing, buddy?" Napoleon asked, resting a hand on his sleeve. He shrugged him off.

Tian looked at Gene, shaking his head ever-so-slightly, then walked off set. Gene half expected people to clap. No one did. He stepped in front of the principal actor. Up close, his handsomeness seemed unearned.

"You don't have to, Dad," Athena said quietly.

Everyone stared at her, then him. *Dad.*

Gene sat down on the ground. "Kick me," he said, peering up at the principal actor. "Go on, spit on me." He had done the math. This is what the points commanded.

The crew looked around at one another. After a long moment, the sound guy rehoisted the boom. The lighting team rechecked their equipment. The principal actor cleared his throat.

Gene lay down, prepared to play a role that, in some ways, felt as if it'd been written for him.

And then Athena called action.

Gene qualified to join SAG that day. On IMDb, he is credited as ELDERLY ASIAN MAN. A gift from his daughter; according to union laws, featured background are not required to receive screen credit.

After the film's release, Gene read review after review, hoping to reach a verdict on the film without experiencing it, but the reviews were as mixed as he felt. When he finally purchased a ticket at his local art theater late one morning, he was one of three in the audience. He sat stiffly in a red velvet chair, folded his jacket over his lap and ate an entire box of chocolate-covered raisins before the previews had ended.

At first, the film didn't suture him in, just as he'd predicted. He thought he'd remain detached throughout its entirety but especially during his scene, as he looked at himself pretending to be someone else, knowing exactly what tricks had been turned to tamper with the lie until it could pass for the truth, remembering exactly how sawdust had gilded the air (movie magic!) and how the synthetic lights had felt strangely cool against his skin.

But as Gene watched himself spasming and wincing on the subway platform—his arms tucked helplessly around his stomach, his mouth limp with resignation—he felt knocked over by such exquisite grief that he discovered, to his surprise, his cheeks were wet.

HAPPY ENDINGS

When he opens his eyes, he's standing in a brightly lit hallway. The walls are painted baby pink and the floors are checkered black-and-white. Down here, the air smells like the aftertaste of something sweet, something artificial. He follows the hallway down, where it turns left and feeds straight into the parlor entrance: two automated frosted glass doors like those of a dentist's office. The interior could pass as a dentist's office, too: modern and clean with BreathOble Plants pulsing in the corners. The receptionist's desk is a half circle rimmed in aquamarine light. Music, a subdued instrumental, plays demurely from hidden speakers.

A silver plaque on the wall announces WELCOME TO HAPPY ENDINGS.

The man is both relieved and disappointed. Relieved the place looks legitimate, more than one would expect from the basement of a sex doll factory, and disappointed because he nonetheless craves the residue of danger that clings to illegitimate places. This aspect of his personality—hardwired for risk—lies dormant in his personal and professional life. It only awakens in places like this one.

The receptionist stares down at her hands, the long white arch of her neck exposed like a helpless swan's. She doesn't glance up at him until he's right up against her desk. She looks to be in her late twenties, though the newest line of TrueSkins makes it impossible to tell anyone's real age. She's pretty, in an uninteresting way. Her name tag reads ANASTASIA.

"Do you have an appointment?" Her English is good, the accent North American. He suspects an AutoTranslator is implanted in her throat.

"No."

"Which one of our services would you like to try?"

The man frowns. Given the name of the place, he hadn't anticipated a diverse array of options.

"We have Happy Endings Deluxe, Sublime and Infinite," Anastasia prompts him.

"Infinite."

The man slides over a digital glass card, illuminated with thin, pulsing lines of light, and drums his knuckles against the counter. The automated doors part to reveal another customer, a thickset woman. He's surprised; he thought only men would frequent this place.

"Sign here, please," Anastasia says.

She places a tablet on the counter, an electronic Terms of Agreement. He scrolls down, presses his index finger beside the X, shoves the tablet back. He's getting impatient. He's seen the closed door to the right of the counter and he wants to know what lies beyond it.

HAPPY ENDINGS

Tomorrow morning, he has a meeting at Hong Kong University. He researches DNA, its springy coils and serpentine double helixes. He started his career in academia, then briefly segued into the private sector before upgrading to independent research, unbound by the slog of peer-reviewed articles and government grant applications. Despite all odds, he's still hopeful, still bent on delivering a cure for his mother, whose body has been ransacked by so many operations and artificial implants, she's sixty percent human.

"I'm a cyborg," she rasps when he visits her, separated by a thick pane of glass. He never manages to laugh at her weakhearted jokes. His mother is the only family he has left. Her life is nonnegotiable. If she leaves him, who will anchor him to this failing world? For her, he has rearranged his life: tirelessly tracking down the latest studies, patents and procedures, even if they're only legal outside the U.S. For her, he has forsaken building a family of his own. When she tells him—reprimands him, even—to be a little selfish, he has to stop himself from reprimanding her lack of gratitude.

He first came to Hong Kong seventeen years ago, when he was completing his postdoctorate. He'd been younger then, twenty-nine, but the city had felt older. Whole swaths hadn't yet been bulldozed and refashioned high above sea level in an intricate archipelago of bridges and man-made islands, the rising ocean frothing beneath them. Back then, he had also come to meet with researchers. His visit was meant to last one month, but after he received a university grant to continue his research, he stayed for the whole year.

The work depleted him. His mother's first operation was complicated by the fact that the only company that manufactured artificial nucleic acid was based in Hong Kong. The patent had been denied in the U.S., blowback from the latest wave of unchecked Sinophobia. He spent hours mired in the bowels of bureaucracy, both medical and political. His worry manifested in a phantom cough that defied explanation. His hair went next, defecting in pale clumps.

From time to time, he was allowed relief. Professional, uncomplicated relief.

He had never had any problems sleeping around: he exercised, kept himself shaved and groomed, possessed the kind of square, blunt features deemed conventionally attractive. He simply didn't have time for the banalities of trying to fuck a stranger: coffee, movie, dinner, etc.

When it came to the sex trade, he also did his research. He avoided brothels where girls were underage or victims of sex trafficking in favor of government-regulated establishments. The sort that offered health insurance and a pension, where security guards and cameras ensured the women's safety. During his visits, he was courteous and gentlemanly, always brought a single heart-shaped chocolate wrapped in gold foil, always clarified what he could and couldn't do, always remembered to ask for a name. He prided himself on his restraint, his control, his vigilance—as a researcher and as a man.

Of course he'd heard about the other possibilities of paid sex, both concealed and publicized, that leaked through the city: sex in skyscraper penthouses, in palatial beds with six girls at a time. In saunas and karaoke bars and self-automated taxicabs. Underground dungeons and silk harness webs and gravity-free pods. Still, for months, he remained loyal to his government-regulated establishments. Perfunctory. Hygienic. Easy.

HAPPY ENDINGS

Then, dipping out from a bar in Soho one night, a man in a holographic face mask had slipped him a digital advertisement, a glimmering rectangle he discreetly pocketed. Later, he inspected it in the privacy of his apartment: the digital ad was a portal into an entire dimension he'd been missing out on. TotalEmbodiment VR sex hotels, silicone-hydrogel sex dolls and the first line of TooReal bots. The images undulated in his hand—lavish and profane. His jaw grew slack from the pure creativity of it all.

Still, he remained skeptical. Why have sex with a 3D image, with a lifeless doll whose insides are constructed from mesh and wires, when warm-blooded women were readily and safely accessible?

He posed this question to Xavier.

"Because of what you can do to them," he explained.

Xavier was a childhood friend who traveled to Asia at every opportunity, eager to ditch his wife and two toddlers for a week. Deemed a public safety hazard, sex work had been outlawed in North America and what was left of Europe. But in parts of Asia, Xavier explained, laws concerning sex robots hadn't yet been passed.

"What you can do to them," the man repeated, his eyes blinking at the possibilities.

Xavier laughed at his childlike expression. "Exactly. You can do anything to them." He paused. "They're more expensive for that reason."

"Why?"

"Replacing parts costs money."

Oh, he had money.

When he wasn't at the lab, he was being sucked off by three purple-pink VR monsters, with four breasts each and as many orifices as he could dream up. He cleaved a sharp line between that person, the one sweating above a tentacled sex bot, and the person who diligently holo-called his mother at the hospital every day.

That year, his flesh separated from his self and floated above it, regenerating only after it had been purged and exhausted down to nothing. His old habits ebbed away. He no longer showered before he arrived. He abandoned the heart-shaped chocolates. He forgot to ask for a name. But it made no difference, he reasoned afterwards—they weren't real.

The sex bots and avatars blurred together, a whorl of hard and soft, in an unending torrent of pleasure. It was mind-numbing—and a perfect distraction from the real reason he'd come to Hong Kong—but all the same, after the initial sheen of fresh excitement dulled, he found himself growing bored.

A month before he returned home, he met up with Xavier when he was passing through and asked him for the best fuck he had ever had, human or nonhuman, it didn't matter. Xavier showed him not a reservation website or preview video clip, but an address in a part of town he'd never visited.

"What's so special about her?" he asked.

"Go find out yourself," Xavier challenged him with a grin.

Instead of an ultramodern facility, he arrived at a nondescript brothel on the fingertip of Victoria City. A honey-tongued madam greeted him and collected his money. As soon as he entered the room, the girl said he could use her as he saw fit, declared with proud defiance. Under a pink lightbulb's glow over a flimsy mattress, he examined her face and body for a single flaw and found none. She didn't partake in the performative writhing and moaning he'd grown accustomed to. She had simply offered herself up before him as if she didn't care what happened to her.

He realized, finally, why Xavier had singled her out as exceptional: it was impossible to tell if she was a bot.

Figuring out whether a girl was human or not was increasingly difficult, especially since some had started passing themselves off as bots; better pay and less hours due to recharging time. You couldn't tell by the texture of her skin or how wet she felt between her thighs; they had perfected that tech early on. The only way to know for certain was to look her dead in the eyes, ideally in natural lighting. They hadn't optimized the dilation of the pupils just yet.

"Are you real?" he panted as she fucked him breathless.

She laughed with her head thrown back. He didn't like being laughed at.

He understood in that moment why men returned to human girls. The difference lay in the danger—that glint in their eyes, a cocktail of hunger and fear. After all, you couldn't scare a bot.

He had left her, he felt certain, a changed man.

Seventeen years later, as if spurred on by Pavlovian instinct, he wanted relief again—he deserved it, didn't he?—the moment he landed at HKG airport. He entertained thoughts of sniffing around a dark alley, conducting business the old-school way, oblivious to the girl's age or how she'd arrived in her present circumstances. Taking her against a rain-slicked wall or beneath a streetlight's embrace. The thought, he had to admit, aroused him.

But it was against his principles. He was an ethical person. A caretaker, a son. A respected scientist.

"Where should I go?" he asked Xavier over holo-phone, now married to his third wife, his children fully grown, but still a frequent traveler to Asia.

"Happy Endings," Xavier said before he could finish.

"You're kidding me. A massage parlor?"

"Something like that. Trust me, you won't want to come out for days," he assured him. "It's pure bliss."

Behind the first door are more doors. He stands in a hexagonal room, tinted to the colors of a peach. "This way," Anastasia says and presses her palm against the glass-plated wall. A panel glides open to reveal a pristine bathroom with cotton robes lounging against the wall.

The man steps inside, considers whether he should shower at all. Something about smelling like aftershave makes sex feel too commercial. The animal scent of him, of her, unwashed and ripe in their filth, isn't unwelcome to him. Eventually, though, he undresses, inputs his ideal temperature and lets the automated shower sud and scrub him; might as well since he's paying for it. He debates masturbating so as not to ejaculate too early, then changes his mind. What would be the point at a place called Happy Endings?

When he exits, Anastasia is standing in the exact same spot, her hands folded across her waist, her smile serene. He wonders if she's the latest model of a TooReal bot. She leads him across the room and slides open another invisible panel.

"This is Eden. She'll take care of you now."

Before he can turn around, the panel slides shut.

"Hello," Eden says.

He notices first her hourglass shape and what he estimates are 32F breasts. Her body looks molded to perfection, as if a sculptor had pinched and pulled at the clay of her flesh—the work of TrueSkin, no doubt. Like Anastasia, she wears a PVC button-up white dress, an upgraded version of an X-rated nurse's costume. He barely registers her face, identical to the surgically enhanced faces of all the girls in Hong Kong: unnaturally sharp nose, eyelids cut high above her eyes, pink plushy lips, all set in an inverted triangle of a face. These days, he finds it harder and harder to tell them apart.

What preoccupies him is the room. He tries to gauge the size of it before realizing his eyes can't locate the corners of the walls or the depth of the floor. The room is spherical, with only a single massage table at its center. He taps his foot against the translucid surface: solid. Strange.

Strange, too, is the color: a shocking, medical white. He had assumed a massage parlor this expensive would exude a more ethereal aura.

"I'll take your robe," Eden says. Her accent is London posh.

He still finds it uncanny to hear an Asian woman speaking perfect English, but stops himself from complimenting her on it.

Eden's fingers lightly lift his robe from his shoulders and a flint of desire sparks through him. He smiles down at her, his eyes gorging on her cleavage. He wants to find out if they're real—if she's real.

She gestures at him to lie down on his stomach. The massage table is microbead soft. His head is cushioned in a plush padded contraption. He hears the squish of a dispenser followed by the sound of Eden smoothing oil between her hands. When they alight on his back, they're firmer, more authoritative, than he'd expected. Her hands knead up and down his back, coaxing out the knots and ropes of tension. She extracts the pressure from his neck, his spine, his calves. In spite of himself, he feels himself grow sleepy in his relaxation. He closes his eyes and dreams of walking in an endless hallway.

"Wake up."

Eden stands over him holding a warm towel.

The man blinks and rubs his eyes.

"Please lie on your back now."

He smiles at her—with the massage over, they can address the real reason he's here: a happy ending. Though, sizing up Eden's appetizing body, he wants more than a simple hand job now. And based on Xavier's emphatic recommendation, she must offer something better.

He palms the small of her back and guides her towards him. "I'd like you to be naked." He's skilled at voicing commands as requests. Not that he needs to ask permission from a TooReal bot, if that's what she is.

Eden smiles at him. He looks directly into her eyes for the first time, but with the light annihilating everything into a white haze, he can't get a read on her pupils. He knows another way to find out if she's real or not, though. He slides his hands underneath her dress. Before he can unbutton it, she does it for him. He already knows what position he'll twist her into first. He reaches for her, drowsy with desire, when she clasps his wrists and pins them to the table with surprising strength.

"Please lie on your back now," she repeats.

He stares at her. The new line of TooReal bots is something

else. He doesn't like playing the submissive but decides to acquiesce this once.

"I'll be right back." Eden disappears through a curtain and he closes his eyes, grinning like a child about to tear into his birthday present. "This will only hurt a little."

Before he can register what's happening, she plunges a needle into his left arm. He can't move; his veins are coursing with a liquid that solidifies his flesh into cement.

"What are you doing?" he gasps.

"You asked for Happy Endings Infinite," Eden says pleasantly.

She looks down at a tablet, tapping swiftly at the screen. He can't make out the interface before she adjusts a headset over his eyes, delivering him into pitch-black, and presses cool, jellylike pads across the length of his body. He recognizes it as a VR setup, though his penis is left untethered, not suctioned into a cozy RealPusssy pod. The inert massage table is moving now, as if it's sprouted wheels. He detects a humming noise followed by a dry click. He swivels his head around, enveloped in dimensionless darkness, certain his entire body's been encased. He tries to lift his hands, to sketch a picture of his new surroundings, but the effort is futile.

"Now I will read the directions. Please pay close attention," Eden says. Her voice is muffled and distant. Fuck—he's definitely in some kind of chamber.

He forces a few deep breaths. He apparently paid for VR sex—really expensive VR sex—so he might as well enjoy it, right? Try to fucking enjoy it, he commands himself.

"—move on to the next scenario, touch the arrow at the top of your vision. To exit the scenario completely, touch the exit circle at the bottom of your vision. Now please enjoy your Happy Endings."

WHERE ARE YOU REALLY FROM

Lazy, soft-bellied waves. Salted air carried on a cool breeze.

He opens his eyes. He's lying on his back in a straw cabana, dressed in white linen. He sits up and looks around. The beach before him is deserted and pristine. Alabaster sand, water pierced with slats of sunlight, the sky a shockingly blue dome. What most people would call paradise. He feels thirsty and a moment later, a tropical cocktail sweats in his right hand. He takes a sip, unable to resist. Fuck, it's good.

I'm hungry, he thinks, testing the parameters of the world. A half second later, a delectable spread materializes on a long table inside the cabana. A roasted pig choking on an apple forms the centerpiece. The smell is unbelievable, but he's not ready to dig in just yet. He stands up and stretches, finishes the cocktail off, pops the pineapple on the lip of the glass into his mouth. He's never tasted anything as sweet.

Okay, this isn't so bad.

He steps out of the cabana and places both feet in the sand, regulated to an ideal temperature. At the shore, an array of digitally enhanced exotic fish flicker past. The ocean looks coolly inviting and he finds himself wishing for a swimsuit, when, as predicted, he's instantly outfitted in loose swim trunks. He wades into the silky water and angles his head towards the sun: not too hot, not too bright. He's never experienced VR this real, with an unmatched level of sensory detail and visual perfection.

All right, Xavier, I can see why you didn't want to leave. But a man can get a little bored in paradise if he's all by himself.

Just then, he hears soft laughter drifting from the cliff that juts out into the ocean. He swims over in a hurry, anticipating what he'll find there. Inside a darkened grotto, glowing with pearls of light, three naked young women splash each other with water. Wavy, silken hair drapes across their breasts. They look modeled after Polynesian women. A little darker skinned than what he usually goes for, but he can't complain.

He wants them to start kissing each other. Not even a second later, they comply. The tallest fondles another girl's breasts before taking them into her mouth. The third girl joins in before they stop and look over at him, shyly beckoning him with their hands. He wades closer, practically salivating. When he's within arm's reach of the women, a notification flashes before his eyes.

Engage? Y / N.

He stabs impatiently at the pulsing Y button hovering in the air.

A new notification pops up in red: Function has been disabled.

The man frowns and swipes away the pop-up, exploding it into multicolored pixels. He lunges at the women, still kissing each other in turns, but his hands move through them as easily as moving through air. Their coding is so flawless, their images don't glimmer or freeze for even a second. When they continue to caress one another, as if he's mere background noise, anger throbs through him.

He swivels around the grotto, eyes groping for a switch, an intercom, an emergency lever. But his only exit is via a barely visible circle at the bottom of the screen and a right-pointing arrow, equally inconspicuous, at the top of the screen.

He takes one last look around paradise.

He almost loses his grip and cracks his head open on the reddish-brown dirt, though if that were the case, he'd simply remanifest in the situation he finds himself in: on the back of a wild mare, moving at incredible speed. Having gone extinct several decades ago, horses exist only in his imagination. He's never ridden one before, but his virtual self knows how to rhythmically move with the horse's spring-loaded muscles.

He blinks and swivels his head around. A desert landscape, prickly cacti and tumbleweeds flying past. The air is dusty hot, though conveniently none of it enters his eyes or nose. He looks down: leather chaps, cowboy boots. Ahead of him, the sunset, a burning ball of gold.

He gets it now. Happy endings? Riding off into the sunset? Ha ha. Very clever.

A loud whoop arises from behind him. He turns around to see another horse, another man astride it. He's naked from the waist up and wears a headband with a white feather tucked in its side. Red paint is slashed on both his cheeks. What's he supposed to do with this guy? Fuck him? He notices then that the object bouncing behind the guy isn't a pile of fur, but a woman clad in deerskin.

Kill him and save the girl. That's how the story goes, right?

He's a little tired and wishes he were back on the beach, licking roasted pork juice off his fingers, but no back arrow is available.

"Guess I'll kill him and fuck the girl," he says aloud.

A lasso appears in his palm. He shrugs, tosses it behind himself, then whips it forward. The rope encircles his feathered rival in one single, immaculate gesture. He's yanked off the horse and thuds violently against the ground, once, twice, his eyes crimped in pain. The man lets the lasso snake loose from his hand and doesn't look back.

Up ahead, the horse carrying the girl canters to a stop. He

swings off his own horse and saunters, tries to saunter anyway, over to the girl. She looks up at him, grateful tears shining in her sepia eyes, and offers him her hand.

"Thank you for saving me," she whispers. "I am in your debt."

He ignores this; he isn't here to make conversation. He wants to see her splayed naked on her back against the horse, her hair tangled in its sleek mane. She obeys, wordlessly. She unravels her two braids, abundant hair framing her silhouette, and unties her scanty dress. After another mental command, she spreads her legs. He approaches her slowly this time, reaching out his hand towards the smooth concave of her thighs, when the same notification pops up.

Engage? Y / N.

He closes his eyes and prays the system won't fail him again.

Y.

Function has been disabled.

"Fuck!"

He slams his hands into the back of his head, doesn't feel a thing. When his breathing has mellowed, he turns to contemplate the girl. She looks up at him, eyes still misty with gratitude (her default setting?), her hands limp by her sides.

Play with yourself, he thinks.

She complies.

The man unbuckles his belt. A happy ending given to yourself isn't so happy, though it's better than nothing. He grins, the promise of instant satisfaction before him, but when his hand reaches down: nothing. He unbuttons his jeans to examine himself for the first time. His eyes are met with a cruel blank. He pats at the flat space, incredulous. He feels desire boiling inside him, so where the hell is it coming from?

"God fucking damn it!" He pitches his cowboy hat to the ground, sending up a whirl of dust.

The girl looks up at him, her face placid and good-natured even as her fingers energetically thrust in and out of herself. They need to run tests on that algorithm; the effect is unsettling. He sighs and looks around for the arrow, suspended above the setting sun.

He keeps his eyelids drawn for several moments, almost dreading opening them, wondering if he'll find himself mid-motion again. Whose genius idea was it to engineer that scenario? But the sensation of plushness swaddling him is too tempting to resist. He opens his eyes.

He's lying in a grand four-poster bed, gloomy with drapery. The room appears medieval, with an armored suit standing at attention in the corner and a faded tapestry of a battle warming a stone wall. Beside a trifecta of stained-glass windows, a fire sputters to life inside a blackened hearth.

I could just sleep, he thinks. I never get enough sleep in real life. And these blankets are so damn soft, I could sink into their cottony embrace forever.

Just as he slips into the elusive space between sleep and consciousness, a hard rap on the door intercepts him.

"Your Highness?" a thin voice calls.

His curiosity rouses him. "You may enter," he plays along. He sits up in the downy bed with some difficulty.

A young girl in a simple dress pushes open the heavy door. A chambermaid? he guesses. Fourteen or fifteen, blond, blue-eyed, rosy-cheeked. Not his type.

"Your Highness, I've been sent to get you ready for the ball." She addresses the floor instead of him.

"Ball?"

"Yes, your Highness, the ball where you will choose a princess."

He smiles in spite of himself. "What do you mean by 'get ready'?"

"I must bathe and dress you," she murmurs, blushing rose from her ears to her chest.

He imagines if he were to reach for her, another pop-up notification would ask if he'd like to engage, followed by another denial.

"All right, let's get it over with."

But when he swings his legs down, a different pop-up obscures his vision: Fast-forward? Y / N.

He doesn't have much interest in being washed and dressed, so he selects Y.

He makes another mental note to tell the higher-ups not to make the crown so heavy. He wouldn't be surprised if it were cast in solid gold. He could take it off but . . . it's a crown. And he's a king. Or a prince. Regardless, he's got an image to uphold.

The rest of him looks royal enough. He wears an ermine-trimmed sapphire cape, black tights, a frilly shirt with a snarl of strings, buckskin boots. A set of rings on both his gloved hands fractures the light. He could get used to this, being waited on day in and day out. The very notion feels earned, as if he's waited his whole life for everyone around him to recognize what he's always known.

Bring me wine, he thinks, and a different maiden materializes with a thick crystal goblet sloshing with liquid. He takes a long drink. The wine is surprisingly good—for VR.

A horn blares from a corner. A squat man, clad in clownish pants and a poufy hat, unfurls a scroll of parchment paper. "And now, Our Highness will choose his princess, his one true love he shall live happily ever after with."

The man snorts. Is she going to arrive in a pumpkin carriage?

Beyond him, in the main stretch of palace—a cavernous, marble expanse severed by a river of crimson carpet—awaits a sea of women. They're stitched into jewel-toned dresses, with burdensome skirts and stiff corsets, their breasts coerced almost to their chins. Their hair is twirled and pinned into complicated designs. The women, he notes, not without some disappointment, are all European.

The one standing at the front, a redhead in an emerald-green dress, curtsies before him. She rises slowly, allowing him a magnanimous view of her cleavage, and licks her plump lips. He feels himself grow warm.

Strip, he thinks.

She obeys.

He feels himself grow warmer still.

Come here.

She walks towards him.

An image arrests him: her sucking him off on his throne while hundreds of people watch. Not a bad view.

Okay, I'll play your game one more fucking time. He beckons her forward with his index finger.

Engage? Y / N.

Y.

Function has been disabled.

The man cries out and hurls himself at the woman, passing

through her swiftly. He looks back in a rage. She's rooted to the same spot, naked, staring neutrally at his throne.

He tears off his clothes, his doublet or frock or whatever it is, his gloves and pants and boots until he's stark naked save for the crooked crown atop his head. He looks down at himself: still neutered, as if his eyes are surgical instruments. He feels mad with desire, mad with anger, unsure anymore if the two aren't the same. He charges down the steps towards the sea of women as they applaud him. Idiots.

He swivels around, taking in all the obliging bodies. At his fingertips and yet unavailable. Definitely not paradise. More like hell.

"Start fucking each other," he shouts. His eyes are wild, as if daring the system to execute the command with this many bodies.

For a moment, everyone's image glitches, their bodies fuzzy with neon. Then, all at once, the women are unspooling their hair, unlacing their bodices, unpeeling their stockings. He spies a few of them disappearing underneath skirts. One by one, they sink naked to the ground, writhing, hands grasping at fur rugs. Most are paired off, but some are getting creative with groups of three, four, six. A chorus of moans echoes through the sepulchral hall.

A few of the men, guards and squires, abandon their posts to join the orgy. As a knight in full chain mail clanks by, shedding his heavy garments one by one, the man recovers his discarded sword. The hilt is encrusted with rubies, the blade is a burnished silver. He tests its weight, whistles it through the air. The sword is the realest object he's felt in this game so far.

He drags his new toy against the floor as he surveys the excess of pleasure around him. His eyes fall on the grand banquet table in the center of the hall, overflowing with decadent confections, bouquets and candelabras.

"Incorporate the feast into the fucking," he sneers. His mind is ravenous. He wouldn't be surprised if foam had collected at the corners of his mouth.

A moment later, he doubles over laughing as women are pummeled by eggplants, as men are doused in gravy and licked clean. A maiden balances a bunch of grapes over another's parted legs. The knight is earnestly fucking the roast duck. At the top of the stairs, a joker sporting the head of a beady-eyed goat masturbates into the mouths of three half-naked women on their knees.

He feels desire welling up in him so much he might go blind with it. He wants to fuck. He wants to fuck anything. He knows, with shameful desperation, that if he could choose to live or to fuck one last time before getting killed off, he'd choose the latter. He wouldn't even hesitate.

He pauses to observe a coupling on top of the banquet table. A servant thrusts into a woman from behind as her hands knead the thick tablecloth. Her breasts plunge into a tower of whipped cream pastries. They're both in states of undress, her skirt hitched up and her corset unfastened, his belt and pants pooled around his ankles. The woman is pale, with raven-black hair and a haughty nose. She's stunning.

He places his hand beneath the woman's head, cradles it, wills her to look at him. She smiles at him, and then, like a curse, she's laughing at him. A pitying, too-human laugh. Remembering his nudity, he looks down at the shameful blank between his legs. He feels like Adam must have felt in the garden. The woman's bright black eyes fix on him. Mirth dances across her exquisite features. Something about her is familiar.

With both hands, he lifts up his heavy sword and slices it cleanly through her neck. Her head bounces twice on the table. Her eyes flash at him midair, indignant, before her head hits the cold marble floor and rolls away. The servant continues to thrust into the woman's headless body, blood bubbling from her lovely neck.

The man smirks and walks off, dragging his sword against the thick carpet, against the knot of limbs on the floor, leaving rivulets of macabre red. He mounts the stairs and collapses on his throne. Below him, the scene is carnivalesque, disgustingly gorgeous. An obscene fall from grace.

Exhaustion hits him. He should retire upstairs, sleep for a few days or weeks. When he wakes up, order a dragon to fly him around the kingdom. Maybe toss a few peasants into the dungeon for the hell of it.

He pushes himself up, wraps a bearskin cloak around his shoulders and exits down a dim hallway. Candlestick sconces cast a hazy glow against the walls. The spiral staircase to his private quarters is damp and chilly, though his steps are dry against the smooth gray stone. Halfway up, he hears someone else's steps behind him. No doubt another virgin maiden eager to wash and dress him for bed.

"Not now—" he sighs, turning around before stopping so abruptly, he falls over onto his back.

The woman he decapitated looms over him. He recognizes her royal purple dress. She's moving, alive, though she's still headless. Above her breasts is a stump clotted with blood. In her hand is a carving knife, glinting in the watery candlelight. The man twitches in disbelief and scrambles upright, then bounds up the stairs, panting, his heart quaking in his chest. *I just have to make it to the bedroom*, he thinks, forgetting an exit floats below him.

The headless woman's steps draw closer and closer, the icicle point of her knife grazes the nape of his neck, penetrating the defenseless barrier of his skin, and then—darkness.

He wakes up gasping, convinced he's on the verge of death. A whole minute passes before he calms down enough to realize the simulation is over. His VR headset has been removed. He's supine on the massage table, a body-length glass case with three metal bands snapped over it. He tries to move his arms and legs but he's still paralyzed, though the sensation has transformed from that of cement in his veins to a liquification of his bones. He finds he can shout, though.

"Eden!" he cries before descending into a whimper. "Eden."

He thinks, unbidden, of his mother. Her perpetual state of existence isn't so different from the current one he finds himself in: immobilized in a hospital bed, jabbed with tubes, isolated from the rest of the world. He wonders, for the first time, if keeping her alive is a punishment.

He jerks upwards, wrestling against his restraints, when he spots Eden behind a translucent wall lit up with live video feeds. She walks back and forth, looking between her tablet and the wall. After what feels like an excruciating eternity, the live video feeds cut out. Eden's figure crests across his vision. She wears the same stark white dress he watched her unbutton earlier.

"Well, aren't you creative?" she says. "You're the first person to behead someone."

"Let me out."

"We've had food orgies before, but never on such a large scale. Bravo!" She claps half-heartedly.

"Let me out, you cunt."

"No, I don't think I will."

She smiles down at him. "I recognized you from the moment you walked in. Do you recognize me?"

His gaze glides over her like a scanner, emotionless. *Does he recognize her*—give him a break. He's seen hundreds of girls like her in his lifetime. How is he supposed to remember what each and every one of them looks like? This—the anonymous impunity of paid sex—only works if he sees them not as individuals but as objects. He looks away, surprised at the unfiltered valence of his own thoughts.

She comes closer, puts her face right up to the glass. "Still nothing?"

With one hand, she starts to tug at her hairline. She looks like she's scratching her skin off and he involuntarily jerks away from her—the sight makes him unbearably itchy. Then he realizes that's exactly what she's doing. A flap of her forehead has been peeled off, exposing viscous, clear slime underneath. She's removing her TrueSkin.

He's seen the 3D commercials. He knows you're not supposed to do it yourself. You're supposed to return to the same sterilized facility, let them snip you out of it. For a monthly payment plan, you can even maintain the TrueSkin in a temperature-controlled shaft.

He waits for her to finish sloughing her face off, but he sighs, certain he'll never recognize her, TrueSkin or not. There were so many whores, with so many invented names, and so little time. When he lived in Hong Kong, he never saw the same woman or bot twice, never needed to.

Eden lets her TrueSkin hang at her throat, then pats her face dry with a towel. "How about now?" she asks, hovering over him.

The disbelief he feels is so absolute, it doesn't register at first. No. Impossible.

"You look surprised."

He opens his mouth. Shuts it. But it is possible. She's here, in this room. The only woman who awed him. Her face as remarkable as he remembered: indifferently beautiful. Though one side of her face looks off-kilter, like it's been frozen.

Eden laughs, short barks followed by gleeful gasps. As if she's laughing so hard, she's sobbing.

"You thought I was dead," she chokes out, wiping her eyes. Then she straightens up as her voice turns somber. "Well, of course you did. You killed me."

The man tries to shake his head, but only his eyes move, darting from left to right like hunted prey. How—he'd been so sure—

Eden laughs again, tenderly, as if reminiscing about a happy memory. Though she knew he'd come—eventually—she cannot believe the moment has fallen into her lap. Years of waiting and now, here he is. Impotent and paralyzed in her custom Happy Endings VR chamber, everything he sees or does controlled in her little tablet.

Some might call her actions a form of revenge, but Eden prefers the word consequence. "Revenge" is amateurish, melodramatic in its very conception, whereas her actions are no different from cleaning up a spill, ironing out a wrinkle, righting a book that's tipped over.

Apart from the handiwork of gravity around his jaws and eyes, he looks the same: unnervingly pale eyes, with near invisible eyelashes and brows. Not wearing a TrueSkin, she surmises, but no doubt subsisting on a healthy dose of LifeEssense each day. She circles the chamber, the tablet safe in her hands.

"No one can hear if you scream," she says offhandedly, like she's discussing the weather. She relishes the flare of fear in his eyes, sweet as chocolate on her tongue. "And don't bother calling for Anastasia. I've turned her off for now." She pauses and frowns at the flap of skin dangling at her throat. "I didn't get a TrueSkin because I wanted to look young or because I didn't like my body." She cocks her head at him. "I got one so you'd never be able to find me again. And because the left side of my face became paralyzed." She sighs. "That sometimes happens with asphyxiation."

Seventeen years ago, in a brothel on the edge of Victoria City, he had straddled her, his veined hands flexed around her neck, playing what seemed like a little boy's game. A little boy who wanted to play god. She had let him, was even amused by it. She thought her profession was funny in that way. Sex was a constant negotiation, a high-wire act with the thinnest of lines separating pleasure from violence. You could cross from one to the next, and vice versa, within seconds. Every time she had sex, she made herself vulnerable to either extreme.

Prior to that, he had fucked her in every conceivable orifice until blood stained the mattress. She had been distracted by the strangely beautiful pattern, like a camellia. Each time he had finished with his filthy act, he would gauge her reaction, his gaze a provocation. She knew he expected, no, *wanted*, to see her cry and wail and beg. Each time she refused him this, he improvised some new unspeakable act. She wondered if he was secretly filming her to sell the video online or if he was planning to slip something into her bottle of water, all the better to haul her off into an unmarked van. Or if he'd make her shove scissors inside of herself or play with his excrement under threat of hurting her if she failed to comply. The other girls told her it wasn't unheard of from these rich foreigners, these insatiable gweilos with their unimaginative god complexes. Some of them asked for girls who were mute, unable to communicate a safe word, or for girls as young as eight. But the most recent fad was paying local straight couples an eye-watering amount to let the man fuck the girlfriend to near death as the boyfriend helplessly watched, the very definition of cuckolding, live and up close. The gweilos were always trying to prove something. But what? And to whom?

She wasn't stupid—she read the reviews they left on brothel websites, the comments they wrote in online forums, leaving instructions for other foreigners on who to contact, what command to give an AutoCab, what phrases to whisper to the girls and in what language, the rate of STDs, the extent of what you could get away with in Hong Kong, how involved the police were if anything went awry. Some of the forum posts possessed all the intricacies of a professional travel website, including detailed maps, directions, photos and translations for men who couldn't bother to learn the language, but instead of a family vacation, the website was built for sex tourism. These men had dreamt up a separate lexicon for women like her, an imagined mythology that rendered them alien. The mythology sent hundreds of sexpats flocking to her home country each year, hoping for a revelatory sexual experience, as though her body were any different from the bodies of the women in his country. No, those women were cherished enough to earn the title of girlfriend and wife, sister and mother, daughter. She was a stopover on the way to nuclear happiness.

Afterwards, these men folded back into their everyday lives

without notice or fuss. Men who were doctors and teachers and politicians, but worse, kind when they wanted to be. Loving when they chose to be. Doting fathers and beloved husbands and respected friends and colleagues. How they behaved on "vacation" didn't negate these facts, something Eden found more terrifying than the men's warped desires.

This man wasn't unique, he was like the hundreds of others she had encountered. When she thought he had finally worn himself out, he told her he was going to fuck her while he choked her. The pleasure would be immense, he assured her, then she could choke him. Fair and square.

She didn't care either way. He clamped his heavy hands around her neck and got off on it for a few minutes, moaning erratically. Then he registered her smile: contemptuous with a hint of pity. His grip slackened and she laughed. His hands tightened and tightened until her body thrashed of its own accord, until her eyes rolled to the back of her head and her heartbeat shook. The last thing she remembered was the look in his eyes: Something inhuman. Something animal.

Later, the madam told her he'd left in a conspicuous hurry, jumping into the first available AutoCab. The madam hastened into the room and screamed at the sight of her lifeless body. She had to decide whether to save the girl or pursue the man. In the end, it was an easy decision—she was the most highly requested girl at the brothel, after all.

At the hospital, the doctors declared it a miracle she had survived, even with all the life-defying tech they'd amassed by then. She was hospitalized for over a week. During that time, the nurses and doctors were all a little afraid of her: she had been legally dead for eight minutes and forty-nine seconds.

She had crossed over to a valley forbidden to the living and—how could she not have?—emerged brand new. Unyielding in places she'd been forgiving. Opaque in places she'd been transparent as glass. The few family members she had left, an older brother and an aunt, she scrubbed from her mind like erasing a hard drive. Her childhood—drowsy, sun-drenched days skirting narrow alleys, stealing candied sticks of fruit when the vendor's back was turned, holding her brother's hand as they leapt over a water hose—she sealed away so tightly, she could never access those memories, or that self, again.

She collected the money she was owed from the madam, bought a TrueSkin and went into the far more lucrative private escort industry, where she christened herself "Eden." A name that signified a pleasure so sublime, it existed only at the beginning and the end of the known world.

After working as an escort for three years, she siphoned her savings into a brothel of her own. A virtual one catering to gweilos, with an unoriginal name they'd instantly recognize. Some of her fellow sex workers balked at the idea. Why feed them a fantasy of their own invention? But, with no exit to the game, she had decided to play the game herself. A survival tactic. In some ways, performance art.

She simply refused to waste her miraculous existence (how many centuries of women had fucked and shirked death to birth her, only for her to die and rebirth herself?) condemning the condemned. Instead, she would adjust her settings and update her software. She would evolve. If she was going to get fucked, she at least wanted to consent to it.

The day the brothel opened, Eden ran through every simulation herself, combing through the programming for flaws. Afterwards, she lay in the VR chamber paralyzed not from the shot, but from heart-palpitating anticipation. The man who'd strangled her, should he come to the massage parlor, was not the first man to hurt her. That was a man in the neighborhood where she'd grown up, who strolled through the streets pushing a metal cart of frozen fruit pops in the summer. He wore his hair in an oily ponytail and walked with his left foot dragging behind him. When she was ten, he had given her a gift—her favorite mango-flavor, free of charge—and then, in the abandoned textile factory, he had sought payment for his kindness.

Eden hadn't thought of the man in many years but she allowed herself to think of him now, just this once. She pictured watching him enter the parlor on the security cameras. Preparing the shot, flicking the needle clean as he vibrated with excitement. Snapping the chamber over his naked body and clicking the locks into place. Before she knew what was happening, she was crying. She had not known it was possible to cry from joy.

No, the man who strangled her was not the first man to hurt her. But he would be the last.

Anastasia is where Eden left her, in the stockroom. Beautiful, simple Anastasia. Eden designed her to have enough force to knock down someone ten times her size—useful for the times a client became uncontrollable before the paralysis shot. But she also designed her to be desirable; she wasn't immune to beauty.

Eden punches a series of commands into her tablet and Anastasia wakes up, sees her and smiles.

"Prepare the shot," Eden says.

Anastasia starts to stand up, when Eden touches her hand.

Anastasia turns towards her, perpetually open and eager to please by nature. They used to spend nights together until Eden realized she was simply reacting to an old biological reflex. Over the years, her interest in sex had whittled away, little by little after every encounter with a client, until her libido seemed an idea rather than a fact. She couldn't switch off the instinctual need for intimacy, and though she'd sworn off humans after her brief flirtation with death, she might have continued seeking it through Anastasia or other bots. Instead, she took on work as her lover. She watched her hired programmers with such intensity that she learned their language quicker than they could teach it, then mastered it completely. Coding was when she felt most godly, at the computer's helm, diving into its slipstream, rearranging reality, her fingers moving across the keyboard as nimble as a musician's gliding across a piano's ivory limbs.

When she wasn't working, she passed the time (or: on a cynical day, waited to die) in a VR chamber—her own private one located beyond a curtain in her bedroom. She coded spaces for her exclusive use: a garden patio, a café at night, a field of endless sky and grass, a single chair for her to rest on.

She told herself, initially, that she was just running tests. Product analysis. But she simply found this faux reality preferable to hers. Metal and silicone-hydrogel weren't at the mercy of memory but she was only human, after all. She wanted to take a scalpel to her ability to bruise. This—the ability to power down—was the only aspect of Anastasia's existence that she envied.

Anastasia couldn't grasp why Eden wasted so many hours inside the VR chamber. She also couldn't fully grasp her job. After their hundredth client, she asked in her perfectly pitched voice, "Are we exploiting the intrinsic loneliness of the human condition?" and

Eden could only marvel at her, at the endless surprises that lay coiled inside her coding. She had kissed her rather than answer her.

Anastasia is still looking up at her, waiting. "Yes, Eden?"

She drops her hand. "It's nothing. Thank you, Anastasia."

When Eden opens the chamber, the scent of ammonia wafts into the air. Of course he pissed himself. Still a little boy.

With a single dexterous movement, she shoots another paralysis dose into his arm. Just before she repositions his VR headset, Eden takes one last look at him.

"We've only just reunited after all these years, but I'm afraid we're going to have to say goodbye now."

"No," he whispers. "Please, you don't understand, you've made a mistake—" Darkness swaddles him. "Help!" he screams, but in response, the chamber lid locks into place.

"Enjoy," Eden purrs through the glass.

"You've made a mistake," he whispers again. He wouldn't leave a woman to die. He wouldn't.

Tears dribble silently from the corners of his eyes. He wants his mother. For several moments, he has only darkness to keep him company. Panic bites at him. Though the chamber is dead silent, his ears ring. His heartbeat is so loud, he thinks it might combust. He coughs once, twice, his phantom ailment reawakening.

When he opens his eyes, he's standing in a brightly lit hallway. The walls are painted baby pink and the floors are checkered black-and-white. Down here, the air smells like the aftertaste of something sweet, something artificial. He follows the hallway down, where it turns left and feeds straight into the parlor entrance: two automated frosted glass doors like those of a dentist's office. The interior could pass as a dentist's office, too: modern and clean with BreathOble Plants pulsing in the corners. The receptionist's desk is a half circle rimmed in aquamarine light. Music, a subdued instrumental, plays demurely from hidden speakers.

A silver plaque on the wall announces WELCOME TO HAPPY ENDINGS.

THE DOLLHOUSE

My daughter's dollhouse is perfect. The eternally green grass in the front yard is protected by a white picket fence. Pink plastic bricks prop up an iridescent roof with scalloped shingles like the scales of a mermaid tail. On the first floor is the dining room, the living room and the kitchen. On the middle floors are four bedrooms and a bathroom inlaid in mint-green tiles, complete with a claw-foot tub. The top floor is the nursery attic, where miniature cribs lined in ribbon and lace sit in an obedient row. If you go around the back, you'll find an amoeba-shaped pool and some striped chaise longues. See? Perfect.

Jenny has christened all her dolls with stripper names: Candy, Violet, Destiny, Misty. She doesn't realize these are stripper names, of course. To her, they are "cute." Her only male doll is named Dreamboat Joe, which works out well because there is only one male doll in my story.

Candy, Violet, Destiny and Misty all lived together in the dollhouse, in a place called Dreamland. I lived there, too. The dollhouse wasn't a home but for many years, it was the only home I knew. It was a place of waiting and expectation. A place constructed not just of plastic but of secrets, both the consequential kind and the inconsequential kind.

Jenny is at an age where she still likes to hear the same stories over and over. Her favorite story is the one about the dollhouse. Each time I tell it, we both pretend she's never heard it before. I didn't really live in a dollhouse with dolls, but I like to tell the story in a way she can understand. Whenever the story veers too adult in parts, I alter the details or skip over them. Even without a child as my audience, I prefer to tell it this way. Sometimes the truth gets in the way of a good story.

All my best stories are about other people. My daughter isn't interested in stories about me and I don't blame her. I've never thought I was very interesting. In fact, I'm really quite forgettable. I'm not saying this as a display of faux modesty; it's true. If you came into my work and I cleared your table, you probably forgot me the moment after you exited the restaurant. If I committed a crime on the street that you happened to witness, I doubt you could pick me out of a lineup. I would never commit a crime, though—I'm not daring enough. My life is small and contained, but it's a good life. I live with my husband, our two-year-old son, Matthew, and Jenny. Everyone says she is my spitting image: we share the same crooked incisor and the same graceless laugh. We have the same tendency to offer our generosity whether or not it's deserved.

THE DOLLHOUSE

Each time I tell Jenny the dollhouse story, we lie on the carpeted floor next to her actual dollhouse, her most prized possession, beneath the living room bay window. As I narrate, I hold up her dolls to act out the scenes. These busty and leggy dolls—with their polyester hair and inflexible limbs—stand in for the dolls I knew, who couldn't look more different. Their static smiles sometimes jar with the situations they find themselves in, but Jenny doesn't seem to mind. I move the dolls and their endless accessories into different configurations, different rooms, as Jenny watches entranced.

Wrapped in the gauze of afternoon light, insulated from the rest of the world, is my favorite way to spend time with my daughter. At nine years old, she is testing out the waters of independence and unsure if she likes it—shyly closing the door to her bedroom when a friend calls, but insisting I stay in the dressing room with her. I am all too aware that as she ages, her need for me will turn delicately inward and near invisible, while any outward signs of my need for her will grow hulking and hairy, embarrassment embodied. Already I see signs of it.

So even when I'm in an irritable mood and want nothing more than to lie still in the dark, even when I'm exhausted from working a double shift the previous night, when Jenny asks me to tell her a story, I never refuse.

Violet and I shared a bedroom in the dollhouse. Jenny dresses our dolls in black-and-white maid costumes, complete with aprons, stockings and Mary Jane shoes. Violet even gets a feather duster.

Before a doll arrived at the dollhouse, we would clean her room and the communal bathrooms. The rooms would be prepped with a robe, slippers and towels. Cotton rounds, extra-heavy pads and stretchmark cream were discreetly stowed inside each dresser. After Dreamboat Joe picked up the doll from the airport, I would show her to her room and point out all of the accommodations. Each bedroom was outfitted with its own TV, a kettle and a mini-fridge stocked with snacks and bottled water. The dolls stayed for a month to three months, depending on how much they'd paid.

The dolls asked us to bring them whatever they wanted, whenever they wanted. We cleaned up after them, we fed them, we sometimes bathed them. I never complained; after all, our only purpose was to attend to their every need. Violet, on the other hand, loved to complain with childish glee about the dolls, who had all arrived with a secret and would depart with the same secret camouflaged in a different form. I disliked this habit of hers. Complaining would suggest I had desires that weren't being met and I didn't want to desire anything. That might sound odd, but it made me perfect for my job.

On nights I couldn't sleep, I'd get up and walk aimlessly around the dollhouse. I'd hear snoring, the quiet murmur of a TV, some crying or whimpering, but for precious pockets of time, I'd come across only pristine silence. Compared to all the other times of the day—when the dollhouse hummed with relentless noise—the dollhouse in the dead of night felt like it had entered another realm altogether. Objects looked purple-tinted and impermeable, as if they might dissipate when touched. I liked to sit by the pool—I didn't know how to swim—and take comfort in its constant blue flatness. Sometimes when I stared up at the sleeping dollhouse, no one wanting anything from me, I'd feel a strange panic. At heart, I have always needed to be needed.

THE DOLLHOUSE

"Like a sleepover!" Jenny folds her arms, pouting. "Not fair."

I don't let Jenny attend or host sleepovers just yet. She doesn't know what people are capable of.

"Not really," I say.

"So you *weren't* friends?"

"No, we were—in a way." The only doll who resisted our friendship was Fantasy.

"Why?" Jenny asks.

"We didn't know enough about her," I explain, then ask if she wants me to describe the dolls, knowing she will say yes.

Misty loved to eat fruit but only when Violet and I had painstakingly peeled their skins, even from grapes. She was a gossip obsessed with everyone's problems except her own, but so cheerful in disposition that her flaws were easily forgiven. Another agreeable doll was Destiny, who did nothing but stare slack-jawed at the TV all day. She sped through pirated soap opera videotapes faster than we could buy them. She tried to insist we watch them with her because she wanted to agonize over the plot with someone. Other dolls made our jobs harder than they already were. Candy demanded we clip her fingernails and toenails before buffing her calluses, as if we were running a twenty-four-hour spa. After the first time Violet had been subjected to this task, she cornered me in the kitchen and said, "Rock, paper, scissors."

"Why?"

"If I tell you, you won't play."

"Then I won't play."

"You aren't any fun," she teased me.

Dreamboat Joe had employed us when were eighteen and

nineteen years old, newly arrived in Dreamland. Four years had passed since then. Though Violet and I were only a year apart in age, she acted as if I was much older because I was careful to never break Dreamboat Joe's rules. When some dolls begged for cigarettes or a sip of alcohol, Violet would relent. She smoked herself and had even completed high school. Though she was more educated than me, I found her careless and wasteful. She threw away half-eaten food and snacked in bed, even when she wasn't ill. She told inappropriate jokes to the dolls and dressed inappropriately, too, in scoop-necked tops and skirts a size too small. She told me I could borrow her clothes and makeup, but I made it a point to dress conservatively. Because Violet was my only constant in the dollhouse, I felt sisterly towards her and hoped I could serve as a good model of behavior.

"Was Candy the worst doll?" Jenny asks.

I shake my head. We nicknamed one doll Spoiled Doll because she demanded we massage her back, arms and legs twice, sometimes three times a day. She openly flirted with Dreamboat Joe in spite of his wedding band. Another doll was nicknamed Anger Issues Doll. If she could not have exactly what she wanted—if, for example, we ran out of strawberry jam and only had raspberry—she'd throw a spectacular tantrum, hurling insults and nearby objects at us. My left collarbone still bears a pink-white scar, the mark of a flying spatula.

Sometimes I think the dolls were displacing their frustration onto on us, resentful of the price they'd paid—$9,000 to $27,000—to travel alone to Dreamland, where they could not go anywhere by themselves, where they commanded little authority over the language, where they had to rely on strangers to translate for them. If they wanted something and we could not procure it, they had to believe we weren't lying out of laziness or apathy. If they had to visit the doll doctor, Dreamboat Joe was responsible for conveying the precise measurements of their tenderness, pain and nausea. If we told them to stop worrying, they had no other choice but to square their worry away. I wonder, still, if they trusted us. I like to think they did.

Though Violet and I called dolls by their nicknames, we knew all their first and last names. How could we not? We knew their favorite foods and drinks, the smells and textures they abhorred, the rhythms of their bodies and the patterns of their sleep. We knew what crushing expectations awaited them at home. We knew if they were excited or terrified or so exhausted that they could not feel anything but exhaustion. We knew who had never experienced anything so painful and who had lived through worse.

"Tell me the dolls' secret," Jenny says, right on cue, her chin cupped in her hands.

The dolls all arrived with a well-concealed belly and departed with a baby doll in possession of Dreamland citizenship. A baby doll who could return to Dreamland legally, who could enroll in Dreamland universities without paying the hefty international fees, who could obtain Dreamland jobs without a company sponsoring their visa. A baby doll who could one day sponsor their parents' visas.

Giving birth in Dreamland was not illegal, Dreamboat Joe liked to repeat, running a hand through his slicked-back hair. He wore gray-tinted sunglasses, even indoors, and his forehead was pearled with sweat no matter the time of year. Dreamboat Joe ran the foreign website that explained the legality of his business, how to hide a prominent belly and how to correctly answer a Dreamland customs officer. The website logo featured a doll gripping the handle of a suitcase on the left side of a Dreamland map, and as she exits on the right side, cradling a baby doll in lieu of the suitcase. But sometimes the dolls didn't care about passport applications, sponsorships or birthright citizenship. Sometimes they simply coveted a second baby doll, which wasn't allowed in the land they'd traveled from.

I once asked Dreamboat Joe if his business was legal, why he insisted on "playing a game" where we rounded up the dolls and hurried them into the plastic pink van and the sky blue sedan. Why had he made Violet and me go through the trouble of obtaining our driver's licenses in Dreamland?

"Don't worry about things until I tell you to worry about them," he said dismissively, as if he were speaking to one of the dolls. After he left, Violet complained he was acting like her father. I told her this was Dreamboat Joe's way of caring for us.

Two phases separated life in the dollhouse. Violet named them the Before Period and the After Period. To pass the time while we worked, we played out hypothetical situations in both periods, trying to gauge when we were more miserable.

Sometimes the Before Period was better because a doll might still have energy to swim in the pool, walk around the neighborhood or enjoy excursions to the mall to stock up on baby doll clothes. Sometimes the Before Period was worse because of all the ways the dolls' bodies revolted against them: the unending moodiness, heartburn, constipation, insomnia, hemorrhoids, strange and vivid dreams. With all the different dolls we met, Violet and I were witness to all the uncommon symptoms, too: nosebleeds, blurry vision, sore teeth, the sudden growth of whiskers in unexpected places. Oh, and the vomiting—that I will never forget.

Sometimes the After Period was better because the doll had paid for a nanny or a wet nurse, selected from a trusted list Dreamboat Joe kept circulating on his payroll. In addition to the dollhouse where I worked, he owned three other dollhouses in the area.

A doll in the After Period could finally indulge in what had previously been off-limits. She might be floating from the hospital drugs, her heavy aches and spasms a thing of the past. She could rest and recover until she had to breastfeed again, or not at all, if she chose formula. She might consider the next few weeks a vacation.

But most of the time, the dolls felt worse during the After Period. They lay in bed and bled through pad after pad. After two ruined mattresses, we convinced Dreamboat Joe to buy waterproof coverings on top of which we placed the bedding. The dolls spoke of feeling splintered and cleaved apart. Of being haphazardly sewn back together, crooked and narrow in places they weren't before. One doll dislocated her pelvic bone. Dolls with C-sections mourned the seven-inch mottled gashes in their stomachs, and nearly all the dolls, their excess folds of skin. When they went to the bathroom, they often cried. Other dolls cried when their breast milk remained stubbornly stopped up, when their baby dolls bit too hard, or not at all. Most dolls refused painkillers, believing it a weakness indulged only in Dreamland.

Candy was one of these dolls, even though her birth had necessitated an emergency surgery after a uterine rupture. One morning, when I was helping her change into adult diapers, she abruptly pushed me away and sank back down on the toilet.

"What if my son never uses his passport? What if he moves to Dreamland only to come back home?" she asked. "All of this will have been for nothing."

I didn't know what to say besides that of course he would, especially after he learned everything she'd sacrificed. I wasn't sure if I meant this. Although I believed parents were obligated to sacrifice for their child, I believed a child didn't owe a debt on his existence.

Candy laughed but her eyes gave away her skepticism. "You have to say that. It's your job."

I wondered if she thought I was trying to trick her. If she thought the entirety of Dreamboat Joe's dollhouse business was one clever scam. After all, the business was predicated on a single, dogged belief: life was superior in Dreamland. Everyone needed to believe the price they'd paid—the price we'd all paid—would be recouped many times over.

Working at the dollhouse, I learned the ways a woman's body is a dollhouse: one with infinite rooms and infinite ways to sabotage her.

I had no firsthand knowledge of the dolls' pain; I wouldn't meet my husband until a few years after I'd left the dollhouse, when I was waitressing. My own pregnancy was uncomfortable but manageable. I had luminous skin, plump as an oyster bed, and my hair turned as lustrous as an oyster shell, though I couldn't stand being touched by my husband. My labor time was under four hours. I was one of the lucky ones.

THE DOLLHOUSE

And then, of course, there were losses. Some dolls miscarried. Other baby dolls emerged blue in the face or lived for a few precious days only to die in a labyrinth of plastic tubes. Violet and I were unprepared for these crises, just like we were unprepared, in many ways, to work at the dollhouse at all. I feared for what awaited those dolls back home, the wrath of husbands and mothers-in-law exponentialized after the money they'd squandered. Some dolls claimed they would be better off never returning home at all.

Even when a birth had no complications, pain didn't always leave a physical trace in its wake. Instead, it surfaced silently in the dolls' faces: wan and vacant, listless and erased. They did not take pleasure in holding their newborn dolls. They did not coo at them or tickle their little feet. One doll kept the curtains drawn in the daytime and stopped showering, but even before she'd given birth, I knew she was different from the other dolls.

Her name was Fantasy. She was thin with equally thin, sickly hair, as if she suffered from a vitamin deficiency. When I first saw Fantasy, I was struck by her proudly protruding chin and eyes that seemed, to me, perpetually mocking.

In the Before Period, she was doggedly withdrawn. Every afternoon, the dolls would gather in the living room for an afternoon tea party to trade gossip, eat cookies and drink tea. The sound of spoons striking porcelain cups, set against a backdrop of cheerful chatter, is indistinguishable from my memories of the dollhouse. Other communal activities included stretching and light exercise, poring over baby books on Dreamland names, even sharing university brochures. Eighteen years later, these dolls' children might become each other's academic competition, but for a brief period, their fervid hopes for their children bonded them together.

Fantasy never participated in these moments of socializing or in any of the outdoor excursions. Violet and I assumed she had paid for the cheapest package since she was only staying for one month, but later, we realized she was simply uninterested. Another peculiarity about Fantasy was her body's dearth of cravings. When we asked what might tempt her, anything at all, she always replied, "Don't bother yourselves." We were accustomed to the dolls' unceasing wants—something was always too warm or cold or tight or loose—but Fantasy apparently had none.

After dinner, she would retire to her room and shut the door. We never heard her turn on the TV; perhaps she read. The few times she had to exit her room for us to clean, we found it tidy and sparse. No books took up space on the night table; perhaps she kept them in her dresser or suitcase, but I didn't dare check. I never looked where I wasn't supposed to. The only activity I suspected Fantasy enjoyed was swimming. When cleaning her room, I noticed a faded swimsuit and a striped pool towel hanging on the back of her chair, and yet I never once saw her swim.

During one of our before-bedtime talks, Violet insisted that Fantasy must be stupid. At dinner, conversation had turned to Dreamland universities and the difficult exams required for entrance. Even harder were the essays, which required perfect fluency in the Dreamland language.

Fantasy, who rarely spoke, had interjected, "That's not true."

"Yes, it is," Misty said in her sunny manner. "My nephew applied just last year."

"No. You must have heard wrong." The quiver in Fantasy's voice came as a surprise to everyone. She was clearly upset she hadn't been aware of the essays, but when asked why, she kept her reasons to herself. The other dolls shared a knowing glance before continuing to eat.

"She's so uneducated," Violet said now, yawning. Sometimes Violet seemed to forget that I, too, was uneducated. Beyond this, I suspected that Violet—with her valentine heart-shaped face and facile charm—felt personally offended that Fantasy didn't hunger after her friendship the way all the other dolls did.

Our conversation was cut short when Dreamboat Joe knocked on our bedroom door. I hadn't heard his convertible pull up to the dollhouse. He looked distracted and kept flipping open and close his gray cell phone with one hand.

"Did you notice a van outside today?" he asked, without saying hello. We shook our heads. "Call me if you do. And tell the other dolls to keep an eye out."

"What's happening?" I asked.

Dreamboat Joe flicked his hand. "It doesn't concern you."

Jenny stuffs Dreamboat Joe back in his butter-yellow convertible, with immovable white wheels that dig lines into the carpet. She pushes it away from the dollhouse as her father enters the living room. When he asks what we're doing, Jenny ignores him and tells me to keep going.

I sometimes sense my husband's sorrow that he cannot find the door to the room only Jenny and I can enter. But, in truth, I don't know how to change this, having never known my own father, and even if I did know how, I honestly don't know if I would.

We look up at her father in silence. He smiles at us before leaving me to continue my story.

WHERE ARE YOU REALLY FROM

After Dreamboat Joe left, I couldn't fall asleep. Around two a.m., I got out of bed and drifted without purpose through the dollhouse. On the second floor, I heard crying followed by fevered attempts at reassurance coming from Destiny's room. I knocked on the door and opened it to see Destiny pacing the room as she rocked her crying baby doll. He had colic but Destiny's package didn't include a nanny. She looked like she'd hopelessly chased after sleep for days.

"Do you want me to try?" I whispered. She nodded, grateful. I took him in my arms and rhythmically patted his back. He quieted a little and I decided to take him for a walk around the backyard in case he started up again. I was about to pull open the sliding glass door when someone else pulled it open from the outside. A scream rose up my throat, but then I saw that it was only Fantasy: wearing her faded swimsuit and long striped towel around her shoulders, her hair stringy with chlorine. So this was when she went swimming, in the middle of the night. I nodded at her and she quickly walked past me towards her room.

The next morning, I knocked on Fantasy's door to strip the sheets and discovered her still in bed. I made my excuses to leave, but Fantasy told me to come in. She was sitting up, the sheets tucked neatly beneath her. I stood hesitantly by the door. Fantasy wore clothes forgotten by a past doll: a long-sleeved hot pink shirt with a yellow smiley face in the center. The happy color looked incongruous against her severe face.

"How long have you been working for Dreamboat Joe," she asked. Her manner of speaking—blunt, uninflected—transformed the question into an accusation. She looked me over with equal bluntness, as if dissecting me open with her gaze.

"Four years."

She nodded. "I saw you comforting Destiny's baby doll last night." She said this with some effort, her eyes fixed on the blank TV screen. I waited, unsure of how to interpret this comment.

"Thank you," I finally said.

"Do you want children."

"Of course. One day."

She nodded again. "You can sit down." I chose the corner of the bed, closest to the door. "I couldn't do your job," Fantasy continued. I finally understood what she wanted: conversation. She'd been here for a week and had hardly spoken to anyone.

"What do you do back home?" I asked.

"I work in a factory." I felt myself involuntarily frowning. Even though Fantasy hadn't known about university essays, her mannerisms belonged to those of a wealthy doll.

"What kind?"

She shrugged. "I don't know. I screw in one plastic casing on top of another. Hundreds every day."

I shook my head. "I couldn't do *your* job."

"So we are both doing exactly what we should be doing," Fantasy said, cocking her head and smiling in an amused, distant way. It was the first time I'd seen her smile. She had very small, childlike teeth.

"Yes," I agreed, searching for another topic of conversation. Fantasy, who had come across as odd and stuck-up, not nearly as lively as the other dolls, now intrigued me. "And your husband? Does he also work in a factory?"

Contempt crossed Fantasy's expressionless face. "Work? The only work he knows is drinking. That's his job. Drinking, drinking, drinking."

I laughed because it was the kind of response expected from me when the other dolls complained of their husbands: lazy, worthless, bossy, selfish, reckless, bad-tempered, lustful, lustless, weak. Before working at the dollhouse, I had not known all the ways a husband could disappoint his wife and even after four years, what I knew was secondhand.

Fantasy's face sealed itself back into the absence of expression. "Is that funny to you?"

"No, of course not." I stood up a little unevenly. I thought we'd entered the territory of confession—that heady, intoxicating space inside a conversation—but we clearly hadn't. Perhaps Fantasy never entered it with anyone. "I'm sorry. I wasn't thinking."

My apology didn't soften Fantasy's impassive countenance. She turned back to stare at the blank TV screen. Only after I left did I realize I'd forgotten to strip the bed.

"She sounds so weird!" Jenny interrupts me.

"She was a little weird, yes. Now, do you want me to tell you about the time Candy's mother-in-law broke into the dollhouse?"

Jenny shakes her head. "No. Tell me more about Fantasy."

Fantasy continued to carve out excuses to speak to me. I felt both grateful and guilty she only sought me out when no one else was around.

I learned more about Fantasy—that she was twenty-eight, that she was an only child, that her family had disinherited her for marrying a male doll they disapproved of, that she had obtained the funds to pay for her stay at the dollhouse through a loan shark—but she avoided speaking in depth about herself. Instead, she wanted to ask me questions.

Fantasy's curiosity about my life flattered me more than I felt comfortable admitting. Most of the other dolls only feigned curiosity as a gesture of politeness, our interactions held at a distance mutually agreed upon between strangers, even when I possessed the most intimate knowledge about their bodies. But I didn't mind; like I said, I don't think of myself as an interesting person.

When Fantasy asked me about my upbringing—always in the same blunt manner—I worried I would bore her, but she listened so intently to my answers that I sometimes forgot I was speaking to a stranger. I found myself remembering details from my childhood, memories solidifying from semitransparent to opaque as though colored in by my words.

I didn't cause my mother much grief, or, I think, much joy. I was raised under the belief that admitting to desires of one's own was shameful, while servicing others' desires was virtuous. The more I sacrificed my desire for someone else's, the more virtuous I'd be. In this way, I learned to acquiesce to others and anticipate their needs before mine. And yet, this trait, honed by my mother, equally infuriated her. If I didn't bend to her will quickly enough, she grew exasperated with me. But if I bent to it too quickly, almost thoughtlessly, she grew exasperated just the same. "How did I raise a daughter so different from myself?" she often asked in these moments. My mother not only resented how different we were, but blamed me for it, as if I had willed myself from inside the womb to become someone she was not.

I paused when I said this and laughed, flushed with the uneasy intrusion of my own self-consciousness. I apologized for speaking about such trivial things. I was wasting Fantasy's time. Did she want to rest? Was there anything I could get her?

Fantasy would wave her hand at this and simply pick up where the conversation had left off, as deftly as picking up a lost stitch with a needle. My protests and her dismissals became an expected ritual between us. A part of me wondered if I was interesting because Fantasy believed I was, or if it was her interest in me that acted like a catalyst, transforming me into someone interesting.

But one afternoon, after I insisted once more that I must be boring her, she asked in a pointed voice, "Why do you do that?" When I was too stunned to answer, she asked again, "Really. Why do you do that? It's exhausting."

In that moment, I glimpsed an image of how Fantasy—of how everyone—saw me. So committed to my own self-deprecation that it could only read as false and manipulative. A tiresome, ingratiating woman. No wonder the other dolls held someone like me at arm's length.

The other subject Fantasy wanted to talk about was Dreamland. She had all kinds of questions: What are Dreamland citizens like? I heard fat and thickheaded. Have you met any children born in Dreamland? What are they like? Everyone says ungrateful and greedy. Is it true teenage dolls in Dreamland don't respect their parents or their teachers? Is it true dolls in Dreamland only worship themselves?

Not long before her baby doll arrived, Fantasy asked me if I was happier in Dreamland.

Violet had taken the other dolls on a shopping trip to the mall, leaving the two of us alone in the dollhouse. We were in the kitchen, sun-dappled and lavender-accented. It was my favorite room in the dollhouse. I was at the counter preparing that night's dinner. Fantasy stood beside me, mutilating a napkin into strips and pleating them into minuscule squares.

"Yes," I replied automatically. Then I considered her question with greater care. "I think so."

"What do you mean?" Fantasy pressed, impatient.

I tried to stall. "I don't know if I understand what Dreamland is really like."

I had never had a real conversation with a Dreamland citizen, my only proximity to them handing over money and accepting change, too embarrassed to try out the few Dreamland phrases I had memorized. The times I left the house, I had traveled with Dreamboat Joe or in a group with the other dolls.

"I don't know if I can answer your question," I said.

"What if you had been born here?"

"I don't understand."

Fantasy paused her napkin folding. "Do you wish you'd been born here, in Dreamland?"

I thought of the Dreamland children I had observed on our outdoor excursions. I envied their effortless navigation of Dreamland and yet I also believed, perhaps unfairly, that they were spoiled. Misty, whose nephew is a Dreamland citizen, told me they grow up with a specific kind of anxiety around their identity that she and I will never experience. The kind I wonder if Jenny has already weathered at her young age. Still, the very existence of the dollhouse elevated Dreamland children above any other kind of child, didn't it?

When I tried to imagine myself growing up in Dreamland—riding a yellow bus to school, attending dances with boys—my mind skidded to a blank. Fantasy's question was unthinkable to someone like me. I suddenly felt stupid and frustrated with my stupidity. I turned towards the refrigerator, pretending to search for more ingredients. Too much time had passed since Fantasy had asked her question. My obligation to answer her had expired.

Then I heard Fantasy say, as though to herself, "But of course you would have. That's the right answer. Everyone knows that." Her voice was tender, almost yearning. I turned to look at her in surprise.

I realized Fantasy was the kind of doll who disguised her personal opinions and motivations in order to test others. I couldn't pin down what she wanted me to think and what she actually thought. Her desires were unreadable in a house where everyone else's were on full display. This, more than anything else, unsettled me the most about her.

While washing dishes that night, I ran my mind over Fantasy's question until its exterior shell melted away and all that remained was a hard, unforgiving center. All my life, I'd been too afraid to lift up the corners of myself and see what lay beneath. Now I let myself. Was I happy here?

I didn't know if my existence at the dollhouse equaled the notion of happiness. But it did feel important. At any given time, double the amount of dolls lived in the dollhouse, which meant I was responsible for double the amount of beating hearts. Life and death taunted each other, as if they were locked in a game of wits. I like to think I helped both when the dolls were dealt a fair hand and when they were dealt a cruel hand. The former elicited routine relief. But the latter. Oh, the latter. It elicited compassion followed by a private, hot lick of excitement. I'd picture myself holding the doll as she wept, drawing comforting patterns on her back. Reassuring her that it wasn't her fault. In those moments, I did my best work: I became anodyne.

I bought the dollhouse for my daughter's fourth birthday, then added on the different floors and sections with each successive birthday. My husband was resistant to the gift. Shouldn't we encourage Jenny to take an interest in subjects like science, trains, the planets? he pressed. Shouldn't we want more for her than mothering dolls, when she herself is still a child?

I didn't listen to him. How would he know what little girls wanted? And so what if Jenny wanted to play house? At her age, I would have loved nothing more.

In the end, we were both wrong. Jenny never cuddled with her dolls, nursed them with fake bottles or sang off-tune lullabies in their empty ears. She wanted fully grown dolls to maneuver into chaotic situations. The more chaotic, the better. She played God more than mother.

The next morning, I woke up late. Violet was already dressed and making her bed.

"I saw you talking with Fantasy in the kitchen yesterday," she said without looking at me.

My breath hitched. I thought I had been careful to keep our conversations out of view.

Violet continued. "What do you even talk about with her? I can't imagine it's fun. She looks like she's never been happy a single day in her life." Violet jutted her chin out, fixing her face into a mask of severity. Mimicking Fantasy. Without waiting for my response, she dissolved into laughter, delighted by her own meanness.

My hands twitched in my lap. I felt as if I was seeing Violet clearly for the first time. Or rather, because of our constant proximity, I had not taken stock of how much she'd changed over the years. She watched Dreamland TV channels and listened to awful, wailing Dreamland music. She even styled herself after the dolls in popular music videos, with their choker necklaces, flowy dresses and aggressive boots. She wanted Dreamland citizenship purely so she could vote. Not long ago, she had told me she didn't want children of her own because she'd taken care of enough dolls for a lifetime. She said she had "other things" she wanted to do instead. I felt immeasurably sad for her. I was taught that to be a woman is to be a mother. That some other "thing" could eclipse motherhood was unfathomable to me. But I also felt a little envious of Violet's audacity to reinvent the life she'd been handed. She wasn't afraid of becoming unrecognizable to herself.

"Nothing that would interest you," I finally said.

Violet shrugged and changed the topic, already bored. She'd taken out a bottle of purple nail polish and was painting her left hand. "Did you hear what happened to Dreamboat Joe?" I shook my head no. Violet looked pleased she was privvy to information I wasn't. "He got a phone call—from the police."

"Oh." I didn't know how to relate this to myself.

"Aren't you afraid?"

"Of course not. Dreamboat Joe protects us."

"That's what he says."

"Are you saying he's lying? Don't talk nonsense." I got up to make my bed.

Violet laughed—it flustered me more than if she'd snapped at me. "You're afraid to leave the dollhouse," she said, eyes wide in revelation. Then she leveled the sentence at me in singsong, *"You're afraid to leave the dollhouse."*

"No, I'm not."

"Prove it. Let's go out tonight. After the dolls are all asleep."

I stared at Violet.

"Johnny will pick us up."

My disbelief nearly cut my tongue out. "Johnny?" I finally managed. "Who's Johnny?"

"I met him when I took the dolls to the mall."

"Oh. Is he your boyfriend?"

"No. He's a friend . . . with benefits," Violet said, her voice a taunt. I turned away to make the bed so she wouldn't see the color saturating my cheeks. "Sorry, do you not know what that means, Virgin Mary?"

I decided I would never forgive Violet for how much she was enjoying my humiliation. And then, a second later, I decided that I would forgive her. Because I was a selfless person.

I smiled beneficently at her. "How nice. I'm happy for you."

Violet scrutinized me as she blew on her nails. My reaction had disappointed her.

Fantasy's birth was difficult: twenty-two hours of labor before she was given an emergency C-section. When Dreamboat Joe brought her home not even a day later, her skin looked sallow and soft, like it had spoiled. The hospital discouraged the dolls from staying long. They'd started to piece together the truth, this conveyor belt of dolls who didn't speak the Dreamland language, who didn't have a planned birth with a doctor at the hospital, always brought in by the same gruff male doll who took off in a rush rather than an anxious husband who paced the waiting room.

For the first few days, I visited Fantasy frequently, no longer caring if Violet noticed. I brought her warm towels, magazines, hot water. When I asked how she was feeling and was met with silence, I figured she was exhausted from the birth. When I asked if she needed help showering, I believed her when she said she could do it herself.

I only suspected something was wrong when I noticed her behavior around her baby doll. All day long, she stayed sequestered in her bedroom. All day long, I did not hear Fantasy make a single sound. When I came into her room to clean and air it out, her baby doll was swaddled and lying on the bed, about an arm's length away from Fantasy. A whole other baby doll could have fit in that space. Not even a pillow barricaded her from the edge of the bed.

"Do you want me to bring you the bassinet?" I asked Fantasy, glancing at it in a corner of the room. The bassinet was white and ruffled, with silk rosebuds stitched along the sides. Fantasy shook her head. I felt hurt she hadn't asked me if I wanted to hold her baby doll.

"She's beautiful," I said. "What's her name?"

"Dolly." Fantasy's voice, now out of use, came out as a croak.

I prepared to leave when she said I could hold her. I gingerly picked Dolly up and cradled her in my arms. Her furnace-hot hand curled around my own. She was small, around two and a half kilos, and her head was completely bare of hair. "She's beautiful," I said again, though in truth, she was an unremarkable baby doll, as most were. I think I felt affectionate towards her because I wasn't sure if Fantasy did. I sought Fantasy's gaze, but she'd turned to face the wall.

A week after Dolly's arrival, I couldn't sleep again. When I looked out my bedroom window at the pool, I saw a figure mar the water's unblemished skin. I changed into my floral swimsuit, a hand-me-down from a past doll, and headed to the backyard. The water was warmed to seventy-eight degrees. I paddled towards Fantasy but stayed within the shallow end, where my feet grazed the pool's rough floor. When Fantasy resurfaced, she glanced at me without a word. I suddenly felt shy. I didn't understand what had compelled me to join Fantasy when she clearly swam in the middle of the night because she wanted to be undisturbed. I watched her for a while longer, dipping her head in and out as her arms sliced through the water with practiced ease. I realized I still knew so little about her. She was leaving soon, and with her, my unanswered questions.

When she resurfaced next, I said good night and paddled to the pool steps, not realizing I had floated over to the deep end. When my foot met boundless water instead of the rough texture I'd anticipated, I panicked. I kicked my legs as my arms uselessly flailed. The pool couldn't have been that deep and yet the water rising above me felt insurmountable. I was gasping while inhaling a mixture of chlorinated water and pockets of air. I couldn't believe my own foolishness.

Then an authoritative arm hooked around my chest and dragged me to the shallow end. Fantasy's thin arms were unexpectedly strong. She propped me up against the metal railing as I continued to cough. A minute later, I felt a towel drape across my shoulders.

Fantasy was standing next to me. I couldn't meet her eyes and instead kept mine closed. When I opened them, I did a double take. Faded bruises bloomed on her body: rancid yellow and purple splotches traveling across her legs, arms and back. Other marks on her thighs looked like cigarette burns. The sight was a shock—I had only ever witnessed violence inside the safe confines of the TV screen. I turned away and considered saying nothing. But at this surreal hour of the night, I found myself speaking into existence thoughts I normally wouldn't dare speak aloud.

"Did your husband do that?" I asked.

Fantasy walked back into the pool and paused when she was waist-deep, as if considering whether to ignore me or keep swimming. "Who else would do it."

The thought of Fantasy and Dolly returning to him was unbearable. What would a man like that do to his own daughter?

"You have to leave him," I said, "or—or report him to the police."

The words sounded juvenile even as they slipped past my lips. I was speaking as if I was presenting revelatory information, not the most obvious choices Fantasy would've already taken if she could have.

She fixed me with a disappointed look. "I didn't think you were a stupid woman. Are you? A stupid woman?"

I was too rattled by what I'd seen to feel insulted. I heard myself saying she had to think of Dolly, she had to push aside her own fears, she was a mother now. I looked pleadingly at Fantasy. The intensity of her expression, such bald resignation, frightened me.

"My husband doesn't know I'm here," she said flatly. "But he is the reason I'm pregnant."

I stared at her in confusion.

"Do you understand now or do I need to give you the details?" Fantasy's lips tugged up in scorn, as if held by invisible strings. "You know nothing about men or the world, do you? You're still a child."

The meaning beneath her words slowly clarified itself: she was suggesting an unnatural transgression that would never happen between husband and wife, precisely because they were husband and wife. A husband's desire, after all, was his wife's desire. This is what my mother had taught me and what her mother had taught her. The boldness of Fantasy's thinking, her confidence in rewriting the truth, unnerved me. The anger I'd felt towards Fantasy's husband, as if uprooted and unsure of where to land, veered in a new direction: towards Fantasy.

"Where's Dolly?" I abruptly demanded. My heart pounded in wild disbelief at her carelessness.

"She's sleeping," Fantasy said, preternaturally calm, but I didn't wait for her to complete her sentence, I was already tearing across the backyard, past the sliding glass door, up the stairs to Fantasy's room. I flung open the door, bracing myself for some unspeakable horror, only to see Dolly fast asleep in her bassinet, just like Fantasy had promised. Dolly sucked peacefully on a pacifier and yet I found myself scooping her up and pressing her to my damp chest. She instantly woke up and began to cry.

I turned around to see Fantasy in the doorway, watching me.

"Look, she's terrified!" I said.

Fantasy's expression revealed nothing to me. For several moments, only Dolly's cries scratched at the thick air between us. I understood I had crossed a boundary, but my footing on this new territory was unsteady.

Fantasy held out her arms. "Give her to me."

Here. Here is the moment I am certain everything changed. Because I hesitated—how long those seconds felt—before reluctantly passing Dolly to her mother. Dolly's pacifier tumbled from her mouth to the carpet.

"Good night," Fantasy said pleasantly, in a voice she'd never used before. "Oh, and please shut the door. I wouldn't want to wake the others."

I felt my chest rise and fall, my breaths agitated and uneven. I wanted to slam the door—and with it, slam the syrupiness out of Fantasy's voice—but instead I closed it gently. Cowardly.

I went back to my room and crawled into my bed, still in my damp swimsuit. Unable to make a sound, I did something I hadn't done since I was a small child: tuck my fingers into my mouth and suck, comforted by the familiar, bland taste.

In some ways, Fantasy reminded me of my mother. Selfish without any apologetic gestures to excuse it.

The most painful moments of my early childhood were when I was with her—perhaps she was bathing me or cleaning me up after I'd eaten—and I distinctly knew that she was not present. That she had traveled to a place forbidden to me. Distracted isn't the right word. Maybe—it pains me to think—the right word is regretful. The thought of my mother having access to a life shaped around only her own driving desires, desires that didn't factor in my existence, was the most abysmal concept my young mind could conceive of. In these moments, I would do anything to retrieve her from wherever she'd slipped off to. I would whine that I was cold or my stomach hurt or I wanted something sweet to eat. If that didn't work, I'd cry. Then I'd see her attention shift, just as a camera might refocus on its subject, back to me, and I would feel instantly soothed and even a little superior: *Yes, that's right.* I was supposed to be the most important thing in her life and I could not stand when she resented this fact.

"Did you and Fantasy have a fight?" Jenny asks, smoothing Fantasy the doll's hair with a sparkly plastic brush.

"You could say that."

"Why?"

I consider this. "Because we were too different."

I stopped going to Fantasy's room after the pool incident. When I told Violet it was her turn to bring Fantasy her meals, she didn't fight me. Fantasy's package included only two weeks of rest. She would be leaving soon enough.

I joined Violet in the kitchen the next night. She was sitting on a barstool and nursing a beer, one of the Dreamland brands she bought for herself. When she silently handed me one, I accepted, though I disliked the taste. Ever since Violet revealed she'd cultivated a life outside of the dollhouse, we spoke to each other less and less.

"You were right about Fantasy," I said. "She is stupid."

Violet's mouth twitched, as if she doubted the honesty of my words. Then she laughed and mimicked Fantasy's rigid expression, her jutting chin. This time I laughed and joined in, too, though no pleasure came of it.

I closed my eyed and drank, greedily. I didn't tell Violet that that morning, when adding powdered supplements to each doll's glass of orange juice, I had skipped Fantasy's glass. That during dinner, I had served her the piece of chicken that had fallen onto the kitchen floor. That when changing her bedding, I had found a small dead cockroach pressed between the sheets and the waterproof pad and decided to leave it in its soft coffin.

Fantasy had flicked on the light to the darkened room of myself that I never dared enter. Like the dolls whose bodies kept changing, I, too, kept uncovering new rooms inside myself. Except my rooms contained secrecy, and now, small acts of cruelty.

I imagined myself as the dollhouse, the windows lit up at night, expanding with rooms in every direction until its proportions grew so large, it didn't look like a dollhouse anymore. It didn't look like anything.

I wonder if a mother cannot help but see her daughter as a miniature extension of herself. Sometimes I am invaded with such exasperation over Jenny that I feel monstrous, before the feeling dissipates as quickly as it ambushed me. I know I'm easier-going with Matthew, but I like to think with both him and Jenny, I'm better than I have to be. Sometimes I watch Dreamland sitcoms with the two of them and observe how the mothers act. Even when it feels like I'm about to embarrass myself horribly, I try out little things here and there. Leaving notes in their lunch boxes, volunteering at their school.

My weakness, I know, is pressing Jenny too tightly to my chest. I wailed when my husband insisted she had to sleep in her own room at age five. When she was an infant, I could not bear to let her cry herself to exhaustion. Her pediatrician said it would be good for Jenny, the separation would teach her independence, and I looked at him as if he had lost his mind.

When I took Jenny to the park, I avoided speaking to the other parents, who glanced up at their children only when they ran to them with a scraped knee or a runny nose. I, on the other hand, would watch Jenny without looking away once, my heart lifting each time she flew down the slide, her face split apart with happiness as though her little body could not contain its enormity.

Sometimes I want to tell Jenny she has no idea. She has no idea what the size of my love looks like.

The morning of Fantasy's departure, Misty found Violet and me in the kitchen preparing breakfast. "I went out for a walk," she said in a teasing voice. "And I saw that van again. The white one. Parked around the corner."

"Call Dreamboat Joe," I said, but Violet was already reaching for the phone on the wall.

I finished cooking because I didn't know what else to do besides adhere to my usual routine. I wiped down the kitchen counter, then went to inform the dolls that breakfast was ready.

When I knocked on Fantasy's door, she had already finished packing. She sat on the bed staring at the blank TV, her suitcase by the dresser. Dolly was in her bassinet, her little hand tensed tight around her blankie.

"Come and eat breakfast," I said. Fantasy didn't answer or look at me. Annoyed, I shut the door louder than necessary.

When I returned to the kitchen, Violet was still on the phone. She sounded panicked and kept repeating, "I know, I know." She hung up and ordered, "Get all the dolls on the second floor ready." When I could only stare at her, she shouted, "Wake up!"

I ran up to the second floor, banging on the bedroom doors as I shouted instructions, instructions Dreamboat Joe had drilled into me. I understood now that he hadn't made us play a game; he'd been preparing us for the worst.

When I reached my room, I threw my most important belongings into a shopping bag. I took everything with my name on it. Even in my frantic state, I knew not to leave traces of myself in the dollhouse. I grabbed the keys to the van and jammed open the door to the garage with a box of laundry detergent. The dolls crowded together, their faces stricken with fear and worry. I herded them into the van and counted heads: we were missing someone.

I ran back into the dollhouse shouting Fantasy's name. Not a thing in her bedroom was out of place, save for Fantasy herself—she was gone. I had no time to let the shock of the empty room settle over me. When I saw Dolly in the bassinet, I forgot Fantasy entirely. She smiled at the sight of me. I let out a cry, picked her up and breathed in her powdery scent. I rushed back into the garage, trying not to jostle Dolly too much. I placed her in the first pair of arms I saw and started up the minivan as Violet started up the sedan. She would take three dolls and one newborn. I would take four dolls, two newborns and one wet nurse.

I clicked the garage door opener, stifling my breath until I was certain no police cars blocked the driveway. I backed out and turned right, away from where Misty had sighted the parked white van, towards the exit of the housing development, past the unsettling rows of identical houses with identical lawns. As I drove, the morning sunlight cracked and spilled across the hills, pouring straight into my line of vision.

I had only driven a few blocks away from the house when I saw her. Walking down the sidewalk, wearing flared jeans, platform sneakers and that surreally hot pink long-sleeved shirt, carrying only a single plastic grocery bag. From behind, she looked like any teenager in Dreamland.

Misty rolled down the window and called her name. But Fantasy continued to stroll, calmly and purposefully. I didn't slow down the minivan.

"What are you doing?" Misty shouted at me.

"She wants us to leave her," I said, ignoring Misty's look of astonishment.

I was not sure of this until the words broke loose from me, but the second they did, I understood it was what Fantasy had planned all along.

For years afterwards, my behavior felt out of character. I abided by what was right; I should have stopped the minivan rather than entertain Fantasy's selfish desires for a single second. I didn't know what had awoken this bold new defiance—yet more rooms were expanding inside me.

But later, I realized I had not been acting out of character, not in the slightest. I had simply anticipated Fantasy's needs. I had bent to her will.

Through the rearview mirror, I looked back at Fantasy. I don't know if we made eye contact—sometimes I imagine we did, sometimes I am sure we did not. What I do know is I kept glancing back at her shrinking figure until she was just the barest hint of a person.

"Why did she walk away?" Jenny asks. "Why didn't you go after her?" She sets down Fantasy the doll and looks up at me. "You went after her the last time you told the story."

"Did I? So many questions," I say, tickling Jenny until spasms of laughter escape her. "Why? Are you going to leave me one day?"

Before she can answer, I make her laugh again.

The doll police apprehended Dreamboat Joe and his wife at one of his other dollhouses. They were arrested for tax evasion, fraud and lying to immigration officials. You might have seen it on the news. In the video that played on the local channel, Dreamboat Joe wore his tinted sunglasses. His wife shielded her face with both her hands, her long permed hair the only way I knew her. Violet had been right: Dreamboat Joe obscured so much from us.

The other dolls discovered at that dollhouse did not face punishment. Like Dreamboat Joe always said, giving birth in Dreamland was not a crime, though some Dreamland politicians disagreed. They argued that the right to be a citizen of Dreamland had to be earned. We were cheating, they claimed. We were taking a shortcut.

I don't know where Violet drove the sedan. The last time we saw each other was that breathless morning in the garage, just before we separated. When I think of what she must look like now, I'm not sure I could pick her out of a crowd. She'd wanted to blend into Dreamland more than anything, to such an extent that no one could tell her to go home because Dreamland was her home. I imagine leaving the dollhouse finally gave her the chance.

As for the minivan I drove, it was never pulled over. I headed west, then south, past looping concrete freeways and sprays of palm trees, all the way to the ocean. I stopped at a parking lot facing the beach. We didn't have bathing suits or towels with us, but we all wordlessly exited the van and walked towards the water, entranced. Unlike the dollhouse pool, the ocean's surface glittered as if small pieces of metal danced across it. A boardwalk stretched its lanky arms into the water, seaweed clinging to its wooden legs like hanks of black-green hair. The air tasted whipped with salt. That day was my first time seeing the ocean. I turned Dolly towards the water and whispered for her to look, but she scrunched her eyes shut and twisted away.

I passed her to Misty and walked to a battered white truck in the parking lot to buy ice cream for everyone. Dreamboat Joe hadn't left an emergency fund so I used the cash in my purse, past the point of caring if it was unwise. I still remember that ice cream sandwich, a melting slab of vanilla held by two pillowy thin chocolate cakes. I had never tasted anything so extraordinary.

This is Jenny's favorite part of the story. Afterwards, she always begs me for an ice cream sandwich and I always give in. I buy the same kind sold in the truck, wrapped in wax paper. But they have never tasted as good as they did on that day.

"What happened to Dolly?" Jenny asks, her words thick with sugar. She hasn't asked me this question before, but I realize with a start that it's because she's grown older, the margins of her world beginning to expand beyond herself.

I want to tell her that she's healthy and strong, and eating an ice cream sandwich, in a house filled with books and games and a family who loves her. Instead I tell her she's fine.

"Oh. That's good," Jenny says without looking at me; she's concentrating on licking all the melted ice cream from the wrapper. "Did she ever find her mom?"

I think of myself, a housekeeper and a waitress, who had always thought her life uninteresting, until one day, it wasn't. I think of Fantasy's mocking eyes, of her receding teenaged silhouette.

I came across a letter from her a few years ago—at least, I'm almost certain it was from her. The letter was addressed to Jenny. Next to her name was an infantile sticker of a bear hugging a heart. At first, I doubted Fantasy could have tracked down our home address, but some of the dolls have stayed in touch on an email chain and every year, I receive a handful of holiday cards. Looking closer, I noticed the address was written in a slanting, forceful font, as if its author was not accustomed to writing. As if it belonged to the hand of a factory worker. I threw the sealed letter away. Opening someone's mail is a crime and, as I've said before, I would never commit a crime.

I've paused for too long. Jenny looks at me with a slight crease in her brow. Does she know? In agreeing to tell her this story over and over, have I always wanted her to know?

Jenny smiles wide at me, exposing the gap I love between her teeth. "Can I have another?"

"Yes," I say, too quickly, too readily, as if she has offered me forgiveness for a trespass neither of us has named. "Yes."

CASUALTIES OF ART

I.

The taxi scrapes its way through a slender path crowned by birch trees. They bow their shoulders, as if ashamed they've been caught in a flaccid state of undress. When I heft my luggage from the trunk, the rain rinses me through within seconds. The two-hour train ride has left me feeling creased and fur-tongued. I want, badly, to brush my teeth.

The main building features a wraparound porch hugging its second level. I'm struck by its handsomeness: wood-paneled and modern, presiding on a grassy slope with two picnic tables anchoring it on both ends. The enormous front door is girdled by thick iron bands. Past it stretches the interior of the lodge, as polished and bright as a new penny. I place my suitcase against the wall and bend down to discipline an errant shoelace.

"Are you one of the fellows?"

I stand up to see another victim of the downpour contemplating me. I wonder if she's the program manager but then I notice the rain-sprinkled suitcase beside her. I nod and stick out my hand and we laugh a little over our clammy handshake.

Her name is Lauren, she says, and she just heard from the program manager that he's out picking up the other fellows from the train station. Apparently one of the trains is delayed. I tell her I didn't know we could ask for a ride.

"Yeah, I didn't know, either." Lauren smiles up at me as if we've just bonded over a shared secret. She's short, with a generous chest and emphatic, almost protruding eyes. A startlingly stern mouth when not smiling. She's dressed in a vintage floral dress and has secured her ashy blond hair back with a velvet scrunchie. (Character: mothering, would die for animals but only animals, loves her family of hard-core, gun-toting conservatives but pretends she doesn't.) Forgive me: I have this habit of sketching people like characters in a story. My college ex-girlfriend called it sociopathic. I called it having an imagination.

Lauren suggests a self-guided tour of the lodge and because I don't know what else to do, I follow her. Upstairs is a library, two computers and a printer. Downstairs, a kitchen, a bathroom, a dining room and a sitting area with a fireplace. Everything looks identical to the website pictures. Also on the website: the fellows are required to eat dinner together, but not breakfast or lunch. Internet is available in the lodge, but not in our cabins. Partners are allowed, but not children. Cell phone reception is spotty and the nearest town is an hour's walk away. The program promises us that this surrender to austerity, to the bare necessities, will lead us to produce our best work. Well, bare necessities not counting the chef-cooked meals.

The keys to our cabins are waiting for us on the dining table. Four buttery-smooth envelopes are arranged in a square: David

Lee, Lauren Fisher, Carter Andrew Wright, Jacob Moscovitch. *Carter* and *Jacob*—the names alone set me on edge.

I pocket my key and head back to the foyer.

"Do you know where I can get some coffee?" Lauren asks, abruptly, even though we passed by the coffee and tea station while touring the kitchen. I have a feeling she wants me to suggest we drink some, together. Under normal circumstances I would, but today—damp and exhausted—I can't dredge up the energy.

"I think I saw a machine back there."

Disappointment stains Lauren's face for a half second before she hastily wipes it off.

"Well, I guess we should dry off, don't want to get sick on the first day," I say brightly, pretending I haven't noticed. "See you at dinner?"

She nods. As I close the door behind me, I wonder if I've committed some kind of writer residency faux pas.

I trudge up the path behind the lodge, zigzagging from the horizontal lashes of rain and wind. My cabin is the farthest one out, tucked northeast of the lodge. The inside reminds me of the back of a thrift store, self-conscious of its antiquated smells. Whitewashed walls with dark wood flooring, a full bed, a nightstand, a wooden desk and chair, an upholstered armchair—quaint. On the right side of the bed is a narrow, drafty bathroom. This is my home for the next three months.

After showering, I unpack: clothes, toiletries, laptop, two empty notebooks. Bringing two was ambitious. I lie down on the bed and tell myself I've made it. I applied, I got in and now I'm here. These are facts. And yet self-doubt still plucks at me. I can't shake the suspicion that I've tricked my way into the program, an ugly paranoia that followed me from the train all the way into bed like an insistent toilet paper trail. This is another tic I can't shake: trying to catch myself out, to fail to the point of proving that I should stop writing. My college ex-girlfriend—Sohee—said my allergy to failure was to blame.

"You would rather kill yourself than face rejection," she told me once, before waxing on about how I need to accept that to write *is* to fail. She was—is—a writer, too.

When I wake up, the clock on the nightstand reads a quarter past eight. Fuck. I consider hunkering down in the cabin for the night, sustaining myself on my last granola bar, rather than face the embarrassment of missing the welcome dinner. Tomorrow, I'll claim I contracted food poisoning from train station sushi, with a few gastric details thrown in for authenticity. But the thought of everyone kindling a connection without me is worse, so I change into dry clothes and stumble to the lodge. The rain has petered out to a frail drizzle.

When I open the front door, I hear the other fellows' voices before I see them. I close my eyes, as though it's open mic night and my name was just pulled from a hat, and walk in. Everyone is spread throughout the sitting area with drinks sweating in their hands. I make my excuses and stay nailed to the floor, at a loss for where to sit or what to say next, when Lauren mentions that leftovers are in the kitchen. I feel absurdly grateful for this small act of kindness and revise her character description: when her hardcore conservative family crosses the line during the holidays, at least she gently corrects them. This is unusual for me; I rarely revise my characterizations. I've found that most people aren't as complex or unpredictable as they think. People tend to be exactly who you think they are.

I make a plate of cold chicken, sweet potatoes and kale, then select the seat beside Lauren on the sofa, my plate balanced on my knees. She smiles up at me.

The man sitting in the armchair is Jacob. He is exactly what I picture when someone says "New York" and "writer" in the same breath. Tweed coat, white button-up, blue jeans, gently scuffed brown oxfords. His dark hair spirals out into floppy curls and his features, set in a pale face, lean sensitive. He has a willowy neck and rounded shoulders. I have to admit I'm pleased he's a little effeminate-looking. Maybe because he knows this, he plays incessantly with a green Swiss Army knife, flipping it open and shut like the moody protagonist of a coming-of-age film. (Character: loves to inform women they are reading the wrong authors, only drinks whiskey in public, shaves every day without needing to.)

The man standing up is Carter. Decently tall, the body of an athlete, a swoop of dirty blond hair, perfect picket fence of teeth, all packaged in a cable-knit sweater and loafers. He seems well-versed in tugging everyone's attention towards himself. I dislike him, on principle, as I dislike any man of his ilk. He possesses the blinkered goodness of someone whose parents told him "I love you" every day of his life. Those people are, on average, the worst people alive. (Character: WASP trust fund kid, smells like "stock market" sounds, can watch people getting chainsawed open without flinching.) I catch a slip of what he's saying, something about a private vineyard tour in Napa Valley, and I have to stop myself from snorting. At least, I tell myself, I'm a good inch taller than him.

I'm trying to calculate everyone's ages (I think Jacob and Lauren are the youngest in their mid-twenties and Carter is somewhere in his early thirties) when Carter asks, "What about you, David?"

Everyone's been offering up summaries of themselves: studied here, published there. Jacob works as the events manager at an indie bookstore, Lauren completed her MFA degree this past summer and Carter is the editor of a literary magazine I've never heard of. One hundred percent a trust fund kid.

I swallow a wad of cold chicken, then pour myself a glass of ice water from the pitcher on the side table. "I studied Business Economics at Newark. And I, um, worked in accounting. I mean, I work in accounting—my company is giving me extended PTO." I sense, with aching precision, the surprise and even derision that this inspires.

"Right—cool, man. You don't let your job define you," Carter says generously, which only sharpens my dislike of him.

I don't tell the other fellows that my only formal proximity to literature is two semesters of creative writing in college, taken as "guaranteed A" electives, where the praise of two teachers made me delusional enough to think I was good—maybe exceptionally good—at writing. I don't tell them that I stopped writing for five years postgraduation, when I'd firmly sunk into the cushy upward mobility of a corporate office job. And I definitely don't tell them that it wasn't some profound, undying love of fiction that drove me back into its arms—it was finding out Sohee had won a prestigious writing fellowship. That day was the day I started writing every morning. So the reason was hubris or maybe a cousin to it: hubris born with shame.

Instead, I say, "Sorry for crashing your fancy literary party," which I intended to land as a joke but all it inspires is a taut silence. Yikes. I return to my plate of chicken.

The more the conversation closes in on itself, like some hellish self-referential circle—talk about agents, something called Publishers Marketplace, a literary scandal involving stalking and lawsuits I've never heard of—the more my chest compresses in on itself. Though I would never disclose it to this crowd, I know nothing about their world. This program is the first time I've been granted access past its cocky gates and I can't help but feel I'm resented for it. I didn't write my first short story when I was eight and a half years old and I didn't attend a private high school for the arts and I didn't map out my life's trajectory around the singular goal of getting into this room, or a room like it. I can visualize the thought bubbling up over their heads: *He who hasn't suffered enough for his art hasn't earned the right to be here.*

The nagging suspicion that I am an interloper who subterfuged his way into the program constricts my chest again. But then I look at the other fellows and new knowledge spills over me, as cold and unmistakable as the ice in my glass: I must be here for diversity purposes.

The next morning, everyone heads to the grocery store an hour's walk away. They'll take the van, store up on snacks and alcohol. Elijah, the program manager, asks if I want to join. He's red-haired, smiles too hard and seems generally inoffensive. (Character: dabbles in LARPing, closeted bisexual, will make a great dad one day.) I tell him I brought enough food with me, though that's a lie. The bitter taste of last night's conversation still coats my tongue and I can't bring myself to endure another. And anyway, I've never excelled at group settings. As an only child, I've learned to be the arbiter of my own entertainment (and my own misery).

When the van crunches off, I feel a little naughty, like a child who's been granted temporary dominion over the whole house in lieu of parental supervision. I take my time wandering through the lodge, poking around the kitchen, browsing the library's meager selections. I sit down on the padded windowseat overlooking the gravel driveway and take out my notebook, half hoping the mechanics of preparing to write will lead to the act itself.

In my application, I stated my intention to complete a short story collection during my time at the program. I submitted a sample story and outlines of the stories I planned to write. The overarching theme was loneliness, but for good measure, I braided in urgent references to capitalism and technology. Both of which, I argued, contributed to "the new age of solipsism modern man finds himself in." I'm not sure how much I believed my own puffed-up artist's statement, or how much of it I simply succumbed to by dint of laboring over the words for so long. Or, if I were to flatter myself, I could believe the finesse of the lie was compelling enough to sway its architect. By the time I submitted my application, I was convinced that this book was my One True Love. But now, looking down at my notebook, I would rather punch myself in the teeth than write about loneliness or capitalism or technology.

When I told my parents I had gotten into the program, they were perplexed. I had never even confessed I took creative writing classes in college. My father, in particular, couldn't understand the point of hitting pause on my career to dick around in the middle of the woods. But then my mother exclaimed in self-righteous delight that this was all *his* fault: In elementary school, he bought me Choose Your Own Adventure paperbacks, dozens of them, since they were the only books I willingly read. When the plot was predestined, I lost all interest. Even at that age, I was obsessed with the flexibility of truth, its delicateness. Subject to change via a single eraser smudge.

I glance out the window and do a double take: a spectral figure floats up the path to the lodge. Black-haired and pale as chalk. A slight chill braces me. I squint, wondering if I'm seeing things, and rub my eyes. When I open them, the figure is nowhere to be seen. I sprint downstairs, taking the steps two at a time before the front door flies open and I'm standing face-to-face with a woman.

She's smiling, though her smile falters when she sees me. I realize I'm staring slack-jawed at her. Her appearance unsettles me in more ways than one. Messy black hair that hits her waist, a tapered chin, a diminutive slope of a nose. Bright, expressive brown eyes. She wears distressed gray jeans, a light blue denim jacket and peacock feather earrings. If I had to guess, she's also in her late twenties. Her skin and hair are dewy from the rain. She's beautiful.

I wish I hadn't changed into sweatpants.

"Hi?" she finally says.

"Oh. Hi. Come in." I remember I have a name. "I'm David."

She seems reassured I know how to socially function after all. "Sophia," she says and offers me a noncommittal handshake. She smells like she's just eaten take-out food, oily and fragrant. I step aside as she surveys the entryway. "It's gorgeous. Better than the photos." My confusion must have resurfaced in my face because she explains, "I was supposed to arrive yesterday but I got delayed." She lifts and drops her shoulders. "That's what I get for booking a flight with two layovers."

I had thought the program only accepted four fellows. Maybe I misread the information on the website or maybe a fifth spot was added at the last minute. I could ask clarifying questions, but I'm distracted by the cool relief flooding my veins: *I'm no longer the only one.*

"Where did you fly from?" I ask.

She walks into the sitting area and abandons her suitcase in the middle of the room. "Seattle."

"I love Seattle," I respond (second lie of the day).

"You?" she asks.

"Jersey City."

"Cool."

An awkward gap in the conversation hangs in the air. I scan for something else to say, some other normal social nicety exchanged within the first few minutes of meeting a complete stranger, but what comes out is, "Are you Korean?"

Her brows knit together for an instant, then relax. She laughs. When I don't return her laugh, she raises her eyebrows. "Oh, you're serious?"

"My mom's Korean," I quickly explain, anticipating a flustered look of recalibration.

"Cool," she says and nods her head like she's listening to a song only she can hear.

"That's why I asked."

"I see."

Annoyance creeps into me. Is she honestly refusing to answer such a benign question? "So . . . are you?" I press.

Sophia walks to the kitchen. She opens the fridge and takes out a bottle of water, calmly sips from it.

"I'm sorry, did I offend you?" I ask, trailing after her.

Sophia laughs again. "No, it's fine. I just don't answer that question."

CASUALTIES OF ART

The perfect volley of a response comes to me: "Surely you make an exception when the person asking shares the same race as you," but she keeps baffling me and the thought dissolves under the roof of my mouth.

"Huh," I say instead. Just forget it, I tell myself. Give her a tour of the lodge, ask if she's had lunch. Better yet, ask about her writing. I can already guess—memoir disguised as fiction with glimmers of magical realism. I'm willing to bet her author bio notes that she is first and foremost an activist.

But somehow, "Is it for political reasons? Like some kind of protest?" comes out. I worry I sound petulant and command myself to stop.

She shrugs. "Not really."

I can't stop. "I'm sorry, I guess I'm just not understanding—"

Her voice uncorks in abrupt laughter as she grasps my arm, then lets go just as abruptly. "That is so typical."

I feel both offended and slightly turned on. "Typical?"

She reaches for a bag of pretzels on the counter and opens it. She offers me the bag and I grab a fistful before I realize what I'm doing. I despise pretzels.

"I went to college with a lot of guys like you."

"What do you mean 'guys like me'?"

She looks me over carefully. I'm dying to hear her explanation but the idea of someone pinning me down, neat as a dead moth affixed to corkboard, is too much to bear. I don't wait to find out before countering, "Well, I know a lot of girls like you."

"Oh, yeah?" She steals the pretzel bag away from me as if daring me to keep talking.

Ideas cluster in my head: grew up in an all-white neighborhood, can't speak her parents' native language for shit, which she used to announce with pride, but joined Asian community spaces the second Asian heritage amassed social clout.

Before I can prove to Sophia that I see her as much as she sees me, the front door's slam interrupts us. I have never felt so resentful of a door. Diluted chatter and the rustle of plastic bags expand into the silent lodge. I will myself to snap out of it—am I honestly falling for someone, someone who weirdly gets under my skin—five minutes after meeting her, after swearing off the distracting nonsense that is dating and romance and love?

Everyone files into the kitchen to see the two of us loitering by the counter. I'm wondering why Carter looks so elated when he ditches the bags he's holding and beelines towards Sophia. He swoops her into his arms and hoists her up from the ground. A delighted squeal escapes her as they kiss a mere two feet away from me. I notice he holds her not by the waist, but with both hands cupping her ass.

"Baby, you're here!" Carter bellows as he sets her down. "When did you get here? How was your flight?" Without waiting for an answer, he announces, as if he won her in a competitive auction, "Everyone, this is my wife, Sophia."

She starts shaking people's hands and I hear snippets of "Seattle" and "layover" and "gorgeous, better than the photos" again.

I lean against the counter, smiling what I hope is a sincerely warm smile.

Chef Manon has prepared magret de canard, roasted fingerling potatoes, an arugula salad garnished with walnuts and feta, and for dessert, a crumble with blueberries picked fresh from the property. She and Elijah share their meal together on the covered back patio, away from the fellows.

All throughout dinner, I glower at Carter. I glower in my head, anyway. Outwardly, I'm nodding and making appropriate eye contact while maintaining a cordial half smile on my face. When dessert is served, I even chime in with a feeble joke about submission guidelines.

Something about Carter and Sophia grinds against me. I'm trying to puzzle out why. Couples like them are so ubiquitous, I've become resigned to their popularity. Most of the girls I grew up with eventually paired off with men from the Carter-flavored variety pack. Some of these girls I had dated, some of them had turned me down by stating I wasn't their "type" as nonchalantly as stating a preference for nonfat over 2 percent. To cauterize the sting of rejection, I deduced they could only obtain unattractive, overweight or prematurely balding men at the bottom of the white man food chain. In other words, betas who struggled to date white women and therefore had to resort to secondary options.

The times I walked past couples composed of this demographic where the situation was inverted—he conventionally attractive and she not—I deduced he was plagued by a fetish and therefore could not make out her facial features to a distinct enough degree to ascertain whether or not they were aesthetically, and objectively, pleasing. All he could see was the blurry outline of a woman who slotted into his fetish prototype, therefore securing his attraction.

My mental machinations grind to a standstill when I notice everyone's gaze is angled towards Sophia. Jacob has asked if she's a writer.

"No, fortunately I'm a painter," Sophia says drolly. Everyone chuckles. I don't understand what's funny.

"A fucking amazing painter," Carter underscores.

Sophia half-heartedly rolls her eyes and nudges her shoulder against him. Carter responds by kissing her on the cheek, his mouth sloppy with blueberry crumble. His arm has been chaperoning her waist all night. Proprietary or lovesick, I can't tell, but the knowledge that these two will be joyfully fucking tonight in the cabin a few yards from mine makes my sinuses ache.

"What kind?" Jacob follows up.

"I'm working on a new collection of oil paintings," Sophia answers simply before clocking that everyone's gaze is still trained on her, awaiting elaboration. "Well, it's part of a larger project I've been working on for the past few years, called *Ordinary Bodies*." That this is the type of crowd that can handle a little academic jargon, indeed respects it, finally seems to click because she sets down her fork and recites her artist's statement in a practiced, fluid and deeply aggravating manner.

"My work is concerned with demystifying the mythologies of the East Asian body invented by Westernism: our hair, skin and eyes that have historically been conceptualized as separate from our bodies, as if they're autonomous entities. For example, slanted vaginas and impossibly small or nonexistent genitalia, for both sexes. In my last collection, I achieved this through painting different body parts on a massive scale. So, penises were mistaken for vaginas, thighs for breasts, eyelashes for pubic hair. The goal was to disassociate the viewer's expectations of the titles of the paintings from the paintings themselves."

My cheeks grow hot. I drink rapidly from my glass of water, praying no one has noticed. I feel, in a way I intuit is absurd, like Sophia has aired our dirty laundry out in public and given a name to something these people didn't know about and never needed to.

"I know it's a binary and reductive view of gender," Sophia quickly tacks on, a touch of defensiveness buttressing her voice, "but my critique is of preexisting gender systems."

"She received an artist's grant to do nothing but paint for a whole year," Carter gushes.

Everyone's expression lifts in admiration. Show-off, I think, irrationally.

"Now I'm interested in decomposing the East Asian body," Sophia finishes. "Exposing the blood, bones, muscle and guts that run beneath the skin. Like in every body. It's sort of an exercise in equalization through deconstruction."

"I'd love to see your work," Lauren says warmly, though the expression in her eyes is flat.

"Our cabin is basically her studio now," Carter chuckles, casting his full gaze on Sophia. "I'll be writing in the library most days. Anything for my baby." I can practically see hearts dripping from his eyes—the urge to dry heave across the table is strong. "I'm just lucky she agreed to come here. She's always traveling. Hates to be in the same place for more than a few months, isn't that right, babe?"

Sophia smiles winningly at him. I can pick out at least one imperfection in her: her two front teeth are rabbity, bucked. But my pleasure is short-lived when I realize the effect is charming. The image of pressing my tongue against the smooth enamel cuts through me. I bite down too forcefully on my fork, tasting more stainless steel than blueberry.

"Your project is so impressive," I announce, my tone as neutral as a game show host. But beneath my smile, my jaw clenches. Sophia is the worst kind of woman. The kind who rails against white men and everything they represent but goes ahead and marries one anyway, as if she should be applauded for her performative self-awareness. I decide that out of everyone at the program, I hate her the most.

II.

The next day, I face off with my laptop. At the end of the third hour, I haven't dribbled out a single sentence, though I have re-alphabetized all my files. Here, sheltered from all the noise and distractions of the modern world, I am supposed to be breathtakingly creative, astonishingly productive. And yet the unending scroll of a Word document feels akin to suffocation.

I close my laptop, slip on my jacket. Already, I feel defeated.

The rain has finally let up, softening the air into a still and mellow version of itself. I stomp through the trees, my entire body humming at high frequency, and hardly notice the greenery flashing past me, the muddy pools underfoot. At the water's edge, sludge and wood debris have collected. The smell of decay wafts towards me. I sit down on a flat rock facing the silvery lake and the aging pine trees beyond it, picturing everyone else bunkered down in their cabins, industriously toiling away. I know I look the clichéd image of a brooding, failed writer. But I am brooding. And I have failed.

"Taking a break from writing the next Great American Novel?"

I look up. It's Sophia, a large black portfolio sandwiched under her arm. She's wearing a paint-splattered smock and white canvas shoes without socks. Her messy hair is twisted into a bun and she's forgone makeup. I would have thought her beauty would diminish without it, but if anything, it's more straightforward.

She sits down beside me. I hesitate, unsure if I should exude the persona of a coolly confident writer or reveal that I am a loser who blundered his way into this program by accident, or worse, a new DEI initiative. I can't bring myself to do the latter. "Ha ha. Yeah, you caught me." Pathetic.

Sophia leans back on her arms. "So what *are* you working on?"

I hear my voice straighten out as I launch into my usual speech about technology, loneliness, mankind, etc. Afterwards, I expect the usual diplomatic response—*sounds fascinating*—but Sophia presses her lips together before a kind of braying laugh bursts past them. She smothers the sound with her hands.

"What? *What?*" I hear myself turning petulant again, just as when we first met.

She slips into the intimate cadence reserved for divulging gossip. "Okay, don't be mad? But last night, Carter and I talked about what we think everyone's writing is like. And he was sure you write political stuff, like about race. And I was like, oh, no, he *definitely* does not." Sophia pauses here, her expressive eyes greedy for my reaction.

Knowing that she and Carter talked about me both pisses me off and thrills me. But I decide to withhold the satisfaction of giving her a reaction by staying quiet.

"Oh, come on, David. I mean, I couldn't really tell from all that abstract talk, but *do* you write about race?" She cranes her head towards me, as if unwilling to let me forget she is beautiful, even if she is exasperating.

"My characters are just characters," I say after careful deliberation. I don't tell her that in the story I submitted to the program, like in every story I've ever written, all the characters are both nameless and raceless. I don't tell her that the idea of writing about my mother's kimchi stew makes me want to shove my hand in a food processor.

"Uh-*huh*." She nods again with that same knowing attitude.

"So am I only allowed to write about certain subjects and not others? I think that's a pretty backwards stance to take. Limiting, even." Saying this aloud makes my pulse quicken, as if I'm preparing for a fight.

"Obviously not!" Sophia looks irritated, then plucks some grass off of her jeans and turns reflective. "I mean, I've been there. When I was in art school, I only painted 'Western' subjects and styles. I went through different phases, like landscapes, 'American pastorals.' Then I had a pop art phase. A brutalist phase and so on. I felt like, why *couldn't* I paint what my white classmates were painting if I wanted to? Well, one of my Chinese classmates was doing a take on European 'chinoiserie.' Reclaiming it or whatever. She'd sculpt melting Ming vases and burn yoke-back chairs, stuff like that. And I remember being really annoyed by it. Like, I had this feeling she was doing it just to get the third-year fellowship at the Art Institute of Seattle. And well, she *did*."

Sophia picks up a speckled stone. "It wasn't until I started therapy that I finally recognized I had a lot of shame to unpack"—of course she's one of those people who talks incessantly about their own therapy—"I didn't want my artwork to draw attention to my identity. I didn't want people to think I was skating by on it or that I was somehow, I don't know, profiting from it."

She releases the stone back into the lake's open mouth.

"But then I realized if I gave in to other people's belief that they can access everything about me through my art, I would never be able to paint again." She pauses here, as if censoring her next thought. "Anyway, there's a difference between not writing something because you genuinely don't want to, and not writing something you *do* want to write just because you don't want to be judged for it."

"So we're damned if we do and damned if we don't."

"Fair point," Sophia laughs. "But, I mean, like—it's the difference between being an artist who creates for herself versus an artist who creates for any other reason." She eases into a self-deprecating tone. "I didn't get it until I started doing the work of unlearning all my inherited fears."

At first I'm a little startled, warmed even, by how much of herself Sophia has unzipped for me to see. But then I can't help but wonder, how much of her vulnerability is a careful curation?

She looks at me, waiting.

"I do write what I want to write." I intended to say this firmly, but it comes out sounding very unfirm.

"I also thought I was painting what I wanted to paint." She hesitates and for a moment, looks almost shy. "I'm just saying, your writing could—it could access all these complicated feelings and, like, nuanced emotions if you stop ignoring an essential part of yourself." Her voice starts to pick up confidence. "Ask, what are you writing *away* from? What would your writing look like if you wrote *towards* it?"

I contemplate the placid water. A knifelike fish darts beneath the silvery surface. If anyone else said this to me—Carter or Jacob, for instance—I would be mentally covering my ears and humming to drown out the noise. But Sophia, zealous belief beaming across her face, is . . . convincing. In another life, she would have made an excellent cult leader. I realize I don't know anyone like her. Despite her tidy self-curation, and my attempts to circumvent it, there is something ineffable about Sophia.

"Where did you grow up?" I ask her.

Sophia blinks and I wonder if, for once, she feels destabilized. I wouldn't be surprised if she's only comfortable when she grips the wheel of the conversation.

"All over."

"All over where?"

"My dad was a pastor. We moved around a lot." She throws this line away like it's nothing but it's clear she both does and does not want to talk about it further. A sudden inkling comes to me.

"Are you adopted?"

Sophia stares at me like I've just asked if she eats babies. She even shifts a little away from me. "First, it's 'Are you Korean?' and now it's 'Are you adopted?' What are you, the fucking Census?"

"Sorry, I shouldn't have asked, I just—sorry."

Sophia rolls her eyes at this. "Well, as a matter of fact, I am. Adopted. I guess that's why it took me a while to feel like I could paint . . . what I wanted." She opens her mouth but nothing further debarks.

"It's okay. You don't have to explain." Sophia glances at me, a question suspended in her eyes. "Really," I insist.

"How chivalrous of you," she snorts, then nods a moment later. "Thanks."

We sit in silence for a while and I'm surprised by how effortless it feels. But I also feel exhausted, every interaction with Sophia about as predictable as a fun house. Then she sits up and slaps me on the arm. "Hey, we were talking about *you*." Her voice is playfully teasing. I fight the urge to slap her back on the arm, just to have an excuse to touch her.

"And my repressed identity hang-ups?"

She laughs. "You know what, send me your next story. I know I'm not a writer, but I read all of Carter's stuff. And I'd love to read your work." She pauses. "I've actually been meaning to ask you if I can."

"You have?" I ask, my voice a register too hopeful.

"Yeah."

I'm too tired to inoculate myself from the truth: that in spite of myself, I still want to impress Sophia.

"Okay," I hear myself saying. "Deal."

After dinner, Jacob produces a bottle of whiskey and Carter reveals a cigarette case of pre-rolled joints. I'm wary of letting my guard down around them when I'm drunk or high, but after today's debilitating bout of impotency also known as writer's block, I willingly partake. More precisely, I think, *Fuck it*.

A couple hours later, Lauren and Sophia are listening to a soporific playlist in front of the fireplace. Jacob and Carter are playing a drinking game involving quarters and shot glasses. I'm lying on the sofa, my mouth fuzzy, as I pleasantly float somewhere between here and the ceiling, when a discordant crash jolts me up. Everyone looks over at me—a broken glass and its contents soak the rug. The glass exploded so close to me, a jagged shard lies poised across my shoe.

Lauren looks over at me, worried. "Are you okay, David?"

Ignoring this, Carter charges towards the fireplace, a frenzied energy radiating off of him. "What are you guys doing, sleeping?" he shouts. "To the lake!"

"What?" Sophia murmurs, half-awake. He picks her up, chucks her over his shoulder and is out the door. Her shrieks disperse into the night air as the others stumble after them. I stay put because a resting object wants to stay resting and I could, feasibly, rest on this sofa forever.

I'm startled when, a moment later, Jacob and Lauren are standing over me, demanding I get up. When they yank me up by my arms, I can't help but laugh, infected by their joy. I can't help but feel a little touched they came back for me.

The night air is cool and damp. The moon, a marbled white clock in the sky, her face wiped clean. The path to the lake is dimly lit, but I follow Carter's whoops and the flashes of reflected moonlight flicking off the sequins on Lauren's sweater.

Everything is brighter at the lake. The scene expands before me like an unreal photo projection, too perfect to be disturbed. Carter threatens to toss Sophia in, but sets her on the ground just before they hit the water. He strips down to his briefs and leaps in, breaking the lake's glassy surface. When he reemerges, he calls us playground-era insults for not following suit. Unsurprisingly, the insults only affect Jacob. He disrobes and jumps in—pulling Lauren after him, fully clothed. Lauren shrieks, but her happiness is as transparent as her sweater. I wouldn't be surprised if they hook up tonight.

"Come on, babe!" Carter's voice calls, distant.

I glance over at Sophia. "Are you going in?"

"Do you want me to?"

Do you want me to? Is she kidding? My mouth opens and closes, unable to formulate a single coherent thought. I don't know if my or Sophia's drunken state is to blame, but her movements are slow, so slow. Her long-sleeved shirt comes off first, revealing a thin gray cotton bra. Then her shoes. Finally her jeans. I order myself to look away, afraid I'm gawping.

Sophia starts running towards the water, when she abruptly stops to ditch her bra and underwear. I catch a glimpse of her naked form and like a man possessed, I tear off my clothes, leaving only my boxers on, and follow her in. I comprehend the water's glacial temperature and yet I hardly comprehend it at all. I wick the water from my eyes, looking around for Sophia. A suppressed laugh surfaces from behind me. I turn around.

"Hey." I search for some casual or ironic remark but all I can think about is Sophia's perfection, above and beneath the water. "What was that earlier?"

She paddles in place. "Want to race?"

Sophia's talent for avoiding conversation is both cute and irksome, like a party trick she discovered in middle school and refuses to retire.

I'm not the best swimmer in any water-based situation, much less a lake in the middle of the night without a lifeguard present, but I grin and nod, my heart rate spiking. The thought of Sophia and me—alone and far from the others—is more euphoria than I can bear. She takes a deep breath, eyes mischievous, when she abruptly yelps and disappears into the water. My lungs freeze.

"Sophia!"

Just as I'm about to dive under, something grabs ahold of my ankle and tugs. Underwater, velvety blackness envelops me. My arms and legs still. I feel helpless, but not frantic—more a curiously resigned helplessness. But then bodily instinct kicks in and I shoot back up to the surface. Sophia reemerges at the same time, both of us coughing and gasping for breath.

Carter pops up behind her. "Caught you!" he gurgles, spitting out a stream of water.

"What the fuck was that, Carter?"

"Chill out, man, she was captain of the swim team."

"I didn't mean her."

Carter looks at me, all confusion and innocence. "What are you talking about?"

Let me guess, he was captain of the drama club. "Forget it."

I'm hoping Sophia will echo my distaste, but Carter wraps his arms around her from the back and kisses the hollow of her neck. She splashes him with water and whines, *"Car-ter"* as an unconvincing reprimand. His eyes widen when he realizes she's completely naked. He spins her around to face him, kissing her hard. She seems embarrassed at first, her two hands lying flat against his chest as though to hold him at an appropriate distance but then she yelps a second time and I notice she's the same height as Carter. He's hitched her up, her legs braced around his waist. I can imagine, so clearly, what is about to happen under the cover of pitch-black water. It dawns on me that Carter isn't trying to stake his claim to his wife in front of me. He simply doesn't see me as a threat.

I swim back towards the shore, dejected, then heave myself out of the water. I forgot how much I hate the sensation of tugging on dry clothes against wet skin. The moon's brilliance is a floodlight, laying bare my loneliness. The humiliation of believing that Sophia and I were somehow aligned against her husband cuffs my ankles, dragging behind me with each step I take.

When I'm halfway to the cabins, the distant notes of Lauren's and Jacob's laughter almost out of earshot, a hand clamps around my arm and I have to stop myself from shouting bloody murder.

It's Sophia. She yanks me farther away, behind a thicket of

trees. She has on Carter's flannel button-down and nothing else. Before I can ask what she's doing, she presses the damp column of her body against mine and kisses me. The rush is so strong, I'm actually knocked backwards.

"What are you doing?" I whisper. I feel lightheaded but the next words still leave me involuntarily. "Aren't you supposed to be with your husband?" I could kick myself for how sulky I sound.

Sophia groans and lays her head against my chest. "You're so annoying."

I soften. "I know. I'm sorry."

Before I can say another word, Sophia stands up on her toes and kisses me again—quick and sweet—and runs back to the lake. I stand still for a few moments, stunned, then walk through the darkness back to my cabin, with a grin that could outshine the moon.

III.

The program director, a sinewy white-haired woman I've only seen through my laptop's screen, informs us via email that Chef Manon has unexpectedly left due to a family emergency. She emphasizes the difficulty of procuring a quality chef in the area on such short notice. Her apologies. In the meantime, we will not want for frozen entrées.

The initial good-natured cheer of strangers banding together in artistic solidarity, everyone happy to spend more time socializing than writing, has morphed into a new phase: isolated and wary. Everyone covertly squirrels their meals back to their cabins instead of congregating in the lodge. Crusted dishes jigsaw together in the sink. More alcohol is bought and consumed. Empty bottles spill out of the blue recycling bin, which no one bothers to empty, and onto the tacky floor. Maybe the weather is to blame: after a brief dry spell, the godforsaken rain has returned.

I hardly see Sophia. Here and there, I'll catch sight of her at the lodge but she's always with Carter. Once, the two of us were alone in the kitchen waiting for the coffee machine when Sophia abruptly left without a word or her decaf Colombian blend. In the presence of others, she becomes strangely combative towards me. She only acknowledges my existence at dinner to disagree with something I've said—one time arguing a nonsensical point about the difficulty of CPA exams—to the point where everyone has started making jokes about our "competitiveness."

I don't dare seek Sophia out—though I've fantasized about pelting rocks at her window like we're in the third act of a rom-com—because, one, I sincerely believe Carter would put a hit out on me if he found out and, two, I mean to honor the promise I made to myself before arriving here: no more fucking around, in the literal sense.

But honoring this promise means that, unfortunately, I have to write.

In college, Sohee always wanted to write together. She could write anywhere: at the library, a café with free Wi-Fi, on her phone in the subway. I told her I could only write alone, in absolute silence, with my phone on airplane mode. Eventually, we found a compromise where we'd write in my single's dorm room, back to back so we couldn't distract one another. I came to love the ritual, the way I could feel her concentration through every ridge of her spine. After a writing session, Sohee always wanted to trade manuscripts. Even though I offered to read her stories and give her feedback—truthfully, I was more curious to see how my stories measured up to hers—I never wanted Sohee to do the same for me. She said this was further proof I was sociopathic. I reassured her, "Maybe all writers are a little sociopathic."

The next time I face off with my laptop, I decide to listen to Sophia's advice, if only to humor her. I begin a new story about a mixed Korean and Chinese kid who grew up in Fort Lee, New Jersey, whose parents own an all-you-can-eat pan-Asian buffet. I name him David.

Shedding the protective coat of pure fiction is terrifying but also thrilling, the way I imagine exhibitionists feel. Sohee used to say my writing, with my nameless and raceless characters, was "defensive." As if the more I could contain the reader's interpretation, the less the reader could see me through my writing. She insisted I had to "surrender myself to being interpreted."

So okay, Sohee. I surrender.

Observing our low, malnourished spirits, Elijah has determined the medicine for our malaise: a field trip. A "morale-boosting" trip, to be exact. I expect to be annoyed by the idea, but I'm actually looking forward to it.

The morning of, I rack my head on how to slip Sophia my story. Since I don't have her email, I print it out and wait for her in the lodge, migrating from the sofa to the armchair to the sofa again.

Around eleven a.m. (what are she and Carter *doing* in their cabin?) the two of them amble in. When Carter is busy scavenging the fridge, I beckon Sophia over to the fireplace. She looks at me, eyes wide like, *What?* but comes over in the end.

I hand Sophia my story and she stares at it, confused. When she realizes what it is, she smiles and folds it lengthwise, then tucks it into her back pocket and returns to the kitchen without a word. I flog myself afterwards by rereading the story and finding a typo on page two.

For the "morale-boosting" trip, Elijah has decided on a local harvest festival. On the way there, in the seven-seater van, he elaborates on the festival's various activities: corn maze, pumpkin-carving competition, apple picking and bobbing, face painting. Everyone smiles stiffly at one another, hostaged tight into our seat belts. The atmosphere in the van feels politely miserable, like we're on our way to a family reunion no one wanted to attend.

With a delayed start to the day (Jacob forgot his inhaler and we had to drive back for it), we arrive in the late afternoon. The festival is quaint and homely. The low sun burnishes the warm hues of the pumpkins, scarecrows and barn. The brisk air smells of cinnamon and hops. The entire festival reminds me of an autumn-themed candle sold at the mall.

Carter appears to be in his natural habitat, zeroing in on the pumpkin-carving competition without hesitation. He grabs Sophia's hand, but she laughs and shakes her head.

"Come on," he says, "you're my good luck."

"I'll pass. But good luck anyway."

They kiss before separating. I watch as Sophia combs her hand through Carter's hair—a lovingly intimate gesture that makes me want to gut someone with the decorative scythe we just passed.

The others go off with Carter, leaving me, Sophia and Lauren. I'm wondering why Lauren didn't tag along with Jacob when she suggests the corn maze.

"I'm up for it," I say.

"Same," Sophia shrugs.

The three of us head into the maze. We walk through it without a strong sense of purpose or direction, laughing when we come into contact with a screwy-eyed scarecrow, when a cluster of face-painted kids whips past us. We talk inanely about the weather, the punishing frozen dinners, what we've been reading. Lauren walks at a slightly faster clip but slows down to ask how my writing is coming along.

"Good, actually. I just finished a new story."

"Really? I'd love to read it," Lauren says before I can finish my sentence. I catch Sophia rolling her eyes. "Maybe we could talk about it over coffee sometime?"

"Sure, yeah. Anytime."

Whether she's blushing or wind-chapped, I can't tell, but Lauren's cheeks pinken.

"I read David's newest story," Sophia says. Her tone is strange, almost proud.

Lauren smiles at her—she somehow manages the gesture with only her lips while her eyes remain flat.

"I just gave it to her this morning," I say, inexplicably needing to explain.

"Hm. Are you interested in writing, Sophia?" Lauren asks.

Sophia blows air out of her mouth and shrugs. "I'm interested in a lot of things."

"Good for you."

Sophia opens her mouth then screws it shut.

Is it my imagination or do they hate each other? Probably my imagination.

The air grows chilly as nightfall grazes the rim of the horizon. I zip up my jacket. I feel dizzy around Sophia, like I've inhaled paint thinner. Is the reason because she's frustratingly pretty today, with her long hair plaited into a thick braid and her lips painted a burgundy red? She even dressed up, in a plaid dress and dark tights tucked into boots.

No, stupid, the reason is she read your story. I stare at my shoes as I walk, too nervous to look at her, making one blind turn after another.

I'm not sure when we lose Lauren. I only know when I finally look up, Sophia is beside me and no one else.

"Where's Lauren?" I ask.

Sophia stops. "I thought she was walking next to you."

"I thought she was walking next to you."

We look briefly around—no Lauren to be seen—and continue on. I admit I feel a little unburdened, not because Lauren's company is unwelcome, but because alone with Sophia, the list of conversation topics I want to discuss increases tenfold. The types of conversations I don't know how to have—or want to have—when the other fellows are around.

"Random question—" Sophia starts before I can, her voice tentative yet falsely glib. "Do you think Lauren is pretty?"

I sense I am not supposed to answer this question honestly, or rather, that only one viable answer is at my disposal. "Why?"

Sophia ignores this and opts for an alternative tactic: "Okay. Marry, fuck, kill: me, Lauren and . . . Carter."

The answer is a no-brainer: marry Sophia, fuck Lauren, kill Carter. But I sense that this is another treacherous question, that I would be showing my hand too soon by admitting I would marry her without a second thought, and regardless, I think she'd still be pissed I would even consider sleeping with Lauren.

"Do I have to play?" I ask helplessly.

"Yes," she says, without a trace of irony.

I give in and answer her, truthfully, and wonder if I'm drunk off nonalcoholic apple cider or if all this romantic fall festivity is going to my head.

Sophia smiles and keeps walking.

"Okay, your turn," I say. "Marry, fuck, kill: me, Jacob, Carter."

"I'm not going to play," she laughs. "No way."

"That's not fair," I say (how does Sophia always reduce me to a teenage boy?) and I feel real, unmitigated annoyance fermenting inside my chest. "Why did you ask me if you don't want to play?"

Another sticky gaggle of kids flies between us, flattening us against the walls of the maze. A small girl drops her caramel-dipped apple and Sophia retrieves it for her, resulting in a photo-worthy hug. The moment has passed and I know I can't pick it up again without sounding butt-hurt.

After we walk a few places, Sophia says, "It was good, by the way."

"What?"

"Your story. It was really good." She pauses. "Why do you look shocked? You gave it to me."

"You're serious?" My first instinct is, of course, to inject doubt.

"Are you always this surprised whenever someone compliments your work?"

"I didn't know—I mean I wasn't sure about the story—about how it came off." I clear my throat. "Since it was a kind of experiment."

I never thought my life was important enough to merit its own fictionalization. Autofiction is new terrain for me. I find myself confiding in Sophia that I'm not equipped with knowledge the other fellows came preassembled with, they're all leaps and bounds ahead of me while I'm starting the race from the penalty box. I tell her I think I only got into the program to fulfill a diversity quota.

"A starving artist trapped in the body of a corporate accountant," she says, pulling a "poor you" face and patting my back.

I'm not sure what to make of this—is she mocking me?—when her voice turns hesitant. I've noticed it only turns hesitant when she's about to share something that can't be boiled down to an artist's statement.

"I know how you feel. 'Imposter syndrome,'" she says, and I almost don't believe her. Five minutes with Sophia and you'd think she'd never felt insecure a day in her life.

"You don't show it."

"Haven't you heard: 'fake it 'til you make it'?"

We laugh at this and walk in silence for a while. "Well, how was it?" she continues. "Writing 'autofiction'?"

I smile at her.

She crosses her arms and dips her chin.

"Don't say 'I told you so,'" I groan.

"I told you so!" She slaps my sleeve, lightly. A flint of electricity shoots down my forearm and straight to my groin. "But in all seriousness, I thought the story was really moving. The part when his friends find out he works at the restaurant was heartbreaking, actually."

My ears burn, a maddening affect. Why is my body already convinced? Sophia's not a writer—she could very well be literature-illiterate. Or maybe she just has a kink for always being in the right. But as much as I try to ward off her praise, I feel my lips quivering with the force of a suppressed smile.

"I did have a note, though," Sophia continues. Right. Of course.

She appraises my expression before continuing. "David admits he likes when people assume he's full Korean. I thought that was really interesting. Like, is he ashamed of his Chinese side? And how does his dad feel about that?"

An anxious tingle works its way up the back of my neck—where is she going with this?

"And, well, if he is, I just didn't understand why." She checks my expression again, then transitions to a self-aware joking tone. "Maybe it's a well-known thing in 'the community,' but you know, I have white parents."

I think of telling Sophia that she's right. That no one ever thought I was anything but Chinese. That I was so knowable by virtue of my face. Everyone felt they had a right to the story behind it and when I didn't share it, they went ahead and read it anyway. So this was my poor device, my measly attempt at showing them up and proving, no, you can't know me, I'm as unreadable as you are: I'm not Chinese. Which was true. Partially.

But I don't know how to articulate this so I just say, "Right. Got it. Thanks."

"Oh god, you're so annoyed. I can tell."

"No, it's a good note. Really." I can sense Sophia's curiosity hasn't lessened one ounce. I change the subject before she can dig into a deeper line of questioning. "So I guess you're never going to tell me if you're Korean?"

"Well, that was when I didn't know you. Now we're friends."

"And?"

"And what?" Sophia grins and dashes off. I almost shout after her to stop, I refuse to play these adolescent games, this is no longer cute, it's downright obnoxious, but in the end—as she must have expected—I chase after her. She's a fast runner. We turn a corner, fly down a long stretch, round another corner, and find ourselves in a dead end facing an oversized stack of hay bales. We both catch our breath for a moment.

"Why do you always do that?" I ask.

"Do what?"

"You know, avoid . . . talking." I glance around the maze's hedges, unable to meet Sophia's gaze.

"You're the one avoiding me," she counters. "Every time I see you at the lodge, you won't even look at me."

I can't look at her. I think I'm falling in love with her. If I look at her, she'll know. "What? No, I'm not." I'm still fixating on the ground when her boots come into view. Her citrusy, honeyed perfume encircles us. I finally look at her. Even her collarbones are exquisite. Everything about her is so exquisite, it's unbearable.

"Well, stop," she says.

"Stop what?"

"Avoiding me."

I'm contemplating what to say, how to sidestep the trap of earnestness because earnestness is a fool's game—just wrap yourself in so many layers of irony, David, that you can never be accused of anything by anyone—when she pulls me behind the bales of hay and kisses me.

Again, I'm knocked backwards by the intensity of it. My body isn't giving my head any time to think. My tongue is in her mouth and she moans, kissing me more fiercely, then presses herself against me and we drop to the ground. I pull her dress off her shoulders for her breast and she moans again, louder. Her nipple is hard and warm between my fingers, between my lips. I still can't comprehend what's happening when she unbuckles my belt and unzips my jeans. When I hesitate, she tells me she's on the pill.

CASUALTIES OF ART

This is a bad idea flits across my field of consciousness immediately followed by *But it would make a great story* and it's as if my hands have become autonomous extensions of myself and before I know it, I am pushing aside her dress and yanking down her tights, her underwear.

Afterwards, I'm in a daze, drugged.

"I wasn't sure—I wasn't sure if you liked me," I sputter as I sit up.

"Maybe I don't," Sophia says, smiling. She rearranges her clothes, brushes herself off and smooths her braid. Her lipstick hasn't moved a fraction of an inch.

An excess of questions piles up in me—Should I tell her I'm falling in love with her? What does this mean for her marriage? How will we break the news to Carter? He'll have to leave the residency, naturally, seeing Sophia and I together would be too painful—

"Well," she says, interrupting the happy sequence playing in my mind, "people are probably wondering where we are."

With a single sentence, the conversation is shelved. She's playing it cool, ergo I must play it cool.

"Oh. Right."

"I want to try one of those cinnamon rolls," she says offhandedly, like it's any other day. "Aren't they famous or something?"

I watch as she drifts towards the glow of the lantern lights and the soft acoustics of laughter, the two of us buttoned back up into our separate bodies.

On the ride home, Elijah sings off-key musical numbers to himself as he drives. Lauren has claimed the passenger seat, Carter and Sophia take up the middle row, leaving Jacob and me alone in the back. All the fellows are asleep except for us.

"You have a good night?" Jacob asks, jostling me in the ribs. He flips his pocketknife open and shut, open and shut. Usually, this habit of his makes my eye twitch but tonight, I don't care.

"Yeah, I did." Even though my head is still in a Sophia-shaped cloud, I force myself to ask what he'd clearly hoped I'd ask all along. "What about you?"

He smirks like a teenage boy on prom night and nods at Lauren.

I look askance at him. "Did you guys fuck in the corn maze?" And here I was thinking Sophia and I had been original.

"What?" He blinks, confused. "No, we kissed." Jacob sounds more clear-eyed, less nasally, and I realize it's the first time I've heard the pretentious lilt in his voice ebb away. "I mean, we've kissed before. Tonight was just the first time we were both sober." He pauses, flips the knife again. "But I can't tell if she likes me or if she's . . . bored out here and I'm, you know, conveniently here, too."

Jacob's choice to confide in me and not Carter with matters of the heart should endear him to me. But for whatever reason, I find myself resisting. I'm beginning to understand that my dislike of Jacob has little to do with him and is instead rooted in the fact that in another life, had I been born with the means to attend a six-figure-price-tag liberal arts college where I, too, could major in French Critical Theory and study abroad in Paris, I would have turned out exactly like him. Another part of my dislike: Jacob's desire for validation is so obvious, it rolls off of him in pungent waves. The way I worry my own desire does.

Jacob isn't turning out to be anything like the character I imagined for him and I can't help but feel disappointed. I guess the truth is I don't like giving people a chance to disprove me. I'd rather they stay firmly within the boundaries I've drawn for them, like *Sims* characters.

"Lauren seems to know what she wants," I finally say. "I don't think she'd do something just for the sake of doing it."

Jacob takes this in, nods. "So, you ever think about it?"

"About what?"

He halves his volume to a whisper. "You know. Lauren."

Why is this the second time tonight someone has asked me about her? I glance at Lauren's sleeping face, barely visible in the right-hand side mirror. I don't find her features especially attractive or unattractive. And yet, at the same time, I wouldn't *mind* hooking up with Lauren. I'd almost see it as a challenge. In all my years of dating, I've never pursued a white woman. Unlike some of my friends who lusted over the blond actresses and models of the world, I refused to be so predictable. At least that's what I told myself. I can't untangle if this preemptive maneuver was a result of assuming they'd have no interest in me and therefore beating them all to the punch by never putting myself in a position to face rejection.

I clock Jacob staring at me, anxious at the length of my silence. He flips his Boy Scout toy into the air again and it lands knife-down in the seat, a hairline from my leg. "Whoops," he says.

I unslouch and rearrange my posture. "No, I haven't."

We ride the rest of the way back in silence.

IV.

The next week is my own personal inferno. Chef Manon has returned, thank the never-eating-frozen-pizza-again gods, but this means communal dinners are back, too. Every night, I have to somehow keep my food from reentering my esophagus while watching Sophia and Carter share custody of the same dessert spoon because apparently once you're married, you can't eat with your *own* dessert spoon, *no*.

On Wednesday night, we played charades, where Sophia and Carter teamed up and annihilated everyone. Watching them play together was the first time their compatibility evinced itself—they're both attention whores, wildly competitive and cannot stand losing—knowledge I would have gladly traded for ignorance. After they won the final round and hollered, "In your face!" at everyone, the ghosts of their high school selves seemed to make an appearance: he the star quarterback, she the head cheerleader. The image was so painfully clear, I was tempted to check its veracity.

Every time we cross paths in the lodge, I keep waiting for Sophia to talk to me or shoot me a signal—I'd take a blank paper airplane—but she just says, "Hey, David," and comments about the weather like I'm the goddamn mailman. For the first time in my life, I know how it feels to physically *pine* for someone.

On Sunday, exactly a week since the night of the maze, I'm trying to make my way through an overcooked lamb chop when Carter twines his hand around Sophia's waist and engages in foreplay with her hair, slipping and looping the long strands through his fingers. It's not the first time he's done it but witnessing this display of nuptial bliss for the seventh night in a row is tantamount to, no exaggeration, UN treaty–breaking torture. Not helping is tonight's Greek-inspired dinner because guess who honeymooned in Greece and now guess who won't shut up about all the "fantastic" food they ate and the "fantastic" little villages they

CASUALTIES OF ART

explored. If I hear Carter say "fantastic" one more time, I am going to reach across the table and stick my fork in him.

I glance at Sophia, quietly picking at her substitute falafel. She won't look up at me.

"Hey, fun idea," I begin, cutting my lamb so hard you can hear the knife assault the plate, "why don't we play 'Never have I ever'?"

"Oh my god, I haven't played that since college," Lauren says, practically choking on her wine in excitement.

"I've actually never played," Jacob announces with a hint of pride. Right. In college, he probably played "Who can name the most facts about the Roman empire?" for shits and giggles.

"Well, it seems this is your lucky day, Jacob," I smile. "I'll go first." I splay both my palms out, pretending to think. "Hm. Oh, I know. Never have I ever cheated on anyone."

A chorus of "Ooohs" sweeps around the table but no one folds a finger.

Without skipping a beat, Lauren goes next. "Never have I ever had a threesome," she blushes.

When it's Carter's turn, he pipes up, "Never have I ever committed a felony."

But I don't notice what fingers are surviving or capitulating because everyone else in the room has receded into darkness. I am staring straight at Sophia and she is staring straight back at me.

After dinner, I catch Carter fixing himself a drink, alone, and though I have never felt any inclination to spend time with him, I ask if he wants company. I find myself preternaturally curious about him, purely because he has access to Sophia, all of her, and I want to know why. I want to understand what, beyond his puppyish good looks, deems him worthy of bearing the title of Sophia's husband because surely that is not enough of a reason to legally, institutionally and financially tether yourself to a man.

"Yeah, of course," he says, nonplussed.

We shepherd our drinks to the patio. The still night air does little to quiet the racket in my chest.

"So how's writing?" Carter asks.

"I'm trying out 'autofiction,'" I laugh, hoping some light self-disparagement will grease his defenses.

"Yeah, Sophia mentioned it to me—sounds like it's going well."

I feel as blindsided as the time a rogue truck ran me off the highway, but I just nod and take a burning sip of my drink. "How about you?" I've spoken briefly with Lauren and Jacob about their projects, but I've purposefully kept myself ignorant of Carter's.

He seems to relax within this familiar conversational terrain and tells me he's working on a novel about two wheat farm boys in North Dakota, the younger of which suffers abuse from his negligent single mom, while the older acts as his de facto father.

He's attempting to write blue-collar poverty porn? Jesus, no wonder he got into the program.

"Sounds harrowing. In the best way, I mean."

Carter takes this in and thanks me, doesn't seem to doubt it. And then I can't help myself—I want him to doubt it. "What inspired you to write it?"

Carter clears his drink, his gaze elliptic. "Why do any of us write anything, right?"

"Right." I hear the subtext behind his words loud and clear: he doesn't want to tell me. And I don't mind. I don't actually want to know about his likes and dislikes, his family, his—god forbid—

childhood. The more Carter talks, the more his blanks are colored in. This was a mistake, I think.

"'Night," he says, and pauses just before he heads back inside. A wordless beat hangs between us as we consider each other. I wonder if Carter is more perceptive than I gave him credit for.

Twelve hours later, Sophia graces the doorstep of my cabin with the same mien as the Grim Reaper.

"To what do I owe the pleasure?" I ask.

"Oh, shut up." She steps inside and looks around, then locks the door behind her.

"Where's Carter?"

"The library."

"Aw, such a good little husband."

Whatever Sophia bottled up busts open now. "What the fuck were you doing last night?"

I can't help but play dumb. "What was *I* doing? I was playing a game known for creating intimacy amongst friends. What were *you* doing?"

"You are a child," she groans. "I mean it, you have the emotional bandwidth of a child. Do you know what last night was? It was you throwing a *tantrum*."

I peer at her more closely: she looks stressed, her makeup slept-in and smudged.

Fuck. This isn't what I wanted—I don't actually know what I was expecting pulling my little stunt. "I'm sorry, Sophia." She looks startled by my sincerity. In any other situation, I would shut up before risking more vulnerability but this is Sophia—beautiful, confusing-the-fuck-out-of-me Sophia. I pull her into my arms, breathe in her scent of honey and turpentine. We kiss, but it feels brief and perfunctory, and behind it still lingers Sophia's anger.

I confess that I've been miserable. That seeing her and Carter together feels like cruel and unusual punishment. That I didn't mean to put her on the spot, it just happened. Sophia listens to me then gingerly pats my back and untangles herself from my arms. In that single gesture, I feel the room drop ten degrees in temperature.

"Listen, David, um—I know we haven't talked about what happened. And I don't want you to think I—regret—what happened." Even Sophia's voice has turned deliberately oblivious, as if hoping to stop the conversation's bleeding edges. She glances quickly at me as she tucks her hair behind her ears. "But I am married. And well, yeah."

"'And well, yeah'? That's all you have to say?"

She sighs. "What do you want me to say? We did something we shouldn't have—I'm not blaming you, my marriage is not your responsibility—but now I have to live with it." She lifts and drops her shoulders. "If and when I tell Carter, it will be my choice."

Hope flies up in me. "Tell Carter—you mean—to leave him?"

She looks strangely, almost bemusedly, at me. "You want me to leave my husband?"

"Yes! I don't even understand why you're with him. He's the prototypical, privileged, entitled WASP!" Until the words flee from my mouth, I don't realize how long they've been itching to.

Sophia looks both baffled and outraged. "'WASP'? Whoever said he was a WASP?"

A vague, pestering voice tells me to save myself while I still can. I ignore it. "How—how can you stand him? Especially with all your artwork being about—" I drop this hazardous line of thought. "Listen, I'm not blaming you. I'm sure Carter doesn't show every side of himself to you. You're as much a victim in this situation as I am—" I hold Sophia's gaze, but what looks back is so chastising, I don't dare finish my thought.

"Did you just call me a *victim?*"

I feel I've shrunk several feet. "What? No—"

A serrated laugh escapes her. "Do not fucking talk down to me, David. You walk around here all boo-hoo, 'It's me against the world, oh, I don't know anything about literature, I'm the biggest victim who's ever lived, everyone's out to get me'—yeah? But what has anyone here actually done to you?" She pauses and I think she wants me to answer, but it turns out she just needed to catch her breath. "Don't you fucking put that on me. We are not the same. Okay?"

I stutter an "Okay" back, my mouth agreeing before my brain can play catch-up.

When Sophia speaks again, her voice is bone-weary. "David, I hardly know you. I mean, you hardly know *me*. This isn't even— it's not the first time I've fucked up." She pauses and considers me like she's trying to puzzle something out for herself. "The last guy was Korean, too."

The room shifts on its axis. I place my hand against the wall, unsteady despite being sober. "The last guy?" I ask reluctantly, because I'm not sure I want to know more.

She wanders over to my desk and flicks her nail against the back of the chair. "My therapist says I have a tendency to 'self-sabotage'—" She brakes, then reverses into sarcasm. "And my friends say I just want to 'fuck away the guilt' over marrying someone like Carter."

"So why did you marry him?"

"David." She shoots me a you-can't-be-serious look. "I refuse to get into this with you."

"Okay, fine."

"Fine."

We stay like this for a while, each of us stubbornly bridled. Then a few seconds later, as if she's lost control over her vocal cords, Sophia starts talking. "I met him at a friend's bachelorette party in Cancun. Another friend—well, ex-friend—had her eye on him the whole time. Mackenzie. She couldn't believe he was interested in me and not her. I know, what a bitch, right? So just to spite her, I gave him my number. Mackenzie was so convinced he'd lose interest in me after we slept together and I guess I wanted to prove to her that I could date him if I wanted to. And then, well, things just kept . . . progressing. We started seeing each other and before I knew it, two years had passed."

My jaw tightens—is she actually absolving herself of the fact that she chose to date Carter? As if she's in an arranged marriage?

Sophia picks up a pen on my desk, clicks it, unclicks it. "I didn't understand why Carter wanted to marry me instead of someone like Mackenzie. It's like I have to maintain the upper hand all the time. Even though he's never hurt me, I know he adores me and he's so fucking good, sometimes it makes me hate him. Like I want to punish him for loving me. Isn't that sick?"

I can't trust what I'm hearing. Sure, Carter publicly fawns over Sophia, but I've always assumed his toxic alpha male tendencies are unleashed in private. "What do you mean 'good'?" I ask weakly.

Sophia draws a deep breath, exorcises it. "You think there's more to Carter, but what you see is what you get. He doesn't have, I don't know, ulterior motives when he's nice or when he's an ass.

Like, some people aren't very complex because the world never asked them to be. You know?"

I shake my head.

"Right." She clears her throat, then revises her tone again, as if she's reading cue cards behind my head. "Anyway, you think you understand me, but you don't. You've got some idealized version of me in your head when the truth is I'm sick. I'm a compulsive cheater and a liar." She laughs, a short and ugly explosive. "My therapist really lucked out, didn't she?"

"Don't say that." I collect Sophia's hands in mine. I want to tell her to stop this tedious self-deprecation, this masochistic self-therapization, and be real with me, I just need her to lay down whatever weapon she smuggled into this room and *be real with me.* Instead I say, "Sophia, I love you." The moment the words exit my mouth, I'm not sure I mean them, but I could sense her closing the door to me and I desperately needed to throw out an obstacle to keep it from slamming permanently shut.

Sophia stares at me, her mouth twitching like she doesn't know whether to laugh or cry. She passes me back my hands and slips on an irritatingly soft cardigan-of-a-voice. "David, I think this was a bad idea."

"No, you don't mean that—"

"David!" she half shouts. For a split second, she looks afraid of me. Then she seems to choose her words very carefully. "You do not know what I mean. You're acting like . . . I mean, have you even seriously thought about what you're suggesting? I live across the fucking country." I blink at her. "Are you planning to move to Seattle? Right, I didn't think so. You're not *thinking*, you're *romanticizing*. It's like you don't live in reality—" She stops and readjusts. Studies me. "I think you need . . . rest."

I back away from her. "No. Don't—don't talk to me in that voice."

"What? What are you talking about?" She's grown so exasperated with me, she doesn't even bother camouflaging it.

I know that voice. Right before we broke up, Sohee defaulted to it every time we argued, as if she was my nurse and I was her patient in need of a sedative injection. My chest detonates, collapses in on itself. This is what I get for breaking my rules. I had implemented them for a reason. Why had I made an exception for Sophia?

"It's cool." I walk to the door and open it for her. "Forget everything I said. I was just joking. Ha ha. Got you."

I'm on the floor, my back against my bed, nuzzling a bottle of Japanese whiskey I lifted from the kitchen pantry. Probably costs a lot of money, probably belongs to Jacob—not that I care. I've already drunk a quarter of it. I stare at the ceiling fan as a repetitive bass-like beat tickles the outer fringes of my consciousness. I don't remember putting on music. Or maybe someone's throwing a rager next door. Then I hear a faint "David?" and realize someone's knocking on the door.

"Who is it?" I singsong.

"Lauren."

"Well, come on in, the door's open!"

I smile up at Lauren from the floor and brandish the bottle of whiskey in greeting. She laughs nervously, then looks around, one arm hooked around her middle. Her other arm balances a paper plate covered in foil. "I just wanted to bring you dinner." She sets the plate down on my desk.

"Thanks, Lauren, that's really thoughtful of you," I say, and mean it. "Sorry I skipped dinner . . . I, um, wasn't feeling well."

She sits cross-legged across from me, her eyes crinkling in concern. "Should you be drinking?"

"Oh, I'm fine now." I hold out the bottle.

She takes a long swig, doesn't even flinch. I've never noticed Lauren has lovely eyes: shining hazel pools. She's always been kind to me. A humanitarian, selfless, non-confusing person. I never did follow up on getting that coffee with her.

"Anyway, I hope you feel better—" she says, starting to stand up.

"Wait, don't go."

She looks at me too quickly, too hopefully.

"Come here." I cup my hand around her neck and kiss her. Falling into Lauren is like falling into a safety blanket. Motherly, after all.

But ten minutes later, when we're naked and interlocked, she is anything but. She hitches her legs up with her knees beside her ears, bites me on the shoulder, sucks on my fingers, licks her own nipples. She talks dirty to me the entire time, as consistent and on cue as a porn star. When I come, she pretends to, too. She howls my name so loudly, I'm tempted to tell her to keep it down. But even in my intoxicated state, at one point I paused to marvel at her skin against mine, her pale rosiness as unfamiliar to me as I am to her, swiftly followed by shame for marveling at something so unremarkable.

Lauren after sex is schoolgirlish. She lies on her side next to me, the sheets tucked loosely around her chest. She's also uncharacteristically talkative. She's already overshared, albeit uninterestingly, about growing up in Skokie, Illinois, in a two-parent middle-class household, with three older brothers and two Labradors.

"I mean, sometimes I hate that I had such a boring, ordinary childhood. Not like you." She nuzzles her nose against mine and smiles dreamily.

"Like me?" I suppress a whiskey burp.

"Yes! I would give anything to have the kind of experiences you've had." She sits up and no amount of feminist reading can stop my eyes from wandering down to her bare chest. "Growing up in an immigrant family, working in a restaurant as a kid, having to translate when the *police* showed up." She stares at me like I'm a mouthwatering steak. "You're so lucky, David."

I don't recall mentioning my story was autofiction. Sending Lauren my writing was a mistake. I laugh, more nervously than I intended. "How could I be lucky?"

"Well, because that kind of writing is so *in* right now. It's what all the publishers are looking for! Hey, you should submit it to this upcoming fiction contest for diverse writers—"

My head feels like a blacksmith has set up shop in it. "What do you mean by 'it'?" I interrupt her.

"You know . . . trauma."

I chew over this. "Hey, you could always become a heroin junkie for a couple weeks. Or kill someone in a car crash. Voilà— instant trauma!"

Lauren stares at me in dismay.

"Sorry—joke." Not really. I think I'm going to throw up.

"I mean, no one's interested in hearing sad white girl stories anymore," she says, gazing meaningfully at me.

I recognize this as my cue to disagree. "What? No. *No.* It's all about"—my head keeps skipping on its own record, I'm still far too drunk to hold a coherent conversation—"how you write it. You have a unique . . . point of view?"

Lauren sighs and moves closer to me. "Anyway, tell me more about you."

I pretend to stretch, freeing my arm from around her. "What do you want to know?"

"Everything! I mean, I know a little about you, but there's still much I don't understand." Lauren pulls away and cocks her head at me. "You're actually very hard to read. Like a closed book."

A passage comes to me, oft-read and underlined, and I find myself quoting parts of it aloud: "'You are surreptitious, B+ student of life . . . illegal alien, emotional alien . . .'"

Lauren laughs a little hesitantly. "What?"

"It's from *Native Speaker*. By Chang-rae Lee." What I don't tell her: the quote is taken from the note written by Henry Park's white wife, when she left him and took inventory of all his flaws, as succinct and ruthless as a surgeon's incision. After reading that passage, I became a little obsessed with it, as if it were a prophecy written for me and only me.

"I'm not familiar with her—is she a Chinese writer?"

In that moment, I am terribly sober. "I don't feel good." Lauren looks up at me, anxious. "From the alcohol," I hastily explain. "I should, um . . . probably chug some water and hug the toilet."

"Do you need aspirin?" she asks, laying a hand against my forehead.

I slowly extricate myself from the bed. "No, no, I don't want you to see me covered in vomit. I've got a whole hangover kit—aspirin and everything," I lie, flashing her my best everything-is-under-control smile.

"Oh my god, David, you're bleeding." I follow Lauren's stare:

sure enough, the faintest trace of blood drips from two incisions on my right shoulder. "This is so embarrassing." Lauren covers her eyes with her hands. "Does it hurt?"

"This? I've had shaving accidents worse than this." I dab the spots away with the edge of the bedsheet. "I'm fine, really." I pause. "Next time, I'll bite you. Deal?"

Fuck me.

"Okay," she smiles and climbs out of bed. She gets dressed so self-consciously, sucking in her stomach as she bends over to slip back on her underwear, one leg wobbling, my heart nearly breaks in two.

I walk Lauren to the door and we kiss again. She laces her hands around my neck and lingers. "This was—this was really fun."

"Yeah, we'll, um, have to do it again," I say, then curse myself. Why the hell did I say that, especially after the "Next time, I'll bite you" thing? I can't lead her on. That would make me an asshole. And I'm not a fucking asshole.

At the door, I watch as Lauren heads to her cabin. She turns around and waves; I smile and wave back. Then, when I blink, I catch sight of a pale, black-haired figure floating towards her. I rub my eyes: it's Sophia.

Is the universe bent on giving me an early heart attack?

I watch as she and Lauren pause beside one another, their mouths moving almost imperceptibly in the dark, before Sophia walks straight towards me. When I see the look on her face, I want to close the door and double bolt it. But then she's in front of me, shaking her head in one excruciatingly slow motion, her arms crossed. "You're unbelievable." Her eyes scan the unmade bed behind me and I remember I'm only wearing boxers and a robe. Shit.

"Did you guys just fuck?" She rips the words from out between her teeth.

"What—no—why would you—" I falter. Oh, what's the point of lying to Sophia. Beautiful, confusing-the-fuck-out-of-me Sophia. "I mean, maybe? I mean, yes." I step closer to her. Under the veil of moonlight, her beauty is inexcusable. I reach out to touch her cheek. "But, Sophia—I didn't mean to—I was drunk—and depressed—I thought you hated me—"

She laughs and jerks away from me. "Jesus fucking Christ." She starts to walk off, then turns around to add, "I came over because I felt bad."

"You felt bad?" I ask, hopeful again despite all odds.

"I don't know why," she snaps. "I don't even know why I—" She looks like she wants to say more but then she screws up her mouth in that way she does when she changes her mind.

"You don't even know what, Sophia? What?" To my chagrin, she keeps her sentence to herself. "Come inside," I plead. I wonder if I should mention that, yes, while sleeping with Lauren was unwise on my part, between the two of us, Sophia is the one who is married. But I don't think now is a good time.

She pins me with a scornful look that makes me feel more naked than I already am. "It's so obvious now."

"What is?"

"Your whole sad boy writer act. Why you do it." She pauses. "I can't believe I fell for such a cliché."

I look down at myself as her words penetrate through the fog of my inebriation. Her perception of myself makes me feel nauseous and indignant all at once. How dare Sophia see me that way? I didn't sign off on it. I feel like I've been presented with an evidentiary photo of myself I didn't know existed and I don't like it.

Before I can convince her I'm not who she thinks I am, she's halfway across the clearing.

"Sophia," I whisper loudly, too afraid to yell. "Sophia, come back, please. I'm sorry!" I head after her just as the light in Lauren's neighboring cabin blinks on. Shit.

I stumble back into my room. The bottle of whiskey greets me, open-armed and nonjudgmental. "Hello, old friend."

V.

The next morning, I wake up inexplicably hangover-free, as bright-eyed and bushy-tailed as the squirrels courting each other outside my window. I shower, inhale some cereal and brush my teeth. Within twenty minutes, I'm out the door. I check my watch: not yet five a.m.

Outside Carter and Sophia's cabin, I tap on the window. If Carter appears, I'll concoct some kind of emergency excuse but I don't even let myself entertain the specifics.

Come on, Sophia, I think. Wake up.

I'm about to turn around when the cabin door creaks open. I stay rooted by the window, praying the figure rounding the corner will be the one I want to see.

"What the fuck are you doing?" Sophia hisses. She snatches at my wrist and drags me away from the cabin, then lets go. In her rumpled Beavis and Butt-Head T-shirt and cotton shorts, she looks sleep-deprived but sexy, in a stayed-up-all-night-at-the-rock-show kind of way.

We stare at each other and Sophia suddenly pushes me on the shoulders, sending me backwards a few steps. She does it again, harder, and I can feel all her rage and exhaustion through her fingertips. I can taste it: like iron.

"That was fair. Want to go for round three?"

"I hate you." She scowls but I can see the effort she's putting into it.

"I know—that's why you like me." When she groans without refuting this, my heart sings. "Come on, I want to show you something."

I head towards the driveway where Elijah's van is parked. At first I don't hear Sophia's footsteps following after me and I panic. But then she's by my side, asking me if I have any idea what time it is. Instead of answering the rhetorical question, I unlock the passenger side of the van.

"How'd you get Elijah's keys?" she asks suspiciously.

"He leaves a spare in the lodge."

She sighs as I open the passenger door for her, so deeply I'm impressed her slight frame can harness that much air, then climbs in and slams the door. As I back out of the driveway, she crosses her arms and asks where we're going.

"You'll see." An empty answer but she doesn't ask again.

After a half hour on the highway, I stop at a gas station. We take turns visiting the mercifully clean bathroom, then collect armfuls of snacks: donut holes, fountain soda, ranch-flavored chips, candy bars. The testy and skeptical Sophia from earlier is nowhere to be seen. When I try to apologize again about Lauren, explain that it was nothing more than a lapse in judgment—very heartbroken, under-the-influence-of-80-proof-whiskey judgment—she waves me off, says she's already forgotten. That's when I remember: Sophia said she has a habit of self-sabotaging.

After another twenty minutes on the road, I spot the desired turnoff. I had looked it up a few weeks ago, jotting down a mental note to myself to check it out before the program concluded, but hadn't memorized the exact directions. The appearance of a sign announcing our destination is a relief. I look over to see if Sophia has noticed, but she's busy contemplating the box of donut holes. She holds out a cinnamon-flavored one to me, her fingertips grazing my lips, and I have a picture of us meeting in an alternate timeline when we were younger, maybe in college, and this is our first overnight trip together.

Down an empty road effusive with wildflowers, a left, a right, and then we're at an open clearing hemmed in by a copse of trees, shuddering with morning sunlight. I think Sophia knows where we're going by now, but she still gasps when she sees the surprise: a small, perfect waterfall plunging into a small, perfect natural pool. The color is shockingly aqua, artificial in its intensity. We both wordlessly sit down before the milky froth, the rare gem of the water's surface.

I look over at Sophia, just content to be in her presence, when she abruptly jumps up. "Want to skinny-dip?" she asks, her voice lightly teasing.

I look at her, thrown off. "What? No."

"Let's a play game, then."

I stare at her.

"Oh, I know, let's scream at the top of our lungs!"

". . . You want to reenact *Garden State*?"

Sophia stops mid-walk, her expression closed off. "What are you talking about?"

And suddenly the disparate facets of Sophia rearrange themselves like an optical illusion, shifting from disorder to order within the blink of an eye. I stand up, brush off my jeans. "I'm talking about how you want to be a Manic Pixie Dream Girl." I'm half hoping Sophia will be impressed I know the terminology (I don't mention it was Sohee who taught it to me, along with the Bechdel test).

"Oh, shut up, David. Stop acting like you know everything." Sophia's voice is devoid of all mischievousness now.

"Hey, I'm just playing along." I take a step towards her. "What was it you said last night? I have a 'sad boy writer act.'"

She rolls her eyes, strikes a crossed-arm pose. I roll my eyes, too, strike the same pose. Then I can't help but laugh at the two of us, at this absolute repulsion to be seen by the other that lives alongside this desperate desire to be seen.

Sophia starts laughing, too. When we're both somewhat recovered, she faces the waterfall again. "Why did you want to bring me out here?"

I don't know or maybe I don't remember. What I want now is to kiss her, but I sit down on the blanket I brought and take out my two notebooks. I pass the blank one to her. "In case you want to draw." She arches an eyebrow, but accepts it and sits beside me.

The din of the waterfall is both deathly quiet and deafening. The anomaly of the moment feels like we've slipped through some back door in the fabric of space, cut out a little corner just for us. For the first time in I don't know how long, I feel happy.

A while later, I look over at Sophia's drawing: two men sitting across from each other in wooden chairs, staring directly at one another. Short black hair, set jaws, straight brows. The one on the left clenches his fists; the one on the right splays his hands in his lap, palms to the skies. They're me, I realize. They're both me. The illustrated Davids look confident and clear-eyed. Their faces are drawn with strokes of—dare I say?—tenderness. I've never experienced this before—my notion of myself wrested away from me and interpreted through someone else's eyes.

Sophia looks up. "Hey, no peeking." She closes the notebook and reaches for mine. "What are you writing?"

"Nothing. Observations." I keep the notebook just out of her grasp. She narrows her eyes at me and I give in. "I started a new autofiction story."

She jiggles her cup of fountain soda, takes a sip. "Go on."

I tell her it's about two writers, David and Sophia, who meet at an artists' colony. Sophia is married. David makes poor decisions. Both are bad at love. Both have exes who describe them as red flags.

To my surprise, writing autofiction has been addictive, accompanied by addiction's trademark attributes: Guilt and Shame. Each time I continue the story (pouring my words down Sophia's throat, pinning *her* to a corkboard, tweaking my real-time behavior to various degrees), I feel as if I've succumbed to a weakness I didn't know I had. Autofiction writer David is a cannibal: eager to digest and regurgitate every relationship, every interaction, every waking moment.

When I finish talking, Sophia just stares at me. "You better not publish it anywhere," she finally says.

I cross my heart, Scout's honor, then gesture at her sketch. "You better not—what's the word for publishing art?"

She shoves her shoulder against mine.

"You're really good," I continue. Truthfully, I'm blown away by this small sketch. Tiny crosshatches render remarkably realistic shadow and depth, while her proportions are spot-on without having measured a thing. Her talent is undeniable. I see it living inside her very hands. That's not hours of work transformed into the facade of talent, I think to myself. That's talent you're born with. An unwelcome visitor taps me on the shoulder: envy. For once, I refuse to engage with it. "Can I have it when you're done?"

She shakes her head. "I don't really think art belongs to one person. I think it should belong to everyone. Cheesy as fuck, I know, but I'm allowed to say at least one cheesy thing a day, okay?"

"Okay," I smile.

Sophia looks up at me. "Thanks . . . for . . . all of this. It's actually really nice." She pulls up her knees and reposes her chin in the valley between them. We watch a squirrel ambush a tree, stop to survey us, then continue on its way. "You know, I have a painting that's going to be shown. Tomorrow."

"What?" I turn towards her. "Where?"

"A gallery in Tribeca."

A crossfire of words ricochet in my mouth—She has to go—What is she doing sitting here—I'll drive her to the city right now, Elijah's van be damned—

Sophia shrugs. "It'll be there for eight months, I can go later. And anyway, I told Carter I'd stay here with him for emotional support. You wouldn't guess it, but he really, really hates being alone. He's actually kind of codependent." With the mention of her husband, an awkward breach enters the conversation. I decide the only thing to do is talk around it as if it's not there.

"I assume there's an opening reception and everything?"

Sophia nods.

I find myself standing up, buoyed with the radiant morning light. "Let's go." Sophia stands up, too, stumbling a little. "Me and you, let's go." She searches my face as I keep at it. "I don't think you'll want to miss this. Come on, you owe it to your art."

Maybe my resolve is infectious, because her expression veers tentatively excited. "I mean—it *would* be cool," she admits.

"You could tell Carter that . . . oh, I know, that you have a family emergency! Or wait, he's probably in contact with your family. Maybe you could say—"

Sophia interrupts me. "No. I'll tell him the truth."

I don't think I heard her correctly. "What?"

"I'll tell him I'm going to the gallery opening." She holds my gaze. "With you."

I know better than to press Sophia on what this means for us (*is there an us?*) but my smile flexes so wide, it hurts.

On the walk back, Sophia extends her hand towards mine and though it's the first time, it feels devastatingly familiar, like there is no universe in which we're not meant to walk hand in hand beneath a canopy of trees dusted in sunlight.

When we reach the van, I pull open the passenger door for her, but she climbs past it all the way to the back. This time I take off her clothes, gently and intentionally, and she does the same. If the first time was hurried, this time feels achingly slow. I want to project every inch of her into the negative film of my memory. She clings to my shoulders and back as if afraid she'll lose her hold on this plane of existence if she lets go. I am stupidly and sublimely in awe of her.

When we arrive back at the lodge, it's still early, just after eight. Everyone is asleep, the little back door in space and time sealed back up so seamlessly it's like we were never there. We kiss again before separating.

"Tomorrow."

"Tomorrow," she nods.

"'Bye, Sohee," I say absentmindedly as she leaves.

Sophia turns around. "What did you just say?"

"I said 'bye."

"I thought you said—never mind."

I watch as Sophia walks to her cabin and closes the door, her expression unreadable. The notion that I could have called her my ex's name is so unthinkable—proof of all the hang-ups still ramming against the emergency exit of my mind—that I don't let myself psychoanalyze it. I couldn't have. I wouldn't have.

Back in my cabin, I fall asleep and only wake when it's dark. My love-drunk giddiness is so obvious, it's not safe for me to be seen in public, so I skip dinner and compensate with a bowl of instant ramen on my bed. Afterwards, I open up my laptop and crank out a few new scenes. Sophia's character continues to confound me. As for David's character, I think he's capable of change after all. Despite my aversion to the concept, I decide to submit the story to the diverse fiction contest Lauren mentioned. The deadline is tomorrow night.

The next morning, I oversleep. I stumble to Sophia's cabin; the curtains are parted. When I cup my hands around my eyes and look around, neither she nor Carter are anywhere to be seen. Instead my eyes fall on a nude figure, pale with long black hair, lying on her back, rendered in frantic and broad brushstrokes. She's been intersected down the middle, exposing rivers of blood, coils of intestines, shards of bone. Sophia's artwork.

This? This is what will liberate us?

I flinch from the window and walk farther into the woods, assessing my options. Running into Carter at the lodge will be as comfortable as running into a man I'm about to assassinate, especially if Sophia's present. Or maybe she's already broken the news to him. Or maybe she's waiting for me in the van, ready to go. I check my phone: the battery is dead. Shit.

I sprint towards the lodge and imagine Carter in a corner, rocking back and forth. Or more likely, axing the place apart à la *The Shining*. Is it fair to him? No. But he's a good-looking guy, I tell myself. He'll recover.

What greets me, however, is far worse: everyone sits around the table eating breakfast. All is normal. Too normal. Carter is shoveling scrambled eggs, bacon and hash browns into his mouth. Beside him is Sophia, distractedly picking at a bowl of yogurt and granola. I make a point of sitting across from her, but her eyes evade mine.

"Morning, David!" Elijah says. "Chef Manon made buttermilk pancakes."

"I've lost my appetite."

"Suit yourself," he shrugs and heads back to the kitchen.

"How did you sleep?" comes a shy voice from my left. Only then do I realize I'm sitting next to Lauren.

"Great. So fucking great." I pour myself a glass of orange juice and chug it. "Sophia, how are you this morning?"

Carter pauses his chewing and clocks me with an amused, quizzical look.

Sophia finally looks up at me. "I'm fine." She manages to speak in an even-keeled voice, though her eyes look unnerved. Or maybe lethal. Or maybe contrite. I'm so out of it, I can't tell.

Carter smiles at Sophia. "We're heading to the city today!" he practically shouts.

"Oh, really?" Lauren asks benignly. "How come?"

I think I'm seeing red. I think I'm burning a hole through this chair that leads straight to hell.

Carter turns to Sophia and clasps her hand on top of the table. "We're going to see an opening at a gallery in Tribeca. They're showing one of Sophia's pieces—"

I don't hear another word that comes out of his mouth. Everything sounds indistinct, waterlogged. All I see is Carter's hand on Sophia's and her hand not pushing it away. The sight alone is unforgivable. And just like that, my heart has been mashed into a meat grinder. I understand now, so clearly, why some people become murderers.

That night, I make some last-minute changes to my story about David and Sophia before I submit it to the diverse fiction contest. Not a love story, after all—a horror story.

VI.

The program shuts down for a week in December. We'll regather for New Year's Eve as a celebratory send-off into the new year, with a reading and holiday-themed dinner.

In New Jersey, I settle into my parents' living room pullout bed since my old apartment is still subletted out to a guy I found on craigslist. Life clicks into a predictable rhythm. The ease of it feels a little like stepping back on a treadmill that never stopped revolving. I sleep in. I work out. I watch gratuitous amounts of K-dramas.

Instead of thinking about S——, I send a "Hey, what are you up to?" text to Nora, the last girl I was casually sleeping with (admittedly, poorly timed at 11:47 p.m.), and she texts back, "Lose my number, dickhead." I redownload a dating app and swipe right without motivation, flicking through a digital carousel of women as if browsing furniture. When anyone reciprocates, my first instinct—as with my writing—is to inject doubt. *Is she on the rebound? Did she just attend her first K-pop idol concert?* And the worst scenario: *Did she unpack her self-hatred in therapy and conclude that sleeping with me is proof she's healed?* I recognize that I'm scratching a familiar scab: chasing validation just so I can hold it up to a black light and examine it for unseen flaws. But acknowledgment, as I have learned, does not give rise to change.

When I have nothing else to distract myself with, I pick up a few shifts at the restaurant. My parents insist I don't have to, but somehow, seeking shelter at the place I once loathed—where the faded and discolored decorations remain unchanged since I was a teenager, where the beef and broccoli is still a little too salty and the tempura batter is definitely too soggy, where the register still sticks when you slam it too hard—is comforting.

Two nights before Christmas, I hear someone call my name. I turn around. The culprit is Eric Kim. I head over to his table and recognize Jason Nguyen and Matt Tsiang, too.

"Is this a class reunion or what?" Eric laughs. He offers his fist; I bump it. "I thought you moved to Jersey City?"

"No, dude—he's living in some cabin in the woods. Right?" This is said by Matt.

"Yeah, just for a few months." I stand awkwardly before them in my stained apron and damp kitchen clogs, feeling like I've gone abroad and forgotten my native tongue. They're all dressed in button-up shirts, their hair slicked back or shaved, clunky watches shiny and hopeful on their wrists. "So, uh, do you guys need refills or anything?"

Eric disregards this. "What time do you get off work?"

They bring me to Crystal Palace, a sprawling restaurant with private karaoke rooms that we christened "the back rooms" in high school. We frequented it nearly every weekend because they didn't card. In the all-purpose main room, popular for wedding banquets, is a stage where the host embellishes lackluster memories and the bride and groom play sexually coded games and drunk uncles croon love songs in the wrong pitch. We walk past it, vestiges of a bygone party displayed for all to see. I've always thought an empty post-party room is the loneliest kind of room there is.

We're assigned room 9. Like in all the rooms, black faux-leather benches form a half rectangle around an ornate glass table. I choose a corner in the back and play with the lights, settle on spinning disco. Eric orders beer, soju, fries and chicken nuggets for the table. I order a Calpico Soda and the guys laugh but they all order a glass for themselves.

"Melody and Lisa are coming later," Jason says, sliding his phone back into his pocket. A vague memory of them rouses itself from my high school days: pretty, unkind girls who intimidated me.

After our food arrives, everyone idly flips through the laminated pages in the binders, drinking with one hand while browsing with the other.

"How long are you in town?" Eric asks.

"Just until the weekend."

"What kind of program did you say you're doing?" Matt follows up.

I take a sip of somaek. "Um, writing."

"Like, journalism?"

"Fiction. I was working on a short story collection. About—well, it's not that interesting, but I wanted to examine modern man's desolation." I hate myself.

The three all look at me a little uncertainly, as if waiting to see if a punch line is coming around the corner.

"Well, when your book comes out, I'll tell everyone we went to high school together," Eric offers graciously. He was always like this, the guy who befriended every clique.

"Yeah, you were really good at English," Matt chimes in. We were in Mrs. Nelson's tenth grade class together. He plagiarized all his essays, but she never caught him because she never suspected him. All of us, actually, used to get away with so much shit because no one ever suspected us good little model minorities.

"Yeah. Good for you, man," Jason agrees.

I shrug, hoping to strike a middle ground between modesty and nonchalance. I don't like the way they're all looking at me, their assessment legible in their eyes: *This guy thinks he's too good for us. Says shit like "modern man's desolation."* They smile distantly at me as they drink their beers, no doubt questioning why they invited me to hang out in the first place. My discomfort feels nostalgic. Even in high school, despite listening to what everyone else listened to and wearing what everyone else wore, I was always cosplaying.

"The people there were crazy, though," I announce, too loudly because none of us have so much as touched a microphone.

Through the beer glass tipped back at his throat, I see Eric raise his eyebrows. He sets the empty glass down. "Oh, yeah?"

"Everyone was white." No need to mention Sophia. My darling, backstabbing Sophia. The guys all lightly laugh and shake their heads. "And I don't just mean white—I mean *wh-ite.*"

They settle into their seats, salivating for a good story. So I proceed to put on a show for them. To tap-dance, to tumble a top hat across my shoulders, to twirl around an elegant cane as my legs kick high towards the ceiling. In reality, what I put on is not some grand performance, just a petty and vengeful one-man show.

When their laughter ceases, Jason asks me, "So was this program only for guys?"

I had limited my parodies to Carter, Jacob and Elijah. The chivalrous switch in my head blinks, bright and constant. A reminder to abstain. To have a little decency. But, still intoxicated with the venom of my own malevolence, I switch it off. "Actually, I hooked up with this white girl," which provokes what I wanted: grins, boisterous noises of approval.

Jason slaps my back. "Well, how was she?"

The words leach into my mouth like acid. "She had huge tits."

The guys roar—this is what they like to hear. My disobedient mouth keeps flapping. "I don't know if all white girls are like this, but she acted like a porn star the entire time. It was honestly embarrassing."

"I'm telling you, white chicks are fucking crazy," Eric says. "I was seeing this one I met at work. She was into some weird shit, I can tell you that—"

The guys continue to trade stories, save for Jason, whose preferred "mix" is Blasian girls.

I pour myself more beer, arrange my face in the semblance of a smile. Beneath all the jocular wisecracks courses something meaner and grimmer—casualties of, one, growing up in a country that's collectively cucked you by pronouncing you undesirable before you were even born and, two, bearing the brunt of one too many stereotypical jokes one too many times. It's like I emerged from the womb with a permanent chip on my shoulder that no amount of dating or sex or validation will budge. If I had been born in Seoul, where my parents met, all of this would be a non-issue. I wonder if they realize their decision to immigrate inadvertently fucked up my love life.

The unsavory conversation is only cut short when Melody and Lisa arrive and we finally utilize the karaoke room for its purpose. Everyone has a decent voice, not surprising when they've amassed years of practice. They hew closely to the nineties and early two thousands, with a few older classics and recent hits snuck into the roster. Then Eric and Melody duet in Korean and Matt sings a Jay Chou song in perfect Mandarin and I find it harder and harder to govern my smile. The music is a decibel below earsplitting, throbbing my temples along with the bass. Onscreen, pale women in sundresses meander longingly through empty wheat fields, interspersed with shots of geese taking flight. I know it's impossible, but every single one is the spitting image of S——. Why do you look so sad? I want to ask her. What is it you're looking for?

An hour ago, I was gleefully sinking my teeth into the other fellows and flinging their flesh across the room. But now, slumped in this faux-leather booth and bloated with soju, I feel as shitty as I have ever felt. I threw Lauren under the bus. For what? Entertainment? Fucking-a-white-girl clout?

"Come on, David, sing something!" Melody wags the microphone under my nose. Her short dress has ridden up past her thighs and her mascara has smeared. I watched her earlier when she checked her appearance in her phone, weighted down by so many baubles and trinkets, I was astonished she could hold it up. She's cute, if sloppy. I wonder if I should make a move. A memory rolls over me: senior year, she was suspended for beating up another girl. The custodians never managed to wash out all the blood from the concrete curb. Now she's a dental assistant.

I take the microphone and punch in number 7179: "Creep" by Radiohead.

I struggle to latch my voice onto the ponderous beginning lines. My singing—by far the worst out of the bunch—noticeably kills everyone's buzz. I catch them looking at each other, then me, then each other, but I'm past the point of caring. I stand up, wobbling a little, and clamber onto the padded bench. I extend my arm plaintively up to the ceiling during the chorus, curl it back towards my stomach during the second verse. I buckle my knees. I tug at my hair. I pinch my eyes shut as multicolored constellations dance across my face. I sing my broken little heart out in the dark.

The last time I go into the city is on a Saturday night.

I was mindlessly scrolling through social media when I saw an announcement for a chapbook release: a tastefully designed flyer, the author's black-and-white photo wreathed in a circle. Even if I left now, I thought, I'd arrive late. I hesitated over going, then forbade myself to overthink it, and headed to the PATH station.

The reading's in an expensive part of Brooklyn, gentrified so long ago that hardly anyone remembers it pre-gentrification. The bookstore's ambiance is casual yet intimate, the scent of fresh coffee wafting up from the café on the first floor. Upstairs, in a half-enclosed space, rows of wooden folding chairs face the author and the moderator. I sneak in as quietly as I can and stand in the back.

I almost don't recognize Sohee. Her hair is a shock of white-blond. She's also wearing makeup, which she shunned in college for some feminist reason or another. Electric blue lines her eyelids and clear pink glosses her lips. She has on a thin blue dress and even from all the way in the back, I notice she's not wearing a bra. New tattoos stagger down both of her arms and one of her thighs. I have this wriggly feeling like we've never met, like if I say "Hello," she'll turn to me and ask, "Do I know you?"

I take off my jacket and try to focus on why I came: to listen to a reading. The chapbook is called *Skin/Contact* and, according to the event poster, is themed around "the racialized body's betrayals, secrets and triumphs." The cover looks as if it vomited out a puddle of various skin tones. Being confronted with Sohee's talent after all these years feels like she's rubbing my face in said vomit, but also, like I'm gazing at a cathedral. When she finishes reading, she looks up with a coy smile and does not seem a bit surprised by the applause.

She is so good. When we first met in our creative writing class and the teacher lavished more praise on me, I knew it chafed her pride. And I believed it meant, objectively, that I was a better writer than her. But now a different, more likely explanation strikes me: our teachers—our older, white teachers—didn't understand Sohee or her writing. She didn't give a fuck then and it didn't serve her well. But it has clearly served her well outside of our classroom's insular bubble.

After the Q&A, audience members swarm Sohee, gripping copies of her chapbook for her to sign. I'm all the way on the outer edges, unable to hook her attention. I wonder where Sohee learned to laugh like that: with her throat exposed, her mouth open to the hinge.

When at last I get a chance to speak to her, she's slipping on her coat, a pouf of neon orange. "Sohee?" I say, and pray my breath doesn't retain evidence of the dollar slice I ingested earlier.

She turns around. Her expression retracts, then stills. I'm not sure what this means. Finally she allows me a curt "Hi."

All the rhapsodic, adjective-heavy praise I had preplanned evaporates, leaving behind, "That was great. Really good stuff."

"Thanks." She shrugs on the rest of her coat.

"Listen, I know you're probably busy"—I glance at her group of tattooed and pierced friends, waiting for her by the nonfiction display—"but if you're free, I'd love to catch up."

Sohee looks at me like she's slid me beneath a projector. She could always see right through me.

The bar next door has neon pink light fixtures, gummy checkerboard floors and smells, very faintly, of bleach tinged with urine. Sohee selects a table by the window. I thought she would be parting with her friends, but they follow behind us into the bar, then head towards the old-school arcade machines in the back. I don't know if I should feel insulted. Are they here for emotional protection or was this their original destination?

Sohee tosses her canvas tote bag down on the floor and orders a White Russian. I'm too nervous to do anything besides echo her order.

"So, what do you want?" Sohee barely looks at me and places her phone face up on the table. This doesn't bode well.

"You look—you look beautiful."

Nothing.

"Are you . . . dating anyone?" Sohee stares at me like she cannot believe me. I also cannot believe me. I think I swallowed some cheap pickup artist manual ten years ago and am doomed to repeat it for all eternity.

"I have a girlfriend."

"Oh. Oh!" This is new information. Though her coming out has nothing to do with me, it feels like it has everything to do with me. "Well, good for you!" I say brightly. I stop myself from giving her a high-five then worry it's offensive I haven't.

Sohee folds her arms, unamused.

"Same, actually. I mean, I have a girlfriend, too." I could stop this lie now but I can't seem to physically stop. "She's a painter, really talented actually, I think you'd like her work—it's about demystifying Orientalism or something, ha ha, sorry, I'm bad at paraphrasing. It's a pretty new relationship but it's already getting serious, I mean, the most serious since—you know—" I pause. "She reminds me of you."

Sohee stares at me. "Okay?"

"Listen . . ." I clear my throat. "I want to apologize."

She doesn't skip a beat. "For?"

"Breaking up over text . . . That was immature of me. Really immature."

She laughs. "Oh, *that's* what you're apologizing for?"

The server returns with our drinks. I gratefully suck down a mouthful.

"The text breakup wasn't a surprise. I mean, we were in college. I didn't expect much, from you or any other guy." Sohee shakes her head. "I just thought you were *actually* going to apologize." She examines my face for longer than is comfortable before her eyes dilate in shock. "Oh my god," she says slowly. "You still think I don't know."

My head feels feverish. My tongue, swollen. I return to my drink as if it contains the antidote to my fatal distress. "This is really good—do you think they use oat milk?" I ask, hopelessly trying to maneuver the subject away from the cliff it's galloping towards.

"I can't believe you thought I'd never find out. It's not like the literary world is *that* big."

"What are you talking about?" I ask in as innocent a voice as I can muster.

Sohee's jaw drops. "Don't, David. Don't pretend you don't know exactly what I'm talking about." How did she find out? Impossible. The only way would be if she had—"I interned at *The Filmore Review*."

Fuck. Me.

"I was in charge of digitizing their system. Setting up mailing lists with all the emails of past contestants." She taps a ringed finger against her glass. "I came across your email. But mine was nowhere to be found."

I've been leached of all bodily function. My lungs, hands, legs—nothing works.

"Were you *that* insecure, David? Afraid your girlfriend might win over you?" Her voice is a hard line but her bottom lip is trembling.

My brain feebly spouts out half-hearted excuses: I could tell her it wasn't my fault. I could tell her that after we stayed up all night revising our stories, after we printed them out at the library, after I volunteered to drop them in the mailbox before the eight a.m. pickup so she could steal some sleep before class, I could tell her I really did, I could insist a careless postman's error is to blame . . .

I had repressed the memory for so long that it lunges out at me now, fully formed, clamping around my throat and suffocating me. I can still feel the weight of both envelopes in my hands. I even remember the stamps: American flags, three on each manila envelope because we were afraid of underpaying. And that day, the weather was overcast, chilly—I had borrowed one of her hoodies, the gray one that smelled of weed and fabric softener no matter how long I wore it. I slipped my envelope into the mailbox's narrow mouth without a thought. Next I stuck Sohee's in halfway, and then . . . why . . . *why* . . . did I stop? I took hers out and stared at it for a brief second. Without giving myself time to reflect, I shoved it into the trash can beside the mailbox. I quickly walked off and went to class. I still remember which one: Comparative Economic Systems.

We stayed together for three years, the longest relationship I've ever had, and I loved her more than I've ever loved anyone. When she first passed me a note in our creative writing workshop, asking if I wanted to hang out after class, I was both flattered and apprehensive. I didn't understand what Sohee saw in me, so I took it as a sign that I must be better than I thought. Under the floodlight of Sohee's love, I was shucked clean of my deficiencies. I was absolved. This narrative was preferable over the alternative: admitting that clear-eyed Sohee was afflicted with a myopia that extended only to men.

When I ended things before our senior year, it was only because the guilt broke me, not because I wasn't still in love with her. Sohee was blindsided; she texted back that my lack of empathy was pathological and I agreed with her, which she shot back proved her point. The year that followed—when I was a numbed-out wreck, swiping through half the East Coast, sleeping with any girl who looked my way—further proved the depth of my love, the depth of my remorse.

At least, that's what I told myself—an airtight narrative. But wasn't the truth that I was treading water long before? To keep up with her brilliance. To grind the inferiority out of my voice when I congratulated her on being the first in our class to be published in an online journal. To shrug it off when I found out her ex-boyfriend was white—something I couldn't help but make passive-aggressive comments about, constantly, like a tic. When we had sex, I compulsively imagined the two of them together, how he'd touched her first in every place I had ever touched, and how this guaranteed, whether she was conscious of it or not, our comparison.

Despite all her ironic self-awareness, Sohee never understood she was forever swinging the key to herself in front of me. The ghosts of her past lovers parading past with smiles as patronizing as towel smacks in the men's locker room. When she said she'd only ever dated white guys before me, I knew she expected me to feel proud of the fact that I was the first to break the monochromatic pattern. And maybe I did, for one brief, victorious moment, before it was swiftly replaced by skulking resentment, even when she later claimed she couldn't help it, she grew up in Connecticut for god's sake (an explanation I thought was a cop-out, an easy way to exonerate herself without self-interrogation). Sohee believed in "letting go of the past," but I had no concept of how. Unlike her, I wanted to polish my agony into something white-marbled and monumental so I could worship it, lay my head down before it.

Months later, when *The Filmore Review* mailed out the results, a couple people in our creative writing class received rejections—real, addressed letters in the mail. Mine arrived, too, though I never told Sohee. When she asked if I'd heard back, I said something like, "No, but they must get so many submissions that not hearing back is a rejection." Sohee had shrugged—disappointed, but not terribly so. She knew her success as a writer was not a matter of if, only of when. I both envied and loathed that confidence of hers—where had she siphoned it from? What right did she have to it?

I, on the other hand, was devastated I hadn't placed at all. *The Filmore Review* Emerging Writers Fellowship was only open to writers who had never been published in a print literary magazine, which was why it figured so popular in undergrad creative writing classes, and in addition to publication in their fall issue, it included a six-month-long mentorship under the guidance of the fiction editor and an introduction to a literary agent. Nearly every author who had ever been published before thirty had secured it and for this reason, when it eluded my grasp, it seemed like the death knell on my potential, my talent.

When Sohee asked if I was planning to enroll in the Intermediate Fiction class, I told her I didn't have time. She, on the other hand, took every available class in the department and eventually became the prose editor of the undergrad literary journal. I thought of submitting—sometimes going so far as to upload a short story, only to chicken out at the last minute before the deadline ticked past—because the thought of Sohee having the authority to accept or reject me was intolerable.

After she graduated, I knew from lurking on her social media account that she moved to the city and cycled through minimum wage jobs, sacrificing health insurance and stability for her art. She organized readings, built a community with other writers, took workshops, kept submitting to journals. She put in the work. I wonder if Sohee applied to the writing residency. If I've robbed her of her spot.

"Well?" The sharpness of Sohee's voice draws me back to the pulsing neon bar.

I manage to eke out a pitiful "Sorry."

Sohee's eyes are watery—the notion that I could be the cause of any strong emotion is still unthinkable to me. I have to remind myself that her tears aren't something to wonder at or to render in pretty prose.

"It's not like I think I would have won. That's not the point, you know."

"I know," I whisper.

"It's just . . . the *principle*. And the fact that you could still continue to date me and sleep with me and just hide it—" Sohee blinks, sending her tears down her cheeks. I fight back the urge to blot them away like I used to.

"Are you going to write about this?" I ask, trying to modulate it as a lighthearted joke, but it comes out as a pathetic plea.

"What the fuck? *That's* what you're thinking about right now?" The look in Sohee's eyes swerves clinical. "God. You really are a sociopath."

"Maybe you're right," I laugh weakly.

A quartet of friends pushes into the bar, letting in a flurry of wind-chilled air.

"David, in all seriousness"—the carefully modulated shift in Sohee's voice sets me on edge—"I think you need to unpack where your hatred of women comes from."

I stare at her in disbelief, the bar's pulsing music now twice as loud. "I don't hate women."

But it's like Sohee can't even hear me. "I'm not trying to sound condescending when I say this, but I really think you could benefit from therapy. It's helped me. A lot."

"Right." I force out a laugh, my gaze careening across the bar. "Watch out, everyone, David's 'crazy.' Bring the straitjacket!"

"Don't turn this into a joke. God, you *always* do that—it's such a fucking crutch." When I don't dare say another word, she keeps going. "And you *still* talk about yourself in the third person? When will you get that your life is not a fucking piece of fiction and that people aren't fucking characters?" She leans back in her chair as if to capture a fuller picture of my shortcomings. "I swear, you're allergic to accountability. David, nobody is making you hurt other people. *You're* the one doing it."

Another apology would be negligible in this situation. My eyes stay superglued to the table, unable to meet Sohee's. They only unstick themselves when I hear a voice I don't recognize.

"Hey, are you okay?"

A worried-looking South Asian woman with a septum piercing stands beside our table. Sohee transforms at her girlfriend's presence, her face suffused with gratitude and relief. She collects her things and stands up. I steel myself, eager for Sohee to lash me to bloody strips—my sinful self is begging for flagellation—but she denies me this. I watch as she and all her friends leave. I wasn't worth the oxygen in Sohee's lungs. I don't blame her.

On the train ride home, I try to callous my mind against thoughts of Sophia, but it's an exercise in futility. I keep picturing her and Sohee meeting. It's not out of the question—they both run in artsy NYC circles, they're both around the same age. Hell, they even make similarly motivated art. I see them waiting in line for the bathroom at some AAPI feminist event in Chinatown, complimenting each other's style. They exchange info, get matcha lattes, become friends. They find out, one drunk and slippery night stumbling back to the F train, that they both dated me. They crow, "What were we thinking?" as they clasp each other's arms and later, "At least he gave us something to write/paint about!" Maybe, I think a little sheepishly, in this scenario I am their reluctant muse, inspiring all sorts of angsty, cathartic art.

But I can also imagine, just as clearly, that they'd eye each other up and down in the bathroom line. That they would leave without speaking to each other, let alone exchanging numbers. They're both devastatingly brilliant, both devastatingly ambitious. Whenever an artist is confronted with a similar artist, they're perceived as a threat: only so much opportunity to go around, etc.

In college, Sohee's and my creative writing professor claimed that two writers cannot sustain a relationship.

"Why?" I'd asked.

"Because when you break up, which you will, each of you will race to see who will write about—and publish—your breakup before the other. Who will get the first say and the last say. And, worse, who will say it better."

I remember feeling indignant, even desperate, to prove him wrong. I hate that with Sohee, he was proven right.

VII.

The day I return to the program, I miss my train. The next one is delayed, then canceled. By the time I arrive, the late winter sun has already kissed the lip of the horizon. The sky is a blue velvet cloak, fringed in orange. A distant wood-burning fire thickens the air. I could live in the countryside, I think for the first time in my life. And then, a second later: who am I kidding? I refuse to buy a gun and I don't have a death wish.

I drag my suitcase up the gravel driveway and stop outside the lodge. The déjà vu that hits me is unfamiliar: as if I've been here before but in some other timeline, not the one I presently find myself in—half-sick with anxiety over seeing Sophia again.

When I go inside, the soft clatter of forks and knives drifts from the dining room: dinner is in progress. I wonder if this is a curse I've caught: doomed to always show up late, to always have to play catch-up.

I don't announce myself straightaway. I idle beneath the awning and observe everyone: Lauren, Carter, Jacob, Elijah. I daresay I missed them, even Carter, with his cloudless optimism. But Sophia. Sophia is nowhere to be seen.

"Happy New Year, everyone."

"You're back!" Elijah gestures for me to sit. "We were worried you'd never come."

I think I explain that my train was delayed, then canceled and rebooked, and I think I serve myself from the glass dishes on the table but I can't be sure because all I can think is: *Sophia. Where is Sophia?* Is she resting in her cabin? Could she be waiting for me in *my* cabin? Or, I think frantically, she's gone into town. No, she's arriving tomorrow. Or maybe she's in the bathroom, fixing her hair, and I've made a big production out of nothing.

The conversation has picked back up where it left off. I try to find an opening into it but I can't be certain if everyone is discussing investments or invertebrates, monogamy or Monopoly. At some point, I look down and realize my dinner plate has been exchanged for a bowl of chocolate mousse dolloped with cream.

Elijah returns from the kitchen with two more bowls, setting them down in front of himself and Carter. His hand lingers on Carter's bowl.

"Should I bring another for Sophia?" he asks in a politely tentative voice.

Thank god, I think, Elijah has asked the one question that's surely on everyone's mind, not just mine. I feel, a bit dramatically, that if there is a heaven, Elijah's entrance is guaranteed.

Everyone looks up at Carter, then away, as if not wanting to pry.

Carter pushes back his sleeves. I inspect him more closely: unclean shave, sprinkles of dandruff on his shoulders. Whatever's going on, he's not happy about it.

"Sophia," Carter begins, in a voice I've never heard him speak in before, "won't be returning."

A sinkhole opens up beneath me.

"Oh," Elijah says—I can see the gears of his brain whirring and clicking—then adds, "I'm so sorry to hear that. We'll all miss her."

Everyone nods. I masticate the insides of my cheeks to stop myself from demanding why. *Why?*

"She's in London. For an art exhibit," Carter responds to my silent appeal, with none of the joy he used to infuse into hyping up his wife's career.

"Oh, well—well, that's wonderful news!" Elijah smiles and glances worriedly at his dessert, as if debating the acceptable moment to begin enjoying food again.

I shovel the chocolate mousse into my mouth and glare at Carter. A hot corkscrew of anger burrows through me. I feel certain: this is all his fault. Over the break, he must have caught Sophia trying to get ahold of me. Or maybe he found her sketch of me and melodramatically obliterated it into pieces. He called a divorce lawyer and told Sophia he was taking everything, and as if that wasn't enough, he was changing the locks to their apartment, but not before texting her family group chat that she was a cheating liar, causing them to disown her, which, naturally, triggered all of Sophia's abandonment issues. She demanded to come back to the program to see me, but he said he'd sue her for emotional distress if she so much as looked at a train ticket. Instead, he shipped her off to London. The insecure bastard.

The second the table is cleared, Carter pours himself a drink and sulks by the fireplace. Even Jacob, who typically lags behind him like a fraternity pledge, seems to know better than to approach Carter in his current state.

I, on the other hand, walk over to Carter, my knuckles aching to make contact. With every step, my anger grows more outsized. As I zero in, my vision telescoping the entire world down to him and him alone, it takes on a dimension of relief—because this situation could only ever boil down to two grown men locked in fisticuffs. Just because we're at a writing residency doesn't mean we're more evolved.

But as I'm about to cut into Carter's line of sight, my vision is blocked. I jerk back, synapses stalling. Protruding eyes. Stern mouth. Broad chest.

"I need to talk to you."

I look down at Lauren as the siren whipping round and round the inside of my head fades.

"Hello, David? Are you there?" she says, more loudly.

I unclench my fists. "I'm here."

We sit outside at one of the picnic tables. The second we settle in, moths hover near the lantern light above us. I swat one away.

"So, what's going on?" I ask, anxious to return to my (violent) task.

Lauren keeps brushing her hair from her face. She's hacked it off and dyed it, drastically, following the example of fictional female characters after an interpersonal disaster. Dark brown and blunt doesn't suit her. She seems stiff, as if she's holding in an uncomfortable pocket of air. It dawns on me that she's about to confess her feelings. That, during all of winter break, she must have replayed images from our night of carnal pleasure and agonized over why I never called. I look into her hazel eyes. She's a nice girl. I've treated her poorly. But in my distracted state, the guilt I feel is faint and difficult to access, like I'm remembering the flavor of a long-ago, discontinued candy.

"Lauren, I think of you as a friend," I start to say, when she abruptly blurts, "David, that night was a mistake" at the same time.

I blink, wondering if I've misheard her. "Come again?"

Lauren tidies her hair behind her ears. "The truth is—oh god, this is so embarrassing—but I was upset at Jacob, he was being so avoidant and couldn't decide if he wanted to actually be with me or 'keep things open' and I just, well, I just wanted to act like I could play that game, too."

I clear my throat several times. "I see."

"Don't worry," she says quickly, "I didn't tell him. I was going to, but—so the thing is, we're together now." Lauren pauses here and blushes. Someone shoot me. "We saw each other over the break and he took me ice skating, it's so unoriginal I know, but he asked me to be his girlfriend and . . ." She glances down at the table and smiles as if reliving the butterflies-in-her-stomach moment, then seems to remember my existence. "And, well, I wanted to ask you: could you keep what happened just between us?"

I stare at her for a few seconds before regaining my voice. "Of course!" I mime zipping my lips and chucking the key, then deeply despise myself for it.

"Thanks, David. You're a good friend." Her generosity leaves a rug burn inside me because I haven't been a good friend to her or anyone else here.

"I'm happy for you guys," I say and kind of mean it.

We stay like that for a moment, as if adjusting to this new dynamic, and something about Lauren and Jacob finally getting together is a comfort. Not everything has to be ambiguous or disastrous or contract claused to death. Sometimes you can just ask the person you like to be your girlfriend when you're ice skating at Christmas. In some other storyline, I wish I could have asked Sophia to be my girlfriend while ice skating at Christmas.

"So. Pretty unexpected, right? About Sophia not coming back," I segue, hoping my voice doesn't lay bare my devastation.

"Did you hear? She and Carter are separated," Lauren says, suddenly conspiratorial and, beneath it, smug.

"Oh?" I manage.

She leans close and turns the volume of her voice a couple notches down. "The day everyone left, I forgot my phone charger and had to ask Elijah to turn the van around. I guess they thought they were alone because I heard them having a huge fight. Carter kept asking Sophia to stay, he said he wanted to try marriage counseling, but Sophia didn't want to, she just kept, like, shutting down all of Carter's solutions. He's been a total wreck since he arrived this morning, even though he thinks none of us notice." She waits expectantly for my shock. "Can you believe it?"

I swat away another moth. "Why, yes. I can."

Because even though the news of Sophia's absence ambushed me from behind, I'm not surprised at all. I remember something Carter said early on: Sophia could never stay in one place for long.

When I reenter the lodge, I walk over to Carter. He looks just as Lauren described: post-meltdown. Not a "hire a hitman to off my wife's lover and bury his body in concrete" type of guy after all. Faced with his dreary posture, his cloudless optimism nowhere to be seen, the guilt I've been holding at arm's length finally tackles me to the ground. At the end of the day, privileged or not, he is just a man.

I think back to the first day I met Carter, how I hated him on instinct. It turns out I am as guilty of doing to others—to Carter, to Jacob, to Lauren—what I don't want others to do to me. All my characterizations, all my attempts at flattening someone out—because people are harmless in one dimension—are just that: one-dimensional. That's what it means, I realize, to catch myself out.

"Hey, Carter," I say. "How are you, man?" I offer him the box of chocolates I bought at the train station.

He looks up at me, as if grateful someone cares enough to ask after him, and in that moment I have confirmation he doesn't know I'm half responsible for his misery. He grabs an entire handful of cream-centered chocolates. "I've been better."

In another life, we could darn close our wounds with the thread of mutual heartbreak. In this life, I sit down next to him and grab a handful, too.

Everyone disperses after dinner to rest up before the New Year's Eve celebration in a couple hours. Elijah keeps saying we won't want to miss it—he managed to wrangle enough funding for champagne, balloons *and* sparklers.

I head back to my cabin and lie down in bed with the curtains pulled shut. I don't even flick on the light. The next two months spread out before me, daunting and pointless. I don't know why I'm here if Sophia's not. Writing—in the purposeful, publishing-focused way we've all come here to do—feels irrelevant. The only thing I've worked on in the past two weeks is my story about David and Sophia. But, if I were to let honesty override all other cognitive functions, the autofiction story doesn't really feel like a story anymore. It feels more like a convenient device for endlessly playing out the many lives of a single choice, a single mistake. Or maybe it's my attempt to rewrite history and assert control over what felt uncontrollable. Or maybe I should stop kidding myself and admit that the story is nothing more than mental masturbation. Artless self-plagiarism.

CASUALTIES OF ART

When I open my eyes, it's nearly midnight. I've missed the New Year's Eve celebration. I roll over onto my stomach, ready to sleep through the end of the year and wake up in a new one, when a hard object wedges itself under my rib cage. I turn on the light to see a flat package bound in brown paper and white string.

I sit up, graze my hand across the package, then untie the string. Inside is me—two of me on stretched canvas. Square, about twelve by twelve inches, rendered in acrylic paint. Thin, squiggly red lines and shapes swarm the dark, blasted background—a lake or sky, I'm not sure. Facing off on two chairs are two Davids: one with his hands open, the other with his hands squared to fists. It's Sophia's finished sketch from the day at the waterfall. I thought she didn't give anyone her art, believing only museums worthy of it.

I jump up, my heart igniting with joy. Because I know, without a doubt, that the painting is a message from Sophia: *Come find me.*

I start to pack before I remember I haven't unpacked a thing. The others will understand—one day. I walk down the gravel pathway as quietly as I can, gripping my suitcase in my arms. As I call the number for the local taxi company, I look up and see, in the swath of sky above the lake, explosions of light.

All the way to the city, to London, I look out the window.

At Heathrow, I stop inside a bathroom to brush my teeth, change my clothes and spritz on cologne. It's already late morning the next day. I don't know where Sophia is staying but I have a feeling that if I hit enough modern art galleries, I'll find her. I have to.

The first gallery is a miss. The second and third are, too. Each time, I ask if an American artist named Sophia has an upcoming exhibit at this gallery. Each time, I brandish the painting as if it's a Missing Persons poster.

When I reach the ninth gallery, it's just about to close. My legs ache and I'm ninety-nine percent sure I'm dehydrated and it doesn't help that my last form of sustenance was a stale airline muffin. I hear the confidence in my voice deflate as I ask, once again, if an American artist named Sophia has an upcoming exhibit at this gallery.

When the front desk receptionist answers yes, I almost don't register it.

"What? Are you sure?" I ask and she frowns at my pink-veined eyes, my wrinkled clothes.

Then I hear someone call my name. "David?"

I turn around and there—there is my Sophia.

When I open my eyes, it's nearly midnight. I've missed the New Year's Eve celebration. I roll over onto my stomach, ready to sleep through the end of the year and wake up in a new one, when a hard object wedges itself under my rib cage. I turn on the light to see a flat package bound in brown paper and white string.

I sit up, graze my hand across the package, then untie the string. Inside is me—two of me on stretched canvas. Square, about twelve by twelve inches, rendered in acrylic paint. Thin, squiggly red lines and shapes swarm the dark, blasted background—a lake or sky, I'm not sure. Facing off on two chairs are two Davids: one with his hands open, the other with his hands squared to fists. It's Sophia's finished sketch from the day at the waterfall. I thought she didn't give anyone her art, believing only museums worthy of it.

I stare at the painting. I don't know what to make of it. I hurry to the lodge, enter Elijah's off-limits office and find Sophia's number on the contact sheet. Even though it's late, I pick up my phone and call her. With each ring, my heart feels like it's going to leapfrog out of me.

After the fifth ring, she picks up. "Hello?"

"Sophia."

"David?" A pause. "How did you get my number?"

I ignore this. "Thanks . . . for the painting."

Sophia doesn't speak for a few moments. Then: "You're welcome."

I wait for her to tell me what it means. She doesn't. "So what does it mean?"

Sophia sighs.

I don't know how to ask if it means: *I'm sorry.* Or: *Maybe we could have, in another life.* Or: *I love you, too.*

"I want a definitive answer," I finally say. "A clear conclusion. You know, closure."

"Oh, David," she laughs sadly. "I can't give you that."

"You're doing it again—being evasive."

Sophia's voice turns a sharp corner. "You want me to be evasive."

". . . Why?"

"Because you don't actually want to know what I think of you. Do you?"

I pause, bereft of words. "Oh."

"Goodbye, David."

"Wait—"

Another sigh. "Yes?"

"Don't do this. You're self-sabotaging again—"

"I'm what?"

"You told me your therapist says you self-sabotage all—"

"No, I didn't," Sophia interrupts me. "I have never said those words."

I fall silent.

"Goodbye, David."

"Wait, Sophia—I'll talk to you again, right? You're not going to, like, block me, are you? Just tell me what I did wrong. Why did you—"

Before I can say anything else, she hangs up.

When I open my eyes, it's nearly midnight. I've missed the New Year's Eve celebration. I roll over onto my stomach, ready to sleep through the end of the year and wake up in a new one, when a hard object wedges itself under my rib cage. I turn on the light to see a flat package bound in brown paper and white string.

I sit up, graze my hand across the package, then untie the string. Inside is me—two of me on stretched canvas. Square, about twelve by twelve inches, rendered in acrylic paint. Thin, squiggly red lines and shapes swarm the dark, blasted background—a lake or sky, I'm not sure. Facing off on two chairs are two Davids: one with his hands open, the other with his hands squared to fists. It's Sophia's finished sketch from the day at the waterfall. I thought she didn't give anyone her art, believing only museums worthy of it.

At first, I feel nothing. And then . . . outrage, heady as a fever. *A painting?* Sure, Sophia doesn't owe me anything, including an explanation, but I would rather have nothing than this. At least nothing is unambiguous, pure in its decisiveness. Leaving behind a figurative painting feels like Sophia is still playing a game with me, wherever she is. The mature course of action would have been to talk to me face-to-face instead of letting a painting do it in her stead, if that was even her intention. For all I know, this is one big practical joke. For all I know, she's laughing at the thought of me racking my head over it.

I decide I will get the last laugh.

After the program ends, I end up expanding the story of David and Sophia into a novella. By the time I query the project and sign with an agent, I've changed their names into Daniel and Sarah, though the characters remain readily identifiable. Two years later, when the novella is published, the launch takes place at a bookstore in Lower Manhattan. As I prepare to read a selected passage, I look up to see a figure gliding through the aisles in the back—spectral and pale, her long black hair its own character.

Afterwards, when Sophia comes up to me at the book signing table, I pretend I don't remember her.

When I open my eyes, it's nearly midnight. I've missed the New Year's Eve celebration. I roll over onto my stomach, ready to sleep through the end of the year and wake up in a new one, when a hard object wedges itself under my rib cage. I turn on the light to see a flat package bound in brown paper and white string.

I sit up, graze my hand across the package, then untie the string. Inside is me—two of me on stretched canvas. Square, about twelve by twelve inches, rendered in acrylic paint. Thin, squiggly red lines and shapes swarm the dark, blasted background—a lake or sky, I'm not sure. Facing off on two chairs are two Davids: one with his hands open, the other with his hands squared to fists. It's Sophia's

WHERE ARE YOU REALLY FROM

finished sketch from the day at the waterfall. I thought she didn't give anyone her art, believing only museums worthy of it.

I'm not sure what to do with the painting. After the program ends, I stick it in a cardboard box at the back of my closet, where it lives among old greeting cards and childhood memorabilia. Each time the box moves with me to three different apartments, so does the painting, but by the third apartment, I've forgotten about the stowaway.

I stop writing. For all the turmoil and brief spasms of pleasure it once brought me, I don't miss it at all. Writing might have made me a more interesting person. But it certainly didn't make me a better person.

I continue to work in accounting, though for a different firm, and meet my wife through an old-school Korean tradition: a group blind date at a hanjeongsik.

Eleven years later, we're in London with our daughter. Traveling with a young child is not ideal, but my wife, a marketing director, has to meet with a major client in the city and we decide to make it a family trip.

It's a Sunday and we're at the Saatchi Gallery. My daughter is fussing and my wife's feet are sore. She insists on taking our daughter to museums for her "cultural enrichment," even though I think, at age five, she'd be happier elsewhere. I'm in an irritated mood, babysitting both the stroller and a sticky half-eaten fruit bar, searching for the restrooms while they trail behind me, when I look up and see myself. Two of me, that is, eight feet tall.

At first, my eyes merely skim over the painting, cursory in their intake, but then my stomach pitches forward. I haven't thought about Sophia's painting in years.

The two Davids still face off with each other but now they appear to me in a new light: not so much tenderly but clinically rendered. Despite their difference in pose, they both exhibit the posture of someone ill at ease in himself. Someone defensive because he is insecure and ungrounded because he is defensive.

I walk towards the little white plaque next to the bottom right of the painting, and brace myself for something eviscerating, something that will reinterpret everything I've just interpreted, but the painting is simply entitled *The Writer*.

A hot prickle rises up in my throat, and then, all of a sudden, I'm laughing. So Sophia did see me, just not how I wanted her to see me. Maybe I saw her, too, just not how she wanted me to see her.

My daughter tugs on my sleeve. "What's funny?" she asks, because—like her father—she hates to be excluded from a joke.

"Nothing, sweetheart."

When I open my eyes, it's nearly midnight. I've missed the New Year's Eve celebration. I roll over onto my stomach, ready to sleep through the end of the year and wake up in a new one, when a hard object wedges itself under my rib cage. I turn on the light to see a flat package bound in brown paper and white string.

I sit up, graze my hand across the package, then untie the string. Inside is me—two of me on stretched canvas. Square, about twelve by twelve inches, rendered in acrylic paint. Thin, squiggly red lines and shapes swarm the dark, blasted background—a lake or sky, I'm not sure. Facing off on two chairs are two Davids: one with his hands open, the other with his hands squared to fists. It's Sophia's finished sketch from the day at the waterfall. I thought she didn't give anyone her art, believing only museums worthy of it.

My first impulse is to write Sophia a long letter, drippy with apologies and demands for apologies. The type of letter I wrote to Sohee in college, post-breakup, sent to bullet point my own grievances and massage my own emotional complaints. But I have no way of contacting her. Sophia doesn't even have an online presence—not a single social media account or artist's website. Late one night at my parents' place, when my masochistic tendencies were at an all-time high, I looked her up and could only find a mention of her at that art gallery in Tribeca, where she was referenced by her initials. I still don't know Sophia's surname. The difficulty in finding any proof of her existence feels almost ghostly, which is fitting because, it hits me, I've been ghosted.

When I think back to the day at the waterfall, and of what transpired afterwards in the van, the scene is repainted in a different gloss. No longer softly rose-colored but bittersweetly transparent. Sophia's expression was a little unreadable or maybe I just didn't want to read it. Because the sex we had is sex I've had before: the kind when you're saying goodbye to one another before either of you has said the word aloud.

All this time, I've tried not to think about that morning because it would stir up questions too brutal for me to think into reality: if she meant to leave with me and changed her mind, or if she never meant to leave with me in the first place. I want to know why, I want her to talk to me, I want her to miss me, I want to at least petition for the right to stay in her life. I just don't want to be crumpled up into the "Mistakes I've Made" drawer. But it occurs to me now, at this shamefully late stage, that what I want from Sophia is not her concern. She is not saddled with the burden of my desire. I alone am saddled with it.

I prop the painting up on the nightstand and come to a decision: I'll leave her alone. Sophia must have had her reasons for cutting contact with me. That much I can give her—the right to her own perspective. I couldn't give this to Sohee, but I can give it to Sophia.

I open up my laptop, connect to my phone's hot spot and write a different email, addressed to *Dear Editor*, to please pull my recent submission from the diverse fiction contest. Then I search for the story of David and Sophia in my files. I right-click and hit delete, then empty the trash. I expect to feel disappointed—all that work for naught—but the only side effect I feel is a swell of relief that exits my body with a shudder.

The time on my laptop reads five minutes before midnight. I look out my window at that moment to see everyone walking towards the lake, ferrying bottles of champagne and sparklers in their arms. I pull on my winter coat and boots in a hurry and follow after them, a little ways away. The stars are low and bright in the sky tonight, though the moon is shy, playing hide-and-seek behind a patchwork of clouds. When they reach the lake, I find a flat bed of ground to sit on. I like observing the others from afar, the tall trees huddling close around them as if in protection. Their figures are silhouetted like black puppet shadows against the bruised night. Their sparklers cut into the air, streaking ribbons of light behind them.

Watching the others as they begin the countdown to the new year, I realize I don't feel any desire to document the moment as its own story, to edit it into a narrative with a beginning, middle and end. I'm just happy to be a witness to this: life, unfolding.

And then I get up to join them.

ACKNOWLEDGMENTS

All my gratitude for the generosity, support and insight of everyone who helped bring this collection to life: Martha Wydysh and Ellen Levine, Casey Denis and the Penguin Press team (including Chris Chin, Darren Haggar, Victoria Laboz, Lauren Lauzon, Lavina Lee, Sheila Moody, Christina Nguyen and Mollie Reid), Carrie Frye, Aleia Murawski and Sam Copeland, Oliver Munday at *The Atlantic* and Autumn Watts at *Guernica*, my NYU professors and cohort, with special thanks to Nathan Englander who read early versions of "Mail Order Love®" and "The Dollhouse," the NYSCA/NYFA organization for supporting an early version of "Casualties of Art," my first short story teacher Kim O'Neil, readers Kelley Baker, Nadine Browne, Marva Dixon, Sabrina Imbler, Yuxi Lin, Glenna Moran Pop-Stefanov, Camille Nguyen, Silvia Park, Larissa Pham, Kimberly Wang, my friends, my family in Taiwan, my parents and brothers, Hamlet and Totoro, JB.